AN UNHOLY REDEMPTION

ANDREW KEENER

Published by My Spirit Books 2012

First published in Great Britain in 2012 by My Spirit Books, Maidstone TV Studio, Vinters Park, Maidstone, Kent ME14 5NZ
www.myspiritbooks.com

Cover design by Dana Keener

Printed and bound in the UK by Biddles, part of the MPG Books Group, Bodmin and King's Lynn

British Library Cataloguing-in-Publication Data
A catalogue record for this book is available on request from the British Library

ISBN 978-1-908810-04-5

Acknowledgements

I would like to dedicate this book to my wife for her time, patience and support during the entirety of the book, to my beautiful son Kyle and to all my family and friends who believed in me when I had doubt.

Thanks also to Jacky Algar, Paul Blows, Jessica Dobbs, Kenneth Macfie and Ian Ritchie for pre-ordering this book.

Chapter One

A shimmering sun began to rise on the eastern horizon over a desert far away from civilisation, releasing its light through the tall black mountains, their shadows like dark giants moving in perfect harmony with the movement of the sun. Watching from the west, a figure sat in solitude on a rock admiring this wonderful luminary of nature in the sky. Then a sarcastic smile came across his face as a thought began to burn in his mind. *Is it not ironic that God gave us the sun as a giver of light and life, yet it is made of the most lethal destructive power known to man. If only that power could be harnessed and used to destroy mankind.*

His smile grew wider while he enjoyed this momentary thought of global destruction. The mist hovered like a ghost over the surface of the sand and then began to lift and fade away. He bent forward and reached out with his long white bony hand to scoop up a handful of sand and watched the many golden grains shower through his fingers.

"This day each grain of sand represents one soul that is going to die."

He lay back to rest his head on the rock face and looked up to the heavens, shutting his eyes as he pondered a world with no heaven, just men living on earth doing as they pleased with no-one to answer to. *Ah, now that is my idea of paradise.*

His thoughts of world domination were disturbed when he sensed the presence of someone standing nearby.

"Speak," he said, without moving and keeping his eyes shut.

"My lord we have found another."

"Who is it this time?" he asked, angry at being disturbed while in a moment of contemplation.

"Forgive me my lord, it is me, Simon. I have come to tell you that Adrian has been caught trying to leave our brotherhood to join the other side."

"Hold him, Simon. I will be there in a while."

"Yes my lord," Simon said, then spread his wings and took flight back to camp.

He watched Simon flying off in the distance. As Lucifer's anger grew at the thought of Adrian's betrayal, the white of his eyes flickered a shade of red like that of a fiery ruby. Jumping to his feet, he stretched his arms and began to unfold his wings. His wing span grew to at least forty feet, casting a shadow over the desert floor and scaring a scorpion which burrowed frantically in the sand to escape. Standing in his full glory, he gave a last look of contempt to the heavens and cursed. He then took flight amidst the cloud of sand created by the power of his wings.

Back at the secluded camp Adrian looked intently at the angel assigned to guard him.

"Marcus, my dear brother," he said. "Why have you chosen this path? Don't you know that it is wrong? This holy war that Lucifer is instigating today against God cannot be won. Millions will die and all for the sake of his pride."

After trying for a moment to ignore his prisoner, Marcus looked at his captive with burning eyes. "You stupid fool! It amazes me how God and his angels manage. All this talk about love, freedom and everybody living as equal, it is a disease spreading into the hearts and minds of anyone prepared to be sold a lie. Talk of a brighter future and being delivered unto the Promised Land is just a dream engineered to control the masses with futile hope."

“Marcus, Paradise and the Promised Land do exist. If only you would open yourself to it.”

“Have you seen it?”

Adrian bowed his head from Marcus’ intense, intimidating stare. “No,” he replied reluctantly, “but I do believe in it and have faith in our God the father. Faith that he will bring us to the Promised Land.”

His words were disturbed by a gust of wind which began to move the sand around their feet. The grains did a frenzied golden dance. They both looked to the sky and saw Simon descending. Adrian watched and listened to Simon with increasing dread, in full knowledge that Simon was returning from reporting to Lucifer about his disloyalty.

“The only promised land you will be seeing today is a certain agonising death when our lord returns,” Simon said as he landed. “Lucifer does not take too kindly to traitors.”

Simon folded his wings away when the chains and shackles that held Adrian fast to a rock started to shake and vibrate. Looking over his shoulder and in the direction Simon was staring, Adrian began to see a small black figure flying in the sky, like a vulture circling for the right moment to descend and feed on its prey. The figure grew larger as it slowly descended.

Adrian’s body began to tremble more violently as he realised what was approaching. He looked around at the surrounding angels who were kneeling to greet their master. This was who would decide his fate. Adrian closed his eyes and began to pray that God would come and save him. All at once everything became still and there was a dead silence. The wind had ceased and all Adrian could hear was the sound of his heart pounding like a drum. A gentle gust of warm air moving slowly over Adrian’s face caused him to relax. Believing he had been saved from the evil clutches of Lucifer, he smiled, ready to thank God for his deliverance.

“Isn’t life cruel,” Lucifer said as Adrian opened his eyes.

Adrian's joy sank when he saw Lucifer's heavily scarred face and his full head of black hair in front of him. With two fiery burning eyes, Lucifer stared intently into Adrian's. The warm air had been Lucifer's breath emanating from his nostrils as he stood nose to nose like a tiger watching its prey.

"Things never turn out how you expect them to." Lucifer started to laugh out loud. He then pulled his face away and turned to see if his servants were still kneeling in submission and reverence. Then he turned back to Adrian.

"Look Adrian, you see how much my subjects respect me. They see their god before them, a god that is very present and alive, a god who will deliver them into their own paradise. They don't have to pray for my help, I am already here. Tell me Adrian, where is God now, the god who you just prayed to for help? I can't see anyone, can you?"

Lucifer silenced the other angels' laughter with a wave of his hand. He then signalled for them to rise.

"Maybe he will listen to me." Lucifer turned to the heavens and shouted, "Oh God, can you help this poor soul?"

After a brief silence, Lucifer mockingly put his hand to his ear waiting for a response.

"You see, Adrian, my theory is right. Your God has abandoned you just like he did me and just like he is doing with all humanity."

"Why do you mock the Most High, Lucifer?" Adrian asked nervously, his hands and head sweating profusely as he gulped to get moisture into his mouth, to speak again. "You were once in great favour."

"Yes I was, but God in his infinite wisdom decided to cast me out of heaven like some disgusting foul creature. Why? Only because I wanted to know what God knew. All that love, knowledge and wisdom should have been for everyone, not just for God. That is simply selfish and arrogant."

Adrian listened to Lucifer rant with some sympathy, which rapidly turned into fear again when he noticed Lucifer's anger growing and his eyes begin to glow a brighter red than ever before.

"Bring me my sword!" Lucifer shouted angrily at two angels. They saluted and immediately took flight.

The angels arrived at a small opening in the ground, slightly hidden among some rocks. Guarding the entrance of the cavern stood two enormous dog-like creatures shackled in chains which gripped tightly around their necks and feet. The two angels cautiously approached amidst the frenzied barking and snarling. They saw that the beasts' eyes were of the deepest black and their razor sharp fangs snapped as they barked and released saliva on the desert floor. They looked ready to devour anything that got too close. Stopping just out of reach of the snapping fangs, one of the angels lifted his right hand in the form of a salute and began to utter an ancient word, a word known only to a few trusted angels, the meaning of which was Lucifer's privilege alone. The angel's eyes immediately flashed red. At once the beasts bowed down in perfect submission, their faces deep in the sand as they breathed in unison.

The other angel walked past his companion – who was still holding the salute, his eyes still ablaze in a red trance, not blinking or moving once – then threw himself into the mouth of the cave. As the angel descended at speed, the intensity of the heat greeting him became almost unbearable. When he finally reached the ground, he used his wings to fan and disperse the dense smoke blocking his sight. When the last of the smoke faded, the angel looked in awe at what rested on an altar in front of him. Glowing from the surrounding fire, Lucifer's sword was at least six feet in length and made from the purest of gold. Transfixed by its beauty, the angel ran his finger along the smooth blade. The handle was gilded with the finest metals and embedded with rubies running along its perimeter. In gold writing around the circumference of the handle was a single word: *Animositas*. The angel watched the reflection of the fire bouncing off the blade while he stretched forward his shaking hand to retrieve it from its fiery depths. He gripped the handle firmly and removed the sword, pausing to feel its glory. In one swift movement he lifted the sword in the air. The sword was now vibrating and pulsating as if alive as the angel moved it side to side, cutting the air in front of his face.

"Beautiful," he said. He then returned, holding the sword closely to guard it against damage. In a blast of smoke, he shot from the opening of the cavern to the bright sun hanging in the sky and landing on the ground next to his brother angel. He gently put one hand on his chest and leant forward to whisper in the ear of his entranced companion, "I am here". The mesmerised angel dropped his salute and regained consciousness, shaking his head as he opened his eyes. His red eyes returned to normal and the slow breathing of the two beasts became faster and more erratic until they were biting and snarling at their chains. The angels then took flight back to camp and a waiting Lucifer.

Lucifer did not have to wait long before the two angels had landed and one was kneeling in front of him offering him the sword in submission.

"Beautiful, isn't it?" Lucifer said to Adrian as he took the weapon. "This sword has been around since time began. I and only one other," he looked at the heavens, "know its true name and power and capabilities. In the right hands, it can wipe out millions of humans, those disgusting creatures God proclaims to love so much. It can also kill a multitude of angels."

Lucifer teasingly waved the sword in front of Adrian's face, allowing him to see his own scared eyes in the blade's reflection.

"Take a good look at this blade and its perfection Adrian. It mirrors my perfection and is fit only for my worthy hand, don't you think?"

Adrian began to tremble when Lucifer lowered his head to whisper in his ear.

"I want you to remember this day as the day when I was God, the day when I had the power to save or kill you. My voice is the last thing you will ever hear as I sentence you to death, a death worse than death or life itself, where you will have no knowledge of anything not even knowledge of yourself."

Adrian began to weep as Lucifer thrust the sword into his heart as if it were a hot knife gliding through butter. Lucifer shut his eyes and made a connection with the sword by concentrating on its power. In a flash, the blade burst into flames and glowed the brightest of reds.

"With this sword and the power of my will I damn you to Hell."

Adrian let out a deafening scream, startling some vultures sitting asleep on a dead tree in the distance. In an instant, Adrian's body and wings began to turn into grains of sand that danced in the wind and then fell to the desert floor.

Far across the vast desert in the east, an opening in the sky began to appear, allowing a ray of light to descend on a camp settled among the dunes. An angel slowly emerged from the ray to greet his brothers saluting his arrival.

"In honour of the Most High," was the harmonious cry from the angels below.

"What news of the west, Gabriel?" the angel from the sky gently asked one of his brothers below. "Are there any changes in Lucifer's movements?"

"Not much my brother, Michael. But he and his brothers are growing in strength all the time with their ongoing recruitment of souls. There is also some sad news. One of our scouts has just reported the death of Adrian."

Michael's face sorrowed and his sapphire blue eyes began to weep at the thought of the death of a brother. He looked down towards the holy ground where the battle would take place. A terrible image of war and death encroached into Michael's mind causing him to close his eyes to be rid of it. Opening his eyes again, he lifted his head to face the west where he knew that Lucifer and his brethren were readying themselves for war.

"Tell me Gabriel, why has it come to this? So much blood will be spilt today."

Michael again had to fight off a thought of the sand turning into a river of blood.

"It is inevitable, my brother. It has been written and spoken about since time began," Gabriel said.

Michael turned with a glowing radiant face like the morning sun towards Gabriel as he heard his words. "Why do you look at me so intently, Gabriel?" At this, Gabriel dropped his stare.

"I notice my dear brother that you look worried. You don't doubt our victory today, do you? Or did the Most High speak of something that troubles you?"

Michael and Gabriel both bowed their heads in reverence and placed their right hands over their hearts to show respect in mentioning the Most High.

"Gabriel," Michael said putting his hand on Gabriel's shoulder, "The Most High has held me to secrecy about the events that are going to unfold on this day. All I can say is that whatever the outcome, we all must keep the faith. You must follow my every command and trust in God's infinite wisdom. Can you promise me that you will do this?"

"I will Michael, you know I will."

They both turned to see another angel approaching. Michael watched as Daniel swiftly approached with his sword.

"Your sword, brother," Daniel said. Michael thanked Daniel after taking his blade.

Michael held his sword aloft towards the heavens, turning it from side to side. The sunlight bounced off the edge of the blade. It was almost a replica of Lucifer's in size, length and weight. The only difference was that instead of having rubies on the handle, it was inlaid with blue sapphires which shone in the light of the day.

"Come Gabriel, the Most High's work is to be done. Let us ready ourselves. Go and call the assembly of angels. It's time we all gathered in prayer to prepare us for what lies ahead."

With a bow of the head, Gabriel flew until he came to rest on a high cliff top. He bent down to pick up his golden trumpet, where it had been sitting waiting for the return of its master. He took in a deep breath, raised it to his dry lips and exhaled.

Lucifer turned to face the east as Gabriel's sound travelled through the air on a westerly wind and met his ears. A big smile made its way across Lucifer's intense face on hearing this great sound. He thought of mass destruction and how it grew ever closer.

"Gather the brethren Simon, the time has come to demonstrate to God and this planet who has ultimate power." Lucifer slowly breathed in as if inhaling and visualising the smell of death that would soon be wafting through the air.

"It's a great day to create a hell on earth," he said quietly.

Lucifer lifted his sword to touch his face as if making a salute. With the blade resting on his nose, he closed his eyes and connected with his innermost power, making his soul come to life. Within seconds, electric bolts surfaced from the ground, snaking around his feet and gradually climbing up to his groin, his upper torso and then around his face, until his whole body was surrounded by red light circling around him like a tornado. Lucifer's eyes blinked open to reveal a bright crimson light in his powerful stare. Just as quickly as they opened, his eyes closed again. The eerie silence was almost deafening, silencing the wind. It was as though everything had ceased for a final moment in time; past, present and future had now joined together to witness the end. A muffled growl issued from Lucifer's stomach, getting louder making its way up into his chest, then throat, until finally Lucifer threw his head back. He opened his mouth and released a deafening scream, causing his sword to burst into flames that burned the brightest shade of red. Lowering his head, he slowly opened his eyes to view his army of angels around him. Some looked on him in fear; others glorified themselves in their leader's fiery gaze.

"Behold," Lucifer said in a voice like thunder, "you see before you your leader in all his glory. Do not be afraid. This day you will be delivered and you will have your paradise – that I grant you. Come with me and let my will be done."

Lucifer lifted his sword and pointed it at his brothers. As he uttered a word only known to him, some of the flames fired off the sword and entered the hearts of his brethren. In an instant their eyes flashed red, connecting them to Lucifer's energy. Lucifer, accepting his followers' allegiance, turned to face the holy ground below, and using his sword he shot out a red flame that lit up the ground creating an almighty bang of thunder, causing the holy ground to shake and tremble until it finally cracked and opened, revealing an eerie red glow of light surrounded by smoke. From amidst the smoke and red light, a moaning started to sound, the sound of dammed souls who had been serving Lucifer for an eternity in the fiery depths of Hell. These souls started to surface and hover above the holy ground, bending in submission to their master, ready for his command. It was not long before the surface was a wave of red souls glowing in anticipation for the chance to expel their anger into the world. Lucifer roared to his army of souls below: "It has begun."

A strange feeling resonated through Michael's body on hearing the roar of Lucifer and as he knelt in prayer. It was a feeling of such intensity and urgency that he broke from his meditation and looked west. Realising that the time was near, he turned to his brothers. "Come brethren, let us join minds in honour of the Most High."

The other angels stood to join Michael, bowing their heads whilst placing their right hand over their heart. As they reached a perfect unison of minds, Michael closed his eyes and held his sword to his face.

"Father, it has begun. In your name and in the name of love, we serve you."

Above the angels' heads, the blue sky opened. A blue light began to glow brighter. Slowly, it descended on Michael and his followers and then it began to vibrate on a different frequency. Becoming quicker and urgent, it gathered in momentum, collecting its energy until it burst like a clap of thunder. Michael watched with joy as it escaped its confinement from the vast sky and descended like a shot. On opening their eyes they looked to the heavens to see the souls of the saints and the saved exiting Heaven and descending towards the holy ground and the red souls below.

Then with a commanding voice, which resonated with a new kind of authority, Michael spoke, "The time is upon us, a time to defend what we know is good and true. It is time to preserve the word of the Most High and keep Paradise safe from the hands of the unworthy."

As the burning sun reached its highest point, Michael flew high above the ground with sword shining blue ready to strike. The blue sky surrounding them was shining brighter than ever before, as the destiny of their souls was igniting to complete their mission. Approaching them head on was Lucifer and his gathering. Their half of the sky was of a blood red colour, lit by flashes of lightning ripping through the dense sky. As the souls raced to each other, Lucifer could see the shining red and blue eyes dancing in the air like rubies and sapphires. He then turned to look through the flapping of his wings to see if his angels were still as faithful as the souls below. Feeling satisfied and proud of where he was on this day, he broke into a laugh that rumbled like thunder.

"Michael!" Lucifer shouted his war cry as he accelerated to meet his main opponent.

"Lucifer!" Michael returned his shout as the two came together in slow motion.

As their swords connected, spraying sparks rained down to earth. Angels from both sides were fighting using their swords and wings as weapons. All around fell from the sky, as their injured wings could not keep them in flight. The battle of the souls below also raged in confusion amidst the rising dust from the desert floor. Out of the dust, blue and red ghost-like souls entangled in a battle for survival to join the surrounding mists that were embroiled in a battle of their own. Gabriel looked up to the sky at the blue energy which was much stronger than the quickly diminishing red energy. *We are going to win,* he thought as he pulled his sword from the chest of another defeated angel.

Hours of fighting ensued. In the heat of the battle, Lucifer looked down to see his shrinking army of souls and then looked behind to see the few remaining angelic brothers. *I have to win, I must have ultimate power.* He swung his sword in rage at Michael. Fending off this attack Michael rushed at Lucifer and flew straight into him, stunning him.

"Gabriel," Michael shouted, "fly down and order the retreat."

"Why? We have almost won; retreating is not necessary."

"Just do it!"

Gabriel folded his wings close to his body and descended with speed to the battle below. After issuing the order, Gabriel rejoined the battle above where Michael and Lucifer were crashing together like thunder. Gabriel wondered whether to assist Michael, but a stern look from Michael told him otherwise. Michael fended off another attack from an enraged Lucifer, then, for a moment that seemed to last forever, Gabriel watched in horror as Lucifer's sword first struck Michael's left wing and then a second strike severed his right wing.

"Michael!" Gabriel screamed as Michael's wings began to flap lifelessly. As Michael fell from the sky, he turned to look at his brother Gabriel and the blue light from his eyes began to fade, revealing two white tear filled eyes.

Michael fell to the ground, whispering Gabriel's name. The sword fell from his dying hand, returning to its dormant metal. With a look of horror and disbelief, Gabriel saw the blue light in the sky fading fast, engulfed in the brightness of the red.

"What do we do now Gabriel?"

Gabriel turned to see Daniel looking exhausted and demoralised.

"We have lost," Daniel said, "none of our swords can match Lucifer's and with Michael gone we have no hope!"

Gabriel barely heard him. With effort, Gabriel broke from his moment of contemplation and lifted his head to the heavens which were now nearly red.

"Why?" Gabriel shouted. "Oh, God save us, win us this day."

A cackle, which broke into a roar of laughter, interrupted Gabriel's call for help. Gabriel turned to see Lucifer, sword poised in hand ready.

"You see," Lucifer said, "God has abandoned you. So why do you love God so much? Why don't you come with me and I will grant you paradise? You and your brothers have fought well. Let me reward you."

"Never!" Gabriel replied, looking up to the sky like a lost lonely boy for one last hope of aid from the Most High. Then he turned to the few brothers that remained and ordered a retreat. "Grant me the permission to recover Michael's body," Gabriel pleaded.

Lucifer nodded in agreement with a smirk on his face and arms open in a mocking gesture. His eyes followed Gabriel flying down to the now silent battlefield below.

As he approached the ground, Gabriel's heart sank at the sight of all the bodies, of angels together dead on a sea of flesh and feathers. Through tears, Gabriel spied Michael lying lifeless next to his sword. He gently lifted

Michael over his shoulder, grabbed hold of the sword and took flight. Ascending into the sky, he looked up and observed the last of Heaven's souls retreating into the last of the blue sky. Gabriel closed his eyes in horror, his heart swelling with remorse at such a failure on this day. He reopened his eyes to see Lucifer in front of him.

"You know you had the choice to be on the winning side Gabriel," Lucifer mocked.

"I really hope you find your peace Lucifer, and one day you will realise what you have done on this day." Gabriel gently made his way towards the heavens with Michael still cradled over his shoulder.

"Realise what I have done. I have defeated God's army. I think I am at peace, don't you? We will now have our paradise, a paradise on earth with me as God."

Gabriel took one last look at the death and carnage and defiant Lucifer below, then he submitted to the closing blue light which was getting smaller and smaller until it was a small pinpoint in a sky. It finally collapsed in the fullness of a red sky.

It is done, Lucifer thought. The sound of cheering and merriment below drew his gaze to the ground where he could see his faithful angels waiting in anticipation of his return. With a triumphant heart and glorious wings, Lucifer swooped down to join his companions.

"My lord, your throne awaits you," Simon remarked as he landed. Lucifer saw Simon standing next to a golden throne, in front of which stood the two beasts that had previously guarded the sword. Now they were free, calm and pleased to see their master as he landed and patted their heads.

"Yes Simon, I will take my rightful place. The one that was destined for me as a god and ruler on earth."

"Yes, my lord, we are all waiting to see you in your chair as our ruler."

Lucifer rested his sword on a mounting attached to the throne and took his seat. The congregation knelt in perfect submission and swore allegiance once more to their leader. Simon lifted the crown fashioned from all the precious metals and stones found on earth and gently placed it on the head of its new owner.

"My faithful souls you have dominion on earth. As a reward you may now drink from the riches of life – greed, lust, avarice and all earthly pleasures are yours now for the taking. This is my command to you on this victorious day when my paradise came to earth."

Dark shadows flickered on the ground as the souls danced around the blazing fire. Its flames reached up to meet the dark blanket of the night. As each beat of their drums sent them more into a more frenzied state, Lucifer turned to his angels who were sitting beside him.

"These souls are very easily satisfied. You give them what they want and they will follow you even to death and beyond. I am very proud of what I have achieved this day. I have proved that the Most High made a mistake in casting me out of heaven. I have become the most powerful god alive. I succeeded to let God and man know who I am and he ordered his angels to retreat in fear of my superiority."

"Yes, my lord," all the angels said in harmony.

Lucifer's moment of self-flattery was disturbed by the silencing of the drums. He turned to see what had happened. Out of the darkness of the star-vacant sky, a tiny bright light was making its way towards them. Suddenly, there was a flash of light which temporarily blinded everyone. When Lucifer's eyesight recovered, he saw his angels and souls screaming at the white light which ploughed along the ground turning their bodies to ash in the very place they were standing. Lucifer, stunned with disbelief, took a while to gather his senses, then with horror he reached forward to take the sword from his throne and leapt to his feet.

"Nooo!" Lucifer roared. The last thing he saw before he collapsed was the ash of his pets float off in the wind.

CHAPTER TWO

"LUCIFER WAKE UP, WAKE UP!" Cautiously, Lucifer opened one eye to see who was addressing him. But he could not see anything apart from white light and the throne on which he was sitting.

"Who is there?"

"Why don't you recognise the voice of the Most High?"

Lucifer thought for a while then a look of disbelief came on his face on hearing a soft but authoritative, recognisable voice. "It's a trick. You would not let me back into heaven, you cast me out. You are here, but your mind and spirit is so full of evil and hatred you are not able to see Paradise and me. Nooo!" Lucifer said angrily, as he struggled to stand from his throne, but the chains bound tightly around his wrists and ankles held him fast.

"It is no use struggling to free yourself from that throne. You can't escape the confinements of your own greed which that throne represents. You wanted power and authority. Well, now you're trapped in the chair of your own self-indulgence."

"How can this be? I beat you and your angels in glorious victory. What a sound it was to hear Gabriel command a retreat and watch as he and your other cowardly angels disappeared into my red sky."

"But you did not win. Look where you are now still trapped under my power."

"That might be so, but I defeated your commander, Michael. That in itself is a victorious act."

"Hello Lucifer," Lucifer turned his head and heard Michael's voice resonating out of the white light. Michael's voice was almost remorseful at tricking Lucifer. "It was a great battle; you fought well but underestimated the power of the Most High. I am very much alive."

Lucifer struggled to find the right words. "How can this be? I struck you down with my own sword and joyfully watched as you fell lifeless to the ground below. Gabriel even carried your body back into heaven."

"Gabriel did not even know that I was still alive. I was the only one who knew of the Most High's plans, which were given to me before descending to earth. My instructions were to give a command of retreat to the army at the right moment then allow you to defeat me, but not kill me, for I was under the protection and love of the Most High."

"But why not just defeat me in battle? It would have been easier."

With commanding authority, the Most High's voice silenced them both. "Why do you think I planned this, Lucifer? With a blink of an eye I could have laid your body out to rest a long time ago."

"Perhaps you and I are not so different after all?" Lucifer said. "It seems you were playing a sick game in which you wanted to humiliate me again like the time when you cast me out of heaven."

"No!" The Most High's voiced roared like a lion. "I wanted you to grow in confidence, power and authority. I allowed you freedom on earth to corrupt nations and in my great design you became the most powerful leader of angels and men. Your power and glory on earth was second to none, but that is what I wanted you to think, even to the point of allowing you to defeat Michael and his army. This was all staged to make you realise that even while you were in your most powerful and glorious state of mind, I still had the power and authority over you. With very little effort I still could take away everything you had. It is a harsh reminder of how powerful I am and how powerless you are, a fact you seem to have forgotten in your own arrogance. So all your life, thoughts and actions were, in fact, an illusion. I am very sorry Lucifer, but you have been my puppet in a demonstration of my authority over you, and my love for humankind on earth."

Lucifer's veins throbbed against the skin of his head and arms as a violent rage rushed through his body. He struggled to free himself, but the chains that held him remained tight. In fact, as he anger grew, so did the strength of the chains, reminding him that his anger was the very tool holding him tight.

"Love?" Lucifer spat. "You don't love humans, you don't even know the meaning of the word. You abandoned them a long time ago, as you did me by throwing me out of Heaven."

"Lucifer, do you still not realise that I did not throw you out of Heaven?" God was now trying to communicate in a more reassuring voice. "You left when your mind turned to envy of me and my love for mankind. The very action of looking upon me with envious eyes was your own downfall. You allowed this envy and jealousy to turn into fear and anger at the very thing you did not understand, my mind. The word of my mind is what keeps the earth turning, lets the fire warm their hearts, the air fill their lungs and the water quench their thirst. This knowledge has lasted since time began. By what authority did you assume you had this knowledge?"

"I did not think it was a right," Lucifer said. "I just didn't understand why this knowledge cannot be shared. If more angels had this knowledge they could have helped you look after mankind more effectively."

"How dare you judge me," the Most High's voice roared like thunder "My great design for earth and mankind works perfectly and is in no need of a secondary caretaker who wants to be my equal."

"I did not want to be your equal. I just wanted to know what you knew, and in denying me, you turned me into this evil soul, as defined by you, that I am today."

"No, Lucifer." The Most High's voice was now speaking more sorrowfully. "I did not deny you the knowledge of my mind. You like everyone else do not have the capability of understanding me and the essence of what I am. If that happened there would be no reason for me to exist. What place is there of a god in the minds of gods themselves because if they had total knowledge that I possess then they would be like me and not need me."

"But if this world you created and the whole of existence is so perfect, why have I had so much influence and power in creating so much killing and hatred on earth?"

"When I created men, I gave them souls. With their soul, they were given free choice to choose whether to do right or wrong. You see, Lucifer, you and I are not to blame for human nature, because we are not human ourselves. Inside each and every one of them I have installed a life energy, which comes from me, the very source. This life energy does not recognise good and evil, it just is and exists. It is only the mind of man that defines this source as good or evil with positive or negative actions."

"What do you mean I am not to blame for their evil actions? I am the very embodiment of evil. I make them do those things on earth. I glorified myself in their sins and watched eagerly as man turned against man creating a hell on earth."

"I am sorry Lucifer, but you are wrong again. Some humans choose to be good and others choose to be bad and this reflects on the balance or vibration resonating in human minds, If more humans decide to do bad, more evil is created and vice versa. It is a very delicate balance. I want to show you something."

Lucifer looked down at his feet and watched as the white light started to disappear. It gently faded away like a cloud dispersing in a sky, allowing a vision of the world to appear. In this vision, Lucifer could see humans on earth fighting in war.

"What do you think they are fighting for Lucifer?"

"I hope they are fighting against your system of faith."

"Not quite, close though. On one side of the battle you have an army who are fighting in God's name; on the other, you have an army who believe in worshiping things they can see like the stars and planets. Who is in the right? Are the army who fight in God's name, whatever that god is, just in their actions? Or the army who have no concept of a god? If the army of God lost, then everybody would assume their god was weaker, or worse still did not exist. The worship of planets would become the new religion where everybody would fear to offend Mars or Venus. Because that side became victorious, it would have to be accepted as good; it must be, because it won and that proves it exists, doesn't it? What you see here is a shift in human philosophy. Both sides are doing what they think is right; it is only their judgment of each other that determines who is right or wrong There is no conception of good or evil, only two sides fighting for their purpose and belief."

Lucifer again struggled with his chains, trying to secretly slip his arms through the clasps holding him in place. The vision switched to reveal two men constructing a building. The Most High continued his explanation.

"One was from a very wealthy family and the other was bought up in poverty. Because of their different upbringings, they learnt different values. The wealthy man learnt that respect and popularity were measured by how much money and friends you had. The poor man however learnt to respect the little things he had, very few friends and only what nature had provided for him. They had both been given a task by me to construct a building fit for me. The wealthy man used his abundant finance to employ hundreds of expert craftsmen to draw up the plans, construct and build a glorious edifice. The finest stones, precious metals, gold and silver were shipped in from other countries. The glass was cut to precise measurements. The building was all completed within two years. However, the poor builder had only a few helpers and workers. Slowly and diligently they gathered wood from a local forest, cut and carved the wood until their hands bled. They worked through all weathers, not stopping through all the blood and sweat, until its completion after five years. With that vision Lucifer, who do you think loves me more and who is the better builder to build a home for me?"

"Why are you asking me about love? "Lucifer shook and lowered his head in an act of frustration and boredom, "I do not know of it anymore, I don't want to. I am tired of feeling like a student of morality. Haven't you forgotten I am the one who stands against the very thing you stand for? I do not need lessons in morality because I don't want or have any."

"Well, let me tell you anyway. The poor man loves God more because he designed, built and completed the building with a lot more of self-sacrifice. Whereas the wealthy man only paid for other people to design, build and complete the construction. Now if you take everybody else away on the earth and just leave the two men in their buildings and I decide to visit as a mortal, where do you think I would feel safest if either building started to collapse?"

"I suppose you would feel safer in the wealthy man's building. I know I would because it is bigger and stronger."

"No, I would feel safer in a poor man's house because of the fact he knew his building. Through all his self-sacrifice, he gained complete knowledge of its foundation and that which made it strong. The wealthy man through his complacency did not know of the true meaning of the foundation laid a foundation which made it weak. Here is the lesson, Lucifer. Don't you think that as God I thought of everything when I designed the world as a safe home for mankind?"

"You spoke about this delicate balance earlier and how it can change between good and evil. Look at the state of this safe house of yours. Now I want to show you my vision." The Most High allowed Lucifer to state his case as the clouds temporarily joined together then opened again to reveal visions of men killing men, people dying of hunger through poverty and disease and natural disasters like earthquakes played out beneath them.

"Don't you think these acts demonstrate my power and authority, on earth even though I am chained to this damned chair? I am still in control." Lucifer smiled as a rising feeling of confidence and power entered his body again. "Your house, as you eloquently put it, is becoming more and more godless. People are asking if you exist or, even better, cursing you for their misfortunes, when all the time I am in control and to blame. It is wonderful when I hear them saying that you are to be blamed for my actions. When they say God has forsaken them and the devil is in control that he must be because God would not allow this to happen, that is my victory. I put it to you the Most High that my will is stronger than yours. It is this will, inherent in every mortal that manifests into what you see in this dark vision."

"I think you still do not understand me properly. Let me try to elaborate in a way you might understand. Prepare yourself for what I am about to tell you it will confuse you but I can assure you I speak the truth. We are not the ones in control of our destinies, the humans are."

"What! Nonsense."

"As I have already explained, when I created everything and from the beginning of time," the Most High continued. "I created man and gave him a soul and he was perfect. Unfortunately, he decided he wanted to be more human than spiritual, taking part in earthly pleasures such as the gratifications of flesh, wealth and greed."

"I thought you said they were perfect? It did not take me long to show you their imperfections; tempting them was so easy."

"Wrong again, that is what you have been led to believe. But in fact you only exist because of the dark side of human nature. You did not create the evil in them. They created you out of their own evil actions. Think about it how would mankind justify their bad actions and how would they decide if an act was bad or good? Men, in their search to understand their own human nature, could not understand or accept that they were solely responsible for their own actions. So what they arrogantly decided was to place the blame somewhere else, and they created YOU."

Lucifer s eyes opened wide, his mouth dropped, but then he started laughing at what he thought was an absurd statement. *How could that be?*

"That's ridiculous."

But Lucifer's laughter turned into anger as he began to question his own existence. "No, no." Lucifer shook his head to reassure himself of any doubt. "You lie, I am in control, those disgusting creatures you created are not in charge of my destiny. How dare you suggest such a thing?"

"It is true. I gave them free will, which contains an inherent longing for knowledge of what and where they come from. This search for knowledge led them to explore all aspects of human nature, although unfortunately some of these acts involved carnal knowledge. In their pursuit they discovered some actions were not to everyone's liking, so they said the devil was responsible, a fitting scapegoat for the dark side of their nature. It's ironic they seem to have forgotten that they still have this knowledge. It has just been buried and blinded in their futile search for what they already have."

"So if I am just an illusion of the human mind, how is it that I can remember you throwing me out of Heaven?

You said my own jealously and envy cast me out."

"That is true, but do you not remember the other reason why you left Heaven?"

"What other reason?" Lucifer asked with contempt.

"The other reason you were cast out, all those thousands of years ago and times before that."

"Why was that? I cannot remember."

"All in good time. First I want to draw your attention to what is happening now. Humans are becoming so evil in nature and their love for me has taken a dramatic shift. It is evident that my existence is becoming less and less while your strength in their minds grows all the time. After you finished your war and rampage on earth, you left behind you a nearly godless world."

"You said it was all in your big design, a big act to make me feel powerful on earth. If I remember rightly, you called me a puppet."

"That is true, but there is a bigger picture here which I only know about and unfortunately it cost quite a few human sacrifices."

"A few? Let us be real, how about thousands?"

"You should feel honoured. It was all in your name. However, their loss will not be in vain, although they all helped play an important part."

"An important part in what?" Lucifer asked urgently and angrily.

"That I cannot tell you at present because it is only for me to know the plans I have for you."

"Untie these chains and I will show you who has plans for whom."

"Lucifer, when are you going to learn? Maybe one day you will."

There was a deathly silence, which to Lucifer seemed to last a lifetime, as he tried to look into the light to comprehend what was happening.

"Lucifer I have decided on your punishment."

"What! More punishment? How could the punishment be worse than it already is? What could be worse than being defeated in battle, humiliated and held here against my will, told that my whole existence has been staged to get me to where I am now, in this damn chair? Oh, I nearly forgot, I do not exist do I?"

"Silence!" The Most High's voice roared, causing the chains holding Lucifer to vibrate. "Your punishment is to be cast out of where you now sit into the body of a mortal. I cannot think of a more fitting punishment than to become that which you hate the most. You will still have the mind you have now, but flesh and bone will be your prison. As you walk about on earth as human, you will help them in their most trying, difficult and dangerous times. To enable you to do this you will still have your spiritual gifts and powers, but instead of using them for evil you will use them for good. It's time the balance shifted and the humans started believing in me again. I cannot think of a better person to make this happen. This will go on for as long as you want it to. If you do not decide to help, you will simply stay in human form. When I feel satisfied you have done what is needed, you will be allowed to return to angel form and what you truly are. Lucifer, it is time for you to think of a new name as you are prepared for your new existence."

Lucifer fought very hard to keep his eyes from shutting, because he feared the thought of being entrapped in a human body and being earthbound in human form utterly repelled him to the stomach. A fear started to burn deep in his mind as his eyes were forced to close.

Chapter Three

Aware that he had awoken, Lucifer stalled opening his eyes for as long as he could. He wondered what nightmare might reveal itself. He thought that maybe he had been dreaming whilst asleep on the throne after winning the battle. *Yes, that's right, I am asleep. I am still the victor and supreme ruler of earth, God failed and I won.*

Reluctantly, he opened his eyes. It took a while for him to adjust to a different light, one that was a little dimmer than that of the Most High's. Lucifer soon realised that he had not been dreaming. He found himself floating above a vast array of beds occupied by sick people and watched as a man assisted by a nurse coughed up blood. She was comforting him in his pains. *Oh I see a hospital where sick people get better, not my place to be I enjoy death and suffering not places of healing*. His attention was drawn to a man being administered some urgent treatment. Doctors and nurses were quickly and efficiently trying their best to save this man's life. One nurse ripped open the man's shirt whilst a doctor slid a small piece of metal into his arm. Another doctor reached out and started to charge the electrodes.

"We're losing him!" one of the nurses shouted.

"Not when I'm on duty. This one HAS to survive," a doctor replied.

Lucifer started to sneer at the effort being

expended on bringing a human back to life.

Let him die, Lucifer shouted angrily at the deaf ears of the humans below. *I cannot stay here for all eternity.*

Lucifer turned to fly away, but noticed he did not have his wings. He was rooted at the very place he floated and couldn't turn away from the sight of the man being resuscitated. A feeling of panic and sickness came over him as he struggled with his confinement. *Why am I able to fly without wings and why am I unable to move?*

"This one HAS to survive if it is the last thing I do in this godforsaken world," the doctor said. "Clear!"

A sudden pulse of electricity suddenly rushed through Lucifer's being, causing him to recoil in unbearable pain as the doctor operated the paddles.

You have got to be joking. The pain subsided, allowing him to grasp the full extent of what was to become his fate.

"I am not going in that body," he shouted to the heavens.

The doctor moved the paddles to the man's chest. The Most High's voice repeated in Lucifer's head: "Become that which you hate the most."

"Clear!" the doctor shouted again.

"Arrghhh!" Lucifer screamed as the pulse resonated through him again, slowly pulling him down to where the human was lying. Waving his arms in the air, he tried to frantically take hold of anything that would halt the awful process to which he was now being subjected. He watched with horror as his feet began to merge with the man lying lifeless on the bed. The process became more intense and painful until just his head was left to merge. Looking up now at the doctor and nurses working on the body, which was to become his prison, his watched the doctor lift the paddles above his chest.

"One more try, give me all you have, nurse," the doctor said as a nurse turned to the electrical panel and turned the knob to full power. The doctor rubbed the metal plates together and placed them on his chest.

"Please God let him live!" he shouted. "Clear!"

"Nooo!" Lucifer's cry was to no avail as he now become at one with the human body and took his first human breath.

"We've got him, doctor. You did it," the nurse said.

"Thank God, I thought we'd lost him." The flat line on the screen was now bleeping and moving in a regular rhythm.

On opening his now human eyes, Lucifer observed the doctors and nurses all looking down at him. A doctor took hold of a pocket torch and shone it into his eyes. Lucifer turned his head to avoid the intensity of its beam.

"Get that thing away from me," Lucifer protested angrily.

"Welcome back, you gave us quite a scare. We thought we were going to lose you. That hole in your head nearly cost your life; those muggers had left you for dead."

Lucifer turned to the sound of the nurse speaking to him. She was bent over him, smiling and rubbing his forehead.

"Get away from me, you disgusting creatures," Lucifer said as he pushed the nurse away. "Do you not know who I am?"

"Why don't you tell us?" one of the doctors snapped at Lucifer's apparent ingratitude.

"I am Lu ..." Lucifer attempted to say his name aloud but the words just did not form correctly in his mouth. He tried again, "I am telling you I am Luc ..."

Still the words did not come, which made him remember God had forbidden him to say his true name.

"Lewis? Leonard? What about Luscious?" the doctor asked. "Can't you remember? I think he must be suffering from amnesia."

"I am the Lord and Prince of Darkness, the most evil angel that can ever enter your dreams. I have lived for thousands of years and God has decided on this punishment for me, that I should be incarnated in this disgusting body of flesh where I now reside."

"Okay," the doctor replied, "I think that bump on your head might be a bit more severe than we originally thought. We had better keep you in for a couple more days for observation. Nurse, will you administer our patient a small sedative to help him relax?"

Lucifer felt the needle enter his arm.

"Ouch, that hurt," Lucifer said. This was the first time he had felt pain on a physical level. He did not like it one bit; it gave him a feeling of such weakness.

"Don't be such a baby, surely the lord of darkness has felt and seen much more pain?" smirked the nurse.

"I don't like your tone, lady. If I had my powers I would turn you to ash in the very place where you stand." The nurse gave Lucifer a concerned look.

"You must not keep talking like that. People will start to think you're crazy and you don't want to end up in an institution, do you?"

Lucifer realised that he was not going to be believed and that he had no powers to prove what he said. The nurse tucked in the blankets of his bed as the sedative started to work. Once again he felt his eyes becoming heavy.

"Can you remember your name now?"

"It's Luther," he said reluctantly as he watched the nurse switch the light off in the ward.

"Well, good night Luther. See you in the morning."

He turned to face the window by his bed, looking out at the sun as it made its way down behind the horizon. He pondered on the memory of sitting on that rock in the rising sun of the desert just before the battle. As the last ray of light vanished into the darkness of night, he could not believe his predicament, confined in a bed as a human in a mortal world.

The sound of someone on the television news roused Lucifer from his sleep. He watched carefully as the reporter talked about the political struggle in a country in the Far East between Governor Rasheed and General

Silas, the first who wanted things to stay as they were and the second who wanted to change a nation which was full of false prophets and politicians, responsible for corrupting their society. Silas's spokesperson said that Silas wanted to establish a new political and religious stronghold over nations without interference from established customs and the Western world.

The nurse angrily turned off the television with the remote control and the television screen went blank, much to Lucifer's annoyance.

"That General Silas is a horrible man. He is a butcher and a religious fanatic, hell bent on genocide, greed and dictatorship. He doesn't want peace, and if you ask me it marks the beginning of the end."

"He seems quite a powerful character with admirable qualities, a leader of men."

"The only thing he is going to lead us to is the end of the world if we aren't careful. I don't know how he became so powerful. Please don't tell me you're a follower of his? Governor Rasheed is a much more peaceful man."

"Well, let's just say I knew someone like him a long time ago. Tell me nurse, what year is this and where the hell am I?"

"I see you are still suffering a little from memory loss. It's the sixth of June 2006 and you're in a hospital in London in the United Kingdom."

"Is it really?"

He couldn't believe that four thousand years had passed since he'd battled with Michael. It felt strange because the conversation with the Most High seemed like only hours before. *So this is the future? I wondered how it would look. Now I see machines working together with humans to save lives in hospitals and people communicating from inside a wooden box with a glass front.*

The sound of coughing broke his thoughts. He turned to see the man he had seen whilst floating on the ceiling coughing up more blood. The man noticed Lucifer's intense stare and quickly wiped away a tear, embarrassed. He was frail and in his mid-thirties, with dark, fading eyes, pale skin, and lips that were almost blue.

"What is wrong with that young man?" Lucifer asked the nurse who was making his bed more comfortable.

"Oh, that's poor David. He has terminal cancer. The doctors don't think he'll last till the end of the week. I feel so sorry for him, being so young and the cancer being so aggressive. He has so much to live for – a loving wife, a daughter and parents that love him dearly."

"That is a terrible shame." Lucifer tried to make himself sound sympathetic, but all he wanted to do was roar with laughter at the poor man's fate.

"It is shame God can't help him," Lucifer said. "Where is God when you need the Almighty the most?"

"Please don't blaspheme in front of me," said the nurse, offended.

Lucifer's eyes filled up with water as he fought hard not to laugh. The nurse crossed herself. Lucifer turned to face David who had now stopped coughing and was smiling at him. Lucifer stared intently back. When the nurse wasn't looking, he drew his finger under his throat and let his tongue fall out of the side of his mouth. Shocked, David started coughing violently. The nurse rushed to raise the bowl to his mouth. She gently sat on his bed and comforted him as much as she could. After a while the coughing ceased and the nurse lowered David's head onto the pillow, allowing him to breathe more easily apart from the odd crackle from deep inside his chest.

The nurse returned to Lucifer's bed.

"Is anyone else going to die soon?"

The nurse filled his glass with water. "Why do you want to know?"

"Just call it natural curiosity. Tell me nurse, do you enjoy your work saving people? People you don't even know. What do you get out of it?"

"There is nothing better than the feeling you get when

you manage to save somebody's life, or heal sick people and watch them get better."

"I can't see it myself,' Lucifer said. 'You are not able to receive thanks from dead people for all the hard work you have put in. What about other sick people, are you ever thanked for your time and effort? Does God thank you when you are lying in bed after saying your prayers?"

"Stop it! I told you before; don't talk about God in that way. I agree that in the last ten to fifteen years, people's behaviour has progressively got worse towards my profession. I don't get thanks at all, even from you. The whole world is going crazy if someone would rather leave someone to die in the streets than help them. I can't understand how this world has become so selfish to the point of complete arrogance."

"Exactly, and yet you still choose to do your job faithfully and zealously, why?"

"I guess I'm an eternal optimist. I hope that one day something will change, and there will be a time when the word of God will be known in this world once more. A time when people will again start to believe in their own humanity."

"Rubbish. Why don't you just accept human nature as it is and realise nothing will ever change. Look at General Silas. He is becoming more powerful with his religious beliefs."

"You sound as if you enjoy accepting the fact that nothing will change. But I tell you I feel something big is very close on the horizon. It's going to change the way we think forever. God won't sit back and let these awful things in life carry on. I am sure God has a plan and that plan will soon be revealed."

"Not if I have anything to do with it!"

"What was that?"

"I just said I don't want anything to do with it. I gave up on believing in God a long time ago. When can I get out of this hospital? Having all these people around me is making me feel quite sick."

"Oh, we are feeling grumpy today. You should be able to leave tomorrow after the doctor has inspected your injury and given you the all clear."

"Good." Lucifer turned his back on the nurse, indicating he didn't want or need anymore attention.

The sound of the bedside clock's second hand ticking seemed progressively louder as Lucifer mused on how time here was so slow. Yet the past four thousand years had seemed to disappear in a blink of an eye. The rest of the day dragged on. Before long, the sun was making its way down in the west. Medication and food had all been distributed and the doctors were leaving the ward after completing their rounds. It fell silent during the darkness of the night. Lucifer was unable to fall asleep due to a patient in the corner snoring. David's breathing was also getting worse. As an angel, Lucifer didn't need sleep, but now he was in human form, tiredness and fatigue were setting in. He turned onto his stomach and pulled his pillow over his head to muffle the sounds around him. For a while, Lucifer rested. He was soon awoken by the sound of David's coughing penetrating through the pillow. Lucifer sat up. David was struggling in the darkness to find his panic button, knocking over a glass of water in the process. Lucifer looked around to see if any of the other patients had woken to see what was going on. All remained silent and asleep. All of a sudden the coughing ceased and Lucifer turned to see David looking right at him. Their staring eyes were held together for what seemed a lifetime before David broke the silence.

"Help me please, I am so afraid," David said. "I don't want to die and leave my family, please. I feel so alone, I know you can save me."

Tears of sorrow and despair fell from David's eyes as Lucifer watched him, emotionless.

"I have no desire to save you." Lucifer knew that

David was near to death and now possessed a deeper understanding of who Lucifer was. "Look at you, a real disgrace to the human race. Why don't you die with some dignity? Or maybe even ask God to come and save you."

"But God came to me in a vision and told me you have the power to save me. Please think of my family."

"Well that vision and God are lying to you. There is nothing or no-one that can save you now. You are most probably better off dead and out of this godless world anyway."

"Please!" David fell back onto his bed and everything went silent.

Lucifer watched in the semi-darkness for a brief time until a small spark of light started appearing from an opening in the ceiling. This light started to grow and expand in brightness, reflecting in Lucifer's eyes as he watched intently. It was at this point he felt something, something that he had never experienced before: fear. Lucifer cowered as the heavenly light got so bright illuminating the whole ward. He cried out to the other patients but they remained peacefully asleep, totally oblivious to what was happening. Just then David's soul left his body and floated over to Lucifer's bed, he looked down at Lucifer with forgiving eyes.

"I forgive you and I love you. One day you will know the meaning of this and the word of God and truth."

Lucifer was now feeling sick to the stomach as he watched an angel descending through the light in the ceiling to escort David to the Most High and Heaven above. In that instant Lucifer recognised Raphael from his long golden hair, green eyes and gold crown which sat proudly on his head,

"Hello my brother. I see you chose not to help and save this man. Do you not remember the punishment given to you from the Most High and the conditions that come with it? Why prolong your pain?"

Lucifer became more defiant.

"Forget it Raphael, you tell the Most High that I will find a way out of this wretched body and return to my former glory. When I do there will be hell to pay."

"Peace be with you brother," Raphael and David were now ascending hand-in-hand into the light. When it vanished, the ward was in semi-darkness again. Silence had returned, apart from an occasional snore.

Lucifer smirked at the ceiling where the angel had disappeared and was about to turn over to go to sleep when he suddenly clasped hold of his chest. The skin started to pull tighter around his skeletal frame as a tremendous pain shot from his head into his heart, causing him to recoil in pain and shut his eyes.

In an instant, an image of David as he was just before he died began to form in his mind. Lucifer could see the pain and sorrow on David's face and as the image got stronger, all of David's pain, fear and sorrow entered Lucifer's heart. He struggled with the enormity of these feelings and the pain they were causing him. The more he tried to fight them off, the worse the pain. Lucifer was so used to inflicting pain on others that he could not understand the alien feelings resonating through his being.

The pain began to ease as the image passed, then a second wave of feelings began as another image began to form. It was of David's family, looking at his grave. His young child was tearfully arranging flowers on the grave while the rest of the family looked on in sorrow. Just then they all seemed to turn to look at Lucifer. Within an instant their sadness made its way into Lucifer's heart. Their sorrow at losing one they loved so much caused him to feel he was being torn apart from head to foot. He thought he was going to die when other images started racing through his mind, pictures of people being tortured and killed – all in his name.

"Arrghhh! Leave me alone, go away," Lucifer moaned.

The visions started to fade away as Lucifer let out his cry. As they left, Adrian's angelic face came into his mind.

Lucifer remembered slaying him with his sword just before the battle. The vision confused Lucifer because he could not understand why Adrian came to him with a face of such forgiveness and love after what he had done to him.

"Luther, Luther wake up. Are you all right? I think you were having a nightmare," a panicked stricken face of his nurse was looking down on him as she shook him. "That must have been a real bad dream. Or just bad memories of a dark past?"

"Can you stop your idle conversation? Isn't it obvious I'm not well? Also you might want to check on David, I think he's dead."

The nurse rushed to David's bed, stretching to reach for the panic button to call for help. In minutes nurses and doctors all came running and after an examination by one of the doctors, David was pronounced dead. It was tearfully recorded by one of the nurses. Watching the nurse cry for the loss of her patient, Lucifer still could not comprehend why such a person would dedicate their life to help other people. Still pondering on this, he laid his head down on his pillow and stared thoughtfully at the ceiling. Wanting to close his eyes he knew he couldn't. The images were still burning deep in his mind.

The previous night had been a restless one for Lucifer and he hadn't managed to get much sleep. Now the smell of slightly burnt bacon and eggs made its way into the ward as a nurse wheeled a breakfast trolley to each patient's bed. The squeak from one of the trolley wheels got louder as it approached Lucifer's bed.

"Would you like bacon and eggs Luther? I had an uncle called Luther, a bit of a character though always getting himself in trouble with money and the ladies. Come to think of it, men as well. Such a shame about David don't you think? Would you like orange or pineapple juice?"

"Will you just shut up? Take everything away. I'm

tired and irritable and I'm not feeling well and you're not making me feel any better, you irritating little man."

"Well excuuuse me, you can be like that if you want. I was only trying to cheer you up." He raised one eyebrow up in disapproval and glared at Lucifer as Lucifer continued with his barrage of words.

"Do I look like I'm being cheered up? No, you're annoying the hell out of me."

The squeak started up again as the annoyed nurse moved onto the next bed and started to bore one of the other patients with his ramblings. *Damn God*, he thought as he bashed his head backwards into the bed pillow, *Could the Most High not of thought of a worse place for me to be incarnated as human? So much sickness and people wanting to be nice. I think I'm in a different sort of hell.*

"How are you this morning Luther?" A tall man in a white coat, holding a clipboard approached his bed and spoke in a rough deep voice.

"I have felt better. When am I going to be able to leave this place?"

"That's why I am here, to determine whether you're fit enough to leave. I just need one more examination to see if you're one hundred per cent. Good news is that your x-rays were clear of any brain damage. In fact, it was remarkably healthy. Look to the left then to the right, please."

The doctor held the pocket torch to his eyes. Lucifer tried to turn his head away as the smell of coffee and cigarettes from the doctor's breath met his nose.

"Pupil reaction is good. Any feelings of dizziness, or sickness?"

"Only from the smell of your breath. All these people who are constantly invading my space and not giving me any peace."

"Very funny," the doctor said. "Well if that test comes back normal you will be glad to know you can leave this afternoon. You seem fine and have healed very quickly.

It's remarkable how the wound on the back of your head has healed. There's only a scab left, though that's in a very unusual shape". Lucifer felt with his hand where the scab was. "I've never seen anything like it. Anyway, hopefully the nurse will be along shortly with discharge papers for you to sign. Is there anything else I can do for you?" Lucifer frantically grabbed his bed sheets with urgency at the thought of getting out of the bed and hospital.

"You can tell me where my clothes are, I don't seem to see any around."

"Your clothes have been destroyed because of the damage and blood stains from your mugging. The nurse will take you to our gift aid cupboard where people have donated clothes for our patients, so you can choose what you want. I'm off to see the other patients now. It's been nice meeting you Luther."

Lucifer looked as the doctor held out his hand to be shaken. He gave him a disapproving look. The doctor pulled his hand behind his back in embarrassment and walked off. *The sooner I get out of here and find a way of becoming an angel again the better.*

A couple of hours later, a nurse approached his bed. "Your papers, Luther. Your tests all came back negative; these papers are all ready for you to sign."

He took hold of the pen from the nurse. *I wonder if I can write my true name?* He started to write it but his bony hand started to shake and would not move even when he tried to move it with the other one. All he could manage to write down was the letters "Lu", so he carried on with Luther Fallen.

"Well Mr Fallen that's all the paperwork out of the way. We now have to get you ready to leave here. Has the doctor told you about clothes?"

Lucifer nodded.

"Put on that dressing gown, I'll be back in a minute."

Lucifer waited until the nurse had closed the curtains, then got himself out of his bed and slipped on his dressing gown. He sat on the end of his bed waiting for the nurse to return and wondered what he was going to see when he left the hospital. The curtain sprang open as the nurse pushed it to one side.

"I see you're ready. Good, come with me and I'll find you some new clothes."

Walking past the bed where David had been, Lucifer struggled with the memory of those images as they started to make themselves known again. Shaking his head, he followed the nurse down the shiny corridor, looking occasionally left and right to the side rooms until they stopped in front of a door on the right. On the front of the door there was a small golden plate, which read, in small letters:

Charity is to give from the heart
To all of us in this world which we are all a part.
When all hope is gone and there is only despair
Thank God for you who give and care.

Lucifer lifted his left eyebrow in a disapproving manner at the poem. "I think I can take it from here."

He pushed past the nurse and shut the door behind him, much to the nurse's objections. Inside, he could see a vast array of clothes, all of different sizes and colours. He found some black, neatly pressed trousers. *Well if I am the Prince of Darkness, it's going to have to be black.* The trousers fitted perfectly, as did a black polo neck top. He turned to face a tall mirror fixed on the wall, where he saw for the first time the face he had as a human. It was almost unbearable for him to look in the mirror at the mask of flesh. With his hands, he felt every bone and feature of his face. He was in his mid-thirties with dark hair and dark eyes. He stood about six foot in height, looked muscular and had the tattoo of an angel on his arm. Lucifer felt anger building in his veins at the thought of all memories of him as the angel Lucifer being wiped from existence. Four thousand years had vanished, hadn't they?

The glass stared to fall to the floor, as he rammed his clenched fist into the glass and it remained there as the final pieces fell to the floor. Moving away from where the mirror had been, he finally finished dressing himself with black socks and shoes. Walking to the door he reached for the door knob and spied a long black woollen coat which reached nearly to the ground. It had a high collar with a red label attached which read: "Simon's gift, please give to someone in despair and I hope it will comfort someone in a time of great need".

Thank you Simon, he thought remembering his right hand angel.

"Well, don't you look smart, Luther. All ready to take on and face the world again are we?"

Face the world, If only she knew what I had planned for the world and for humanity. He opened the exit doors and took his first human step in the outside world. *If only she knew.*

Chapter Four

As the hospital door behind him shut, Lucifer pondered his situation. *I have no money or food. I am a stranger to all and all I have is these clothes I stand in and this coat draped over my arm.*

For the first time in his existence he felt alone. Looking up at the scorching sun, he remembered the time when he was lying on the rock with the sun above him in the desert just before the great battle. It was then that he had glorious wings with the ability to fly, he could command generals and vast armies, and was feared by many. Now the sun just warmed up his weak corporeal flesh and there was nothing he could do about it.

"You look lost, friend, and that's a nasty bump you have on your head." His thoughts were disturbed by a frail scruffy-looking old man. His clothes were torn and dirty and he stood there staring at Lucifer with great curiosity and intensity.

"You could say that I am a very long way from home and for the record I'm not yours or anybody's friend."

"Where is home then?"

"Just somewhere out of town."

He had given up on the idea of trying to explain to people who he was and where he came from.

"Christopher is the name."

The man weakly held out his hand for a handshake. Lucifer looked down and noticed the dirty red fingerless gloves he was wearing. He then looked up at the man again who was extending his arm further. *If he wants me to take hold of that he can think again, mortal flesh is disgusting enough and dirty mortal flesh just intolerable.* Feeling intimidated by Lucifer's icy stare, Christopher withdrew his hand and wiped it on his trouser leg.

"I'm not one much for saying hello or greetings either. If you won't say hello, will you please indulge an old man's wishes and let me buy you something to eat and drink? I know a little café not too far from here and you look a little pale. Maybe it's all that hospital food you've been force fed in there."

Lucifer decided to follow this old man. He had no other leads and this man might have local knowledge which would be beneficial and he didn't know why but somehow it felt right. As he sat opposite this old man in the café, he smiled at the irony of his situation. The Lord of Darkness was not only being looked after by a mortal, but also by a weak old mortal. *Can my humiliation get any worse?*

"What are you going to have? I'm afraid I can only afford two coffees as well as a few biscuits, is that okay?"

"Yes I guess so. Can I ask you something, why are you helping me? You don't even know me."

"Well, there's not much love and light in the world these days. Two much killing and blood spilling. I think a little bit of friendship helps dispel some of the darkness covering the world at the moment. Besides, I had a vision which showed me of a great work I had to do."

"What vision are you talking about?"

"After the night of a bright shooting star falling from the sky, I was to go to a place of healing, where I would receive a gift from a stranger who was lost."

As Christopher was explaining himself, Lucifer noticed that the old man could not take his eyes off the long coat which he'd got from the charity department in the hospital.

"Nice isn't it?" Lucifer interrupted Christopher's

transfixed gaze. "It was given to me in that hospital, some charity thing."

"Yes, it's very nice, but what do you want with a heavy black coat especially on a hot day like today?"

"I like it. Besides it was free, given by some gullible charity person called Simon. It said so on the label. He wanted to comfort someone in a time of need."

"Hello chaps, what would you like to order?"

They both turned to see a waitress standing beside them, pen and pad poised to record their order. Christopher ordered two large coffees and some biscuits.

"You do have the money to pay for these don't you?" She was looking at them suspiciously. "We're not a charity, you know."

"Just get us the damn order, woman." Christopher slammed the money down on the table and then smiled at the waitress. Lucifer looked curiously at the man. "Now if you don't mind, me and my friend here are trying to have a sensible conversation."

The waitress lifted her eyebrows and slowly walked off to place their order.

"Service in this place is terrible," Christopher said. "I don't come here that much but at least it is cheap. Now where were we? Oh yes, the coat. You say it was donated by someone called Simon to comfort someone in despair? Oh well, perhaps it's symbolic of the world which is now in a time of great need. I can't understand why there is so much killing, violence and hatred among humanity. It's got worse since General Silas' power and popularity among his people has grown along with his nuclear capabilities. Mark my words, the end is on its way and we are all going to be blown to pieces."

Lucifer watched as the old man started to laugh, showing his black rotting teeth behind his white and yellow stained beard. He cringed at the black teeth and bad breath in front of him.

"Maybe that coat will protect you from the nuclear

fallout when we are all dead. Are you sure you want it still?"

Lucifer noticed the man staring at it again, which made him pull the coat more closely onto his lap.

"Of course I do, I believe it will be of great use in the hard times ahead."

The waitress came over with their order.

"Two coffees and some biscuits, you get extra, cutie, on the house."

The waitress winked at Lucifer as she placed their drinks in front of them. "Will there be anything else?"

"No, we're fine now, please go away," Christopher said.

The waitress stopped looking at Lucifer, giving Christopher a cold look of disapproval before walking off.

Lucifer noticed the old man curiously looking at him stirring his coffee as he added the cream and then the sugar uncertainly in a manner that suggested that he had no clue what he was doing.

"Are you suffering from some amnesia or something? You've got a very big bump on your head."

"Maybe I am suffering from that word you suggested. The bump was courtesy of some mugger who took everything I had."

Lucifer played along with the story. After all, he couldn't tell his companion that he had the privilege of sitting opposite an ancient, all-powerful angel who in all his existence, had never wanted or needed to eat or drink. He watched and copied everything Christopher was doing and then he put the cup to his lips and drank coffee for the first time. The sugar tasted so sweet, it made his mouth water and he craved even more, adding in total seven teaspoons to his cup.

"Steady on, you'll soon have teeth like mine if you drink that much sugar."

Christopher once again smiled with kind eyes at the curious man in front of him. He thought to himself that this man was like a child learning new things for the very first time. "Did you enjoy that?"

Lucifer was about to answer when his cup fell from his hands, smashing on the table below. A surging pain ran through his head, causing the mark on the back of his head to sting violently. As he turned his head, trying to avoid the pain, he looked out of the big window of the restaurant towards the sky where he saw a black cloud merging in front of the sun. The cloud grew at a fast rate, causing Lucifer's heart to beat faster and faster until his mind gave way to a vision.

The vision formed into a play enacted in slow motion. He watched as raindrops fell from a darkened sky, falling to the earth and gathering speed until finally coming to a violent stop on the body of a man lying face down in a muddy puddle. Next to this body was Lucifer's long black coat and a large lifeless tree shadowed the area where he lay. The vision became more lucid as Lucifer saw himself reaching out his hands in order to turn the body over. A bolt of lightning overhead flashed through the sky as Christopher's face lit up, causing Lucifer to drop his lifeless head in the mud. Blood slowly made its way from the wound still visible on his head like a tiny river until it finally converged into a puddle of perfect circularity. In the dead centre of this puddle was a white card. Lucifer leant forward to pick up the card, but the vision started to fade. The surging pain left Lucifer's head as he came to from his dream state. As he looked up, Christopher was looking over him with concern and the waitress was holding a glass of water to his lips.

"You okay friend?" Christopher said. "We were worried there for a moment, you just collapsed in the chair."

Clearing his eyes, Lucifer looked outside the window of the café again and there were no dark clouds, just the sun beaming its radiance onto the world. "I still must be feeling the effects of that bump on my head."

"Do you need to go to hospital again?" the waitress said. "I can drive you, my car is out back." The waitress was smiling at him again, clearly hoping his answer would be yes.

"No, I'm fine. I just want to get out of here. There is so much for me to do and time is running out. Are you coming?"

He looked at Christopher. Lucifer knew he had to have Christopher by his side because the vision symbolised something important and even though this could still be more trickery from God he decided to try and find out more about that card. It was obvious it was of great importance, although to what extent he did not yet know.

"Thank you for asking me to accompany you," Christopher said. "I don't have many friends you know and I don't want to be alone when I ..."

Lucifer looked at him curiously, waiting for him to finish his sentence.

"When you what?"

"Oh never mind, I am just an old man rambling utter nonsense."

"Where do you live, Christopher?"

"I don't have a home as such. I'm what they call homeless, so I spend some of the time sleeping on the streets, but I do have a favourite place to rest my weary head. It's in a park not too far from here. It's so quiet there at night away from the traffic, only the company of the stars in the sky to keep me company. Would you like to see it?"

Lucifer's mind switched back to a memory of the starry night he had won the ancient battle and was sitting on his throne, just before the Most High appeared and wiped out his army imprisoning him.

"You look deep in thought, what is your name? I don't think you have told me yet."

"It's Luther, but can we please stop with all the questions and especially the romanticising about starry nights. It is making me feel quite sick."

"Don't you like beautiful things? I love nature and all the wonderful things God created, but I suppose we all have different tastes and opinions."

"Hmm, you are right about one thing. It is okay to have a difference of opinion, me and the Most High don't see eye to eye and the Almighty up there gave up on me a long time ago, so I suppose we will always have a difference of opinion."

"Did God let you down, or did you turn against God? All I can say is no matter what God has done to me, I still have faith and through that faith I made lots of good friends in the past. Unfortunately those friends have deserted me, but I still keep my faith."

Lucifer ignored his question and watched as the old man looked up to the crystal blue sky. He was breathing in the air and smiling whilst closing his eyes, as if he was remembering friends and lovers from a time in the past. He sighed, opened his eyes and took hold of the pocket of his jacket as a tear rolled down his cheek.

"Look at me getting all sentimental. You must think I am an old fool."

"What makes you so emotional and what are you holding so intensely in that pocket?"

"Not much really. Some things are better just left in the past. Come on, let's head for the park. It's getting late and I could do with a lie down. I'm not as young as I used to be."

As Lucifer followed behind Christopher, trying to avoid the smell emanating from his worn and torn clothes, he thought about what was in that pocket. *All the signs are there, from the time of Christopher introducing himself, the vision of Christopher's death.* He also wondered how he might kill Christopher, assuming it was him, after God had forbidden him from harming anyone, let alone killing someone.

Christopher stopped walking and turned to face Lucifer. He had a kind smile on his face. It was as though he was trying to gain Lucifer's trust and respect. Lucifer felt sick to the stomach. Why would this stranger be showing a complete stranger kindness? He felt sick because Christopher's smile was causing him to question something in his mind. He had never before tried to understand kindness. He had always destroyed it out of hate, now he was being forced to think differently. "I don't think so," he said quietly under his breath as he looked towards the heavens.

"Over there, look. My resting place," Christopher said. "Wonderful, isn't it? A comfy bench next to a rubbish bin where the generous people throw away their unwanted food which makes me a nice supper."

Lucifer watched Christopher rummaging through a rubbish bin. Out the corner of his eye, Lucifer noticed something that made his eyes widen. There stood on the other side of the bench the leafless tree which he had seen in his vision. It was a lot bigger in real life but nevertheless it was exactly the same tree, the length of its trunk split in two, leading into branches bare and hanging down like a skeleton's hand. Christopher had stopped looking for food and had noticed Lucifer staring intently at the tree.

"Weird isn't it, middle of summer and no leaves? No one knows why it has never grown leaves. Some say the tree witnessed a tragic and sad event a long time ago and vowed to stay in a state of mourning until that wrong had been put right. Only then it would start to live again."

"Superstitious nonsense. It does look very odd though, maybe it's just a reminder of death and stands as a warning to anyone who thinks they can ever be happy."

"The local people also think that this place is very haunted, which is good for me because they all stay away especially at night, enabling me to have a peaceful night's sleep. Is it me or is it getting colder? Maybe it's all this talk of haunting and tragedies. Rain is on the way."

Lucifer looked up, shading his eyes from the sun and noticed a dark cloud gathering in density and shadowing all beneath it. Christopher had begun to wrap his arms around himself, warming his body from the cool chill floating along on an early evening breeze.

"Yes, a lot colder than I'm used to, it looks like there's a storm on the way. Don't you have any shelter for yourself, Christopher?"

"No, it's fine. I've slept in colder conditions than this and a little bit of rain won't kill me. Anyway, hopefully God will be kind and keep the rain away."

"I wouldn't hold your breath. The Most High is not in the habit of listening to peoples' prayers. Besides I can predict weather and it won't be long before it is raining and –"

Lucifer stopped what he was saying when he noticed that Christopher's eyes were fixated on his long black coat again.

"Why do you keep staring at this coat? You were looking curiously at it earlier in the restaurant."

"I don't know, it feels so familiar. Like it should mean something to me. You know when you meet someone for the first time and it feels like you've known them for a lifetime or maybe in another life?"

"No, not really. When I received the coat the message attached to it said *for a friend in a time of need* and was signed 'Simon'. I once knew a Simon and he was an obedient ..." Lucifer was just about to say "servant" when he changed his mind and said "follower".

"Come Luther sit with me for a while. It looks like you have a troubled mind and need to share the burden that's lying heavily on you." Christopher had outstretched his hand to the park bench nearby.

"I will sit for a while, but only if we don't speak about me and my past. There's nothing there you want to know. Besides, I can't remember much anyway."

"As you wish, there will be no more discussion about you."

Lucifer knew somehow that Christopher was lying and his knees clicked as he sat down and positioned himself next to this frail old man.

"You know, Luther, all my life I have been a charitable person helping people wherever or whenever I could. My love and possessions have always been theirs as they have been mine, although I think I have been guilty of loving too much and giving what I have to those in need. Unfortunately that led me to my downfall where people took advantage of me so much that I became poor and penniless, but I have been a God-fearing person and God has blessed most of my life with happiness and for that I am truly grateful. However, I fear now that my time to ascend is getting very close indeed. I was going to tell you earlier, but it didn't feel right. In fact, I feel that this very night is my final hour on this earthly plane. It's true you know when they say people are aware when their time is near. I feel it; I just hope God makes my passing as peaceful and comfortable as possible."

Just then a raindrop left a dense cloud from up above and made its way downward, gathering speed until it exploded on Christopher's head. It wasn't long before both of them were covered in raindrops.

"I don't know about a peaceful and comfortable death. It's certainly going to be a wet one." Lucifer refrained from allowing himself a smile at the thought of Christopher's watery death. "You see, even in your last few hours on earth God isn't listening. After all that kindness and faithfulness you've shown – what a waste."

He was now shouting his blasphemies at Christopher above the sound of the heavy rainfall.

"Don't curse God, Luther. Nature sometimes has a mind of her own. I won't tolerate anyone speaking bad about God, especially in my final hours. I didn't tell you earlier when I spoke about my vision of a falling star. I was told that the gift I would receive from this stranger would be black and of great comfort. Would you grant me this final wish and fulfil the vision by giving me that coat in a time of great need."

Lucifer looked at the long black coat lying over his arms, the raindrops rolling off it like crystal teardrops dancing in the dark. He thought, *Why should I give it to him*? After all, it was a gift from Simon and the message and sign was very clear.

"Nooo," Lucifer shouted at the top of his voice. "It's mine and I won't let you have it."

Lucifer took hold of the wound on the back of his head as it began to burn. It was as though the feeling of God's presence was encroaching into his mind like a hot iron, in order to observe whether he would help this man who had shown him so much kindness.

"I won't give in to him," he screamed. "Test me as much as you want."

"Please, please this is all I ask of you. In God's name can I have the coat?"

Lucifer took one more look at the old man's face now beginning to turn pale, matching the colour of his white hair and beard now drenched with rain.

"No, why don't you just die you stupid soul?"

"Giving it to me will be your salvation."

Christopher now took hold of Lucifer's coat and tightly gripped it in his hand. The sky above had now turned a sinister colour black, with the clouds moving and merging violently releasing their rain. Lucifer and Christopher were now in a slippery tug of war, the coat tugged to and fro in a battle of wills. On one side, Christopher was trying to get hold of it like his life depended on it. In a stubborn arrogant frenzy, still wanting power and control, Lucifer pulled back. Lucifer's mind drifted back to when he and Michael were fighting in heaven on opposing sides. Only this time the battle was not with swords but over a coat. As Christopher got the upper hand, a blue light started emanating from the coat bringing Lucifer back from his memory. Realising that Christopher's will was prevailing, Lucifer took a firmer grip and summoned all his strength, creating a change in the light and turning it to a crimson red.

"Pleasssse ... Luther."

Christopher was now using his final attempt against Lucifer's will, making Lucifer focus all his mind.

"Nooo," he roared like a lion.

In a moment, time seemed to slow down and

everything happened at once. A flash of lightning ripped through the sky above as Christopher's hands lost control and the coat left his hands. Finding himself off balance, he slipped in the mud and fell backwards, crashing his skull on the litter bin behind him, causing the bin to uproot and roll down the hill. Christopher slumped face down in the mud. Standing in the rain above the body, Lucifer smiled, which caused a white light like electricity to begin to glow in the dark and resonate, moving slowly over the surface of the coat, making him release it to the ground. Just then Lucifer remembered the vision he had earlier in the café.

As he stretched out his hand to turn Christopher's body over, he knew why he was doing this. He wanted to find out what he had been guarding so carefully in his pocket. Like in the vision, as Christopher's face was lit up by a flash of lightening, he saw blood running down the side of his mouth dripping into the muddy water below. Lucifer searched frantically in every pocket. It was strange but he had this notion that whatever was in the pocket was an answer of some kind for him. However, the search proved fruitless. With disgust, he dropped Christopher's head back in to the mud and began to think what to do next.

His eyes followed the scarlet life fluid leaking from Christopher's skull and he tried to recall the rest of his vision. He noticed in the hole, where the bin had been, there was a perfect circle. At its centre lay a white card bobbing under the surface of the water as the rain drops battered down on it. Lucifer leant forward and took hold of the card. The rain stopped immediately. The sudden silence hurt his ears. The only sound was the dripping of water falling from the card into a muddy puddle, creating tiny shock waves of ripples edging outwards. From its reflection, Lucifer noticed a light above and its presence made him shiver. Cautiously, he looked up and a figure within the light started to take shape, a figure Lucifer knew all too well.

"Lucifer, oh Lucifer, you don't know how long I have waited for you to come into my life and for that I thank you."

Christopher was now like a ghost floating above glowing with a beautiful shining white light. His face was radiating like the sun, causing Lucifer to squint and shield his eyes.

"Thank me, why? Don't you realise you are dead because of me? What did you mean you've been waiting a long time for me to come in to your life? You didn't even know who I was."

"Someone, a long time ago, told me that I would one day meet a poor stranger coming out of a place of healing, holding just a black coat and nursing a wound on the back of his head. I was told it was my duty to look after this person and show him kindness. In turn for my kindness, I would receive a black gift from him and gain my freedom. So every night for twenty years I have watched for a falling star. Only then I would go to the hospital entrance in hope of meeting such a man, the one who would grant me this wonderful gift."

"You stupid fool, what did your kindness reward you? Nothing, you didn't even get the gift of my coat."

They both looked at the coat still lying on the floor next to Christopher's body.

"Don't you see, Lucifer? The gift wasn't the coat, it was my freedom. The blackness was my death before light. I had to see darkness before I knew what light was. That was the real gift of freedom you gave me, without knowing it. Through your evil, greed, anger and refusal of charity, you gave me the ultimate gift of all: love. Only in my death I now know of God, love and freedom. For that I thank and love you as the lost soul you are."

Tears were rolling down Christopher's ghostly face, as his light grew brighter with emotion.

"Love, what is love?" Lucifer shouted out in anger and confusion for a want or understanding of this word he had heard so much about. "I don't know what it is, and

I would rather destroy something than understand it."

"Christopher, it's time to go."

From behind Christopher's head appeared a face Lucifer knew. The familiar green eyes and golden hair of Raphael lit up illuminating the darkness,

"Still God's little faithful puppy, Raphael, guiding souls back to the Most High, his majesty."

Raphael looked at Lucifer with eyes filled with sorrow. "Brother, you still don't know who you are, do you? In time you will understand, I bless you with love."

"I don't want your pity. I am Lucifer, enemy of God and the great corrupter of souls. When I return in my angelic form, you and all the other brethren will kneel before me or die by my sword, do you hear me?"

Lucifer continued to shout at the two disappearing figures as they faded into the sky. He heard Christopher whisper in his ear.

"Don't forget to follow the signs. God has asked me to remind you of his plan and your fate, which lies entirely in your hands alone. I hope you find your way home. I know I have."

The light faded away into the dark clouds which dispersed rapidly. The sun started to set behind a red and orange sky; the sounds of birds could be heard again, preparing their nest for a night of rest. The bench rocked as Lucifer sat down. He turned over in his mind Christopher's last words as he looked down at the body looking pale but now at peace. *Stupid fool, why on earth would he choose that end for himself? Just because someone told him to. Anyway, what's on this card?*

He turned it over and it read: "My dearest Christopher, if you are ever lost and in need of a friend, you will find me at this address, 26 Sanctuary House, Michael Street. Your friend, Sophie. X."

Well, I'll play God's little game and follow the sign. I guess this is the place I'm heading. Lucifer cautiously bent forward to pick up the black coat from where it lay on the ground through fear of anymore white light waiting to shock him. To his relief, nothing happened, but as he took it a leaf floated past his head and landed on Christopher.

"You have got to be kidding me," He looked up at the tree, which was now in full bloom, branches reaching to the heavens as though in praise and thanks for this day that had come to pass. Lucifer shook his head and smiled at what he thought was another attempt of God's so called great plan – a plan which he was going to tear apart – as he walked towards a setting sun.

Chapter Five

Lucifer had walked aimlessly all night through the dimly lit streets of London, resting only to ask a couple of people for directions. Finally, he stood in front of a door of a huge house, a few miles out of the city of London. Above the door was a gold plaque which read: *Sanctuary House*.

His attention was drawn to a flowing fountain in the middle of a large lawn, which had recently been cut. It was surrounded by rows of tall pine trees, all lush and green, reaching for the skies like soldiers standing on guard. The house itself was not so well looked after. Wooden window frames were old and falling apart. Cracks in the plaster rose from the ground like veins showing through skin. He'd started to approach the door when beneath his foot a loud squeak sounded. He'd stood on the head of a battered old doll. Its hair was almost blonde, except for the stains running through it. She was wearing a blue dress and hair ribbon to match.

"Damn thing," he said under his breath as he angrily kicked it to the side.

Lucifer's fist boomed repeatedly on the heavy door. It was not long before he heard the sound of feet running towards the door, and then there was silence. Impatiently he waited for a while then lifted his fist again for a second attempt. Just then a bolt rattled from the other side of the door and the door slowly opened as far as the still attached chain would allow.

Lowering his head to look through the gap, Lucifer could see nobody.

"Hello, is anybody there?" he shouted.

"You can't come in, you know," a little girl's voice said. He looked down to see half of a little girl's face looking up at him, as she hid behind the door. Lucifer could see the twinkling of a sky blue eye nearly covered by long ringlets of blonde hair.

"And why not?" he replied impatiently.

Lucifer could now see her face and her nose was sticking through the opening. She was wearing a blue dress and her hair had a blue ribbon almost identical to that of the doll.

"You have to knock three times," she shouted. "It's the rule."

"Well, I don't follow rules. They are for sheep and people who want to be led –"

He was in mid-sentence when the door slammed in his face, Lucifer clenched his fist in anger and shouted, "Look little girl, I don't have time for this!"

"Knock three times and I will let you in. It's the rule," a muffled voice sounded from behind the door.

"What is so important about three knocks anyway?"

"It says in the Bible: knock three times and heaven you shall enter."

"Well I don't believe in heaven, but I'll play your stupid game if I can eventually be allowed in."

Reluctantly, he slammed his fist against the heavy wooden frame three times.

"That's better," she said.

The door opened again, but only to the length of the chain much to Lucifer's annoyance. He looked down again at the girl who was smiling in appreciation of Lucifer playing her game. She giggled.

"Now you have to solve my riddle and give me the secret password, then –"

Lucifer interrupted her little speech. "Look, I won't tell you –"

The door again shut hard in Lucifer's face, Lucifer dropped his head in resignation.

"Okay, okay open the door and give me the riddle, I'll try to solve it."

The door slowly opened to reveal a cheeky grin.

"Very well, here goes," she said. "I am her, she is me, she is small, I am tall and a speechless friend she will always be to me. I wonder what the password could be?"

It didn't take Lucifer long to work out she was talking about the doll which lay on the floor next to his feet.

"I guess the password is 'doll' as you keep looking at it. You have to try harder than that if you don't want to give the game away."

Smugness made its way across Lucifer's face at the thought of having a victory over this little girl. The feeling was short-lived.

"Wrong," as the girl replied, "You only have one more guess. You were close though."

Begrudgingly, he picked the doll up from the floor and studied it for a while by lifting up its skirt, looking at her shoes until finally parting her hair where he noticed some writing stitched on the bald head: "If I am lost and lonely, please return me to my friend, love Jemima."

"Is it Jemima by any chance?"

"Hooray!" she shouted.

"Angela, what are you doing out of class? And why are you standing with the door open?" said an adult female voice behind Angela. The little girl turned around to look at the person spoiling her game.

"It's a stranger and he gave the right knocks. He knows the secret password. Can he come in?"

"Get away from there", the woman said.

Lucifer tried very hard to peer behind the door. As he leant forward, Angela snatched the doll from his hand and ran off down the corridor. The chain fell against the door and the door slowly creaked open. Lucifer's eyes widened and his mouth dropped as the door fully opened.

"Hello, how can I help you?"

In front of Lucifer stood a woman, cautiously not trying to look into Lucifer's eyes. She looked as if she was in her mid-twenties and wore a long black gown and a white hood which almost covered the whole of her head apart from her face. Around her neck hung a silver crucifix.

Lucifer found it hard to speak. After all, she was the last person he would want to be standing in front of.

"I'm not sure I've come to the right place," he said, handing her the white card.

"Yes, this is the right place, Sanctuary House, the local orphanage. Who or what have you come to find?" she asked politely as she handed him back the card.

"I'm looking for Sophie. I was told I could contact her here."

"The only Sophie we have here is Sister Sophie, but I doubt she'll see you because her life is dedicated to God after having her heart broken a long time ago." The nun looked curiously at Lucifer, staring at his long black coat which was still muddy from the events of previous evening. "What did you say your name was?"

"It's Luther. You have to tell her Christopher sent me, because I'm lost and I was told that if she saw this card she would recognise it."

She stood there for a little while longer trying to decide. Lucifer forced a smile in an attempt to reassure her. She finally relented and stood aside, inviting him in.

"If you wait here, I'll go and find her."

As he watched the nun quietly walk off down the corridor, Lucifer's attention was drawn to a picture on the wall. It depicted the crucifixion. He studied every detail and looked up at Jesus' sorrowful face. *Nobody really knew what you looked like, I remember you well and all those happy times we spent together. Yes I enjoyed tormenting and tempting you in the desert. How I smiled at your fall from grace, especially when your people turned against you, wanting your blood by torturing you on the cross and what for? What did all that forgiveness of sin and that awful word love accomplish? Nothing! It only delayed the inevitable where man would destroy man through greed, corruption and the best of all religion.*

"Excuse me."

Lucifer's thoughts were interrupted by the quiet voice of returning nun. "Sister Sophie has agreed to see you, please follow me."

"Can you please give me a one second?"

He turned to face the picture again and bowed his head respectfully. When he noticed the nun had turned around to give him some privacy, he lifted his eyes and whispered under his breath.

"Don't go too far, brother. I'll be seeing you again soon, once I find my way back into heaven after defeating God's plans. I'll find you and this time I won't be so kind." He then raised his voice. "Thank you sister for your patience. I've finished now."

"Very well, it's just down here."

She turned and started walking down the long corridor with classrooms either side. As Lucifer walked passed one of the doors, he felt someone watching him. He turned to see Angela again. She spoke in a sad whisper.

"I know who you are, and how it feels to be lost and unloved. I don't care what people have said about you in the past, you see there is still something good in you."

Lucifer stopped and glared at Angela. She gave him a perfect smile which lit her face up; her eyes shone as if she had a soul of an angel. She then turned and ran off down the corridor with Jemima lovingly held under her arm.

"Angela, Angela!" The nun had spotted her running down the corridor. "That girl is so naughty and is always getting in trouble, not to mention missing most of her classes. We don't know what to do with her, she has no discipline. Believe me if she wasn't living in this house with God's blessing, I would say she was the devil's child."

As the little girl's figure faded in the distance, Lucifer made a mental note that he had to get this girl on her own and ask her what she meant about knowing him.

"I don't know, I think there's nothing wrong with having a little bit of a free spirit. Sometimes it's good to walk away from the rest of the sheep, experience life in a different light so to speak."

"Hush your mouth, Luther; I wouldn't let Sister Sophie hear you say that. She takes great pride in how well most of the children behave and believes that no one will always stay bad. That's why she's taken Angela under her wing to try and improve her behaviour. Here we are."

They stopped outside an archway with a wooden door. The nun knocked on the door and waited for a response.

"In you go."

Lucifer nodded and walked past the nun who shut the door behind him. Sitting in a bay window behind the desk, an elderly nun was half facing the window, looking out at the sunlight.

"Please, come in and sit down," Sophie said.

She didn't turn from the sunlight. Lucifer noticed she held the white card pressed against her chest. She was looking up at the blue sky and smiling thoughtfully. Lucifer remembered how Christopher had kept the same card in his chest pocket and how he had looked up at the sky in the same way. With a deep sigh, the nun finally turned her chair around, placed the card in a golden box on her desk and slowly lifted her eyes to meet Lucifer's. Lucifer was struck by the piercing blue eyes looking at him. He had only once seen a shade of blue like that before and that was the light which surrounded Michael and his army of angels.

"Relax," Sophie said calmly, "you look a little anxious, like you have just seen a ghost. Please tell me, how is Christopher? I haven't seen him in over thirty years."

"He is dead," Lucifer replied, emotionless. The nun

closed her eyes and bent her head in respect. After a moment's pause, she opened her eyes again, this time filled with tears.

"Did he die in a safe place? And was it peaceful? I pray to God it was so. Were you with him?"

"Yes, I was with him at the end. He went very peacefully and just before he died he gave me this card and whispered to me, 'Go to this address, Sophie will help you find what you're looking for'."

Lucifer was hoping the nun would offer a clue so he knew where he needed to be or what he should do next, but she simply nodded.

"Hope you don't mind. I took the liberty of ordering some tea for us. I feel we have so much to talk about, so tell me how I can help you."

"No, wait one second. I first have to know the connection there was between you and Christopher in order to help me understand my chance meeting with him and how I eventually ended up here."

"Well, I don't know where to start."

"The beginning would be nice," Lucifer grunted impatiently.

"Quite the impatient one, aren't you? You sound just like Angela, demanding something straight away. Well, the first time I met Christopher, his name was Matthew. We were both in our twenties and first became acquainted in our local church. I haven't always been a nun, at that time I was a naïve girl looking for my place in the world, so I thought I'd give God a chance. It was after one of the services that Matthew introduced himself to me. I'd noticed him watching me and he took a chance to ask me if he could buy me a cup of tea."

"You were leading an exciting life then?"

Sophie's mood changed and folded her arms in defiance, "If you are going to interrupt me I won't continue."

"Please, continue," Lucifer said, oozing insincerity.

"I don't know why, after all he was a total stranger, but it felt like I had known him for years after. He was also very polite and handsome. Besides it felt right, does that sound odd?"

The nun continued without waiting for Lucifer's reply. She had now stood up and was looking out of the bay window again. "I remember looking into his eyes as we sat opposite each other, drinking our tea. Matthew explained he used to be a reporter for a national newspaper, but after seeing so much violence and sadness, he had decided it was not the right job for him. I would never forget seeing the sadness in his eyes. He was like a lost soul who needed rescuing. We talked about everyday things, but what struck me the most exciting about him was his enthusiastic talk about coincidences and signs. He told me about a book he was reading, I think it was called *To See the Unseen*. He explained that the book talked about how everything is planned out for us; all we have to do is look for and follow the signs. It also contained meditation techniques to enable us to be able to tune into these signs more efficiently."

Sister Sophie stopped her narrative at the sound of a knock on the door. "Come in," she said.

The nun who had first greeted Lucifer was entering the room carrying a silver tray of tea and an array of biscuits.

"Thank you Sister Phillipa, on the desk here would be fine."

Lucifer watched as she steadily carried the tray past him to lay the tray down.

"Sister, will you please take Luther's coat to the laundry room for a wash. It looks like he has been fighting in the mud with someone."

"No," Lucifer replied with urgency, "it's okay, I would rather keep it on. It is something that is mine and mine alone."

"Don't be silly. It can be washing while we talk. And otherwise I won't elaborate anymore on my story. You can collect it after dinner this evening. You will stay for dinner won't you?"

Again before Lucifer had a chance to answer, Sister Sophie carried on. "Good, that's settled."

Sister Phillipa stood next to Lucifer, waiting for him to remove the coat. Reluctantly and wanting to know more of the story he stood and started to unfasten the buttons. As she took hold of the coat, Lucifer did not release his grip but looked into her eyes to see if there was any womanhood left in this nun. *Had she given herself totally to the God, or did she still have any dormant desire for the embrace of the man?*

"Thank you, sir," she said looking deep into his eyes in full knowledge of his intent. Lucifer then let go of his hold knowing she was a total devotee of her religious faith.

"Will that be all Sister Sophie?"

"Yes, thank you Sister."

Sister Phillipa paused at the door as Lucifer addressed her.

"Make sure it's cleaned well and do me a favour and make sure you don't wash it with holy water."

She gave Lucifer a puzzled look at his strange comment and closed the door behind her.

"Luther," Sister Sophie called out to get Lucifer's attention, please if you don't mind, everyone in this house is taught to be polite to one another. I would appreciate it if you would extend the same courtesy."

He nodded with a wry smile which caused him to wince in pain, he had nearly forgotten about the wound on the back of his head.

"Are you okay, Luther?"

"It's nothing just a wound I suffered at the hands of a mugger. Every so often it gives me pain."

"If you like, we can get our matron sister to have a look at it for you?"

"No!" Lucifer snapped because of the fear of people messing about in his head with their mortal hands. Realising he had raised his voice, he now spoke in softer tone. "The hospital has given me the all clear."

"I will continue with my narrative," she said. "After our drink in the café he walked me home and asked if he could see me again. I agreed straight away and we exchanged telephone numbers. We started seeing each other on a daily basis and finally agreed to get engaged. It was one of the happiest days of my life, a date was set when we would exchange our vows and agreed to save ourselves."

The nun went a slight shade of pink at the sexual connotations, making Lucifer smile at the nun's obvious embarrassment.

"So you were married?"

"Oh no. In the months leading up to the wedding Mathew started acting strangely and totally out of character."

"What do you mean?"

"Well he became more distant and we started to see less and less of each other. He would often make up elaborate excuses for why he could not see me. Also, Matthew became very aggressive towards me, especially when I asked where he was going or why he couldn't see me. It was on a cold November night when I decided to follow him from his house to find out what he was up to. I followed him in my car for about half an hour until he left the main road and drove his car down a small country lane leading to an old estate mansion. I pulled my car over to the side of the main road, got out and made my way cautiously in the moonlight to the house. I hid behind a bush and observed Mathew talking to two men. They were standing in the dimly lit doorway laughing and joking. The two men wore black suits partially covered in some kind of fur around their chest and waistline. It was strange. I waited quietly in my position and the only sound you could hear was their talking in the distance. I wondered what on earth was Mathew doing there and who those two men were. One of the men took hold of Mathew's hands and began to bind them with rope. I felt helpless not knowing what to do, whether I should run and get help. I resisted because I thought it was strange that Matthew wasn't putting up a fight or struggling for his freedom. I watched with amazement when one of the men put a black hood over Mathew's head. The other one banged on the door three times with something he had in his hand. The big oak door opened and I saw something terrifying which to this day I will never forget."

"Terrifying, interesting," Lucifer leant forward, eager for more, "What did you see?"

"Somebody or something stood before the three of them, dressed in the same black suit and the fur regalia, but the head was feline in nature. I couldn't make it out. The head was big and grotesque with pointed ears, an extended nose and it was definitely made up of some sort of fur. I was beside myself with fear at what I was seeing. I wanted to cry out. Just then, the person wearing this mask leant towards Mathew's covered face. It was like he was listening to what Mathew was whispering. Then the masked man moved away and took hold of Matthew's hand and shook it, then nodded to the other two men and went back inside closing the door behind him. More tea Luther? Or perhaps another biscuit?"

The nun had deliberately paused from telling her story. Lucifer could tell she was not really enjoying reliving this experience.

"So what happened next?" Lucifer replied after another sip of his tea.

"For a few moments, the three of them stood waiting, not saying a word, then the door opened again. This time no one appeared. Instead, one of the men took hold of the other end of the rope tightly fastened to Mathew's hand and dragged him inside whilst the other man remained outside and closed the door behind them. I waited for another ten or more minutes, nothing else happened apart from the man smoking and guarding the door. I decided to quietly make my way back to the car.

Driving home, I was still dazed from what I had just seen: men in sinister black suits, tying up people. To me it seemed totally weird and ungodly. What had Mathew got himself into?"

"Well, didn't you ask him what he was up to or who the people were?"

"Yes, eventually I managed to gather enough courage to ask him about that evening although he didn't like people, especially me, prying into his private affairs. I invited him round on a Sunday afternoon for some tea and scones. Before he arrived, I drank about three glasses of vodka to steady my nerves, then I nervously started to ask him. Matthew looked impatient when I found it quite hard to get my words out properly. In the end I broke down and told him everything I had witnessed in every detail.

You can imagine Matthew's explosion of anger, shouting at me, telling me I didn't trust him and what was I thinking of spying on him. He told me I shouldn't pry into things that I could not even begin to comprehend. After a while his anger subsided, then he started to explain to me that he could only tell me as much as he could of the secretive meeting. I listened with great curiosity and my eyes widened as he explained his story in more depth. He told me that the book he was reading contained addresses and telephone numbers of people to contact if anybody reading wanted to learn more about the meditation techniques listed therein. He further explained that after phoning one of these numbers he was introduced to someone down at the local pub. This person was some kind of sponsor or judge of his character to see if he was respectable enough to join their organisation. After this initial interview, the man instructed Mathew to wait for a phone call where he would receive details of where and what time to meet his sponsor. He eventually found out that he would be joining an organisation who praised themselves with the name of 'Watchers'. It was an organisation that claimed to have ancient and esoteric knowledge, and the ability to be able to read signs given to us from the universe. Its main ethos was dedicated to teaching its members this knowledge. It is said that eventually its members would be able to communicate with the angels and temporarily enter heaven."

"Watchers you say," Lucifer mused. "I wonder what they were watching for?"

"Matthew didn't know. People higher up in their ranks knew but didn't tell him. It was the beginning of the end for us, as we grew further apart. I would go to church more and more, he would go to his meetings more frequently. Our marriage kept getting postponed to later and later in the year. It was then that I gave him an ultimatum, me or the Watchers. I was heartbroken when he chose the latter and before long he stopped calling altogether. It was only when I heard from a friend that I found out he had got himself in terrible debt, lost his house and nobody knew where he was."

"He just disappeared without a trace?"

"Yes, for about thirty years. During this time I had mourned and let go of my love for him. Then one day someone approached me and told me that Matthew wanted to meet me at the local park."

"It wasn't on a bench near a lifeless tree, was it?" Lucifer interrupted.

"Yes it was. How did you know that?"

"I am a little psychic, you know." Lucifer was enjoying the opportunity to mock the nun.

"Anyway, as I was saying, I was anxiously waiting in the park. The thought of seeing Matthew again after so many years made me nervous. What did he want? What did he look like? It was not long before my questions were answered. A man dressed like a vagrant approached me."

Lucifer listened as she perfectly described the man with whom he had spent the previous evening in every detail.

"As he approached, I got out my purse ready to give him some money, just to get him to move on. Then he said 'Hello'. That's when I realised the voice I was hearing was that of Matthew. I saw those saddened eyes that I had seen all those years ago, only this time they were now shining, full of kindness and love, with an intensity I had never seen in his eyes before. We soon started to talk about the old times and what we both had been doing in our lives since. He began to tell me how the Watchers had taught him all types of rituals and meditation. He explained how these techniques had helped him to get more in touch with himself spiritually. But after a while they were demanding more time and money from him until he was left a broken man, both materially and spiritually. He conveyed to me how all the members had turned their backs on him, forcing him into living as an ascetic in the local woods. Here he studied the techniques he had been taught every night, seeking enlightenment.

I will never forget how excited he became when he spoke about the visions he was experiencing. He told me how Archangel Michael paid him a visit one night. Michael told him to change his name to Christopher because now he was going to be like Saint Christopher, a helper of people on their journey through life. He further informed Matthew that God wanted him to play an important part in helping a stranger. The signs would tell him where to be and when. I asked him about this stranger, but all he said was that he didn't know who it was, only that he had to wait and watch for a falling star on a particular evening. Then on the following day he had to go to a place of healing. Michael also told him that I was to play an important part in God's plan. In order to achieve this, I had to give my life up for God and become a nun. I laughed at him and said he was crazy, I had no plans of entering sisterhood. I was shocked when he took hold of my arms and stared intensely into my eyes, telling me to watch for a blue light in my bedroom one night then I'd become a believer. After he released my arms, he looked up at the setting sun and stood up to leave. I asked him if it would be possible for me to see him again, he stroked my face with his hand and said if you need to see me come to this tree. Then he left."

"I don't know why I'm telling you all this, but I feel I have to. I remember I was fast asleep in my bed, when all of a sudden the room became very cold, waking me from my sleep. As I opened my eyes, I felt someone or something watching me. This caused me to nervously turn to face the most beautiful blue light you can imagine. It made me feel totally safe and unafraid. The more I looked at the light, the more intense and loving it became until finally I had to surrender myself mentally and spiritually. Then, extraordinarily, this blue light exploded in a cascade of light entering into my eyes. I felt like time had stood still. The light was showing me in my mind's eye this world of suffering – people who are either lost or unloved or looking for some meaning in their lives – I felt so much sorrow in their hearts. Children were walking towards me holding up their arms in need of love. 'Sister Sophie, we need you,' they seemed to be saying. I saw myself kneeling on the floor embracing the children. I would never forget the feeling of total unconditional love I felt with them all. As the vision faded, Michael's face appeared and reminded me of my duty that Matthew had previously spoken about. Matthew's words had come true and who was I not to obey this wonderful vision from God? I have never looked back on my decision to become a nun and finally find my home."

"How did Christopher or Matthew, whatever his name was, come to have that card in his possession, the one he gave to me?"

"After becoming a nun, I went to visit that tree in the park once a week for two months to relate to Matthew what had happened. Sadly he never showed up, so I decided to leave that card with my address on in hope that he would find it. He must have watched me leave the card at the base of the tree next to his bench."

"If he saw you in your God's uniform, why did he not come and see you in the orphanage?"

"I don't know. I guess he was so dedicated to finding his spiritual pathway, he didn't want me or anything else to get in the way of him finding it. I do hope he found it before he died."

Lucifer frowned and gave a wry smile, "Perhaps he did. I expect he is the only one who knows that now."

"Maybe you are right, I do hope so. My goodness would you look at the time. We have been talking for hours. Dinner will soon be served. Would you like to wash before dinner?"

Lucifer nodded.

"I will get Sister Phillipa to show you where the bathroom is. Please Luther, come with me."

Lucifer had just stood up to follow Sister Sophie to the door when his knees became weak. His vision began to fade giving way to darkness as he took hold of his wounded head and collapsed to the floor.

"Hello again."

Lucifer struggled to open his eyes to ascertain where he was and who was addressing him. As his eye sight cleared he saw Jemima, Angela's doll dancing on a side of his bed.

"How are you?" said a little voice from under Lucifer's bed.

"I feel rotten. Come out from under there," Lucifer replied gruffly.

"Who are you talking about? I am Jemima and it is only me and you in here."

Lucifer snatched the doll out of Angela's hand and threw it against the wall, making it squeak.

"Now that wasn't very nice was it?" Angela had now crawled out from under the bed and was standing in front of him, hands on her hips, looking very cross indeed.

"Don't you care about hurting other people and their feelings?"

"Oh yes, I do care about it, particularly when I am doing a really good job of hurting them."

Angela's eyes widened in surprise. "Well I am not going to talk to you anymore, not until you learn some more manners."

Lucifer sat up in his bed as the girl picked up the doll and went to open the door. He realised that this was his perfect opportunity to ask her what she had spoken about earlier.

"Wait!" he said in a raised voice causing the little girl to stop in her tracks. "I was only joking." He realised he had to calm down to get the correct response from her. "Bring Jemima over here. Let me see. I hope I didn't hurt her too much."

Angela paused at the door, looking at Lucifer, frowning and scowling sceptically.

"Well you hurt her feelings so much she's crying. I think you should apologise to her."

"You have got to be joking." He was trying very hard to comprehend the situation he now faced. *Me? Apologise to a worthless piece of material?*

"I don't think so."

"Come on Jemima, let's leave old grumpy on his own."

"Okay, okay," he said as the girl turned around with a smile on her face.

"Are you listening Jemima? The grumpy one is going to say sorry. Well, we're waiting."

"I am sorry," he said very quietly.

"We didn't quite hear that. What did you say?"

Lucifer relented. "I am sorry, Jemima, for throwing you at the wall and hurting your feelings."

"That's better, that wasn't so bad was it? Now what game would you like to play, Lucifer?"

"What did you say? How do you know my name?"

Lucifer threw himself back across his bed and backed up against the wall.

"Silly, it is written on the back of your head," she said and pointed to Lucifer's wound which had been cleaned and redressed. Lucifer put his hand on the back of his head.

"Who else saw it?"

"Only that very nice matron. She allowed me to watch as she took care of you. That's when I saw your real name."

"Did she mention anything about the mark on my head?"

"No silly, they can't see your real name by looking at your mark. It can only be seen through the eyes of people who can see the real truth."

"But you knew who I was when you first saw me, how did you explain that?"

Angela pulled herself up and sat on Lucifer's bed.

"I have known you for a while now. You look slightly different in real life though."

"How have you known me?" Lucifer interrupted impatiently,

"In my dreams, I have seen you in my dreams."

"If I looked different in your dreams, how do you know it is me?"

"God told me in my dreams that a stranger in black would come knocking on our door and through my innocence I would know who he was by the mark on his head."

"Why would God talk to you? After all you are only a child." Lucifer inquired impatiently.

"I don't know, but God told me that you are the naughtiest of all the angels and with my help we can help you find your home again."

"Well little girl, I don't need anyone's help, especially that of an eight year-old girl. I'm sure my ancient and wise mind will get me where I want to go."

"But God said you can only find your way home by

helping humans. You know you really don't look like all those pictures of the devil I've seen. When I saw you in my dreams in angelic form, there was no red skin and there was certainly no horns and tail."

She started to giggle and a glare from Lucifer made her giggle even more,

"And as for hooves as feet, how silly! No wonder people have been scared of you for such a long time. I know what you really look like. You were a beautiful angel like all the others. Except you had a very angry face. What made you so angry? God wouldn't tell me."

"I expect the Most High kept that a secret from you, because he didn't want you to see his cruel side."

"God, cruel?" Angela interrupted in an almost hurt tone. "How could someone suggest God having a bad side?"

"Well I was punished and thrown out of heaven just because –"

"Angela what are you doing in here?"

Sister Phillipa entered the room, stopping Lucifer from finishing his sentence. "Get out immediately and go to your room where you will stay until the morning."

Angela cried out as the nun smacked her legs to move her off the bed. Angela defiantly stayed where she was, hiding behind Lucifer's arm as tears started to form in her eyes from the pain.

"Are you going to move?"

Angela shook her head more defiantly. The nun raised her hand for another slap while Lucifer watched the little girl as she turned towards him, pleading for help.

"Don't look at me," Lucifer said. "Stay as long as you want and enjoy the pain."

In despair, the girl jumped of the bed and turned to both of them, screaming.

"I am going to run away from here and you will never see me again. As for you Luther, I thought you would be different. Perhaps the Bible was right about you after all."

With one last tearful look back, she slammed the door and ran off.

"God save us from that child. Are you comfortable Luther? Sister Sophie thought it would be best if you stay the evening to rest that head of yours. I must say it is healing quite nicely, though it's always better to be on the safe side."

"Where is she going to run off to?"

"Don't you worry about her. She often threatens to run away. We mostly find her hiding in wardrobes or under beds. Now then what did she mean about the Bible and you?"

"I don't know, perhaps she thinks I'm her guardian angel or something."

"I don't think she's in a need of a guardian angel. All she needs is a firm hand. Besides only spiritually enlightened people like us nuns can see the true nature of God and the heavenly messengers."

Lucifer smiled to himself at the nun's comment.

"Anyway you have extra towels at the end of the bed and there are blankets in the wardrobe. Good night Luther, don't forget to say your prayers."

Lucifer looked at her with an unamused face, then turned his light off before she'd left the room.

Lucifer woke to the sound of running feet along the corridor. He could see the shadows of feet under his doorway. He leant over, switched on the light and pulled himself off his bed. Dressing, he left the black coat neatly on the bed. Outside Lucifer's door was chaos, with nuns running in all directions. Some were stopping the children from leaving their rooms while others were opening every single door and cupboard calling out Angela's name.

"Luther, you've not seen Angela anywhere, have you? Nobody has seen her since she left your room this afternoon. Nobody can find her, we've looked everywhere."

The look on Sister Sophie's face was one of despair and pain.

"Have you tried the hidden garden?" said a little boy, pulling on Sister Sophie's habit.

"What hidden garden, Robert?"

"The one she goes to when she's sad and wants to run away from the bullies. It is behind the gardener's shed where the well is."

Sister's Sophie's face became very pale, fearing the worst.

"Oh my, that area has been blocked off for years. We built a wall to stop the children entering there because of the dangerous well and Angela must have found a way through. We might need your help, Luther. Some of those bricks might need knocking down. Thank you Robert, can you please now go back to your room?"

One of the other sisters took Robert's hand and led him away. Lucifer crept back in his room to gather up his coat and then followed the sister down the corridor, wrapping the coat tightly around him. Outside the rain was sprayed around by a freezing cold wind. They arrived at the brick wall to see a small hole partially covered by a bush. It was big enough for a child to crawl through.

"Can you make that hole bigger, Luther?" Sister Sophie shouted over the howling of the wind.

"I expect so," he looked around and saw a heavy spade but paused. *What am I doing? I am not supposed to be helping people. I couldn't care less if Angela was dying.*

"No, this is your problem," he said. "She's in God's hands now and that's not where I want to be." Lucifer smiled as the nun looked at him with horror at his heartlessness.

As he turned around to walk away, he heard God's voice burning in his ear: *You will stay in human form for as long as it takes.* Lucifer held his ears to be rid of the annoying voice, then in angry reluctance he turned back and grasped the spade.

"Stand back!"

With one downward swipe, Lucifer smashed the spade

against the wall causing a whole section to collapse. At that moment, the rain immediately ceased.

"Angela, Angela!"

Nuns rushed through the gap in the wall and ran forward in different directions, calling her name and looking in bushes and behind trees, their torch lights dancing as they frantically searched for the missing child. Sister Sophie run straight to the well and cried out as she spotted Jemima lying at its edge. The other nuns ran to join her, leaning over to look into its dark depths.

"Angela! Are you down there?"

They all listened for an answer. For a moment all they could hear the sound of water dripping to the bottom of the well.

"Angela!" Sister Sophie shouted as loudly as her lungs would allow. A silence which seemed to last a lifetime was finally broken when a faint cry sounded.

"Thank you God, she is alive. Luther, please take this rope and climb down to save her. You're the only one strong enough to make it down and back again."

"Take this Luther, a torch to guide you in the darkness." Lucifer looked around to see Sister Phillipa handing him a torch.

"Very well, just stand back," he said.

He sat himself on the edge of the well and tied the rope firmly around his waist and instructed the nuns to tie the other end of the rope around a nearby tree. The walls of the well were damp and covered with a green slimy moss. As Lucifer gradually lowered himself down, he occasionally looked up to see the concerned faces of the nuns gathered above. As he got lower he could make out the frame of a small body desperately hanging on to a protruding stone. She wasn't moving and all he could hear was a faint cry and cough as she lay in the water.

"Damn it," Lucifer cursed as the wet torch slipped out of his hand, the light getting fainter as it fell deeper and deeper under water. He and Angela were now submerged in complete darkness. Lucifer's black coat was now twice its weight from the rainfall as he hovered just above the water.

"Lucifer is that you?" Angela's faint voice cried out in the darkness. "I knew you would come, God said you would save me. I'm really cold and I've cut my head. I don't think I can hold on much longer, please help me."

Hearing Angela's faint pleas he hung on his rope for a while contemplating his situation. *I have no desire to save this girl in an act of love, but on the other hand this is God's punishment and I am suffering myself. It disgusts me to be in human flesh, however until I help this mortal I am stuck with my situation against my will.*

In the end, Lucifer's desire to regain his power and angelic form won the battle in his mind.

"Okay, I will help you, but I don't know how good I would be. I've never done this sort of thing before."

"Just take me in your arms," Angela whispered from the darkness. "Down here in the darkness, there is just you and me, with only one choice you have to make – whether to save me or not."

Angela had just finished speaking when Lucifer heard her body fall and splash into the water below. Not knowing what to do, he looked up and beyond the nuns' faces to see the clear starry night.

"Okay, Most High, it's time for the beginning of my return"

He untied the knot on the rope around his waist and dropped into the water below. He frantically swam below the surface, hands feeling through the darkness. The water seemed to go on forever until his feet found the bottom. Panic rushed through his mind when he realised he was nearly out of breath. He was just about to make his way to the surface when he noticed a white light around his ankles. It made its way up his legs, spiralling like white lightning jumping off in different directions. Just as quickly as the light appeared it disappeared, but now Lucifer had become calm without a fear of drowning. A tiny hand took hold of his hand and he heard Angela's voice in his head: "Take hold of me in your arms and become who you are meant to be". Lucifer parted his black coat and drew Angela close to his chest, then wrapped the coat and his arms around her. He closed his eyes and heard her voice again: "It's time". Lucifer's mind switched back to the time in the desert just before the battle. The power of this past memory now connected with his present situation, making him feel his energy to the fullest; he now had become at one. His eyes flashed open in a ruby trance-like state, illuminating the water at the bottom of the well and around the two of them in a sea of red, its energy flickering like a ghost. Angela's face was alight with this red energy as she breathed in its life force making Lucifer feel more powerful too. *Yes God, I am still powerful, my name is Lucifer, the one to destroy all mankind. You thought you can take that away from me. Look at me!* he thought with pride and defiance.

His energy began to fade and he found it hard to concentrate. Just then he felt a gentle stroke of fingers on his face, which caused all the red energy to implode into the darkness. He opened his eyes and saw Angela's hand gently holding his face. Her face was now glowing a sapphire blue and she was smiling. He then saw something in her eyes which sent a sensation sparking through his body finding its way to his heart. This pain caused Lucifer to let go of Angela and hold his chest. Angela looked at him through the murky water and held out her hand. Bemused, Lucifer took hold of her hand and they both swam to the surface. As their heads emerged from underwater, they both took a breath of life-giving air.

"Oh thank God, are you both okay?" Sister Sophie called down.

"Yes, sister," Angela shouted up, "we're fine. We're coming up."

Lucifer looked into Angela's eyes through the cold, dark, murky water, occasionally blowing a bubble through his nose.

"Why are you looking so puzzled Lucifer? Is that pain in your heart so bad?" She smiled again. "Don't you think it's odd that some people call it love and others call it pain?"

She held out her hand again. Cautiously he took hold of her and put her over his shoulder. Taking hold of the rope, he started his ascent. Angela held Lucifer tight with her arms in an embrace of love. Lucifer was amazed that the more tightly she held, the more pain there was. For the first time in his existence a tear rolled from his eye.

"Thank God above, she's alive. Thank you Luther, God will repay such kindness."

Sister Sophie had taken Angela from him after reaching the surface and was wrapping her in a warm dry blanket.

"You must be freezing, Luther. Let's get you inside in the warm and out of those wet clothes."

Lucifer began to shake as Sister Phillipa put her arm around him, making the pain in his heart worse.

"No! Get away from me, leave me alone. I don't know what's going on here. You nuns are making me sick."

He pushed the nuns aside and began to run until he reached the edge of a nearby forest. For a moment he paused to look back. Angela was watching him, and he read her lips.

"I love you Lucifer," she had said.

It hurt too much. He ran off into the woods.

CHAPTER SIX

THE MOONLIGHT SHONE like silver glass through the dense darkness of the woods, lighting up Lucifer's shadowy frame as he sat lazily under a tall oak tree. He watched as leaves moved in the breeze making its way through the stillness of the night. What had happened? *I saved someone, which is what God wanted me to do, and yet the pain I felt became worse. I thought I was supposed to be the evil sadistic one, not God. How much worse can this punishment be?*

A rustling in the bushes disturbed his thoughts. A deer had come to see the source of the smell drifting on the evening breeze. Lucifer's eyes began to feel heavy. He removed his damp coat and made a pillow to rest his weary head. He lay down looking up to the moonlit starry night, let out a big yawn and closed his eyes.

He had been asleep a couple of hours when he woke to the peculiar feeling that someone was watching him. He opened one eye to see the bright blue glow surrounding the face of angel Michael, his eyes ablaze like blues sapphires, his long golden hair partially covering his long pointed ears as he stood sword held in hand.

"What do you want? Have you come to gloat at my situation?" Lucifer asked angrily as he turned his back on his arch enemy.

"On the contrary Lucifer, I have come to reward you. The Most High was pleased with your actions this evening. Angela would have certainly have died if you had not intervened. What pleased the Most High even more was the fact you saved one of the chosen ones. She has a very important destiny awaiting her when she is older."

"I didn't save her because I wanted to. I just wanted to be rid of this damn flesh prison."

"All in good time Lucifer. Unfortunately you still have some work to do here first."

"So what's this reward? Are you going to be my servant for the night or do I get to fight you again?"

Lucifer was now on his feet looking up at the enormous frame of his foe.

"No, for tonight alone you are allowed your wings once again, to fly anywhere within the confinement of the earth's atmosphere, to be the angel you are. But remember, you are not allowed to harm anything or anyone. If you do so the Most High will remove your wings for good and you will never again be able to return to angelic form."

Lucifer's eyes began to flash a flaming red as he imagined himself with wings once again.

"All you have to do is close your eyes and speak with your mind and beg for the Most High's forgiveness."

"I will not bow down to the Most High. If I do ask for forgiveness, do I have to mean it?"

"No, Lucifer the choice is yours, you only have to ask."

"But what of this body? What will happen to it?"

"It will be quite safe here until you return to it in the morning. The Most High will ensure you won't lose it."

"I was hoping you would say it would burn away once I left it."

"The time has come. Are you ready Lucifer? The moon is moving fast and your evening is slipping away."

"I am ready." He closed his eyes and took hold of Michael's hand. *Forgive me, Most High.*

Within seconds a tingling sensation ran through his spine, rushing to his head. It was like electricity buzzing throughout his being. His heart began to beat so fast it felt it was going to burst. All of a sudden he felt an immense feeling of freedom as his angelic soul left the mortal frame. His angelic form began to grow amongst a red mist until he was standing twenty feet tall. He saw his eyes reflected in Michael's blade – they were now red and ablaze in all their glory.

"Michael, we stand on opposite sides once again, only this time I don't have my sword. Otherwise I would have been tempted to kill you for real this time."

Michael smiled, wished Lucifer a good night, and vanished.

"Now let's test these wings." Lucifer extended his back muscles and his red wings expanded like a giant fan. Then he knelt with one knee on the floor. *Forgive me, Most High indeed,* he thought with a sneer.

His eyes flashed like a flame and in a single motion he was in flight towards the moon. The ground beneath his feet got smaller and smaller until the land below was almost invisible to the eye. Looking up again, he remembered what Michael had said about the confinements of earth and decided to test his words. With one big flap of his vast wings, he soared higher and higher. This was when he noticed that his wings were getting heavier and he was finding it hard to breathe, even to the point of exhaustion. Realising Michael's words were true, he stopped and hovered where he was, his wings slowly fanning the air around him to keep him in flight.

Okay if I can't go up I can still go round. He closed his eyes and cleared his mind. The red glow got brighter as he breathed his life force in and out. When he was ready, he turned himself horizontal, let out a war cry and began to flap his wings. As he gathered speed, his energy grew and the red glow shone brighter, leaving his being and entering the clouds which surrounded him. Flying through the sky at a vast speed, Lucifer laughed as he turned in somersaults through the clouds. *Time to break the sound barrier*, he thought, closing his eyes again as a fireball started to surround him. Gaining in size until he was ready, he opened his eyes and the fireball entered him, making red lightning flash all around him, shooting him off like a rocket. The land below was a distorted blur because of the speed at which he was now travelling. Looking ahead, he started thinking about hate, greed and all the things he represented, which made him go faster still. It was though all things were possible by tuning into his own energy and life force.

Yet, as he passed over continent after continent, one moment he was in darkness and the next light. He felt there was still something missing from his energy that would make him equal to the Most High. Why would the Most High keep that knowledge a secret?

"Look at me God, look at me!" he shouted, flying on his back, shouting to the heavens and laughing hysterically.

The sun was slowly emerging on the horizon above the woods where he had first taken flight. Again, his wings became heavy until he finally came to a halt. It was like he was trapped in an invisible cage in which he could not move. A sickening feeling came over him again, the same as the one he'd had when he had first entered the human body. As the sunlight became brighter, he turned to face it and bowed to its magnificence. His wings slowly started to fold away, wrapping themselves around him. With a sigh, he slowly fell to earth, accepting that he would soon be inhabiting human existence once again.

Chapter Seven

THE WARMTH OF THE SUN on his face stirred Lucifer from his sleep. A smile made its way across his face as he remembered flying the night before and all the energy associated with it. Was he still an angel or had he returned to human form? He was about to open his eyes when he heard a strong heartbeat accompanied by heavy breathing. In an instant he was sitting upright, eyes wide open, looking at what had been his pillow. The creature lying next to him lifted his head, a head surrounded by a golden mane of fur. Its eyes were transfixed on Lucifer. The mouth started to open for an early morning yawn, showing all of its razor sharp carnivorous teeth. Lucifer watched as its tail occasionally flicked up and down to fan away annoying flies. As this giant creature began to stand, Lucifer started to panic with fear. In his angelic form, he was king of beasts and would command them with one word, but as a human he knew he was defenceless.

He slowly and cautiously crawled his way back from the giant cat which was now fully standing. His mane was black and golden, surrounding the very proud face of a lion in all its glory. A metal frame fence met Lucifer's hand as his retreat was halted. He realised he was in a lion's cage and there was no escape. As the lion's warm breath moved the hair on his head, he slowly met the lion's eyes. Its pupils were encircled in a spellbinding golden and black gaze, transfixed on his every move. Lucifer felt the memory of his power from last night. He breathed this feeling from his mouth into the lion's nose. The lion immediately accepted this breath then precipitated its own into Lucifer nose. Lucifer felt that that they had become one spiritually. The lion bowed its head in a form of respect then rubbed its neck and mane against Lucifer's head in affection. Lucifer threw his arms around its massive neck and, before he knew what was happening, the lion threw him on the floor, playfully wrestling with him and holding him down with its giant paws while licking his face. Their hearts were now beating in unison like the rhythm of nature dancing to music and after much playfulness Lucifer collapsed on the floor exhausted. The lion lay down beside him resting its throat on his shoulder, its eyes watching alertly as if guarding a friend.

"Well, my friend. I can't stay here all day. I need to find my way home back to angelic form."

Hearing his words, the lion stood up and looked toward the sun. He stood proud like a statue, then took in a deep breath and with mouth wide open let out a wild, untamed roar towards the sun. Watching and hearing, Lucifer felt pain once again in his heart. *What are you doing God? I don't understand this pain. How can I have this pain when this sight seems so real and natural to me?*

The lion stopped roaring and looked at Lucifer as if deep in thought. Lucifer felt his gaze and looked deep into his eyes. The lion bowed his head to acknowledge Lucifer's need for departure. Lucifer bowed his head in return, and then swooped down to pick up his black coat. The lion's giant paw stamped down on his coat.

"I understand."

Lucifer let go and stroked the lion's head. "Goodbye friend."

He climbed the fence avoiding tearing his clothes and pulled himself over the top and climbed down the other side. He spotted to his right a signpost welcoming people to London zoo. The lion was now lying down, resting his head on the coat. The zoo gates were just opening as Lucifer walked towards them. A surprised security guard watched as he walked through the incoming daily visitors. Lucifer stopped walking and looked around. In the distance a roar sounded. He smiled and walked through the gates.

Out on the streets of London again, making his way along the pavement, the encounter with the lion went through his mind. Why did the lion befriend him, and why did it feel so natural to be in the lion's company? His mind went back to the previous evening and the memory of flying through the sky in angelic form. It was great to feel that powerful again, but there was still work for him to do if he wanted to fully regain his angelic status and restart his war with God. A shiver went down his spine. He had the feeling someone was watching him and as he turned around, he noticed a man following him. Lucifer smiled when the man stopped walking and made out he was reading a bus timetable at a bus stop. Lucifer turned and carried on walking, fully aware that the man behind had continued his pursuit.

"Read all about it! Falling stars and freak storms hit all around the world last night."

Lucifer stopped at the newspaper stand to ask the boy what he was shouting about.

"It's in the papers mate. Mysterious red lighting storms all around the world and freak shooting stars."

"Do they say what caused it?" Lucifer enquired.

"If you want to know, why don't you buy one? I don't have all day to waste talking to you."

"I don't have any money."

"Too bad mate, read all about it." He was now looking and shouting over Lucifer's shoulder.

"I'll buy that for you."

The young man had caught up with him and joined him at the newspaper stand.

"There you go." Lucifer looked down as the young man paid for and handed him the paper.

"You're welcome," the young man said sarcastically as Lucifer took it silently. "Strange things going on these days don't you think?"

They both looked at the front page headlines.

"I think it's a sign from God, what do you think? Oh, by the way my name is David."

Lucifer looked at the young man's hand outstretched for a handshake. He observed he was wearing a gold ring with a figurehead of a lion with eyes of fiery ruby stones.

"Nice ring," Lucifer remarked as he took hold of the man's hand with a firm grip.

"Thank you, and your name?"

"Luther. Pray tell me, why were you following me?"

David's face went red with embarrassment. "Oh, you noticed that!"

"Well, let us just say you weren't that subtle about it."

"Do you believe things happen in people's life for a reason? Strange things like those storms yesterday."

"Maybe it is a sign from God like you said. Perhaps the Most High is showing anger at all of you – I mean us – humans."

"What! You think God is capable of anger? I'm one of the very few people who still believe in God." Lucifer watched as the young man brought his hand to his lips kissing the ring.

"You like lions then," Lucifer asked.

"Oh yes, I and few others worship them. The lion is a great symbol of courage and strength as well as being regal, don't you think?"

"Yes, it's a very majestic animal. They say it's king of beasts, don't they?"

"Why didn't the lion kill you back at the zoo?"

"Spying on me then following me?" A concerned Lucifer started to edge away from David. "You're starting to make feel uncomfortable, young man."

David took a step back "It's our organisation's mission. We watch out for great omens and signs. I've been visiting this zoo for months waiting for a sign from the lion. You can imagine I was amazed to see you playing with that lion today. That was a great omen indeed. How did you control him?"

"There was no control, just mutual respect, something you're not showing me just now with all your questions. Now go away."

"I'm afraid I can't. My friends in the organisation won't be very happy if I let what I've seen today just disappear. Please. I've nearly made it to master and I want to really prove myself to them. Will you come home with me so we can talk more? My wife does an excellent chicken for lunch."

Lucifer stood staring at the young man for a while, his eyes were crystal blue and shone in the sunlight and his face was almost showing despair at the thought of losing this opportunity of proving himself.

"Lead the way then young man. I'm hungry and intrigued to learn some more of this organisation you speak of – and I definitely won't turn down a free meal."

David's face lit up with joy like that of a young boy who just had received a present at Christmas.

It wasn't long before they were both walking down a short stony path with rose bushes of all colours either side, heading towards a big blue door that had a large brass lion head as a knocker. Once they were at the front door, David stopped, smiled and looked at Lucifer and then opened the door.

"Please come in. Can you wipe your feet? My wife is a bit of a perfectionist, she likes everything clean and tidy."

Lucifer watched as David hurriedly walked to the kitchen, calling his wife's name. The smell of chicken was making its way through the air, making Lucifer's stomach rumble.

"Ruth, I'd like to you to meet Luther."

Lucifer turned to greet David's wife who was a petite

woman with brown, mousey hair and an attractive smile heavily covered in red lipstick. Looking deep into her green eyes, Lucifer immediately noticed a feeling of longing from this lonely woman. She held out her hand and as Lucifer took it into his big hand, a vision entered his mind of their two naked bodies in a lustful embrace. Ruth slowly walked away, slightly flushed in her cheeks from the intensity of his gaze.

"David darling, could you show our guest into the living room?" Ruth said. "I'll make some tea or coffee. What would you like, Luther?"

"Tea will be fine, thank you Ruth."

She smiled and turned to head back to the kitchen. Lucifer watched as she walked away, admiring her figure. An inherent animal instinct inside him almost created a growl from deep within, but Lucifer settled for a lustful sigh. The living room was very spacious and perfectly clean and tidy. The morning sun was shining through a set of patio doors, left slightly open. A breeze occasionally moved the white curtains.

"Please take a seat."

Lucifer chose the armchair nearest the window where he could see the sun. The leather seat let out air as he sat down.

"So where do you come from, Luther?"

"A long way from here. I'd rather not talk about me if you don't mind. All I know is that I was hit on the head and mugged. I can't recall much about where I came from either. Tell me more about this organisation you belong to."

"I'll tell you as much as I can. It's a secret society called the Watchers."

Lucifer's eyes widened on hearing that name again, remembering the conversation earlier with Sister Sophie, David continued. "It's a secret society and I've been a member for a long time. I have to prove myself before I can become the master and be named the man of the east. I only partially know its secrets and beliefs."

"It's just an excuse for grown up boys to get together and get drunk without their wives."

They both looked around to see Ruth entering the room with a tray of tea. Lucifer noticed that David looked slightly annoyed.

"Sorry my dear," he said, "You don't know what you're talking about. It's existed for thousands of years. Many famous people in history have been members and it's a great movement for teaching morals and initiating a brotherhood of men with a foundation stone of brotherly love, relief and truth."

"Sugar, Luther?"

Ruth totally ignored David's speech as if she'd heard it a thousand times before.

"Quite a lot of sugar, I have a rather sweet tooth," Luther replied.

Ruth handed him his cup, then reclined in her chair, gently blowing the surface of her tea.

"I'll sugar my own then," David sarcastically remarked to his wife.

"Tell me more about your organisation David," Lucifer continued. "Do they have a religion or believe in a deity?"

"When you join you have to believe in something much bigger and powerful than man, like a deity, no matter what that deity is. Our philosophy and ritual is based on finding out who we truly are and to search for the light that is from above. This is done in several stages or levels if you like. The more you learn, the higher the level you attain until you reach the status of honourable master."

Ruth let a little laugh that she tried to disguise as a cough.

"You don't believe or agree much with this do you Ruth?"

She looked up.

"Well, 'honourable master', what's all that about? The closest David will get to being an honourable master is a master of his own scared shadow."

"Excuse me. I am still in the room, Ruth." Lucifer

watched with amusement at the look of anger David was now giving Ruth.

"It just strikes me strange that a man would want to join a club where you have to greet each other with funny handshakes and secret words. As for that mask you have to wear, the one you keep in your case ..."

"Mask, what mask?" Lucifer asked. His mind shot back to when he had been at the orphanage talking to Sister Sophie about what she saw the night that Christopher had joined his organisation.

"It's just a mask we have to wear to recognise our rank or level within the organisation. It's symbolic more than anything sinister. Anyway forget about that, our organisation does a lot of charity work. Look at the money we raised for your brother John and his chemotherapy."

David turned to Lucifer, keen to make his point.

"John is Ruth's younger brother and he's terminally ill with cancer. The doctors have only given him about six months. Fortunately, he has Ruth's younger sister Mary looking after him. She's a very kind but lonely soul. Would you excuse me? I have to make a phone call."

David stood from his chair and made his way to the hall, closing the door behind him.

"So you don't agree with your husband belonging to this organisation," Lucifer said, turning to Ruth.

"It's not the organisation so much. It is the fact that he doesn't spend a lot of time with me. He works during the day and most nights he's out with his mates talking about rituals or other boring stuff. The most annoying thing is their annual dinner dance: ladies night they call it. I try to look like I am having a good time and the wine makes that easier. A woman has her needs."

She looked deep into Lucifer's eyes which were transfixed on her. Again her face flushed red and Lucifer knew exactly what thoughts were going through her head. She gasped as she saw Lucifer's ancient passion flicker like a flame in his eyes. Lucifer beckoned Ruth towards him and whispered in her ear.

"My little mortal soul, you couldn't handle the power and passion I possess inside this soul. It's seen thousands of years of death and destruction. Believe me, you will not like what's in here."

She pointed to his heart. "I like a dangerous man."

Lucifer lifted his eyebrows in amusement and sat back in his chair to face the sun.

David had closed the door and was now talking quietly on the phone.

"You say he was in the lion's cage and the lion didn't harm him?"

"Yes he was, Brother Scribe," David replied. "I couldn't believe my eyes. He was play fighting with the lion. They even bowed to each other in mutual respect. Do you think our secret scriptures are being revealed now? All the signs are there."

"Calm down David. I'll get in touch with the other masters and our elders. Keep him there till we arrive."

"Of course I will. Does this help me and my progress within the organisation?"

"My boy, if this is true your name will be put down in the annals of history among our brethren. If he is the one we're waiting for, we have to prepare the way for him. It's imperative you don't lose sight of him."

"I won't, Brother Scribe, see you soon."

David held the receiver to his chest and sighed. He rushed back to the living room where Lucifer was still looking out of the window admiring the sun and his wife was red-facedly sipping her tea.

"Hope you don't mind Luther. I've taken the liberty of inviting a couple of friends over who are interested in meeting you."

"More entertaining than just us, I guess," Ruth sighed. "I suppose I'd better put on my apron again and finish getting lunch ready."

David turned back to Lucifer.

"I was wondering if you might be interested in accompanying me to our meeting tonight. The meeting happens once a year and we get together and go through the ritual. Afterwards we prepare to meet our ladies for dinner as a way to express our appreciation of their time and patience living with us. Of course I will have to get the elders' approval. Maybe we can get Mary to accompany you. She needs a night out as a break from looking after her brother. I am sure we could get a nurse in for one night. Would you honour me and be our guest this evening?"

The thought of gaining further insight into the mysterious society fascinated Lucifer. It might answer some of the questions he had and maybe he'd be able to use this organisation to help him get back into heaven. "I wouldn't miss it for the world."

"Lunch won't be long. I will just go and see how Ruth is getting on. Would you like to watch TV or listen to music?"

"No, I'll just go out in your garden for a while."

A gust of wind blew against Lucifer's face as he slid open the patio door. The sun was burning bright, occasionally blackened by a passing cloud. A cat from next door jumped onto the fence and as Lucifer slowly walked down to the bottom of the garden, the cat following him and occasionally meowing to get his attention. At the bottom of the garden he closed his eyes to reminisce about his old power. But his emotions were dormant. There was no red light, no wings. Just the weight of human flesh around him. He pondered on the night ahead. Why would the Most High lead him on this path? He sighed at the realisation that the Most High was still directing and controlling his life like a puppet on a stage.

"You're not infallible you know, oh great one," he said looking skyward. "When the time is right and when you're not expecting it, I'll seize my opportunity and return as an angel. You will reap my anger tenfold for this humiliation."

Lucifer watched as the cat stalked a bird on the ground. The stealth and patience of the cat was remarkable. In one leap the cat had the bird in its outstretched claws, blood and feather scattered everywhere. Lucifer looked again at the sky and smiled.

"Luther, lunch is ready,"

Lucifer turned to see David leaning out of the kitchen window.

"Okay I'll be right there." He bent down and stroked the cat, which pulled its ears back, warning him off his catch.

Lucifer walked back into the house.

"Put the television on Ruth. I want to see the news and find out if there've been any developments in the east."

David was sitting at the dining table waiting to eat his plate of chicken, chips and peas as Lucifer entered the living room. Ruth was changing channels on the television trying to find the news.

"Hurry up, Luther you must be hungry. That's it Ruth, leave it there, the news is on in a minute. Luther, I suppose you have heard of the growing tension in the east and General Silas, the terrorist. He's scaring people all around the world, especially now he has nuclear capability. I don't think he will ever use them though."

"Why not, after all he is a mad man," Ruth replied.

"Well, if he did, it would mean the destruction of him and his own country. Who'd want that?"

"Someone with nothing to lose I expect," Lucifer argued. "I expect if someone hated humanity so much, it would be better to destroy it than be part of it."

"I expect so but we are all part of God, and destroying man will be like destroying God. No, I think we will leave that to the devil and his arrogance. They say that General Silas is the new antichrist."

"Really" Lucifer said with interest. "Do you think it's possible for the lord of darkness to take human form?"

"If he is as deceitful as we've been led to believe, I guess he could."

"But what about if he'd been forced into human form? What would you think of him then?"

"Well maybe it's part of God's plan to teach that vile wretch a lesson for whatever reason. Only God knows the answer to that."

"Aren't you hungry, Luther?" Ruth had noticed Lucifer was not eating much.

"It's all this talk of religion. It makes me sick to the stomach."

"Quiet, the news is on," David interrupted. They all listened as the news reader started his report.

"In a meeting of government officials representing the world nations yesterday, it was apparent that there was genuine concern over General Silas and his almost completed nuclear capability. He now has missiles that can reach nearly every country in the world. Talks and sanctions are being implemented immediately. One government spokesman clearly stated that military action was a last and final resort through fear of provocation. The eyes of the world are watching General Silas and everything is being done to calm the situation."

"You can switch it off, Ruth. I've heard enough," David said.

"Switch it off yourself. I'm not your servant!"

Lucifer watched and smiled as David did as he was told.

"You have to let him know who is in charge."

Lucifer turned to Ruth. "Have you ever been controlled or told what to do Luther? Or do you like being in control? I like a man who's in control of his life and emotions."

"Ruth, behave yourself," David reprimanded his wife.

"Well, I'm not the man for you as I'm definitely not in control at the moment. That's only temporary though."

"What do you mean?"

"I'd rather not talk about it."

The doorbell rang.

"I'll get it," David said as he walked towards the hall.

"You are a mysterious man Luther. I fear you and yet you excite me. Do you have that effect on everyone?"

Lucifer didn't answer. Ruth looked towards the door.

"It's some of the important men from David's organisation. They've come to see you, David's prize. You are honoured. Well I suppose I better play the dutiful wife and clean this table and make some tea."

Lucifer heard whispering in the hall. Then the door opened and David walked in beaming from ear to ear as he looked at Lucifer. It was like he was giving Lucifer the once over before his important guests could see him.

"Please come in," David said and held the door open. He nervously ushered in three men all dressed in black suits. One man was aged about eighty with white flowing hair and beard to match. He tilted his head forward and looked over his glasses at Lucifer while steadying himself with a walking stick. Lucifer noticed the stick handle was made of brass and was shaped in a lion's head. The second man was in his forties, very straight and upstanding with an air of arrogance and contempt as he stared at Lucifer. The third man to enter the room was in his late fifties. He was holding a black book closely under his arm and had a vast array of pens in his suit jacket pocket.

"This is Jeremiah," David said pointing to the oldest man. "He's our oldest serving member. He knows all the ritual and every facet of its existence."

"Stop it David," Jeremiah said. "You're embarrassing me. Forgive him, he's very enthusiastic. I believe you can never know everything. If you did, what would be the point of existing?"

He held out his hand to Lucifer who kept his hands by his side. Embarrassed, Jeremiah dropped his hand and looked at David.

“Um,” David said, quick to gloss over the awkward moment. “This is James. He’s the current master and head of our organisation.”

“That would explain the arrogant look he’s giving me.”

Lucifer stood up to meet James’ eyes and glared. When James saw his angry look, his whole demeanour changed to as if he were a scolded puppy.

“This is Daniel, he’s our scribe. If you don’t mind, we’d like him to write things down as we discuss them.” Lucifer nodded in agreement.

“Please sit down gentlemen,” David said. “I’ll see how Ruth is doing with the tea.”

“So where are you from, Luther?” James asked.

“Somewhere far from here.” Lucifer was being cautious, not wanting to give too much of his story away. “All I know,” he continued, “was that I received a bump on my head courtesy of a mugger which left me with suffering acute amnesia.”

“I hope the wound wasn’t too severe. Why don’t you let Jeremiah take a look? He’s a retired neurological surgeon.”

Lucifer saw the ruse that was being acted out in front of him, but still he went along with it. Jeremiah took hold of Lucifer’s’ head and held it to one side to see the wound as James continued his questioning.

“So you don’t fully remember anything about where you come from and who you are?”

“I just remember waking up in a hospital bed feeling –”

There was a gasp and Jeremiah’s walking stick fell on the floor. Lucifer turned to see Jeremiah’s looking very pale.

“Let me get that for you.”

David had entered the room again. He bent down to pick up Jeremiah’s stick, then he assisted Jeremiah back to his chair. Jeremiah then looked at Daniel and nodded. Daniel lifted his eyebrows, then quietly scribbled something down in the black book.

Ruth walked in carrying a tray consisting of a teapot, cups and a selection of biscuits.

"Now, don't eat too many biscuits, boys. I don't won't you to fill yourself up before the big dinner this evening."

An eerie silence made its way around the room. It was quite clear that nobody wanted her there. Sensing an air of disapproval Ruth turned on her heels.

"I'll go and phone Mary to see if she'll accompany Luther this evening."

Nobody except David acknowledged her presence. "Thanks darling, see you later."

David kissed his wife on the cheek and shut the door. Lucifer noticed Jeremiah staring intently at him as if he were an excited child bursting with impatience, wanting to ask an important question. The only thing stopping him was the look he kept getting from Daniel. Now Ruth had left the room James continued.

"David told us he first saw you this morning in a lion's cage, playing with a lion. How is this possible? How do you command and control such a beast?"

"I didn't control it, as you put it. It was mutual respect unlike what you showed me when we first met. I knew who he was and he knew who I was, nothing more nothing less."

"There is one thing we have to tell you before we can allow you to attend out ceremony this evening. David, would you mind waiting in another room?" David obediently left and closed the door.

"Now then Luther," James was sitting relaxed in his chair. "The three of us are the head of an ancient mystic order called the Watchers –"

Lucifer interrupted, "When did your organisation start?"

"It goes back thousands of years and began in Egypt. I'm telling you this because our scriptures tell us that after a falling star, and during a pre-assigned time which was yesterday, a stranger will befriend a lion. He will be known by a mark on his head that he has carried with him since time began. During this time, we must relate this story to help him remember and understand who he was and where he came from. Only then will he fully reveal his name and the lost secret for which we have been searching since time began.

The story begins with a man of his time – for now I can't tell you his name, however he was the head of a peaceful tribe. They lived in the east off the land without the need of buying or selling, exchanging things for the benefit of the whole tribe. War, disease and hate were not in their knowledge. They lived in paradise on earth. They worshipped the sun and the spirit of nature which they believed guarded and helped them. They always had enough water and every year the crops did well. No matter how bad the weather had been, there was always enough for people to feed and quench their thirst.

However, there was another tribe that lived across the desert in the west. Its leader was an atrocious character, jealous of his neighbours in the east. He could not understand their way of living and the prosperity that went with it. Why did his own crops always fail? Disease was rife and his tribe was always hungry and thirsty. So he decided to call upon a skilled spy by the name of Joshua. He was the founder of our organisation.

Joshua was sent undercover to the tribe in the east to try to establish and understand where they were getting their power from. After spending many months observing their way of life, he returned to his master to relate his intelligence. The Master of the West listened eagerly as his spy explained how he had seen such wonderful humanity and kindness encompassed in love. They were led by a man emanating great light, who had something about him not from this earth. This leader always had his oldest high priests walking by his side. Every day, when the sun was at its highest, he would leave with these two men and go off to a place in the dessert. Then, in the early evening, he and the two elders would return to the rest of the tribe who would bow on the ground and give praise for their return.

The Master of the West grew even angrier at such news. He ordered Joshua to return and follow the man into the desert to establish why he went there. So the spy obediently did what his master had ordered him to do and returned to the east. The next day, the master and his two elders left the tribe, closely followed by Joshua. After a short distance, the elders stopped and knelt about twelve feet from each other, their faces angled towards the sky, hands outstretched. The Master went to each of them, kissed their foreheads and whispered something in their ear that sent them into a trancelike meditative state, uttering a strange language. He then carried on walking. It was then that Joshua cautiously walked past the two elders, their eyes white and oblivious to his presence, still chanting their mysterious words.

It wasn't long before the Master stopped at a mound of rocks formed in a perfect circle. Inside the circle was a stone altar. At each side of this altar stood two ten feet boulders with something inscribed on them, something that was not legible to the illiterate spy. The spy waited and watched from a distance as the Master knelt in front of the altar with his face towards heaven. It was then that Joshua looked up and noticed the sky's blue veil starting to open. Emerging from its blue depths, a bright light made its way slowly down to the Master below. Watching with a mixture of awe and fear, the spy saw the Master outstretch his hands to accept what was now being bestowed upon him. In a blinding flash, the light shot down into the Master's being making his whole body glow in a glorious white light. Joshua shook with fear as the light left the Master's body in a beam of light and shot into the two elders, forming a perfect triangle of light.

Overcome with fear, Joshua threw himself down into the desert sand. It was then that his fear subsided and love entered his heart. A love of unimaginable power, pure and unconditional. The sand became wet as he wept. The energy within the triangle turned his hair grey and took away all his physical pains and emotional worries.

It was then he realised he was not worthy and should not be witness to the sacred coming together of heaven and earth. Covering his eyes from the light he made a speedy retreat back across the desert to his own tribe in the west."

"Why are you telling me all this?" Lucifer interrupted.

"Our ancient brethren passed down this knowledge with a purpose. That purpose was to communicate this story at the appropriate time and to the appropriate person."

"Well, how do you know I'm the right person?"

"All the signs are there. It will all be explained in the ceremony this evening. May I continue?"

"Please do," Lucifer replied sardonically.

"Due to the prolonged absence of his spy, the Master of the west grew angry and impatient, so he sent two of his guardsmen to Joshua's house to see what had become of him, informing them they were not to return without him. It wasn't long before they returned with Joshua. The Master was shocked by his new grey hair and disturbed look on his face. He ordered him to tell his story. Unfortunately, Joshua was still overcome with emotion at what he had witnessed and informed his master that he could not and would not divulge his experience. It was impossible to explain such beauty and spirituality.

The Master was infuriated by such insolence, so he ordered Joshua's family to be bought before him to help persuade him to speak. Seeing knives at the throats of his loved ones worried Joshua, so he informed his master that he could not tell him, but pleaded that he spared their lives. He would show him the way to where the Master of the East went at high twelve, then his master could see for himself. His master agreed and ordered that Joshua's wife and child should stay captive until his safe return.

The following day Joshua and his master, accompanied by his two guardsmen, hid and waited for the Master of the East to arrive. It was not long before he arrived with his two companions. All three of them knelt and Joshua threw himself to the floor, covering his face with his hands. The Master of the West ordered his two guards men to position themselves behind the two elders and wait for his signal. The sky parted and the light appeared, moving slowly down, ready to be received. Observing this luminous sight, the Master of the West, instead of being humbled by the light's presence, started to feel more powerful and greedy than ever before. He could have greater control over his people, if not the world. His crops and water supply would never be found wanting. With increased strength he would be able to fashion metal into gold and swords to protect that gold. He would be a king.

Trembling in the sand, Joshua cautiously lifted his head to see his master steadily walking up to the altar with a hammer in his right hand. In one movement, he had taken the Master of the East by the throat and was demanding the secret of his light, warning him that death would be the consequence of a refusal. With light still flashing in his eyes, the Master of the East replied, 'I cannot give you the answer you seek, it is only known by me and the light from above'. Anger grew in the Master of the West as he absorbed more and more of the light. He signalled to his guardsmen who simultaneously bought their weapons down on the two elders' heads. If he were not given the secret, he would take it. He brought the hammer down with a crashing blow on to the other master's head, which laid him lifeless at his feet."

"Arghh," Lucifer took hold of his head as the wound on his head began to burn intensely as if remembering some ancient incident.

"Don't worry, it will pass."

Jeremiah was holding him and Daniel was writing excitedly in his book. As the pain subsided, Jeremiah continued.

“With his enemy at his feet, and feeling all powerful after the light had entered him, the Master of the West returned to his tribe and announced that he was now the leader of both east and west. He ordered that the tribe from the east was to obey his new laws and accept him as their new leader. With his newfound power, he went around performing miracles and fooling people with powerful signs and words. Anyone opposing him was to be burnt alive.

Joshua and his family fled both tribes and went to seek solace in the wildness of the desert. On the fortieth day, at high noon, a light shone from the sky and then shot into the desert ground below where the Master of the East had been buried. In an instant he was bought back to life. Confused, he staggered towards the place of his tribe and fell to his knees at the sight which greeted him. His beloved people had been thrown onto a pit of fire. His land was laid to waste and a dark cloud hung in the sky.

‘Why!’ he screamed to the sky, and the wound on his head began to bleed, the blood rolling down his forehead, entering his eyes. The more he screamed, the redder his eyes became, and it was as if time had stood still when anger overcame his sorrows. The blood stopped flowing, but his eyes remained like rubies shining in the sunlight. He picked himself up and made his way back to the ruined altar. He knelt and summoned the light from above. It is said that the light granted him everything he wished for to avenge himself and his people.

He asked for power of the lion. He wanted its absolute strength, courage, ferocity and demeanour to rule like a king. He no longer wanted feelings of mercy or love, only vengeance. Finally, he wanted a sword and wings to easily enable him to destroy all humanity. All of this was granted and as the sky started to turn a crimson red, wings grew from his back and a sword emerged from the sand at his feet. It was adorned in gold and silver on the handle and the end of the handle was fashioned in the shape of a lion's head. Its eyes were inlaid with rubies. The radiance of his aura burnt like a fire all around him and as he held the sword, the blood which ran through his fingers started to merge with the handle and the lion's head.

He swore an oath, 'May my blood and this sword be as one until I have destroyed all my enemies and my work is done'. It was then he turned to the resting places of the bones of his two murdered high priests. With his sword pointing to each, he recited ancient words to bring them back to life, not as humans, but as two fanged beasts fit only for revenge and devouring human flesh. Their chains rattled around their necks; they were bound by the power of the sword and had to obey and protect its owner. It was then that earth's darkest days began.

He took hold of the chains from the beasts in one hand and held the sword aloft with the other one. He took flight and the beasts ran on the ground below. Fire from his sword burnt anyone who got in his way. The beasts tore to pieces any human in their path, and it was not long before a river of blood ran over the sands and smoke rose to meet the darkest of skies. It was said that he and the beasts would not rest until he had found the man from the west who had bought an end to everything he had believed in. He made a throne on earth, vowing to kill mankind for an eternity with his beasts by his side where he would sit until mankind had been wiped off the face of earth. Being full of hate and revenge, he soon began to forget about the light from above which had given him his power. He hated everything and wanted to destroy anything that was not in his control."

Jeremiah stopped his story and gave a curious look at Lucifer as if trying to assess his reaction.

"Do you know why we should be telling you this Luther? Do you know of this story? And do you know his name or ..." Jeremiah took a deep breath before asking the question he had wanted to ask all his life, "... are you the one our scriptures are talking about?"

Lucifer looked at this frail old man whose eyes were full of hope.

"No, I don't think I'm the one you're looking for." He gave them all a look to try and convince them of his words, "If I were I wouldn't remember a month ago, let alone thousands of years. Besides all this talk of men flying with wings, men turning into beasts, lights from above, all nonsense." He started laughing. "Have any of you seen angels? Where did you come up with such an elaborate story anyway?"

Jeremiah recoiled in his seat as hope retreated from his very being.

"I don't understand, all the signs are there. It felt so right. Are you sure?"

"Look," Lucifer angrily spoke. "I think it's utter nonsense and whoever first made up this story was a complete madman."

Seeing Jeremiah's exhaustion, James continued with the story.

"During this mass extermination on the earth, Joshua and his family escaped the wrath of the angel flying above. Our ancient texts tell us that the night before the end, an angel from God visited him in a dream and told him to take his family away from the desert to escape a terrible thing that was going to take place in the morning. The angel told him that because he had observed the light from above, a special gift would be bestowed upon him. He would see and know things not of this world. He was also informed that by acquiring this gift there would be a price to pay. In the morning, whilst invisible and under the protection from the light from above, he would have to observe and record what happened that awful day. After it had been done it was his duty and responsibility to keep the memory of that day alive. He would do this by making his way with his family across the oceans to new continents and new civilisations untouched by the disaster in the west and the avenging angel of the east. It was then he was to tell his wife and children of what had happened, and in turn, they had to tell their children in secrecy.

Eventually, they formed secret meeting places and acted out what happened that day in ritual which you will see this evening. They did this from generation to generation, waiting for a time to come when all the signs would be in place for a reawakening and finally he and the world would know his true name. Jeremiah here is the last of Joshua's ancestors still alive."

"I'm sorry you've had a wasted journey," Lucifer said. "I'm only a mere mortal who's received a bump on the head. Luckily I think the light from above was shining on me and protecting me like Joshua, what say you?"

James sat back in his chair angrily.

"So you find all this funny do you?"

"Well, yes I do actually. I don't believe in anything and I think you're all crazy. All I want to do is get back home."

As he was speaking to James, Lucifer spotted Daniel whispering into Jeremiah's ear, causing Jeremiah to lift an eyebrow.

"Luther," Jeremiah said, "I know you may not believe us, but will you please do us the honour of attending our meeting this evening? You may not be the 'one' we're looking for, but you are a strong omen and it feels right you should be a part of it."

"I protest Jeremiah," James said. "Are you going to allow him into our ceremony when all he's done is laughed and mocked us? Lots of rich, wealthy and wise men would give anything to see what he will see tonight."

"Enough! James you might be the master in charge of knowledge, but I'm the last blood relative of the knowledge. Luther will be coming tonight, that's the end."

James bowed his head in respect of Jeremiah's decision.

"I do hope you will be there Luther."

Lucifer said nothing and with a look of contempt, turned his back on them to stare out of the window.

"Well, I think that's our signal to leave. David!"

Jeremiah called out to David who waited with his wife in the kitchen. The corridor door swung open.

"Are you all done?" he asked with a smile, which soon turned into an anxious look when he noticed Lucifer's back turned against his three guests.

"I guess so," James said abruptly, "see you tonight David. Thank you for the tea."

James turned and left the room, not saying another word to Lucifer. Daniel and David helped Jeremiah from his chair and escorted him to the door. Lucifer again felt someone's eyes watching him and slowly turned his head to see Jeremiah looking at him with a look of small hope.

"You must remember who you are," Jeremiah said. "I will not die without knowing. Please attend tonight."

Again Lucifer turned to the window, but this time not with a look of contempt but one of fearful curiosity, like somehow he knew that the old man was right.

Outside, whilst escorting Jeremiah to the car where James had already made himself comfortable, Daniel spoke to his elder.

"You know Jeremiah, you know the scriptures more than anyone, but we have to remember that we can't force its words to be true. The prophecy itself has to do that. All we are here for is to read the signs and make the path ready for the one."

"I know Daniel, forgive an old fool and his impatience, but I just need to know. Maybe the ritual tonight will help him remember if he is the one."

"Maybe," Daniel said sympathetically as he fastened his seatbelt and looked at Lucifer standing at the window. "Maybe."

Lucifer watched as the car with the three strange men drove off. *Stupid fools, how could they know of my existence? I am a fallen angel, the most evil and powerful of all of God's enemies. My knowledge has no limits and is beyond human comprehension. Admittedly, I did have two beasts acting as guards over my power and sword, and they were my servants when I was flying around conquering nations. But they have never been human, well at least I can't remember them being human. And who were those men from the east and west they spoke about? It must be a story made up in order to attract new members and their money.*

CHAPTER EIGHT

"WELL, DID YOU FIND THAT interesting? They are three very special people aren't they?" Lucifer turned to see David had re-entered the room.

"Interesting yes," Lucifer said, "but tell me David, why do you see them as special?"

"Well, they have been very good to me. They took me under their wing and introduced me to quite a lot of influential people. The most exciting thing is the secret knowledge they have, which one day I hope to obtain."

"And if you received this knowledge, whatever it is, what would you do with it?"

"I expect, depending on what that knowledge was, if it was the power to heal people, I would help as many people as possible."

Lucifer started laughing aloud at David's angry face, which contorted at the thought of his good intentions being mocked.

"You honestly believe that this so-called knowledge will bring you such a gift? Well, I have seen much deceitfulness and trickery. A long time ago, some men decided on a way to obtain money from susceptible individuals. To do this they would tell other people they had a secret, the biggest secret in the world. They further informed them that they too could be part of this secret, but it would cost them a great deal of money. Still not satisfied with the money they received from these gullible men, they told their initiates that the 'secret' could not be learnt straight away, but only in stages. Each stage cost you more money until finally you were too old to learn anymore. Then it was too late. Look at Jeremiah, at death's door and he still doesn't know the truth."

"Why do you say such things? Our fraternity is built on charity towards one another and helping one another in times of need."

"Have you received any of this charity?"

"No, but I know it's there if I need it."

David looked more and more anxious at the thought of his fraternity being not entirely honest in its intentions.

"Well, if you believe in such a philosophy, one that is preached but not practiced, it's your life."

"I don't believe you," David replied. "Anyway, you'll see for yourself this evening. You are going, aren't you? It'd be a shame if you didn't. Many rich and influential people would give anything to have the invitation you have received."

"Do you know David, I think I just might, even if it's just to satisfy my amusement."

Ruth came back into the room from the kitchen.

"Luther," she said, "it's not a laughing matter. David takes it very seriously."

"I'm glad you both find this funny," David said, "I'll leave you to it and go and have a bath. Ruth, show Luther the spare room. He can rest before we leave this evening. Remember, us men have to leave at five o'clock sharp. Is my suit ready?"

Before she had time to answer he was off upstairs towards the bathroom.

"Yes sir," Ruth retorted as she held a military salute for a while.

"I heard that," David's voice sounded from upstairs.

Ruth laughed, and turned to Lucifer.

"Come on Luther, I'll show you where you can rest.

How is your head? David was telling me what had happened. It's such a shame, the streets aren't safe anywhere anymore."

Lucifer followed Ruth up the stairs without answering. His mind was on the events of the evening and what was to come. Ruth led him into a bedroom.

"Here we are. David won't be long in the bathroom. I've put a suit for you on the bed there."

Lucifer looked to the bed to see a suit neatly ironed and laid out carefully.

"I don't know if it's your size but it looks like it might do. I hope you don't mind, it's second hand. It belongs to, well belonged to, my younger brother. Unfortunately, it doesn't fit him anymore due to his illness. He's lost so much weight."

Her voice started to crack with emotion at the thought of her brother's illness, leading Lucifer to muse about human nature and why humans get emotional so quickly over one another.

"By the way I spoke with my sister Mary. She'll be very happy to accompany you as your guest this evening. She is a nice girl, a bit quiet though. You'll be her first date."

"Date? I don't need or want a date. What a horrible thought."

"I'm only teasing."

Ruth's mood had now changed after putting the thought of John to the back of her mind.

"However, you are the first man she has gone out with," Ruth continued. "We think she'll never get married and will die a virgin."

The sound of the phone ringing downstairs made Ruth excuse herself and she left, closing the bedroom door behind her. Lucifer sighed with relief and fell back on the bed. *How much longer do I have to endure being around annoying humans? I want to kill them all. But becoming an angel again is more important. When I work my way out of this punishment, I shall make all their sufferings tenfold worse.*

He turned his head to look at the clock on the bedside cabinet: it was showing a little after three o'clock. Down the hallway, he could hear David whistling and splashing about in the bath. On the wall opposite he noticed a picture of Jesus, his face smiling and his head completely surrounded by a halo of light. Lucifer sat up and reached out for the picture, staring at the image in front of him. *Why did my brother choose to allow himself to be used by the Most High? He did exactly what he was told to do, then in the end the people and even the Most High forsook him, allowing me to exert my power and have him tortured, eventually crucified on the cross. They call me the evil one, but what sort of parent would let that happen to their child?*

The irony of his own situation made Lucifer frown. Here he was being punished for his sins. Yet he was now like Jesus, having to obey God's commands, not out of love and want of saving the human race, but for his own pride and the want of becoming Lucifer the almighty again.

"Bathroom's free," David's voice was accompanied by a couple of knocks on Lucifer's bedroom door. "Don't be long, I've never been late for a meeting and I don't intend to be tonight."

Putting the picture back on the wall, Lucifer gave it one more look then shook his head. Entering in the bathroom, he could still smell David's aftershave as it hung floating in the steamy, humid room. He removed all his clothes and stood looking at himself in the mirror. What a vast difference to his former glory. Instead of towering at twenty feet, he stood in the frame of a six foot man. No wings, only a tattoo of an angel on his left arm to remind him of what he wanted to achieve. The weirdest thing of all was the appendage that hung between his legs. As an angel, he had no sex and gender wasn't important. *How peculiar* he thought, as he relieved himself in the toilet. In the shower, the hot water beat down on his head. The wound had healed well, but had left a mark which he could feel as he ran his fingers through his hair. The muscles in his neck and back began to relax as the hot water took effect.

"Are you nearly done, Luther?" David was outside banging on the door again. "You have about thirty minutes to get ready."

"Okay, okay, I'm nearly done. You're like a dog with a bone, you just won't let go will you?"

Wrapping the towel around himself, Lucifer made his way back to the spare room, his feet leaving small wet footprints on the corridor carpet. He paused on the landing to hear a conversation downstairs.

"Ruth, have you seen my little ritual book? It was on top of the microwave, the last time I saw it."

"It had fallen down behind the microwave. I found it when I was tidying the kitchen earlier."

"You didn't read it did you?"

"Of course not, I wouldn't dare. I know how much it means to you Bro Protector." Lucifer heard her giggle.

"You did. How could you?" David's voice was high and outraged.

"Oh come on David, the words are much too complicated for my small mind. Words are blanked out anyway, so your secrets are still very safe."

Luther returned to the bedroom to get dressed. When he arrived downstairs, he found David pacing across the kitchen floor.

"We should have left five minutes ago."

"Wow! Look at you handsome," Ruth said.

David turned to see. The suit was a perfect fit and Lucifer stood in the doorway, cleanly shaven and feeling very uncomfortable. He wasn't used to people looking at and admiring him, he liked being feared.

"David's shoes fit as well, I see," Ruth said and Lucifer looked down at his shiny shoes.

"I guess so," he replied, clicking his heels together. The black suit gave him a feeling of power and an air of mystery.

"Well okay, now we've got all the niceties out of the way, we have to make a move. Come on Luther." David said. He picked up his black case. "See you at seven thirty, darling. Have you remembered the raffle prizes?"

"Yes dear, they're in the hall where they've been all day."

"Right thanks honey, now is there anything else?"

"Just go!" Ruth shouted. "Your anxiety is making me feel quite drained. Go and enjoy your meeting."

She closed the kitchen door. As Lucifer followed David down the hallway, he felt a pain rush through his head. The pain was exactly the same as the one he'd felt after saving Angela at the orphanage, only this time it felt like the pain would burst his heart.

"Are you all right?" David asked.

"I don't know, I feel strange."

Lucifer turned to face the kitchen. There was now another voice talking with Ruth behind the closed door, a soft delicate feminine voice. This voice sounded like a voice he had heard a long time ago and he somehow recognised it, but what of the pain it was causing him?

"Who's in the kitchen with Ruth?"

"Oh, sounds like Mary, she's arrived early. Come on, we have to go, you can meet her later. I can't be late. Anyway the fresh air might make you feel better."

Lucifer was glad to be led out the door into the open, because the further he went from the house, the more the pain subsided. To his relief, as they drove off down the road the pain completely went.

"Are you all right Mary?"

Ruth had noticed a strange look on Mary's face as she sat at the kitchen table.

"I don't know, I feel quite peculiar. Not in a bad way, more of an excited tingling feeling. It only came on as I walked into your kitchen."

Mary's face was now slightly blushing as she experienced feelings that had laid dormant deep inside her until now.

"Perhaps you are getting excited about this evening? Your first official date."

"It's not a date Ruth. I'm only doing this because I know how important it is for David. Besides I don't even know this man. What's his name?"

"Luther. He's a very handsome man and there is this air about him, I can't explain it, a sort of authority. It's like he can see right into your soul. If I wasn't with David, his feet wouldn't touch the ground."

It was now Ruth's turn to blush.

"Well you will just have to see for yourself tonight, won't you? Mary, how is John?"

"Not too good. I was in two minds whether to phone you and cancel tonight, then John persuaded me to go. He said that a voice in his head had told him that I had to go tonight and if I loved him, I would do it for him."

"Is he still hearing those voices in his head?"

"Yes, they are getting more frequent. He tells me that they say, 'Don't worry, everything is going to be okay', and God is watching over him and soon there will be no more suffering."

"Do you think it's the medication he's on now?"

"Maybe, but they do say that when someone is close to death, they are more aware and know and hear things more than others."

Mary's eyes began to fill with tears. "I feel it would be better now if the Lord would take him soon and remove his suffering. Is that cruel?" She gave a sorrowful, inquisitive look to her big sister.

"Not at all darling, not at all. God knows what is best for John now. His fate is in the angels' hands."

They embraced and cried as the clock on the wall behind them slowly ticked.

The car rocked back and forth as David tried to avoid the holes along the small country lane. In the distance, Lucifer could see the old mansion that Sister Sophie had mentioned. Next to the house was a car park with

Rolls Royces, Bentleys and Porsches all lined up in a neat row. At the doorway there was a crowd of men excitedly watching their approaching car. To Lucifer, David looked very proud indeed.

"I feel like an exhibit from a freak show with all of them watching me."

"You certainly are not a freak tonight. You are our honoured guest. Look, there's Daniel."

Daniel was standing in the doorway with his black book open, his pen rapidly moving from side to side as he recorded events as they unravelled.

"Here we go, this is my parking place."

David slowly pulled up his car in a space which hosted plaque stating "Bro Protector".

"We've arrived thirty minutes early," David said. "That will give me enough time to get ready."

David was looking at his watch and reaching for his black case on the back seat of the car. "Come on Luther, I'll try to take you through this rabble to meet Jeremiah. He should be inside."

The sea of black suits parted as men either side of Lucifer stood aside to let him through. Some of the men had inquisitive looks, others looked arrogant and suspicious, whilst yet others looked at Lucifer in an almost wistful way. Slightly annoyed at all of the attention he was getting, Lucifer wished he had his sword. The wooden doorway was about twelve feet in height. Above its archway there was a symbol embedded in the stone: a triangle that had a lion's head at the top of the triangle, an eagle at the bottom left and a bull's head at the bottom right. Within its centre stood a naked man pointing to the sun.

"What does that mean?" Lucifer pointed to the symbol.

"That will be explained later in the ceremony. Oh, look over there." David pointed to a man who looked very pale and worried. "He's the brother who is becoming the new master tonight. He has no clue of what is going to happen to him."

David seemed to be feeling for the man's despair, after all David himself would soon be meeting the same fate of becoming the man of the east and head of the organisation. Lucifer heard one man joke with the candidate, asking him if he had clean underwear on, which worried him even more.

"Glad you could make it." They both turned around to see Daniel smiling, his book now closed and under his arm. "Don't you think you should be getting ready David?"

"Damn yes," he replied taking a quick glance at his watch again.

"Don't worry, I'll escort Luther from here."

Lucifer saw that even though this man was small and quiet, he still commanded a great deal of authority.

"Thank you, Daniel. See you later, Luther." David rushed off into another room and shut the door behind him. Daniel turned to Lucifer.

"Jeremiah is so pleased that you have turned up. You have reignited an old man's dreams and hopes."

"I don't see why, I'm not what he is expecting ..."

"What?"

"It's just I don't believe in hopes and dreams."

Lucifer refrained from telling Daniel that he was the total opposite of what Jeremiah was expecting. Hardly someone who would save and heal the entire world; he wanted to deceive and destroy the world at its weakest. They both stopped at an inner doorway and through the cloudy glass panels Lucifer could see the flickering of candlelight.

"Are you ready to see something you will never forget?" Daniel asked. "Behind these doors there is a beautiful sight which people have seen thousands of years before, and in the beginning they only opened these doors to worthy men alone. Are you worthy Luther?"

"I suppose we will soon find out, won't we?" Lucifer remarked as Daniel turned the door handle.

Back at the house, Mary and Ruth were getting ready.

"The blue or red one, what do you think Ruth?"

Mary was standing in front of the bedroom mirror holding each dress up in front of her. "What do you think Luther will like?"

"That's a first," Ruth said.

"What?"

"You asking what someone else will think. You are usually so single-minded and do what you want."

"Don't be silly. I just want to look good, seeing it's such an important night."

"Well I know blue is usually your favourite colour. Why not try something different and go for the red one?"

Ruth pushed her lips together while applying lipstick.

"I don't know if I dare."

"Stop being such a prude Mary. For once in your life, live a little."

Ruth had now left the bathroom and grabbed the blue dress from Mary and put it back in the wardrobe. The phone rang. Ruth put her dressing gown on to go downstairs to answer the telephone. Mary held the red dress up to her chin in front of her and held out her leg to see how the dress hung.

"Mary, Mary!" Ruth was calling from downstairs. "It's John's nurse, she says John wants to talk to you urgently."

In a panic, Mary threw the dress on the bed and ran downstairs in her underwear.

"Hello, what's wrong?"

"Hi Mary, John has just woke up from his afternoon sleep and demanded to speak to you. Don't worry, he's okay, he just has something important to tell you."

Mary waited anxiously on the phone, hearing in the background John's voice thanking the nurse while he took hold of the receiver.

"Mary, is that you?"

"Yes, John. What's wrong, dear?"

"I've just had a wonderful dream. I dreamt I had

died and was sitting talking to God. I was told that my suffering would soon be at an end and you would play an important part in ending my suffering. The dream showed you by my bedside crying over my lifeless body. My face looked so peaceful, and behind you I saw a shadow of a man but it was a strange shadow because even though it was black, there was so much light coming from it ..." John trailed off and groaned sharply in pain.

"John! Are you okay? Damn it, I'm going to cancel going this evening and come home straight away."

"No! You must go tonight. It's a matter of life or death. You have to look for the light, God told me. Please, promise you will go? Oh I just heard a voice telling me you have to wear the red one."

Mary was stunned, she shook her head. A coincidence, she thought. "I'll go if you're sure, take care little brother. I love you."

"Love you too Mary, bye."

"Is everything all right?" Ruth had joined Mary and was placing a blanket around Mary's shoulders as she stood in the hallway.

"Yes, I'm fine. John had another one of his dreams. God told him I had to promise that I would go tonight. He also said something strange, that I was to look for the light. I wonder what that meant."

"Strange. Come on, if we hurry we can go for a drink before dinner tonight. Have you decided on what dress to wear?"

"Yes, I think I'll wear the red one."

Lucifer stood in the open doorway of the temple and his pupils dilated as he took in the sight of the magnificent room in front of him. He looked down and underfoot was a red and blue carpet equal in squares like a chessboard. Chairs were laid out equally on either side of him and the carpet. Looking down the centre of the room, he noticed men stood in rows, all of them wearing regalia made from animal fur. Lucifer walked down the centre aisle and the men parted to let him pass as they watched the stranger in their domain. Lucifer ignored them with an air of contempt as he walked by. In the centre of the carpet was a pedestal next to a red-cushioned kneeling stool. To the east of this pedestal was an altar in front of a big wooden chair. On the back of the chair was a picture of a lion's head. In the south of the room there was another pedestal and wooden chair with a matching picture of an eagle's head. In the north there was the same again, but these pictures were that of a calf's head. Finally, in the west, another chair and pedestal depicted a dark figure of a man. All of the fixtures, except the pedestal depicting the man, had candles adorning their mantles.

"Luther please," Daniel had his hand on Lucifer's back, "there is someone over here who is glad you came."

Lucifer was led over to an eagerly waiting Jeremiah whose face was alight with excitement.

"I am so glad you decided to come, Luther. You have made an old man very happy."

Lucifer lifted his eyebrows; it was not his duty to make people happy.

"Thank you Daniel," Jeremiah said, "I will take over from here."

Daniel hurried off to a table and chair in the corner and opened his black book and took out his trusty pen to start writing.

"So what do you think of our temple? Pleasing to the eye, don't you think? Have you seen the ceiling?"

Lucifer had concentrated so much on what was in front of him that he had neglected what shone above. Above the pedestal was the same triangle symbol as on the entrance door. This time it was made of gold, and the candlelight from below danced and bounced off it in different directions. The ceiling was painted to depict various people, animals and symbols. At its centre was a golden picture of a lion's head watching carefully down on all below with its observant red eyes. On each side of the lion was a picture of two men; one white, the other black. Either side of the black figure were two other black figures holding wooden mallets in a menacing manner. There were scenes depicting people praying and screaming while being engulfed in flames. On the other side, the white figure stood holding the chains of two beasts. Out of one of the beasts' mouths was a big golden sword, the other beast's mouth housed a white dove. Above the dark man was a picture of the moon, while the white figure had the sun illuminating him and the beasts below. In between these two celestial bodies, a falling star merged with the lion's head in the centre.

"Every time I come to a meeting, I look up at that and realise I still love it the same as the very first time I saw it," Jeremiah said. "Does it say anything to you, Luther?"

"I must say, you are a persistent man aren't you?" Lucifer said, annoyed. "No, it means nothing to me except the picture of the lion is magnificent and I do have an affinity with lions."

"Good, good, that's a start."

Jeremiah was once again smiling like a child on Christmas Eve anticipating the morning and opening all his presents.

"All stand to receive the *one* accompanied by those who are to follow."

A man at the entrance of the temple stood in front of a row of men all lined up in procession. At the head of the procession was James and behind him was the candidate walking very sheepishly. They all moved forward in time with the organ playing from the other side of the room. *Sheep, just like sheep.* Lucifer smiled as he thought. One by one, the procession got smaller as certain people broke away. First, James took his place in the east, another man broke off in the south, the candidate stood in the west and then a man arrived in the north. When everybody was stood by their chairs, the organ ceased and everybody looked towards James holding a wooden gavel in his hand. With authority he bought the gavel down hard on the altar surface. This was followed by the men at the other points of the compass.

"My brother situated in the south," James said. "Why have we come together?"

"To remember a moment in history when everything was lost, Honourable Master of the East."

"My Brother in the North, what moment in history shall we bring forth to our memories?"

"That moment when day turned into night and light into darkness, Honourable Master of the East."

"Do we know the brethren present to be faithful and true, my Brother in the South?"

"We do, Honourable Master of the East."

"Do we know the temple to be safe and secure, Brother in the North?"

"We do not yet know, but with your authority, we can ascertain the temples position by the correct communication, Honourable Master of the East."

"Then Brother in the North, you have my command to instruct our brother in his duty."

"Brother," the man standing near the temple door stepped forward. "You, having being elected caretaker, will communicate the position of the temple, then afterwards you will relate that communication to me."

The man motioned towards the door. Lucifer looked down and saw the dagger tightly held in his hand, then leant forward to see what was behind the door. The brother holding the dagger used his other hand to slowly open the door, bringing up the dagger as though ready to do his duty and stop anybody rushing forward.

"Brother Protector, how do you report the position of our temple?"

"Very safe and guarded to the best of my ability." Lucifer heard David's voice sounding from behind the door. "It will remain that way even to the cost of my own life, Brother Caretaker." The door was then shut and the brother caretaker came to the edge of the carpet.

"Brother in the North, the temple is found in a safe and protected position and will remain so even to the point of a sad loss of a brother."

He then walked back to his chair. Lucifer watched with amusement as the brother in the north repeated the communication to the honourable brother in the east. Lucifer could see all around him the other brethren moving their lips, repeating the ritual in silence. The gavel smashed down on the altar again, bringing Lucifer's mind back to the proceedings.

"Brethren," James continued, "as the Honourable Chosen one in the East, I declare the meeting open, and safe in the knowledge that we can conduct our business in peace and harmony."

Down the gavel went again followed by the other two gavels held firmly in the hands of the two faithful brothers, then everybody sat down.

"This is the boring bit," Jeremiah leant forward to whisper in Lucifer's ear.

James read a list giving thanks to certain people.

"He is an excellent leader, but he certainly knows whose backside to kiss," Jeremiah said and started to laugh.

Lucifer gave a faint smile, but his attention was more focused on the candidate who sat silently in his big chair in the west looking very thoughtful.

"Why does he look so worried?"

Jeremiah noticed Lucifer looking in the direction of the candidate.

"Well, he has a lot to remember and tonight he's representing the villain so to speak. All will become clearer later. Oh good, now the good stuff, about time too."

James had finally stopped with all the thanks giving.

"Brethren, tonight the ceremony is the appointment of an honourable master. But first let us open in our first state of reverence. My brother in the south, hail all brethren in the first state of reverence while I observe."

"Brethren," said the brother in the south, "shield your eyes from the light above, as none of you are worthy to observe it in all of its glory."

He smashed his gavel down and all the brethren stood and bowed their heads. They took hold of their right shoulders with their left hand, while resting their elbows flat against their chest. Lucifer wanted to laugh, but Jeremiah was looking at him and gesturing for him to copy, which Lucifer ignored, much to Jeremiah's disappointment.

"I, as Honourable Master, acknowledge your submission and respect and now command you to remain in a state of darkness and prayer until man is found worthy."

He bowed his head and slammed down his gavel, then everybody lifted their heads and dropped their arms.

"My brother in the north, has any brother among us not yet advanced to the second state of reverence?"

"Brethren," said the brother in the north. "I enquire of you, are there any of you who have not yet advanced to the second state of reverence?" Three men stood up and followed the caretaker to the door where they turned and faced James, saluted him with the first state of reverence and went out through the big doors.

"My Brother in the South, for the second time I ask you to hail all the brethren but this time in the second state of reverence while I observe."

"Brethren, having hid your eyes from the light above, I ask you to remain the same but now with meditation and contemplation of what we are searching for."

After hearing the gavel, the brethren took their original position of reverence, but this time lifted their right arm and crossed over their left, and took hold of their left shoulder in a self-embrace. Again, they bowed their heads.

"I for the second time acknowledge your submission and respect, and in a way of contemplation through meditation, you still have not found what you were looking for, but I assure you through patience, fidelity and hard work, man will be found worthy again."

Everybody, except for Lucifer, dropped their salutes.

"Only one more to go." Jeremiah said, having sensed Lucifer's boredom. "It's just ritual. We have to do this every meeting, depending on what state of reverence we're in."

"My Brother in the North, has any brother among us not yet achieved the final state of reverence?"

"Brethren, I enquire of you, are there among you any brother who has not yet achieved the final state of reverence?"

This time only one man stood and made his way to the door, saluted and left.

"My Brother in the South I again for the third and final time ask you to hail all the brethren in the final state of reverence."

"Brethren, having hid your eyes and in way of contemplation and having searched your hearts, you can now safely lift your heads and see that light which is from above."

Lucifer sat sitting motionless and watched the brethren as they put up their first sign, followed by the second. There was a brief pause and then James hit his gavel. The brethren dropped their arms, their hands outstretched and their heads facing the heavens.

"Brethren for the third and final time, I acknowledge your submission and respect, and after finding you in a state of meditation and contemplation I feel satisfied. You among men are found worthy and ready to receive that light which is from above and is our watchword. All hail."

"All hail," they all repeated. Again the three gavels struck the wooden surfaces and they all sat down.

"I do hope you will enjoy our ceremony, Luther," Jeremiah whispered. "You're in a very privileged position. We have a very long waiting list of men wanting to be where you are now, watching these proceedings."

"Why don't you allow them into your meetings? I am sure it will benefit you financially."

"Unfortunately, quite a lot of people, even though they have a lot of money, don't have the correct moral aptitude to become a member. I am not saying all rich people are like that. It is just that we are very careful and selective in our choice of members."

"How did you know you could trust me? You don't even know me."

"I have always prided myself on my good judge of character. It's never let me down. Besides, you befriended a caged lion, what more proof would I need?"

"Yes," Lucifer replied. "But lions are fierce predators with an innate killing instinct. They even kill the young of another pride so they can start a pride of their own. Would you trust a lion in your house?"

"No of course not, but if you take the positive characteristics of a lion, like its courage, strength, its ability to protect its own pride and its regal leadership qualities, and apply them positively into a human mindset, that is something quite different and special. This is how I see you. Why did that lion not kill and maim you? And how did you really receive that mark on your head? Hopefully you will understand the coincidences when you see our ritual."

James had stood from his chair with gavel in hand.

"Brethren, we are now ready to receive our newly-appointed worthy, honourable master, but first my Brother from the North, are there any brethren among us not yet honourable?"

"Brethren, are you all honourable men among us?"

This time about twelve men stood and made their way to the doors at the rear, then very neatly and in uniform fashion, they saluted to James and left one by one.

"Honourable Master, residing in the east, the brethren have all been found to be honourable, except one who is still in a state of ignorance and darkness."

"Let this man be known to me for I need to prepare him and myself for what has to come."

The candidate sitting opposite James in the west stood. "I am he who demands knowledge."

"Then step forward, kneel before me and demonstrate the qualifications necessary to receive the light."

The candidate left his position from the west and made his way to the east and stopped in front of James and knelt on the stool in front of the pedestal.

"I ask you Honourable Master of the East to bestow the light and knowledge on me."

"How do you find yourself so qualified?"

"I do not find myself so qualified, but am ready to receive the light and equally share it."

"The light is for qualified and worthy brethren alone. Having found you are not in possession of those qualifications, I have no option but to banish you from my sight and the light therein."

Lucifer's eyes began to widen as the lights in the temple started to dim, to a faintly lit room with just candles flickering away on each pedestal.

"Brethren, turn your back on such a brother found not worthy to be in our presence and do not look back for fear of having your brethren turn against you."

James turned and showed his back to the candidate, then in one movement all the other brethren including Lucifer, prompted by Jeremiah, turned their backs. There was a brief pause, then the candidate stood and slowly made his way to the doors and let himself out. Once the doors were shut James turned to face the front.

"Brethren having found the one is no longer present, you can safely return your eyes to the east and the light that is restored."

As the lights quickly flashed on, everyone covered their eyes at their intensity.

"Well that was interesting," Lucifer sarcastically remarked to Jeremiah.

"It's not over yet. The best is still to come."

Lucifer lifted his eyebrows, let out a big sigh and thought, *It's going to be a long night.*

"My Brother from the North, finding the room with none but honourable men, you have my command to prove the brethren past honourable brothers."

"Brethren, after having seen and received the light, demonstrate your qualifications to the Honourable Master of the East to show him you are worthy and honourable".

At once, and in unison, they all bowed their heads, their right hand rested on their chest covering their hearts.

"Out of our death we receive life, as the darkness gives into light, all hail."

"Then brethren, having seen you as honourable and worthy, I as the Light in the East confirm I am the one until a proven time shall restore the genuine beliefs of our established customs and order. All hail."

Lucifer looked around as they all sat down. *All these men coming together for some play made up to remember some event in the past that never happened. How easily man is led, especially when in pursuit of knowledge and power. People like David are searching for an ideal that doesn't exist. It's just an illusion, but a very powerful one.*

As Lucifer was deep in thought he felt he was being watched. He turned to see Daniel looking at him. Lucifer narrowed his eyes like a lion would to try to intimidate its prey. Daniel just smiled, lowered his eyes and started writing in his book again. Then he stood up.

"Honourable Master in the East, as the scribe and witness I have to enquire of you – during your time as the honourable one, have you found what we are looking for and do you know his name?"

"Honourable past Brother Scribe, I have not, but I have held the position in good stead for the next '*one*' in hope he will be more successful in our search."

"Having not been successful yourself, we brethren ask you to step out from the light, into a brief moment of darkness, to pass on that light to another. Do you have such a man in mind?"

"I do, past Honourable Brother Scribe."

"Where and how is he to be found?"

"Outside the door of the temple in a sad state of darkness away from the light and our worthy eyes."

"Then brethren, let us prepare for what is about to take place".

Lucifer watched intently as James stood and removed himself from the east and headed towards the pedestal, depicting a lion's head in the centre of the floor and knelt in front of it. At the same time, the two brothers situated in the south and north stood and made their way to a kneeling position behind James forming a triangle, all three facing east.

"Brother Caretaker," Daniel continued, "it is your duty to hail Brother Protector and together you will lead the way for the one."

The brother caretaker bowed his head in submission, and then turned to reach under his chair from where he pulled out something which he placed over his head. He then faced the front wearing a tiger mask. The caretaker left the temple. There was a brief pause then the light gave way to darkness. Lucifer narrowed his eyes to observe what was happening. After a while his eyes adjusted to their surroundings to see the candidate being pulled and dragged into the temple by the caretaker. The caretaker and another tiger-headed man, who Lucifer assumed was David, each had a length of rope draped over their shoulders. The other ends of the ropes were firmly tied around the candidate's wrists, who was also hooded with a black silk bag over his head. They pulled him into the temple as if he were a prisoner ready for execution, More than once he fell to the floor. However, the caretaker and David kept on going no matter what distress the candidate was in, dragging him when necessary. *At last,* Lucifer thought as he watched the man being dragged across the floor. *The ceremony is starting to get a little interesting.*

"No one must assist such a man," Daniel said. "Let him feel the pain to remind him of what he has done and imprint in his memory the consequences of his own arrogance and actions."

The procession came to a halt and the candidate was left lying on the floor, breathing heavily, close to the west pedestal where he had previously been seated. All this time James and his two companions had remained kneeling facing the east, not once turning back to observe.

"Brothers, Caretaker and Protector, bring this wretch to his feet so he can stand in readiness."

The two dark figures reached down and pulled the man to his feet, where he stood unsteadily, and untied his hands.

"Brother Protector, thank you for your assistance. Your duty done, you must return and not speak of what you have witnessed here. In due time and patience you will gain the necessary qualifications which will enable you to fully participate in these proceedings."

David saluted in the second state of reverence then turned and left the room closing the doors behind him.

"Brother Caretaker, return to your seat."

He responded obediently.

"He who represents darkness and ignorance, why have you come by this way?"

"To receive the light which is a gift for everyone," said the candidate in a nervous muffled voice from its dark confinement.

"Having been informed previously that you do not possess the necessary qualifications, why do you persist in obtaining the light?"

"I have laboured hard in my life and through meditation and contemplation. I have found myself worthy and capable to receive the light."

Daniel turned another page from the book he was reading and continued. "I know of your want and desire, this I see in your heart. Still I say again, you are not worthy."

"Then as I speak from a place of darkness, I will not ask for the light, I will take it by any means."

"This is your choice, as you exercise your free will. But never forget there are consequences for all actions. Are you willing to accept such a fate?"

"With due respect brother, fate plays no role in my life. My future and destiny are in my hands alone, to do with as I please. With the light from above, I can promote my will and cause by installing it in the hearts and minds of men."

Lucifer smiled. *What arrogance, a worthy soul for my cause.*

"Then brother, do what must be done while we bow our heads in remorse for what is about to come to pass."

Out of the darkness above, a light started to emanate from the mouth of the lion painted on the ceiling. It made its way down to James' head below. The light grew brighter until it was glowing like a halo all around him. The two other brothers who formed the triangle had a similar light above them, but theirs was not so bright. The organ in the background played some heavenly music to aid the ambience. Lucifer watched as the candidate removed his hood, took hold of his gavel from his pedestal, and slowly crept up behind James.

"Who approaches? Who dares enters the light and walk on holy ground?" The candidate slowly crept up behind James, who was speaking with his eyes shut and his hands still held in prayer.

"It is the Master from the West. I have come to claim my right to the light which you possess and to gain knowledge of your name."

"The light is void of all ownership and is possessed by no man. My name is only known by me. Remove yourself from this holy place and speak not of what you have seen."

"I demand of you," continued the candidate, "give me the light and let its truth and let your name be known to me."

The candidate had now taken hold of James with one hand and held aloft the menacing gavel.

"I implore you", James continued, "If you take my life, everything is lost."

"So be it."

The candidate slowly bought down his gavel and struck James on the back of the head. James fell to the floor at the candidate's feet. Lucifer nearly laughed when James acted out his death. The room started to get darker.

"I now stand before you as you lay lifeless at my feet," the candidate said. "I curse the memory of your name and I steal the light from above. You lived in innocence and now you die in innocence."

The temple was plunged into complete darkness and all that could be heard was the sound of movement from the centre of the floor and the quiet organ playing in the background. Suddenly, a loud gavel hammered down, making Lucifer jump. The lights flickered on instantly. It took a while for everyone's eyes to adjust. All the chairs in the north, south and west were occupied again, and the men this time sat with black hoods covering their heads. On the altar in the east lay a body, arms across his chest in the pose of a corpse. He too was wearing a black hood.

"Brethren", Daniel said and stood up. "What we have just witnessed is the loss of a brother, a life cut short in its innocence. May this sight remind you of the start when earth met its darkest hour and the great loss of his name, only to be remembered by a wound. Let this wound on his head remind us of his suffering and death in true innocence."

Lucifer again noticed Daniel looking at him; he was reciting the book without even looking at it.

"He is as hopeful as I am," Lucifer turned to listen to Jeremiah. "We had a long conversation about you after we first met you. We discussed everything that had been witnessed, from David seeing you in the lion's cage, the wound on your head, strange events happening with the weather and a bright shooting star. These are all things spoken about in our great book which Daniel is now reading from. All communicated and passed down from my ancestor Joshua."

"But Jeremiah, I don't believe it," Luther replied. "It's just a story designed to fulfil a need in people's lives, to fill that void. Sorry I don't believe in truth, honour or anything of such nature. My world is built up on dishonesty and mistrust. It amazes me how people can have faith in something they can't see. What a futile existence." Lucifer could see Jeremiah's look of sadness at his comments, which made him feel good.

"Brethren," Lucifer was interrupted by Daniel's voice. "The time is approaching. We have waited for long enough, it is nearly high twelve on the fortieth day. Pray silence and observe so that we may remember what has gone before."

Everyone in the temple stood and faced the altar in the east and waited. The sound of the organ grew louder, playing even more dramatically, faster and louder picking up momentum. The light from the lion's mouth grew bright again. Then the man lying on the altar started to move, his top half lifting like that of Dracula rising from his coffin, until he was finally standing. Haltingly, he made his way back, his hands outstretched feeling and groping his way like a blind man. After a few bumps and falls, he finally reached his chair.

Daniel addressed the hooded man.

"Brother before you sit down, take a moment before you open your eyes to contemplate and prepare your soul for what you are about to see."

After a brief period, a quiet voice sounded from beneath the black hood: "I am ready".

Lucifer was confused at hearing a stranger's muffled voice sounding beneath the hood and was astonished at what took place next. The man started to scream from beneath his hood. He then threw himself to the floor on his knees facing east. His screaming sounded louder as it made its way round the whole temple, then ended in one final cry: "Why?"

The ensuing silence hurt Lucifer's ears more than the previous screams had. The man was kneeling motionless arms outstretched facing the heavens.

"Brother from the East, we have heard your cry in the wilderness to which there is no answer. What is it that you have seen?"

"I have seen a terrible and afflicting sight: my loved ones being tortured and burnt alive."

"My heart feels your pain and weeps for your sadness and loss. What is it you ask of me?"

"Glorious Light from Above, I want my name to be forgotten, to rest in a safe place of innocence, far away from the grips of what I am going to become. Take away my love, install in me hate, take away my mercy, install in me revenge, destroy my weakness, give me strength, destroy my fear, give me courage, let me have control over all the beasts to aid me in my annihilation of man and what he has done and become. All this I ask of you, light from above. Make me the power of the lion over all men, give me wings that I may swiftly pursue my enemies and a flaming sword to remind me of my anger and wrath, which I will use to cut down and smite anyone who opposes me."

"Brother, again my heart feels for your loss. All of this which is asked for shall be granted. Go now, become that which you must, but remember I am always here. I am the Most High."

When Daniel had finished reading his passage, the light coming from the lion's mouth started to fade until it vanished. The hooded man staggered to his feet and blindly made his way to the pedestal in the centre of the red and blue squared floor. Lucifer watched intrigued as the man began to remove his black veil. All the brethren around the temple were becoming excited as the hood was gently peeled away from the face beneath.

Then in unison, as it came off, all the brethren chanted.

"All hail, all hail to the one who has gone. All hail to he who is now, and we pray will return. All hail."

The man in the centre of the room was turning himself around, presenting himself to each compass point and all the brethren who were bowing to him. He had a golden fur mask covering his whole head. It was the face of a lion. Its eyes were red plastic fashioned to look like two inlaid rubies. A well-worn mane encircled the mask.

"Where is my sword?"

The noble voice sounded from beneath its feline frame. The caretaker brother slowly walked forward, still adorned in his tiger mask, carrying a large sword resting on a red cushion. He knelt before his master and presented it. The sword was removed and handled with care and respect. As the caretaker returned to his chair, the lion-headed man recited an oath.

"My soul and this sword in hand are as one, and will not stop until our work is done."

"All hail," the brethren sounded.

"With my sword, I give life to my three brothers who are still in a state of darkness."

He turned to each of the brothers in turn. "My Brother from the South, stand and present yourself to me."

He obediently stood and removed his black hood. This time the man was wearing an eagle head mask covered neatly in layers of feathers, and it had a golden beak and two golden eyes.

"Honourable brother in the east, I represent the eagle and to you I swear my allegiance. With my eyes I will watch over you from the heavens, ready to swoop down and attack your enemies at your back."

"Your fidelity is noted, for which I am thankful. May the air grace your wings with strength and love to fulfil your duty to me. My Brother from the North, stand and present yourself to me."

The brother stood and removed his hooded veil. The

mask this time was in the shape of a bull's head, its horns protruding from the top of the mask.

"Honourable Brother from the East, I represent the bull and I swear my allegiance to you. With my strength, I will roam the earth to watch over you wherever you are and remove any of your enemies in your path."

"Your fidelity is noted, for which I am also thankful. May the earth bring forth all of its fruits to keep you strong and well-fed to fulfil your duty to me. My Brother from the West, stand and present yourself to me."

The man stood and removed his hood. Lucifer was surprised to see a human head with no mask and he noticed it was not the candidate who had been previously sitting in the west.

"Honourable Brother from the East, I represent the man who seeks light and knowledge, I will watch you in your work until a time when I will be ready to receive the light."

"Your willingness to learn is noted," the man from the east nodded in agreement and approval, "for which I am thankful. With time and patience you will be ready to receive the light. Brothers, having been installed into your respective offices, you may take your seats and hold them in good stead until a time of change."

They all saluted and sat down.

"Brethren, before I take my seat in the east, I must inform you that from time immemorial, this chair situated in the east has been occupied by many worthy and honourable men. It has come to represent the light out of darkness, alluding to the knowledge we seek within ourselves. I will guard its memory as honourable men have done in the past. I hope when my time is at an end, worthy men will guard its future. I am thankful that the brethren have shown full confidence in me and will do my best to maintain and uphold the principles and tenets of our work."

Rapturous applause sounded around the temple after he had finished his speech. Men rose in standing ovation in praise of the new master in the east, exclaiming, "All hail".

Lucifer looked around at the faces of the men around him. Some were crying, including Jeremiah. Why? *A weakness*, he told himself, but the pain again started in his heart. A gavel pounded, causing everyone to stop their applause.

"Brethren, as the new Honourable brother from the East, I shall now take my seat, and afterwards you will join me."

He very proudly sat down. There was a brief pause and then all the brethren sat down. "Brother Caretaker, which state of reverence do we find ourselves in our present situation?"

"In the final state of reverence, Honourable Master of the East."

"Then brethren, it is my command, by the power in mc vested, to resume the temple in the first state of reverence. All hail."

"All hail," they all repeated as the gavel made contact with its wooden surface.

"Honourable Master of the East," Daniel said as he got on his feet again. "Having returned to first state of reverence, we have some brothers outside the temple who are not to be found worthy ready to see you in all your glory. It is a time to lock up our secrets in a safe repository united in our hearts and minds."

"Very well, Brother Scribe, your observation is noted. My brother from the north and south," he said and they both stood, "the time has come for us to return to our former selves."

The three of them removed their masks. Underneath, their faces were red and flushed from the heat, and the candidate, now the master in the east, was looking very proud of his new position within the temple.

"Brother Caretaker," the man still wearing his tiger mask stood up to the master's command, "having taken care of our proceedings, we find ourselves in a safe place.

It is my command to you to release yourself and Brother Protector."

With a salute he removed his mask and walked to the temple doors and gently opened them.

"Brother Protector, it is the Honourable Master's command to release yourself of your bond to him and the other brethren."

With one swift movement, David's mask was off his head and being placed in his black case while the brother caretaker closed the door to resume his seat.

"Honourable Master, may all brethren be admitted?"

"With pleasure Brother Scribe, Brother Caretaker admits all brothers."

"Did you enjoy that Luther?" James whispered from behind where Lucifer was sitting; he was leaning forward with a proud look on his face.

"How did you get there?" Lucifer asked, surprised and offended by James being so close to him.

"I crept behind here when the lights were out. So what do you think of our ritual?"

"Do you really want me to answer that? I think the only thing I enjoyed in this charade was when you were murdered. Now that was fun."

"Now look!"

James was stopped from issuing his objection by the wave of Jeremiah's hand.

"Luther, please try and respect what has gone on here. It has happened for thousands of years and all the men here, including myself, are proud to be part of it."

"Proud of a lie. What proof do you have that all this actually even existed?"

"We don't have proof, only faith. That is all we need and I'm sorry you think it's a lie. Even if it was, there's no such thing as a bad lie."

"What do you mean, Jeremiah?"

"Well, look around you. There are people in here who believe in something other than themselves. Something good enough to give their time and money away for. We are all generous in awarding quite a lot of money to charitable organisations and we all do a lot of good work in society. So you see, out of something, truth or lie, good shines through in pursuit of the ultimate truth."

"Well I only believe in myself and nothing more. This only confirms that nobody or nothing can be trusted except myself and the way I want things to be said and done"

"Who hurt you so much, Luther? What has made you so bitter and angry at the world?"

Lucifer noticed the pain appearing again in his heart, causing him to take hold of his chest.

"Are you okay?"

"I'm fine. I just want this stupid meeting to come to a close so I can get some air and remove myself from your irritating questions."

"Not long now. We only have to close the temple when all the brothers have been readmitted – here they come."

Lucifer looked at Jeremiah's face and could not understand why he was still smiling at him and demonstrating kindness after all his insults. They all stopped their conversation and looked around as the man in the east stood to speak,

"Brethren, now our work is done. Please assist me in closing the temple".

Everybody stood and held their sign of reverence.

"Brother Caretaker, see that all the brothers are accounted for."

He saluted, then went and opened the doors of the temple.

"Brother Protector, how are you to be found?"

"Safe and still in a position of trust, Brother Caretaker" came the reply from behind the doors. The brother caretaker closed the doors and walked onto the carpet and saluted.

"Honourable Master, all brothers are safe and accounted for, and we remain so in your care."

"Brother in the West, why do you reside there?"

"Honourable Master, I am here to represent the darkness, like the moon in a night's sky."

"I acknowledge why you are so placed, pray tell us why am I situated in the east?"

"Honourable Brother, you reside in the east to represent the light, like the sun giving its glory to all who dwell beneath it."

"Very well Brother in the West, as our work is done and the sun is going down, you have my command to close this temple."

The three gavels sounded one after the other.

"Brethren, as the light from above us has left us, I close this temple." The organ started playing and the men from the north, south and west left their chairs and walked to the east, where they all lined up, waiting for their companion to leave his seat.

"Brethren, as the designated scribe I record that the temple was closed at seven o'clock precisely and will reopen one month from now at a stated time. Remain standing while the Honourable Master, accompanied by his companions, leaves our temple."

The four of them marched off in time with the music, while the brethren from all sides saluted them. They finally reached the back where the caretaker opened both big doors and allowed them to exit, closely followed by all the other brethren.

CHAPTER 9

"DID YOU ENJOY THAT?" Lucifer's head went forward as David's hand slapped hard on his back.

"It was, how shall we say, interesting."

Lucifer gave him a look. Embarrassed, David removed his hand from Lucifer's shoulder and tried to lighten the atmosphere.

"Well, I suppose we had better go and find our ladies, they should be in the bar. Knowing Ruth, she'll have drunk it dry by now. I can't wait for you to see Mary, she's a cracker, you know."

David winked and nudged his elbow into Lucifer's stomach, which was met by a lifting of Lucifer's eyebrow.

"Where's the toilet, David?"

"Up there on the left. I'll go and find them. Meet us in the bar."

Lucifer sat on the toilet fully clothed. He bent forward and put his hands over his face. *What am I doing here? Someone such as me, lord of all dark angels, sitting in a toilet with no direction in my life, no idea of how to return to myself, Lucifer in all his glory, and continue my timeless battle with the Most High.*

His thoughts were interrupted by a knock to the closed toilet door. "Are you going to be long?"

"I am finished when I am finished," Lucifer growled. "Now go away."

"Charming, I must say." The stranger's voice faded into the distance.

David joined Ruth and Mary in the bar and ordered some drinks. Half an hour passed and an anxious David looked at his watch

"What is keeping him?"

"Maybe he's nervous about meeting Mary?"

"Ruth, you're awful. Please stop teasing me."

"I'll go and find him." David put his drink down.

"No David, let Mary go and find him. It will be fun to see if she can find him without knowing what he looks like."

"Ruth, stop teasing your sister."

"No, it's okay David. I need to go to the toilet anyway. I'll see if I can find him. If nothing else it'll get me away from my sister's infernal teasing. Where was he last?"

"He wanted to go to the toilet, the one at the end of the corridor, on the left."

"Thanks, see you soon."

"Remember, his name's Luther," Ruth shouted at Mary, as she made her way out of the bar. Mary didn't bother to acknowledge her.

The corridor seemed to last forever as Mary made her way through the men in their black suits and the other women heading to the nearest toilet to powder their noses. Lucifer's head shot up and his eyes widened as that same feeling he felt at David's house prior to the meeting started gnawing at his chest. His heart was now beating faster and faster. Outside in the corridor, Mary got closer to the lavatory door. She stopped her advance as that same excited feeling made its way around her body.

"Are you all right?" One of the suited men with a yellow stained beard from too many cigarettes. peered at the flush on Mary's face, as she stood, hand on chest.

"Yes, I'm fine, thank you. Just a lot of people in a small

space makes me nervous. Have you seen Luther? He's the new man."

"No, I haven't. Everybody's talking about him, you know. They say he has great power and that his appearance is the sign we've been looking for."

"Really? I think I'd better find him if he's that special. I was told he was heading for the lavatory."

"I haven't seen anyone going in, because I'm waiting myself. All I know is that there's a really obnoxious man in there. He told me to go away. I doubt that's Luther. Try the reception area or outside, he might have wanted to get some air."

"Okay, thank you. I'll try reception first."

Inside the toilet, Lucifer's heart was now at bursting point, pushing the blood at maximum speed through every vein and vessel in his body as Mary walked past the closed door towards the reception area. The rush of blood to Lucifer's head made him feel light-headed. As he stood, he almost fainted. Falling back he took hold of the sink and steadied himself. It will pass, he thought. As Mary became more distant, it did pass, and he slowly returned to his normal demeanour. Another knock sounded on the door while Lucifer was straightening his tie in the mirror, then Lucifer angrily swung open the toilet door

"Yes! You knocked," Lucifer grunted in anger looking at the interfering man,

"Oh, it's you Luther," the man replied pulling his head away from the door, startled at the sudden opening of the door, "I was just wondering how much longer you're going to be."

"I've finished now."

"Yes, thank you, may I?" Lucifer stood aside to let him pass.

"By the way, there was a fine lady looking for you. I told her you might be at reception or outside."

"What was her name?"

"I don't know. I tell you, she was very fine, with a quiet and very calm demeanour."

"Well, the fine lady can come and find me in the bar. I'm not waiting for her."

Back in the bar, David and Ruth were talking.

"I don't believe it, where can they be? It's been over forty minutes." David was again studying his watch intently.

"Relax, I'm sure they're both fine. Maybe they've gone for a kiss somewhere."

"You really are terrible Ruth. I want them both to enjoy themselves."

"Pour me another glass of wine, dear."

Ruth was aware that David was about to stand on his soapbox about the brotherhood.

"You might want to think about slowing down a bit this evening, it is only just starting and –"

David's objections were silenced by a perfectly timed kiss from his wife. It lasted for about three seconds until David broke it off in embarrassment.

"Not in front of everybody my love, people are watching." David glanced over at a few of the older men facing their way.

"At last, here he is." David was relieved that Lucifer had entered the room and had captured everybody's attention. "Luther please come and have a drink. Did Mary manage to find you? We sent her to look for you."

"No, but I was told someone was looking for me."

"Good evening Luther, you still look very handsome." Lucifer felt Ruth's eyes looking him up and down again, "So what's your poison?" Lucifer gave her a puzzled look and she rephrased her question: "What do you want to drink? The brethren have put five hundred pounds behind the bar tonight."

"I think I'll have water or maybe coffee."

"You are joking right? This is a bar. It sells alcoholic drinks not coffee or water."

"What's an alcoholic drink?"

David looked surprised at Lucifer's question. "You mean to say you've never had alcohol?"

"No I haven't!"

"Well, they have beer, wine, or spirits."

Lucifer looked around to see what everybody else was drinking. James was at the end of the bar and lifted his glass of whisky to sarcastically salute Lucifer.

"I'll have what James is drinking, but fill my glass to the top, not halfway like his."

"Are you sure Luther? Whisky is very strong you know."

"Just get me the drink, David. Anything he can drink I can drink a lot more of."

"Okay, on your head be it."

"It certainly will be in the morning," Ruth laughed.

David passed the drink to Lucifer and he grabbed it and downed it in one.

"Get me another one!"

Lucifer snapped angrily as his eyes fixed on James smiling at him. He could feel James' contempt towards him. *If only I was Lucifer standing here with all my power, I would have great pleasure in making your death a very slow and painful one.*

It wasn't long before the effects of the whisky took hold, making his body relax and sending numbness into his head.

"This is great; does it always make you feel like this?"

"Yes, it does," David said. "It makes some people feel relaxed, confident and powerful, while others feel aggressive or depressed. It depends on what state of mind you are in before you start drinking. I'd advise you to slow down though because you'll wake up in the morning with –"

"Never mind that dear," Ruth had put her hand on David's chest, interrupting him. "I'm sure Luther doesn't want to know about the morning, he should be enjoying the evening. Anyway, shouldn't you be checking if our dinner places are ready and set up correctly?"

"You're right, darling. I'll be back soon. Will you please look after him."

"Oh, I will my dear, I certainly will," she said looking Lucifer up and down and ignoring her husband.

Mary had made her way outside into the moonlit gardens where people had gathered, drinking cocktails and eating hors d'oeuvres under a floodlit canopy. She made her way through the crowds, stopping occasionally to ask them if they had seen Luther.

When her enquiries were exhausted, she decided to walk away from the crowds and go into the surrounding darkness. Finding her way in the darkness, she headed towards a bench at the end of the garden. Sitting down, she looked up at the moon which hung in the sky comforted by a darkness like a dark veiled blanket. She contemplated her lonely life which centred on caring for John whom she loved dearly. Maybe, she thought, God had created a situation where there was no man in her life so she could dedicate it to caring for John. She sighed as she pondered on the thought of a life without a man and any form of love in her life; she had resigned herself to a life devoted to John and his welfare. The moonlight sparkled on a tear as it crawled out from the corner of her eye and rolled down her cheek. *Come on, pull yourself together Mary, you're a grown woman.* She decided to give herself ten minutes to regain her composure and then she would make her way back to the bar.

Back in the bar, Lucifer stared out the window of the bar at the full moon.

"Are you all right?" Ruth asked.

"Don't you think the full moon is spellbinding?" Luther said in a drunken voice. "It sort of captures your mind and holds you in its awe."

"Yes, very nice," Ruth replied, uninterested, "don't you think there are other things to look at and admire?"

She was now pushing her breasts out to maximum effect, waiting for Lucifer to turn round.

"I used to fly above the moon quite a lot you know. I used to fly as close to the sun as much as it would let me."

He carried on looking out at the moon; his eyes could not be drawn away.

"I give up!" Ruth said, angry that her womanly charms were not succeeding. "I think you've had enough to drink, especially now you're talking about flying. If you love the moon so much, why don't you go outside and talk to it? I'm sure it'll want to listen."

"I will. At least it won't try to undress me with its eyes."

"Please yourself, you have half an hour before we eat, don't be late."

Feeling spurned and rejected she turned her back on Lucifer and walked off to a group of three men talking at the bar, holding her out her glass to them to get her another drink. Lucifer glanced a drunken sneer at the people in the bar as he pushed past them and made his way to the exit, stopping only to pick up a bottle of wine from one of the tables.

Outside, the cool evening breeze made its way across his face, making his drunken head feel dizzier. Clumsily, he made his way down the steps into the garden. Men were whispering in their wives' ears and pointing at him as he walked past.

"Good evening." He raised his glass to them, causing their faces to light up with pride because their special guest had acknowledged them. *Fools*, he thought.

Beyond the floodlit area, he walked into the darkness. He stopped in the middle of the garden and lifted his head skywards once again to look at the moon. His memories, fuelled by the effects of the alcohol, rushed through his mind: memories of the great battle, his red army against Michael's blue angelic opposition. When swords came together in a timeless battle of wills. Although he hated Michael, he paradoxically missed him. In angelic form, when fighting Michael, Lucifer felt he belonged and had a purpose. But now he did not have the ability to fight for anything. His powers were gone and his will was being slowly taken away from him. In an instant, he regained control of his thoughts. *No, you might have taken my powers, my wings and sword, but I won't let you take my will away. I still defy you, the Most High, and by this dim light of the moon, I swear that I will be seeing you again with Michael at my feet.* He held his glass aloft to salute the moon and affirm his vow.

Sitting on the bench at the end of the garden, Mary's mind went back to John's words, "You have to look for the light". She watched a small light moving from side to side in the moonlight. Was this the sign was John talking about? A tingle went down her spine and filled her whole being as she stood and made her way to the light, ever aware that the strange feeling she had experienced in the corridor earlier was returning. As she got closer, the same feelings were now rising in Lucifer, but this time slightly dulled by alcohol. Mary's heart was racing as she realised that the connection she was feeling was now associated was with this stranger in front of her. Could this be Luther? Her whole body was aching with anticipation as she approached the dark silhouette standing with his back to her and the moonlight reflecting off the wine glass. Finding the courage to open her mouth, she put on her finest voice.

"Hello, is that you Luther? It's me Mary, Ruth's sister."

Lucifer stood for a while, still looking at the moon and not saying a word.

"Beautiful, isn't it?" Mary tried again. "I always wonder at its spellbinding nature, quite magical."

Lucifer finally slurred, "Magical yes because I am of a magical nature and recognise its true nature, but beautiful I am not."

He turned around to see Mary standing in front of him looking coy. Her face and arms were pale in the moonlight. In the dim light he could make out her soft round face and perfectly formed lips harnessing a beautiful smile while her long dark hair gently moved from side to side in the gentle breeze. As their eyes finally met, the feeling inside Lucifer started to intensify.

"I need another drink," he grunted.

Mary's smile dropped in disbelief as Lucifer turned his back on her and began walking back to the building and the bar.

"Charming I must say. Don't they have manners where you come from? Aren't you going to introduce yourself?" she shouted, but Lucifer didn't even offer the faintest hint of a response.

"So much for John's vision of a light," she muttered to herself. "More like a torch whose battery died a long time ago."

At the entrance of the door, a man was calling everybody to order and requesting that they made their way to the dining room where dinner was to be served. Lucifer had already walked past the announcer and made his way back to the bar.

"Thank you," Mary said to the man holding the dining-room door open. She briefly waited before entering in hope that Lucifer would follow her, but he didn't appear.

Lucifer barged his way to the bar.

"Get me another whisky," he said.

The barman looked annoyed at Lucifer's rudeness and abruptly placed the glass on the bar. Before his back was turned Lucifer had emptied it.

"Another one. In fact, keep them coming."

Inside the dining room, an embarrassed David was looking around at disapproving faces. Jeremiah gave a slight nod of his head in the direction of the door. David rushed out the door in search of Luther. He found him in the bar.

"What are you playing at? Everybody in there is waiting for you."

Panic set in as David realised that Lucifer was now very drunk.

"This alcohol is a marvellous invention," Lucifer slurred. "It helps you to forget things and helps eliminate any feelings inside. Tell me if you drink more and more, will it help you to forget altogether?"

"It's only a temporary thing and you're going to feel like hell in the morning," David snapped. "Now please Luther, I implore you, can we now go and dine?"

"Okay, okay, I'm coming, lead the way."

Lucifer got up from his stool and steadied himself. David nervously opened the door to the dining room and beckoned Lucifer. The light from the chandeliers and the wall-mounted lights blinded Lucifer for a moment. All around him everybody was applauding as he and David made their way to their seats. Occasionally David had to support Lucifer with his hand on his back so he could get to the table safely. They finally reached their seats, much to David's relief. The clapping ceased as a wooden gavel sounded on one of the tables.

"Brethren," Daniel said, "let us pray."

Lucifer let out a small giggle like a naughty schoolboy.

"To the light which is from above, we would like to give thanks for everything we have received and the blessings bestowed upon us. Amen."

Everyone sat down. Lucifer looked at the table in front of him, which was round and covered with a white cloth. There were wine glasses in front of every seat, alternately adorned with blue and red serviettes neatly folded inside. A red candle was alight in the centre of the table, the flame dancing side to side.

"Luther, this is Mary," David said.

"It's all right, David," Mary said, "We've already had the displeasure of an introduction."

Mary was angry at how she had been treated, but also confused because of the strange feeling that intensified whenever Lucifer was around. It was like she hated and loved him at the same time. *How she could love him when she had only just met him? Pull yourself together Mary*, she told herself as they all sat and began to eat their vegetable soup.

"Luther," David said, "this is Stephen and his wife Joan. He's one of our longest serving members. And this is Ian and his fiancée Lisa. Ian is our youngest brother."

They all said hello, and Lucifer lazily waved his hand to acknowledge them and then downed another whisky.

"So Luther what did you think of the meeting?" Steven asked awkwardly. "You must feel very honoured and privileged to be allowed such an insight this evening."

Lucifer looked up at to Steven and rested his chin against his hand with his elbows on the table. "Honoured, I would not know of such a sentiment. As for me being privileged, that's a laugh. You should all feel privileged to be in my presence."

"What makes you so special?" Mary interrupted his speech. "You're rude and arrogant and certainly not honourable."

"Who do you think you're talking to little lady?" Lucifer growled.

"And who the hell do you think you are?" Mary snapped angrily.

"I am Luci –" Again he wanted to reveal his real name, but the words would not come out. "Forget it, I can't be bothered."

"You see David, they.re arguing like a married couple already." Ruth remarked across the table.

Ignoring Ruth's comment, David asked Stephen if he thought their new master of the east was capable of doing a good job. It was evident that David was trying to defuse the growing tension on the table.

"Yes David, I think he'll make an excellent master, a true brother and a shining example of what a leader should be."

Their conversation was interrupted by another sounding of the gavel. David was relieved that the toasts were about to begin. That would give enough time for him to think about how he was going to survive the night without too much embarrassment.

"Brethren and ladies," the new master was on his feet and making his first speech. "The first toast of the evening is to the light from above."

Everybody stood, except Lucifer who remained defiant and stayed firmly seated. After they had all repeated "to the light above", they took a sip of their wine and sat down.

Lucifer looked at Mary's angry face. She was unaware of being watched as she began to eat her soup. His eyes began to make their way down to her low-cut red velvet dress and her cleavage. He closed his eyes and inhaled Mary's scent. The mixture of Mary's flesh and her perfume was intoxicating to Lucifer's mind, causing a stirring deep within. He felt almost animal. This wanting was something he had never experienced before. *How can I stand feeling like this? I hate humans.*

"Do you mind?"

Lucifer opened his eyes to see Mary leaning back in her chair. She'd noticed where Lucifer's eyes were staring and was now pink with embarrassment.

"Luther," David said. "Our newly-made master in the east is insisting that you should make a speech later this evening."

"A speech?" they both looked towards the head table where the master was holding his wine glass aloft in Lucifer's' direction. "What about? I've never made a speech before."

"You just have to try and act as sober as possible," David was speaking in a quiet panicky manner, "Say a few lines thanking the brethren, and me of course, for inviting you here tonight. Just show gratitude for the charity we've bestowed on you tonight."

"David," Mary said, "are you sure that's such a wise idea given Luther's incoherent state? Not to mention his bad manners."

Lucifer turned to Mary and scowled. Immediately,

feeling Lucifer's icy stare, Mary became quiet as a mouse and lowered her head in submission.

"No," Lucifer said. "David, I would be delighted to make a speech. I see how much it means to Mary and I certainly wouldn't like to let the brethren down."

Lucifer smiled with pleasure at knowing how much he was intimidating Mary. Looking across the table, Ruth noticed her sister and how uncomfortable she was.

"Come on Mary, let's go and powder our noses."

Mary didn't need to be asked twice. She was soon up and out of her chair and heading towards the dining room door.

"So Luther, where do you come from?" Ian was the first to break the uneasy silence now surrounding the table.

"From hell and other various places," Lucifer muttered.

"What Luther is trying to say is that he's had a bad life, isn't that right Luther?"

David was trying his best to keep the conversation going as much as possible,

"I can speak for myself. Do you know something? I'm sorry, what was your name again?"

"Ian," he answered, slightly offended that his name had been forgotten so easily.

"Ian," Lucifer continued, "imagine you had something in your life that was so powerful, a power which commanded men, nations, even angels. Now imagine all that power being removed from you against your will, how would you feel?"

"Well, if I had all that power and it was suddenly taken away from me, I would ask myself and the light from above why? I would then think long and hard about whether maybe I'd deserved it and consider what I'd done to upset and offend the Most High."

"You see, this is where God's logic makes no sense and proves the stupidity of the Most High. If God is so benevolent, why would he make mankind, who he loves so much, suffer?"

"That, I can't answer Luther. Some things are left for the infinite wisdom of the Most High. It is not for me or you to question. All I know is that great power is nothing without control. It demands the highest degree of respect and comes with great responsibility. Without these, I would deserve to lose my powers by my own undoing."

"Well said, Ian," Stephen remarked. "I see your degree in philosophy holds you in good stead. I love a good debate amongst friends."

"Thank you Stephen," David said. "Has that helped you with your question Luther?"

"Not really, I want to change the subject anyway. Talking about God bores me and gives me a great headache."

"Excuse me, sir," a waitress said as she collected the soup bowls from the table.

"What's keeping the ladies?"

Again, David was concerning himself with the whereabouts of other people.

"They'd better get back soon, the main course is about to be served."

In the ladies, Mary and Ruth were talking in front of the mirror. "Arrgh!" Mary said. "That man is so rude and arrogant. Who does he think he is?" Mary banged her hands down on the ceramic sink in front of the mirror.

"Calm down Mary, I've never seen you like this before. Your face looks like thunder, like you're ready to explode."

"Well, I was so looking forward to this evening and meeting him. Poor John was telling me about his dreams, all that nonsense about God wanting me to go and look for the light. Ruth, how could I have been so stupid to believe in such fairy tales? Although when I saw Luther's glass in the moonlight moving side to side my heart did skip a beat and for once my head wanted to believe and –"

"Stop!" Ruth exclaimed, interrupting her sister's ramblings. "Look Mary, we don't know anything about this stranger, where he comes from, how he was brought up. For all we know, he could be a wanted murderer or something. I don't know why you're concerning yourself anyway, after tomorrow he'll be out of our lives for good."

"What do you mean?"

"Well," Ruth paused as she leant forward towards the mirror to reapply a coat of lipstick. "I'll ask David to politely get rid of our unwanted guest in the morning – he makes me feel uncomfortable."

"Is that really necessary? You said he had nowhere to go, what will he do?"

"Mary, Mary, Mary," Ruth sighed impatiently, "there seems to be a hint of disappointment in your voice. You sweet thing, always trying to see the good in people or always trying to save someone."

"I know it sounds strange, but for all his rudeness and arrogance I still feel there's a connection between us. Something I don't understand, and yet paradoxically I do. Is this making any sense to you?"

"No, not really. How much have you had to drink anyway?"

"Only a couple of glasses of wine, you know I don't drink much. Anyway, when you met David, did you feel like you had known him forever and your whole body felt alive whenever you were around him? Do you believe in love at first sight?"

"Don't be ridiculous," Ruth replied curtly. "David and I had a friendship to start with and out of that friendship our love grew. There was never that 'wow' between us. Anyway, enough of this stupid talk. We'd better get back before our main course goes cold. Let's just get through tonight, then tomorrow Luther will be out of our lives for good."

Back in the dining room, Lucifer was struggling with his dinner. "How's your beef, Luther?" David asked.

Lucifer was still getting to grips with using a knife and fork. Splashes of gravy were soaking into the white tablecloth.

"It's delicious, don't you think?" Stephen was trying to make polite conversation.

"It's okay," Lucifer said. His mouth was full of food as he spoke and halfway through his sentence some beef left his mouth and fell onto the plate. David despairingly put his head in his hands.

"Hello there, gentlemen," David turned at the sound of Ruth's voice to see the ladies walking back into the dining room. All the men except Lucifer politely stood while the ladies retook their seats.

"Have we missed much?"

"Nothing much, the speeches will start after the main course, so eat up and don't let it go cold."

"Always the organiser, aren't you darling?"

Ruth placed a kiss on David's cheek while looking at Lucifer. He was too busy finishing off the remains of the food on his plate to notice.

"So Luther," Mary had decided to start afresh. "What are your plans for the future?"

"Apart from regaining my angel status and defeating Michael the henchmen of the Most High nothing much really."

Mary let out a little giggle. "No, seriously, what do you plan to do and where are you heading?"

"Why don't you believe me?" Luther asked. In a condescending manner "Just imagine for an instant that right now you sat next to an angel who had done immeasurable cruelty to people. An angel that wanted the death and destruction of everything living on this godforsaken earth. Also imagine that this angel did not know or want to know love and did everything in his power to destroy it. Mary, ask yourself would you still want to be in such a presence?"

"What a strange question, are you all right?" Lucifer nodded and begged for her to answer the question.

"Well I detest all forms of violence, but I would try and understand why this angel is behaving the way he is. I think that someone who is trying to destroy love just doesn't understand it. So therefore I would ask God to help this lost angel find love again because I believe that nobody is beyond redemption."

"What if this angel didn't want to be redeemed and was happy being who he was?"

"That I don't know and I can't answer. All I can say is that in the end, love conquers all. Those who are either frightened or hide in the shadows, too scared to show love, will eventually have to face up to that truth. Only then can they accept it into their lives."

As Lucifer was listening to Mary, he felt pain in his heart and his eyes began to water.

"Rubbish!"

He took another large mouthful of whisky hoping it would suppress the pain he was feeling.

"An idyllic dream for those who are afraid to see the world as it really is. People like you would rather see the world through rose-coloured glasses than go out and feel the pain of reality."

"Well there you go, that's one thing we have one thing in common," Mary retorted.

Lucifer lifted his eyebrows.

"I haven't been with a man, because I'm afraid of being in love," she continued. "To me love is so important that I would rather not know it than have it and lose it. You see, we are both afraid of love."

"I am not afraid of anything and I never will be."

"Luther, is there really no love in your heart at all?"

"No! Certainly not, now can we please change the subject?"

"Why?"

"Because –"

A gavel sounded from the top table, bringing everyone to order and interrupting Lucifer.

"Brethren and ladies," Jeremiah was on his feet. "I

would like to claim your attention as I ask our special guest this evening to make a long awaited speech. I give you Luther."

Everyone started clapping and banging their hands on the table.

"Up you get Luther," David said, nervously pushing Lucifer out of his chair, who glared at David. The applause ceased as Lucifer stood and everybody waited in silence for him to begin. Standing in silence, he looked around the room. Trying to think what to say, he found it hard to concentrate as Mary's words filled his head. He couldn't understand how they made sense, how could they? How could a human know more than him?

"Luther," David spoke just above a whisper to draw his attention.

David's voice allowed Lucifer to focus on his immediate situation. He felt a warm sensation as a hand took hold of his. He looked down to see Mary's hand entwined with his own. For the first time in his existence, if only for a split second, he allowed a moment of intimacy. As soon as it had started it was gone.

"No! What are you doing to me?" Lucifer said and he pulled his hand away. He looked down at Mary's surprised face.

"Luther, this is highly embarrassing," David said. "Will you please stop it?"

Lucifer was now feeling very uncomfortable at the unwanted attention being directed towards him.

"I have to get out of here," he said and pushed his chair to one side. He crashed against the table as he struggled to navigate between the chairs and the other seated people.

"Luther! Come back, I am so sorry Jeremiah," David apologised profusely. Lucifer stopped just next to the head table and looked back at Jeremiah. Instead of Jeremiah looking angry, he just smiled and nodded like he understood.

"No! I don't want understanding, get me out of here," Lucifer said as he stumbled, making his way towards the door. David again apologised to the top table and ordered Ruth and Mary to leave with him.

"Luther! Wait, come back, I want a word with you."

David had quickened his pace to catch up with Lucifer, leaving the two women walking slowly behind. Ruth was laughing at the situation, how her husband had been humiliated in front of all his important brethren. Mary's face told a different story: she had just made a connection that went beyond the realms of this world and she wanted to explore it more.

Chapter Ten

THE SUN WAS RISING across the eastern horizon. Its golden glow started to emerge from behind a landscape of golden sand. A flock of birds flew across the sky, casting their shadows below while an authoritative looking man sat on a balcony, reclining in his chair, watching the sun as it slowly ascended into a clear blue sky. A glass of whisky rested in his hand that he occasionally brought to his lips for a sip. His big black moustache dipped into the drink, giving him a chance to lick it as the glass left his lips. His face was dark from years in the sun, and his eyes were as black and domineering as the night sky. In an ashtray next to him a cigar slowly smouldered, releasing its smoke into the atmosphere. Closing his eyes, he took in a deep breath to smell the beauty of a new morning and give praise to God for another day in power. The latest government polls showed that his popularity was growing and he was getting even closer to ultimate power. Opening his eyes again, he lifted the glass towards the sky and proposed a toast to God and their continued relationship.

After consuming the last of the whisky, he rose from his chair and made his way into the bed chambers, his silk dressing gown swaying in the warm morning breeze as he swiftly walked towards a headless mannequin standing in the corner of the room, adorned with a neatly ironed military blazer. On its chest were pinned medals for bravery and years of service and its lapels were covered in stars denoting the rank of general. He slowly and cautiously scanned every inch of his prized piece of uniform. Satisfying himself it was perfect, he released it from his cold icy stare and made his way to the bedroom sideboard where he rested the glass. He picked up the candles from its surface and made his way to the centre of the floor where a large rug lay. He placed the candles on the floor next to the rug and in one swift movement, he gripped the rug, removed it from the floor and placed it on his bed.

On the wooden floor, hidden under the rug, was a drawing in black. It depicted a five-pointed star surrounded by a perfect circle around its circumference. In three points of the star were the letters N, E and W, denoting north, east and west. At the top point of the star pointing east was a picture of the sun; at the bottom, the moon. The general picked up the candles and placed one on top of the sun and the other on top of the moon. He reached for a match.

"As the sun gives light today, I give light to you in the east."

He lit the candle on the picture of the sun.

"Never fear moon of the west, I remember you when it is night, and therefore I will only light you when it is so."

When he was sure everything was correct, he removed his dressing gown and threw it on the bed. He was now totally naked and the sun shone brightly on his body.

"I came into this world unclothed almighty God from above. I now kneel and present myself in the same way."

He stepped into the circle and knelt at the exact centre of the entwining star, then looking to the sun, he closed his eyes.

"Father of the day sky in your presence and in the absence of mother of the night sky I give you praise."

He bowed forward till his head and hands touched the floor.

"I bow to you in obedience and give thanks for your

blessings and the power you have bestowed upon me. Father, I have been patient, but how long do I have to wait? I am tired of seeing the greed of man and the effect it has on this beautiful planet, the home you created for us. I am sick and tired of the different religious factions struggling for supremacy. Day by day, sickness and disease get worse. Man is becoming a mental and physical plague on your creation."

A tear rolled down his cheek and he found it hard to speak.

"Most High, make me your redeemer and punisher on earth; I will not fail you. Make me the lightning that strikes down the unfaithful. Make me the weapon that puts fear into the hearts of the arrogant and false. Make me the light to show the way for the obedient and act as comfort to the sick."

The flame on the candle swayed briskly side to side, dancing his reflection on the wall.

"I know I am the one for your great work. I implore you, Most High, make me your power on earth to demonstrate your will, the will that must be done. Give me a sign I am still in good faith with you. All this I ask for in the light of day from the east and in absence of darkness in the west."

He closed his eyes and bowed again. There was a brief silence which was broken by a loud knock on his bedroom door followed by a muffled voice.

"General Silas, I have important intelligence to relay to you."

The general didn't reply; he wanted to finish his prayers. Again a loud knock sounded.

"How dare you disturb my prayers Captain!"

"Forgive me General, but this matter requires your urgent attention."

"Very well, give me five minutes," he replied unwillingly.

He blew out the candles, removed them from the floor and replaced them in their position on the sideboard.

Picking up his dressing gown, he quietly laid the rug back on the floor, making sure that none of the picture was visible. He tied the belt of his dressing gown and turned to open the door.

"This had better be good, Captain. I am most displeased at being disturbed during my prayers."

"My most humble apologies, General, but I have excellent news which I feel warranted such an intrusion."

"Very well, speak it out."

"Governor Rasheed has suffered a suspected heart attack and is presently in a critical condition in hospital."

"What! When did this happen?"

"About an hour ago. He had just finished his breakfast when he fainted in front of his wife. It's all over the news. They are saying that with your main rival out of action, nothing can stop you from a victory. You will have total control and power over our beloved country. With the military behind you, you will be a very powerful leader indeed."

"This is great news, thank you Captain."

"Please will you arrange a big bouquet of flowers to be sent to Rasheed's wife for me expressing my deepest sympathy?"

The captain looked a little concerned as the general let out a sinister laugh.

"What! Do you have a problem with that Captain?"

The captain knew very well that when he got that cold icy stare, it was time to appease his leader. "No General, not at all, right away. May I inform you that a news conference and a speech is being organised. The press of the world is gathering in the great hallway where they will wait for you to address the nation."

"Certainly, Captain. I'll be there in about half an hour."

"Excellent, General. May I be excused?"

"Of course. Captain, you do know your loyalty and hard work has not gone unnoticed. When this is all over, you can expect promotion and take control over our army as my second in command."

The captain's eyes lit up at the thought of being promoted.

"Thank you General, you are too kind, please excuse me, I must go."

With a click of his heels and a salute, the captain ran down the corridor towards the great hall. As he closed the door, a wry smile made its way across the General's face. He was amazed at how quickly his prayers had been answered. With Rasheed indisposed, he would surely have victory and absolute power. Nothing could stop him fulfilling God's work on earth.

Back at the house, David was sitting slumped in his favourite chair, his untied bowtie hanging around his neck.

"Well, that went extremely well, didn't it?" Ruth said as she entered the room still dressed in her evening gown.

"No Ruth, it didn't," David snapped. "Luther totally ruined what I thought was going to be a very special evening. Instead my credibility with the brotherhood is now at an all-time low. What on earth happened anyway? Why did he flip and storm out?"

"I don't know. Maybe he'd drunk too much and the attention he got overwhelmed him. We still don't know a lot about him, do we?"

"That still doesn't excuse his totally irresponsible behaviour. Where is he anyway?"

"I've just left him sleeping it off on top of his bed."

"His bed!" David exclaimed with anguish. "Tomorrow he's gone. I don't care if he's a sign or not. I want him out of my house in the morning."

"Your house? I thought it was our house. Don't I get a say in the matter?"

"No my decision is final. When I return from work tomorrow night, I expect him to be gone. Is that clear?"

"Very clear, dear! Anyway, I'm going to bed, are you coming?"

"No, I doubt I'll be able to sleep for a while. I'll just watch television and think about the apology I can make to the brethren for tonight's fiasco."

"Well you can sit there and worry if you like. I'm off to bed,"

"Switch the television on, love, before you go."

Ruth bent down in front of the television and extended her bottom towards David moving slowly side to side. Then with a sexy look she turned towards David.

"Are you sure you don't want to go to bed?"

"I'm quite sure. Can you pass the control on the way out?"

Ruth picked up the remote and threw it at him.

"I wish the remote control could turn you on as well, dear."

She flounced out of the room. David flicked thorough the channels. He glimpsed an array of late night movies and the odd chat show. He switched on the news channel and his eyes widened as he read the headline being flashed across the bottom of the screen: "Breaking news: a country is in mourning as Governor Rasheed is pronounced dead after a fatal heart attack."

David listened as the newsreader reiterated the news in full.

"Yes we can confirm that Governor Rasheed is dead."

The picture on the television screen switched to people lying on the ground and crying in mourning outside Governor Rasheed's house.

"Many of his loyal followers are in shock and distraught. General Silas will now surely gain full control. We will shortly hear from General Silas who is going to address the nation about his country's future. After his speech, we will be speaking to some of the supporters of both General Silas and the late Governor Rasheed to find out what this means to them, and more importantly what this means for world peace."

"I have to stop you there, Ed," the main news presenter interrupted, "we can now go to General Silas' speech."

David watched, absorbed, as General Silas began to address the gathering.

"People of my beloved country and fellow people from around the world."

General Silas was standing on a wooden pedestal, cameras flashes lighting up the room as he began to speak. His faithful captain was standing on his right with a look of excitement mixed with trepidation on his face as he scanned the room for any signs of an assassination attempt. From all the security being displayed on the screen in the General's presence. It was evident that the Captain was still worried. "I speak to you on a day of great contrast. For today, we are a nation deep in grief at the loss of a great friend and leader. But we should now be united in happiness of having a new leader. Myself. I think you all know that although we were rivals in politics and ideas, we remained friends throughout our years in the leadership battle. I sincerely send my deepest sympathy to Mrs Rasheed and all her family members in their time of grief."

He bowed his head and placed his right hand on his chest for a moment of silence. Once it was over, he raised his head and continued.

"I believe that from death comes life. Although General Rasheed's death is saddening and untimely, it marks the end of his legacy and the beginning of a new era for this country and my people. For too long now, we have watched our beloved country torn apart by liberal reformists and dictatorships from outside controlling how we should live. I say to you my people, who are they in the West to tell us what to do when they are breaking all of God's commandments every day? I ask you, does a pig tell a cat how to wash? My people, a new era is on the horizon, a time when we can look to the east and the morning sun and be proud of who we are. We can take back our power as our own. We can once again be a nation at one with ourselves and the Most High in the heavens. We can be an example to the rest of the world."

He paused to look around the room and took a sip of water.

"I stand before you as your new leader and the only suitable person to lead you into this new era. Therefore I am placing our beloved country under my rule."

David could hear a few gasps in the room at General Silas proclaiming himself leader without any democratic process. He knew he didn't have any opposition and he had the mighty fist of the military backing him.

"I am implementing a five point rule which starts with effect from today. I will briefly explain this five point rule to our countrymen. The first rule of our new state is to honour and love the one and only God and obey the commandments. Anybody found to be following any other gods or idols will be judged and punished accordingly. The second rule is that my word is final," at this, a few worried looks were exchanged amongst the reporters. "I will endeavour to bring this country forward to prosper and in doing so I will eradicate sickness, both mentally and physically, and relieve poverty. All these things I will do to try and establish a strong country once again. Under the second rule you will acknowledge me as your leader in good faith and you will pledge to strictly obey my every judgment. The third rule is a rule of independence. By the end of the month there will be no further contact with or interference from the West." This was met with cheers and applause from Silas' fellow countrymen.

"All laws previously imposed by the West will be abolished and new laws of our own will be established. We will no longer bow and succumb to Western pressure and dictatorship. Under the fourth point of law we will become a pure nation again. For too long now we have had impure blood running through our veins. I have decided that all foreigners in our country are to be expelled. This includes those people married to the native people of our nation and the children they have borne. This will enable us to once again reunite that strong pure blood link, making a healthier and more stable society. Once the four points of order are established I will impose the fifth point. This point will be for you as a nation to swear allegiance to me to protect and uphold the whole of its several parts, even to war and the glorious prize of all death in battle. Anyone who does not swear allegiance will be expelled from our beloved country. My people and the people of the world, I want you to know that what I am doing now or what I might do in the future is for the benefit of my people and to the glory of God. Believe me, I will do *anything* to protect this new ideal even to death itself. Thank you."

The General finished his speech and the Captain put his hand over the microphone in front of the General and whispered in his ear. The General gave a nod and then the Captain stepped forward to the microphone.

"The General is available to answer a few brief questions."

A flurry of hands shot up in the air and the General scanned the room with his dark eyes.

"Yes, you in the blue shirt."

"Susan Bridges, Channel 6. General, can you tell the rest of the world why you think you are in a position to take power and impose this five point rule?"

"I have not taken power, but circumstances have put me in a position of power. If I am doing God's work, how can it be wrong in the eyes of man? Yes, you next, your question?"

"Tom Knight, Channel 8. General Silas, before we are all expelled from your country, can you reassure a concerned world about your nuclear capability? We know you have an extensive arsenal, we need to know that they won't be used."

"I can simply say this. We as a nation in the East have nuclear capability as protection as you do in the West. I can safely say that they will not be used unless you in the West attack our beloved country. So it is up to your governments to concern themselves with governing your own countries and stay out of ours. One more question."

The general looked around the room and his eyes made contact with a man sitting calmly in a front row. "You sir, do you not have a question for me?"

The man looked up with his crystal blue eyes and smiled.

"My name is Michael. How much do you love your God and would you really do whatever was commanded of you?"

It took a while for the general to speak. He was spellbound by the blue-eyed angelic-faced man in front of him.

"General, General, are you okay?"

The Captain had stepped forward and whispered in his ear to prompt a reaction. Ignoring him, the General answered Michael.

"Without question, I would obey God even to death itself if that was what God wanted."

"Good, I think you most probably will. Thank you, and God bless you."

"General, General Silas!"

All the press were standing and shouting to gain the general's attention for one final question. Amongst this confusion, the general tried to find the blue-eyed man who had disappeared amongst a deluge of reporters, but he was nowhere to be found.

"No more questions! The General will retire now for an emergency meeting."

The Captain, accompanied by two guardsmen, escorted the General out of the room and into the corridor.

"I was worried about you there sir, did you lose concentration? Or did something happen?"

"What do you mean? I answered all the questions, didn't I; do I look like I am out of control?"

"Yes, you answered all the questions, but why did you stare at nothing with a confused look on your face after the second question? You said you would obey even to death itself if that's what God wanted."

"Don't be absurd Captain, I was answering the question from the reporter in the front row, you know, the one with the electrifying blue eyes."

"General," the captain said sheepishly, "there was no one there".

"Captain!" the general snapped angrily. "Are you questioning my sanity?"

"Forgive me General, I must have missed that question, a momentary lack of concentration due to the importance of such an occasion."

As they walked off down the corridor, the Captain looked at the two escorting guardsmen following close behind. They were both looking at each other in confusion. A subtle cough brought their attention back to guarding their new leader.

Back at home, David was sitting on the edge of his favourite chair, watching the news in disbelief. The reporters were now speaking to followers of General Silas. Some were dancing and shouting praise to God above, while others were on the floor in humble prayer. *How can one man have so much power*? he thought, *All that power in the wrong hands, with ethnic cleansing, independence, total rule and a total disregard for life. God help us.*

His thoughts were interrupted by the phone ringing in the hallway. He quickly switched off the television and rushed to the phone.

"Hello David, it's Daniel."

"Daniel, I am so sorry about what happened tonight. I feel –"

"Never mind that," Daniel interrupted. "Do you have your television on?"

"No, I've just switched it off."

"Did you see the news about General Silas?"

"Yes, isn't it terrible? I think we have troubled times ahead of us."

"Yes, that's why I'm ringing you. I've just spoken to

Jeremiah and it seems that our prophecy is closer than we originally thought. Is Luther still with you?"

"Yes, unfortunately. Ruth left him upstairs sleeping it off."

"Good, it is imperative we keep our eye on him and watch how things unfold in the coming weeks. You must keep him at your house and extend every charity possible to make him feel welcome."

"Of course, Daniel," David replied with a complete lack of enthusiasm.

"Are you okay with this, David? If not we can arrange for Luther to stay with another brother."

"No, no, it's fine. He can stay here with us for as long as it takes."

"Good, that's settled. There is also an emergency meeting tomorrow afternoon about one in the afternoon. You will be expected of course. Thank you again, David, and remember it is of the upmost importance we do not lose Luther. We are relying on you."

"Thank you, Daniel for your and the other brothers' confidence in me. I won't let you down. Have a good evening, good night."

"Good night, David. I'll speak to you tomorrow."

David placed the receiver down filled with a newfound confidence. He switched off all the lights, locked the front door and made his way upstairs. Walking along the landing, he stopped outside the bedroom where Lucifer was sleeping. He gently pushed open the door just to make sure he was still there, because he knew that he was important, but how important, only time would tell.

Chapter Eleven

A small bird was offering its song to the morning sun as it sat on the branch just outside Lucifer's bedroom window. It wasn't long before a chorus of other birds joined in, causing Lucifer to stir from his slumber. He opened one eye. His room was still dark apart from a streak of light shining through the partly opened curtains. He tried to remember where he was and then at once all of the previous evening's events flashed back into his memory: the brotherhood, the meeting, getting drunk and Mary. He quickly sat bolt upright from his bed at the memory of Mary. Who was this woman and why had she made him feel so uncomfortable and sick to the stomach?

"Arrrrgh! My head," he shouted as he put his head in his hands.

"Are you all right?"

His door swung open and Ruth stood in the doorway.

"I heard you shout."

Lucifer shielded his eyes from the light of the corridor.

"It's my head it won't stop hurting and my stomach feels strange, as though it wants to jump into my throat."

"Your first hangover, is it Luther? That's what happens when you have too much to drink. Basically, you've poisoned your body."

"Poisoned, what? Will I die?"

Ruth laughed.

"No, silly. It might feel like you're going to, but the feeling soon goes after a good hearty breakfast and some painkillers."

"Damn, why is my mouth starting to moisten? My stomach feeling is getting stronger."

"I think you had better get into the bathroom quick. It sounds as if you're going to be sick."

Lucifer pushed by her into the bathroom, put his head in the sink and vomited. Ruth smiled as she spoke through the bathroom door.

"When you've finished ruining my bathroom, there's breakfast and some painkillers waiting for you downstairs."

Looking at the bottom of the sink, Lucifer asked himself how he could have let myself get into such a situation. *Here I am, a mighty powerful angel, reduced to being sick in some human's bathroom.*

All these things were a stark reminder of his predicament. He was still imprisoned in human flesh and, for the time being, there was nothing he could do about it. That thought made him sick again. After drinking some water from the bathroom tap, he splashed cold water over his face and through his hair. Looking in the mirror, he decided that although he was in disgusting flesh, he still wanted to look good. Taking one last look, he turned off the light and made his way downstairs to the smell of a freshly cooked breakfast.

"There you are, do you feel better now?"

Ruth was at the fridge with a carton of orange juice in her hand.

"Alcohol is definitely not something I will be partaking in again," Luther muttered.

Ruth allowed herself another smile when looking at his pale face.

"What's so funny?"

"Nothing, it's just that you make me think of a small child who is trying things for the very first time."

Lucifer glared at her with an angry look that could have melted the whole Arctic Circle.

"I'm sorry," she said nervously. "Breakfast won't be long. Please sit down and afterwards I'll find you a change of clothes. Help yourself to some orange juice, tea or coffee."

"Coffee, with lots of sugar."

"I spoke with David this morning and we're both very happy for you to stay as long as you like. I think David has something very important to tell you. He wouldn't elaborate on what it was about, but insisted you stay to hear what he has to say."

"I don't know how long I'll be around. I have something myself to do, something that's of the utmost importance." Lucifer was now thinking that it might be time to move on, but wasn't sure to where,

"What's that? Excuse me." Ruth placed a plate of scrambled egg in front of him.

"Nothing really, just to return to my former glory and take over mankind."

Ruth lifted an eyebrow. "No really, do you have anywhere to go or anybody to see?"

Lucifer pondered on her question as he tucked into his scrambled egg. He realised he didn't. If he left, he would be wandering around aimlessly.

"Well, like I said, you're most welcome here for as long as you wish. Sit there and finish your breakfast. I'm just going upstairs to find you some more of David's clothes, I won't be long."

Lucifer watched as she left the kitchen, then added more sugar to his coffee.

After finishing breakfast, he thought he would go somewhere quiet to concentrate on his power and seek guidance about what to do next. It wasn't long before Ruth returned.

"I have laid some clothes on your bed and a towel to dry yourself after a shower. I'm going out in a while. Mary's picking me up to visit our brother John. I fear he's not going to be on the earth for much longer. His cancer is doing its worst and he's in so much pain, God bless him."

"God bless him! You talk about God blessing him and yet the Most High is the one who most probably caused him to have the illness, the one who is causing him so much pain. You humans really confuse me."

"Luther! I will extend the hand of friendship in my house, but the one thing I will not tolerate is blasphemy. It is not up to us to know God's plan, but if it's God's wish for John to die early then so be it. At least he will be closer to God than I am or ever could be alive."

She paused, allowing herself to calm down. Lucifer stared at her.

"Just make yourself at home. I'll be back about four o'clock to get tea ready. David will be home about six. The brotherhood has summoned him to an emergency meeting after work. Luther, promise me you'll hang around. David so much wants you to be here when he gets home."

"I won't promise anything because I don't know where I'm going or what I'm doing. But after a little quiet time to myself, I'll exactly know where I'm heading."

They both turned to the window as they heard a car's horn.

"That's Mary. I told her not to come into the house after last night. I hope you understand."

Lucifer was relieved as he was feeling sick enough from the drink last night and having Mary in closer proximity would have him running up to the bathroom again.

"Take care, Luther I hope to see you later."

Ruth's words faded into the distance as she ran the length of the hallway, grappling with her coat to put it over her shoulders. The door slammed shut and then there was silence apart from the sound of the clock on the kitchen wall. He heard the faint sound of Mary's car driving off in the distance, then he was finally alone.

In the car, Mary was intent on quizzing her sister.

"How is Luther this morning?" Mary fiddled with her car radio, trying to tune it at the same time as driving.

"He's okay apart from the hangover from hell."

"Serves him right, drinking that much and acting the way he did. It was strange but also sad to see. He was like a frightened little boy running from a fear of the unknown. When I tried to comfort him he totally flipped. Please, Ruth, tell me, did I do something wrong?"

"No, not at all, Mary. As I said to David last night, we don't know anything about him at all do we?"

"You're right, but I feel as though I've known him all my life. That's what's freaking me out."

"Enough talk about Luther. How is John? I really should come over and see him more often."

"Not too good. Every day his physical health deteriorates and he's getting thinner. The only thing that raises his spirits and brings a smile to his face is his visions. They're getting more frequent than ever now. Last night he was saying that God was telling him that he would soon be saved and I had to know a love that defies the boundaries of the earth. Only then would truth reveal itself."

"Poor John, they say when someone is close to the end they hallucinate and ramble on about meaningless things."

"Yes, at least it makes him smile and if it makes his passing easier, I'm quite happy to let him carry on talking about these visions in his make believe world."

Back at the house, Lucifer had finished his breakfast and poured himself another cup of coffee. He picked up the sugar bowl and made his way through to the living room and sat himself down. *I will just finish my coffee, then I will prepare myself to get in touch with my inner strength.*

Looking around the room he observed photographs of David and Ruth lovingly wrapped in each other's arms.

Love, what a stupid sentiment and yet nearly all humans spend their life looking for it. When they find it they are frightened to lose it, and if they do lose it when one of the partners takes it away, it destroys the other person. Yet they still keep on looking for it. Stupid humans.

He finished the last of the coffee then stood up and closed the curtains. He was once again in the darkness alone with only his thoughts to keep him company.

"Right," he said aloud. "Come on Lucifer, let's feel the power of my light, let its glowing red remind me of where I hail from and why I am Lucifer."

He closed his eyes, took in a deep breath and started to meditate. Immediately he was conscious of slowing his breathing. The air made its way in through his nose and out from his mouth. His breath became so light and slow it was as though he was not breathing at all. The sound of his beating heart pounded in his ears like a slow drum in the confines of a temple wall. Soon, earthly thoughts and memories of the previous evening had dissipated into darkness.

Lucifer was now free in his mind to bring forth his energy. He visualised the colour of his being forming in his mind; the more he thought about it the redder it became. His breathing was now starting to get heavy as his energy began to flow and meet its master. It was not long before he was in a trancelike state with a red aura surrounding him. The red glow moved back and forth over his body like waves surging and receding in time with his breathing. The whole room was alight with red flashes bouncing off the walls and reflecting in the mirrors. He started to speak quietly to himself. *I call upon the word given to me before time began, may it bring forth my power, hear me ancient word, the word which is only known to me and the Most High. Do my bidding, show me the way.*

The more he thought about the word, the stronger his energy became, and just before it reached its pinnacle, a picture started forming in his mind. It started off as a small speckled blue light, then it slowly began to grow in size until Lucifer recognised its form. It was Mary's smiling face. At once his energy started to fade. He started to fight off the image in his mind, but the more he tried to fight it off the more strength it gained. His red life force was now fading, it was giving way to a heavenly blue colour.

"No! I will not let this happen."

The sweat was pouring from his head and his breathing had become very heavy and erratic. He squeezed his eyes tightly together for another attempt to remove the image, but to no avail. It was hopeless; the red light had now totally vanished. He was now held captured in a bluc prism of light. With the image burning in his mind, he contemplated his predicament. The blue held him fast like a disease; he couldn't fight it because doing so it only added to its strength. He was certainly not going to accept it, because that would be denying who he really was.

"I curse you the Most High for filling my head with such things."

"Now that is showing a great disrespect," Mary's imagined face had now turned into Michael's and he was smiling, surrounded by a golden glow and looking down at Lucifer

What do you want?" Lucifer asked with contempt.

"All in good time, how do you feel in your present situation?"

"Sick to my stomach and your presence is just about killing me."

"You still don't see it, do you my brother?"

"See what? All I see is your face in front of me, the face I want to annihilate."

"Still wanting to destroy everything and everybody? Have you not learnt that fighting the impossible only leads to frustration and anguish for you."

"It doesn't, it only fuels my power and makes me stronger so I am unstoppable,"

"Strong, unstoppable? That is not how I am seeing you now. You can't even release yourself from the light around you."

"Why, you!" Lucifer lunged forward but was unable to remove himself from the chair, "Let me go now!"

"One day, you will learn that nobody is holding you against your will, you are just imprisoning yourself,"

"Rubbish, I will learn of a way to defy the Most High and defeat your army of angels. What do you want anyway?"

Lucifer felt defiance surge through him.

"Very well, as you still have not grasped the full extent of your punishment, you have to perform another task to please the Most High. It is up to you if you decide to go ahead with it, but remember if you decide not to do it, you will only prolong your pain and suffering."

"Still treating me like a puppet, I see. The Most High is quite twisted don't you think?" He looked at Michael hoping to find some crack in his fidelity.

"You should know me better than that, Lucifer. The Most High wants you to save Mary and Ruth's brother John. He's critically ill and is almost crossing the threshold between the two worlds. It is the wish of the Most High for him to live. He is of great importance and has a story to tell, a story the world needs to know."

"What! You expect me to help that Mary and save her brother. Have you gone mad? Have you not seen what effect that woman has on me?"

"Yes, we have been watching very closely and it is not for me to question the Most High's decision. God be with you Lucifer, I will pray for your salvation, my brother."

"Wait! Come back, how dare you go when I have not finished. I will not do it, do you hear me? I won't!"

Despite his demands, Michael had gone.

Mary held the door open for Ruth as they both entered the long corridor of Mary and John's house.

"Let me take your coat, Ruth," Mary said. "Go through

John's waiting to see you. He's been talking about it all morning. I'll be through shortly, I just have to go to the toilet."

Ruth entered the living room and heard the faint sound of classical music being played on the stereo. She was slightly ashamed to look at the corner of the room where John's bed was placed. Months had passed and she hadn't been to see him. He was lying on his side with his back to her, facing the wall. Mary had turned her living room into a makeshift bedroom because of its easier accessibility to the bathroom and toilet.

"Hello, John," Ruth said quietly, in the hope that he might be asleep so she wouldn't have to face her guilt.

"Ruth! My darling sister, how are you? I've been waiting all morning to see you."

John turned his frail body as quickly as he could.

"Please come over here and give your brother a loving hug. It's been a long time."

She dropped her handbag on a nearby chair and ran towards him where they affectionately embraced.

"I am so sorry John."

"Why are you sorry? Easy Ruth, you don't want to kill me off early do you?"

John was finding it hard to talk and breathe as Ruth held him tight. A tear rolled down Ruth's face as she released him and sat on his bed.

"Why are you crying? What has happened?"

Ruth looked into his sad eyes, sunk inside his gaunt skull. She put her hand on his bony face.

"I'm so sorry that I don't visit you more often John. It is just that it hurts me to see you like this, especially when I remember how fit and active you used to be. It tears my heart apart to see you like this. I'm so sorry."

"If you say sorry one more time, I'll have to give you a slap. Listen, I understand, but remember this disease is not only destroying my body, it's also destroying my mind. It would be very helpful if you visited me a little more, so you can help me remember how I used to be."

"Do you have any tissues?"

"Yes behind you on the table over there. Ruth, I understand, just visit me when you feel the time is right."

"I am so – "

Ruth stopped herself repeating her apologies, as John jokingly started to lift his hand.

"Now tell me about this Luther. Mary has been speaking non-stop about him since their night out together."

"It was certainly not together," Mary had returned and interrupted their conversation. "The way he conducted himself was appalling. I doubt we'll ever be together."

"But Mary, you've spoken of about nothing else since you've met him," John retorted.

"Really? Tell me more," Ruth asked John, adding to Mary's embarrassment.

"Stop it, you two. The only reason I've been talking about him is because I find him mysterious and confusing at the same time. It's like he doesn't belong here. He's like a lost child trying to find his way home. I felt strange because I felt connected to him and yet I didn't want to feel that way because of the way he behaved. He certainly was not a gentleman, someone who –"

"You see what I mean, Ruth?" John interrupted Mary with a wry expression on his face.

"John, you're incorrigible. I'm going to make a pot of tea. You two can talk about me as much as you like, but when I return all conversations about me and Luther will stop, okay?"

"Yes, Mum," John and Ruth said in unison.

"I give up," Mary shook her head and left the room. Both Ruth and John let out a little laughter like two naughty schoolchildren.

"Come on then Ruth, what's he like? Will he do for our sister?"

"Well, she's right, he is certainly mysterious. We don't know where he comes from, and when we talk to him to try and find out he says he doesn't know where he comes from or where he's going. I just think he just doesn't want to tell."

"I'm intrigued, go on, what does he look like?"

"Well, he definitely is tall, dark and handsome."

"Careful, it looks like you have a soft spot for him as well."

John had noticed a slight reddening of Ruth's cheeks.

"Stop it, you know I've been happily married to David for twenty years. He has dark brown eyes, a strong muscular face and a body to match. There's a tattoo on his left arm of an angel which is really nice."

"A tattoo of an angel you say?,"

"Yes, quite beautiful it is too, why do you ask?"

"It's nothing. I just dreamt about something similar last night,"

"Tell me more, what did you dream?"

"I can't remember much of it. All I remember is that in my dream I was in incredible pain and was praying to God to help me. Then all of a sudden, I heard a voice saying, 'It's time'. The clock on the wall had stopped and the pendulum was suspended in mid-swing. All of a sudden, a red mist started to cloud my eyes. I thought I was going to die then, but something strange happened. A hand covered my face. It felt like a natural energy, an energy that started to put my life force back into my body. No sooner had it started than a calmness surrounded me, a calmness not of this world was soon flowing into my heart. It was then the hand and redness started to fade, but as it was fading, I noticed the arm was adorned with a tattoo of an angel. I didn't see it for long because the sound of the clock started again which awoke me from my slumber."

"What medication are you on? I'll have to try some of it if it makes you have dreams like that."

They both started to laugh as Mary came back into the room with the tea. "What are you two giggling about? Some sordid joke about me and Luther most probably ..."

"No, don't think too highly of yourself Mary, the world does not revolve around you. I was just asking John what medication he is on because I want to try some."

"What's so funny about that?" Mary asked puzzled.

"Never mind, let me help you."

Ruth stood up and cleared the table, so Mary could safely place the tray of tea down.

"So Ruth, is he going to stay? Has he decided?" Mary asked as she poured out their tea.

"Well, David was all set to throw him out this morning after last night's fiasco. That was until David received a phone call from the brotherhood last night telling him he mustn't let Luther out of his sight."

"Sometimes I wonder if that husband of yours has a mind of his own? Why does he let the brotherhood tell him what to do?"

Startled, Ruth looked at her sick brother. "I don't know, John. Maybe it makes him feel important, proving himself to all those rich and powerful men is a boost to his confidence. I expect he's still looking for the father figure he never had while growing up. Anyway, enough about David, I want to know how you're feeling, John."

"Like I'm on a rollercoaster. One day, I feel like there's nothing wrong with me and I have no pain, the next I feel like I could die any second. It's strange but my dreams and my little talks with God help me a lot."

"It must be wonderful to have such dreams. Tell me, do you really think God is talking to you?"

"Well all I can say is that – thank you Mary," John stopped in mid-sentence as Mary handed him his tea, "the voice I hear is a voice I know so well, it's like it belonged to me even before I was born. It comforts me when I'm feeling at my worst, and the words are very profound."

"I don't suppose the voice could give us the winning lottery numbers could it?" Ruth retorted jokingly,

"Don't mock me, Ruth! John snapped, "That voice is the main reason why I keep fighting this awful affliction."

"I'm sorry John, I was just trying to make you laugh and cheer you up."

"Would anyone like a biscuit?" Mary interjected to calm the heated situation. She could see her sister was still nervous about visiting her brother and now she must be feeling incredibly awkward.

"It's all right Ruth. Sorry I snapped. I'm just a little tired and my visions and thoughts are very dear to me."

"I understand, sometimes my mouth opens before my brain gets into gear."

"So is Luther staying for a while and we will be seeing a lot more of him?" Mary asked her sister.

Both John and Ruth giggled at Mary's question.

"Stop it," Mary said. "Okay I admit it. Regardless of his behaviour last night, I am still fascinated by him and have an incredible urge to find out more about him. Dammit, I don't know why."

"I think you might get your chance Mary," they both looked at John, "remember yesterday afternoon when I spoke to you on the phone, when I spoke about looking for the light."

"Yes," Mary said intrigued.

"Well, did you find it?"

"I thought I had, but it turned out to be just a glass held in someone's hand moving and shining in the moonlight."

"Who was holding the glass?"

"It was Luther ..." Mary finished her sentence in realisation of what John might have been trying to tell her.

"Are you saying the light is a person?" Mary asked.

"I don't know. Did you have any other experiences last night?"

"Not that I can recall."

"Well, I was told in my dream that you were to look for the light, and when you see it you and only you could interpret it..."

John suddenly groaned in pain.

"John? Are you okay?!" Mary slipped out of her seat to attend to John as he held his chest and cried out in pain.

"It's just those dreadful pains in my chest again. I'm finding it hard to breathe. Don't worry, it will soon pass." John groaned again.

"Shall I call an ambulance?" Ruth asked, panic-stricken at the sight of her brother in pain.

"No, it's okay, it will pass. Just pass me a glass of water please."

Ruth handed Mary a glass of water and watched her sister gently help their brother take a sip.

"May I please Mary?" Mary looked around. "Can I help him with the water? I really want to help."

"Of course. He only has sips. If he has too much it makes him choke. While you're doing that, I'll phone for the doctor."

Ruth sat down beside her brother and took the glass from Mary's hand and held the glass to his lips.

"I won't be long," Mary rushed into the corridor to make a phone call.

"I know I haven't done much for you in the past John, but now I'm pleased to help you."

"Thank you, Ruth," John said quietly in between sips of his water. It was at this moment that they both felt a connection, as if Ruth were fulfilling a missing love between them.

The visions had now faded from Lucifer's mind and his breathing had almost returned to normal. The blue light had now totally vanished and all he could hear was the tick of the clock on the wall. He sat quietly with his eyes closed, contemplating. He knew that he certainly didn't want to do as he was told, and the thought of being near Mary made him sick to the stomach. The realisation of not having a choice made him very angry, but the desire for him to return to his true angelic form was causing conflict within him. *Do I do God's bidding and return to being an angel because of an order issued by the Most High? Or do I try and find a way myself?*

In frustration, he let out a roar like a lion. His eyes flashed open, revealing two bright red lights shining in the dark. It was torture for him to feel a little of his old angelic self confined in a corporeal prison. His mind flashed back to when he was allowed to fly around the earth as a reward for saving Angela.

"Yes, such freedom," he said as the red disappeared. *Maybe I will do as God commands just for now and when I am rewarded I will take my opportunity to escape and will take my revenge.*

He cautiously looked around the dark room to see if Michael or anyone was present and reading his thoughts. Feeling satisfied that no one was around, he drew back the curtains. Shielding his eyes he looked up to the blue sky.

"You won't be there for long, giver of light. You and I have unfinished business. I will take their light from them and they will die from coldness, hunger and loneliness in a world of darkness. The same darkness I have been suffering for an eternity. The Most High won't be able to protect the people of the Earth in their hour of need. Soon all mankind will be cursing God's name and all the time I will be the cause."

He stood smiling to himself and marvelled at the chaos and destruction he would unleash on the world. *My patience is the game I have to play now and when the time is right, I will strike my final blow.*

"How long will the doctor be Mary?" Ruth was looking up at Mary who had returned from making the telephone conversation in the hall.

"He is just finishing with another patient and will get here as soon as he can, maybe in about half an hour. How is he?"

Ruth looked at her brother John; he had fallen asleep with his head resting on her lap.

"He seems to have quietened down after having some water. I think me stroking his hair has comforted him and made him fall asleep."

"That's good, he could do with some sleep. He wakes up some mornings exhausted because the attacks are getting worse and more frequent during the night. Come on, put his head on the pillow, I'll make us another cup of tea in the kitchen."

Ruth gently placed John's head on his pillow, pulled the blanket up around his shoulders, kissed his head and walked into the kitchen with Mary.

"I don't know what I will do when he actually dies. It will be like losing another part of myself. Does that make sense Ruth?"

"Of course it does Mary, you've been caring for him for such a long time, so you haven't had much time for yourself or anybody else."

"I know, don't get me wrong. I don't regret anything and I wouldn't change my circumstances for anything. If I was born again and the same thing happened, I wouldn't hesitate in caring the same way."

"You're such a saint Mary. It must be difficult to have made all those sacrifices, especially all the men I've tried to set you up with."

"There you go," Mary handed Ruth her cup of tea and they both sat down at the kitchen table. "It's not caring for John that's stopped me from dating, it's just that I've never felt drawn to anyone except –"

"Except who? Go on," Ruth asked eagerly.

"Well, Luther is a mysterious man and very secretive. It's like he has something inside him, something locked deep down inside his soul that he hides from the world, and that intrigues the hell out of me. The only way I can describe it is that to me he seems like a lost little boy who has been chastised and spurned for who he is. Whatever happened to him, I feel it hurt him very much."

"Maybe he will stick around and you can find out a bit more about him."

“I would like that very much,” she said excitedly. “If I’m honest, I know I give out all the bravado of not caring, especially after last night, but I do want to see him again. I just doubt he would want to see me.”

“I hope he doesn’t Mary, it just doesn’t seem right.”

“Well I hope so, I really hope so.”

CHAPTER TWELVE

DAVID WALKED DOWN the stone path of Daniel's house, straightening his tie. As he reached the door it swung open.

"Come in, David we've been waiting for you," Daniel ushered David in and looked at his watch. "It's nearly twelve, you were cutting it fine."

"Thank you, sorry I'm late Daniel. I hope you all haven't been waiting too long? I had to finish a report on my computer before I left."

"No, not at all. Let me take your coat and please go through. The others are waiting for you."

David walked into the front room. Jeremiah sat in a chair in the corner and was speaking to the other brethren present.

"Come sit down David. I would like to introduce you to some old friends of mine."

David took a look around the room at the faces he had never seen before. Jeremiah gestured to a man close to him who sat with a pointed nose supporting glasses on the end of it and white short cropped hair that covered most of his balding head. "This is Mark."

David took hold of his hand to greet him. He stood up and smiled, shaking David's hand firmly.

"It's a pleasure to meet you young man, well done."

David smiled with a puzzled look on his face.

"You're welcome, but I'm not sure why I'm being congratulated."

"All in good time," Jeremiah interjected, "and this is Peter." This was also an elderly gentleman with a kind look on his face covered in a long white beard.

"Hello."

"Finally, this is Timothy." He was the youngest of all the men, and had an air of assuredness about him.

"Nice to meet you."

"Now that all the formalities are out of the way, we should begin."

Daniel had crept back into the room and sat down in the corner, pen in his hand waiting to take notes.

"Before I begin," Jeremiah continued. "I must tell you, David, that what I am going to say must stay in this room. It is imperative that this remains a secret within these four walls until Luther, if he is the one, demands to know. Is that clear?" David nodded his head nervously, "It must not be known to anyone else. If it was, it would mean the end of mankind."

David looked around the room. All eyes were on him making him feel like he was being judged.

"You can all depend on me, I swear."

"I know David, I think that's why fate placed you in the right place at the right time. Now is everyone okay for me to start?"

Jeremiah looked around the room and each man nodded in turn.

"Then I shall begin. Before the earth was created at the beginning of time, two energies, made up of atoms, were locked in battle in the universe. The name of these two energies or atoms were matter and antimatter, or if you like, light and darkness." Jeremiah looked around to see if everybody was paying attention and were able to keep up.

"They were constantly in a state of conflict, charging and crashing together one minute and repelling each other the next. For millions of light years this went on, and each time they came together the fighting and conflict became more intense, until one day the two opposing atoms smashed together with such force it caused them to split into tiny pieces. Some of these pieces ceased to exist and just floated off into space. However, the two remaining pieces of both sides came together with the influence of gravity. This final collision brought together the two pieces like a jigsaw puzzle. At last, after millions and millions of light years of conflict, it had taken one moment in time for the big bang to occur. " David looked at Daniel in amazement as the story unfolded.

"These two tiny fragments of atoms, which had now come together, started to shine in a different light to what they were shining before. This light was much brighter and it totally blinded the side of darkness. As the two new atoms shone and moved together in harmony, the mass of the other two opposing sides stopped their conflict to try to understand this anomaly. In this moment of silence and contemplation, the beginning had started: the light and dark atoms wanted to know more about this new light now being emitted. They decided to head towards this new light, but found they could not become part of it as it was too bright for the dark atoms. The atoms of light on the other hand did not want to enter because of the presence of the dark atom. Consequently, most of the dark atoms, realising they could not enter the light, started their fight again with the light atoms. Some of the light atoms, deciding they did not want to enter the light, retaliated. However, a few curious atoms on both sides remained where they were, trying to learn and understand more about this new light, watching, waiting patiently until it would reveal its secret.

"How long would it take for this process to reveal its secret?" David interrupted like an excitable child.

"Thousands of years David, and all these years passed until their patience paid off. Now the two atoms were perfectly unified and were ready to reveal their secret. At once, a chain reaction started in which the light atoms humbled themselves to enter the light and mix with the dark atoms, and the dark atoms had to give up their negativity and find themselves worthy enough to enter the light. It was not long before the two initial unified atoms became billions and billions as more of them released themselves from the universal conflict to join the new light which today we call the sun." David gasped at this revelation, which met with a hiss of disapproval from Peter. David lowered his head in embarrassment and allowed Jeremiah to continue.

"The sun, in its gravitational sphere, could only sustain a certain amount of energy, otherwise it would explode. To resolve this, the sun had to expel some of its energy in periodic explosions. These explosions sent a great energy at terrific speed into space. When this energy had cooled from the immense heat of the sun, it started to form into matter. That matter is now what we call the planet Earth. It had found its perfect place in space, neither too far or too near from her mother, the sun. Earth now began to live and breathe, sustained by the light and heat of the sun. Its water and oxygenated atmosphere began to create life." Jeremiah leant forward to take a sip of water before continuing.

Earth existed without man for millions of years in its perfect surroundings, until one day another explosion of the sun sent forth the original matter and anti-matter from their place of light towards the earth. It took seven days to reach Earth, and when it did it broke through the atmosphere, falling from the heavens and down towards the earth. In its descent, it took in oxygen and started to breathe until finally splashing into the oceans extinguishing its fire. Underwater, this energy evolved until mankind finally emerged from its depths.

Now humanity had been created by the four elements: first, born of fire from the sun, air breathed life into them as they broke through the atmosphere, water gave them the second birth after extinguishing the flames and earth is where now we all stand. All these men and women now walked the earth in total innocence. They all lived in harmony and the peace that still resonated from the energy from which they were born. This energy is what we call love.

Soon intelligence grew and it wasn't long before they were exploring and searching the four quarters of the globe. Individual tribes had settled with different customs, cultures and beliefs. They had learnt how to grow their own food and create things out of wood and metal, and begun to use the four elements to make their lives easier. However, in their laziness, and with their lives now seemingly so complicated, they started to forget where they had come from. Mankind had now created their own paradox: they had forgotten the beautiful light from where they had come and were now studying philosophy and mathematics in the hope of remembering. Their intelligence was taking them further away from the truth.

All was not lost: one man, a leader of the people in the East, vowed never to forget where he had come from. He gave up all his worldly possessions and lived in poverty. He instilled in his people the memory from where they had come and told them never to forget. They were further instructed that they were to live with that perfect moment of peace and harmony that had started at the beginning of time. This remarkable man from the East helped himself to stay in touch with whom he belonged to and where he came from by going into the desert and contacting the light from above. Here, he would make his daily prayers at twelve when the sun was at its highest. Unfortunately, it was at this time and this place where he met his untimely death due to the master of the West.

David, now you see from where we get our beliefs, rituals and customs, which were created just after the creation of the world. I am sure all brothers here today know the story. We practise the ritual every meeting in various degrees and its beauty is impressed on our minds. However, there is another part which nobody knows except myself and the other ancient brethren gathered here today. That information," he leant forward and said quietly, "I will now relate to you David because I believe that it is time to do so.

After those events in the East, thousands of years ago, my ancestor Joshua wrote down all the events that had happened on a scroll before leaving the devastation behind him. He described a falling star which alluded to the fall of the Master of the East and the loss of his loving nature. He now represented the fall of mankind. He went on to write about how this Master of the East had given up everything for revenge after what had befallen him at the hands of the Master of the West. The murderous attack had left a wound or mark on the Master of the East's head. It remained there to remind him of his pain and anguish, and more importantly to help him to eventually remember who he really is. David, you know I have seen this wound on Luther's head. I saw it when we first met him. "

"Yes," David replied in astonishment. "I remember you turning pale and dropping your cane at the sight of it."

"Yes, I did become quite faint with excitement, didn't I? Joshua wrote about two other signs. One was the befriending of a lion and all the beasts of Earth. He said that the Master from the East asked for the power of the lion over man to enable him to destroy mankind after seeing his people being murdered. David, was it not a glorious sight to see Luther in the lion's cage safe and unharmed?"

"Yes, it was quite an extraordinary sight, something I will never forget."

"The third and final sign was about accepting and becoming the light. Joshua had witnessed and absorbed some of the light all those years ago. He knew its secret and things not of this world. No man to date has ever been able to decipher the ancient word; only he who knew its true meaning could do that.

Joshua and his family fled the devastation which ensued, taking the scroll with him. They had a safe journey and settled down with a loving peaceful tribe in the south, far away from the destruction of war. It was here that he and his family started communicating what had happened in the East. However, they did not give the whole story, only a watered down version veiled in allegory, because he did not want everybody to know these secrets. It was not long before people came to his house to hear his amazing story, and he told it over and over again. The years passed, his wife eventually died and his children grown up and went their own way in the world, except one son who loved his father dearly. Now all Joshua had left was his one son and his followers.

Among his followers were three men he trusted with his life. These three men and his son had for thirty years attended every meeting and ritual. They kept silence when it was needed and spoke when it was necessary. When on his deathbed, Joshua called them in. He asked his son to remove the scroll from inside a sacred golden chest placed on the altar in the corner of the room. His son obediently did as his father asked. Taking it in his frail hands, Joshua looked at the four men at the foot of his bed and spoke: 'My son, I love and trust you dearly. With this in mind, in my dying moments I entrust you with the fourth part of the scroll.'

He took a knife and cut along the bottom of the scroll. 'This part contains the secret of becoming the light. Guard it well my son.' He then cut the remainder of the scroll into three pieces, each describing what had happened and each containing a certain way to see the signs of the one returning to Earth. The three other men were each given a piece and charged with its safety. They were then informed that they were to go from this room and take their families to the west, north and east respectively; his son was to remain in the south and take over leadership of his people. In these four quarters of the globe they were to spread the word and re-enact the rituals we know today.

They were also informed that they should not come together at the same time in fear that the whole scroll would fall into the wrong hands. The only time they should all come together was when all the signs were in place. Then should the four ancestors reunite. If that did not happen in their lifetime, then they had to hand down their pieces of scroll to their eldest child from generation to generation until the time was right. This is the reason we are gathered here today. I am Joshua's descendant. Timothy, Peter and Mark are, how shall we say, old friends."

"Forgive me Jeremiah," David said, "but how did you make contact and find out who had their own piece of the scroll?"

"Well David, from each generation, a secret worthy man or woman was selected from their tribe to travel to the other quarters of the globe. When they reached their destination, they communicated using the signs and words to the holders of the scroll who in turn reciprocated. These travellers or messengers were then welcomed into their homes for comfort and refreshment until they decided to return to their own village to relay the intelligence that all was in order."

David's eyes were wide with awe. He was hearing the truth about life and he was now playing a part in it, a part which he did not yet understand.

"If you please gentlemen, it is time for us to communicate like we have done from time immemorial, for the time is at hand."

Jeremiah stood and gestured with a hand to his companions. One by one they stood and approached Jeremiah to communicate a word. Timothy was the first.

"A-Mia-Hey, brothers, I greet you as a Master of the North and as the Ruler of Water. May our work swim in the ocean of life. In line with our great creator, I salute you."

He went forward to each brother and ran his finger under their eyes.

"May the water from your tears I have collected return to the ocean and remind us of the loss of the Master from the East and may they continue till the one has returned."

"All hail," the four of them said in unison. Mark was next.

"Fly-Isis-Fly, brothers, I greet you as the Master of the West and as the Ruler of Air. May our work fly and be carried on the four cardinal winds in peace and harmony. In line with our creator, I salute you for the second time."

He stepped forward and placed a finger on each other brothers' mouths in turn.

"May you breathe in all that is good and breathe out all that is bad, especially the memory of such a horrific end to our beloved Master. My finger is a guard until the return of the one who will release me from my charge."

"All hail,"

"Set-Death," Peter had now begun, "brothers I greet you as the Master from the East and as a Ruler of Earth. May our work grow in the soils of the Earth. In line with our creator, I for the third time salute you."

He took hold of each brother's head and held it affectionately in his arms.

"May this token remind you that we do this in memory of the Master from the East who was buried and comforted in an earthly embrace for forty days until the earth gave him new life."

"All hail." Jeremiah was the last to stand.

"Our-Ra-New, brothers I greet you as the Master of the South and as the Ruler of Fire. May our work be shielded from the eyes and hands of unworthy men. May the heat and fire of our faith help us to continue in line with our creator. Brothers for the fourth and final time I salute you."

He walked forward and covered their eyes with his

hands and one by one he told them: "May your eyes be in darkness until the one decides to reveal himself. We do this in memory, respect and remorse of the darkness his world was plunged into."

"All hail, all hail."

"We now all stand as four," Jeremiah continued, "communications have been made and all is well. I greet you my brothers."

The three other men bowed and said in unison, "We greet you all well brother." Jeremiah looked at each man and asked them, "Do you still hold what is true in a safe place away from the eyes of the unworthy?"

They all said in turn, "I do Brother from the South. Is it your wish to see?"

"It is my right and my wish now the time is at hand. Show me."

They all reached under their seats and removed a black briefcase and placed it on their laps.

"Now as I reunite with you," Timothy said, "I bring my piece of the word to reunite it with the whole."

Peter and Mark repeated the same, then they all stood adorned with white gloves and opened their cases. David's eyes widened as they all removed the contents. Cautiously and gently, each of them held their piece of the ancient scroll in their hands.

"Gentlemen," Jeremiah was now standing, "I believe the time is at hand. All the signs have shown themselves for the return of the One. It is only right and proper if we are all in agreement that the scroll must become whole in its entirety and presented to the One for truth to be revealed to him. However, if he is found not to be the one, we will cautiously depart and continue in our pursuit for as long as it takes. Are we all in agreement?"

"We are in agreement."

They handed their pieces of the scroll to Jeremiah, and David noticed Daniel's eyes begin to swell with tears as he witnessed the coming together predicted by the ancient writings. For thousands of years, the pieces of scroll had passed from hand to hand, but never before now had they ever come together. He could hold his silence no more.

"Jeremiah, is it really true? Am I witnessing the great truth I have been reading about all my life? Please tell me it is so."

Jeremiah looked kindly at his faithful brother,

"My dear Daniel, it is the beginning of the truth. I assure you this part of the truth is true. Only when the One receives it will the whole truth be known to man."

Daniel was now sobbing like a child. "I am so sorry for my emotional outburst, gentlemen," Daniel spluttered. "I am a silly old fool."

"Not at all," Timothy replied, "we have known of this from our father's fathers. You have been in darkness without knowledge of this. I can't imagine how excited you feel right now."

"David my brother, can you now see how important it is to us for Luther to remain in your house until we are ready to present him with the word?"

Jeremiah was not looking at David as he asked the question, but was carefully and cautiously placing all the four pieces of the scroll into his briefcase.

"Yes Jeremiah, I fully understand. I won't let him out of my sight."

"Good, I know, we can all count on you."

All four of them were looking at David, but this time he did not feel intimidated by their gaze. Instead, he felt a new feeling, one of courage and confidence.

"Daniel." Jeremiah looked in Daniels' direction.

"Yes, Jeremiah?" he answered, while wiping the remaining tears from his eyes

"Is it okay if Timothy and Mark stay with you until we'll need to meet again?"

"It will be my pleasure and honour, Jeremiah."

"Peter, you can stay with me at my house and share my hospitality. Is that okay with everyone gentlemen?" Everyone nodded in agreement.

"David, return home now to fulfil your duty. Remember, don't speak of this to anyone, not even to your wife, and especially not to Luther. We don't want to confuse or frighten him off before we have chance to carry out our great work."

"I promise Jeremiah, I will carry out the brotherhood's wishes to the best of my ability. Take care gentlemen, until we meet again."

By turns, he shook all three of the men's hands. Daniel stood to walk David to the front door. Daniel turned to David.

"Good luck, David, you must feel highly honoured with such a charge and to be in the presence of the One."

"I do Daniel." He held his head high and felt a great amount of pride within. "It is a great honour indeed. Take care brother."

They embraced.

"Go on, go home before you have me in tears again."

"Okay, take care Daniel."

"Goodbye, David."

He closed the door behind him, and returned to the gathering.

"Can we rely on him Jeremiah?"

"Yes, I believe we can, Peter." The four men watched David walk down the garden path. "The will of the Most High ensured that he was at the zoo when Luther first appeared. Now that is a great sign, and I am not going to question that or the will of the Most High. I believe our trust in him is not misplaced. He will do what he has to when the time is right."

Chapter Thirteen

"IS THAT YOUR PHONE, RUTH?" Mary asked.

The theme tune from *The Sound of Music* came from her handbag.

"It's probably David phoning me to let me know what time he wants his dinner on the table."

"You are such a slave," Mary retorted jokingly.

"Be quiet," Ruth said to her sister and answered the phone. "Hello darling, what's up?"

There was a brief pause while she listened to David on the other end. "I am with Mary at her home, why? Another brief pause. "I left him at home. I'm sure he's old enough to look after himself." Mary giggled as Ruth pulled a bored face whilst listening to her husband. "Yes boss, anything you say boss goodbye. Oh." Her expression changed to a more serious and slightly confused one. "I love you too darling."

"What's the matter Ruth?"

"I don't believe it," Ruth replied. "That's the second time in all our years of marriage that he's told me he loves me. The first time was on our wedding night."

"Well, that's a good thing isn't it?" Mary asked puzzled.

"Yes, but it actually sounded like he meant it. What has he been up to?"

"You're such a cynic Ruth. I think it's lovely."

"You would, anyway he said –"

They were interrupted by groaning from John next door.

"Mary! Mary where are you?"

"I'm coming John, darling," Mary called out.

They both rushed next door to find John sitting upright in his bed with sweat shining on his forehead.

"He is coming Mary, he is coming. My pain is nearly at an end."

"Ssshh, brother dear, it is just another dream. Ruth, could you pass me that towel?"

She gently laid him back down and stroked John's head until he was silently sleeping again.

"I can't take much more of this," Mary collapsed crying into Ruth's arms. "Sometimes he seems to be getting better, then there is an outburst like that and he tells us that he is about to die. I wish God would take him so he won't be in pain any more. Am I wicked for thinking that Ruth?"

"No, not at all. It must be awful to see him in pain day after day. I don't know how you do it."

"I'm just being silly," she pulled herself away from Ruth's embrace. Come on Mary, she said to herself, You have to stay strong for John.

"It's all right to show some weakness and let out emotion," Ruth was wiping her sister's tears as she spoke.

"Thanks, your words mean a great deal and comfort me. Let's forget about that. What did David want on the phone anyway?"

"He wanted to find out where I was. And where Luther was. It was strange, but there was a sense of urgency in his voice. He ordered me to stay here until he had picked up Luther to come and get me. I guess I will wait here until his majesty returns. Fancy another cup of tea?"

"No, let's have some wine," Mary said, "I have some white chilling in the fridge. We can drink that until David gets here."

David arrived back at his house. "Luther, Luther are you there?" David opened his front door, calling out. There was no reply except the sound of the television coming from the living room. A sinking feeling rushed into David's stomach as he wondered if Lucifer had left the house and disappeared. What would he tell the brotherhood?

"Pull yourself together," he said quietly to himself, "if it's God's will and Luther is the one, he must be still here."

He nervously opened the living room door and to his relief Lucifer was sitting in David's favourite chair watching the television.

"Did you not hear me calling you, Luther?" Lucifer ignored David as he entered the room and turned his attention back to the television.

"Excuse me, I'm talking to you."

"Be quiet man, I'm listening to this news report about General Silas. Now that's an ambitious man."

"Yes and a crazy dictator who is power hungry. We all see him as a very dangerous man."

"I like him. I have a feeling that we will be seeing each other soon, then I will introduce him to the real meaning of the word danger."

"Well, he is only a few thousand miles away in a country that has the highest security in the world, so I don't like your odds very much."

Lucifer gave David a stare of disapproval. Feeling intimidated by Lucifer's cold gaze, he looked away and changed the subject.

"Me and Ruth would like to extend our welcome to you for as long as you wish."

"Oh joy!" Lucifer was slightly getting bored and impatient with his current situation, and now that was going to be extended. Could it get any worse?

"The brotherhood send their greetings to you Luther and wish you well. They also would like you to stick around, so they have charged me with your welfare."

"My welfare? You think I need to be looked after?"

"No, not at all. We just want your stay here to be welcoming and we want to make the path easy for you."

"My path easy? Easy for what?"

Realising he had said too much already, David had to think quickly.

"I only meant that when you decide to move on to wherever it is you want to go, all of us will be only too pleased to assist you."

"Okay ..." Lucifer said with a sardonic tone.

"Luther, I have to go and pick Ruth up from Mary's. Would you mind accompanying me?"

"Mary's?" Lucifer asked with a start.

"Yes, is that okay?"

"Why do you need me to go with you?"

"I did say to the brotherhood that I would look after you. Besides getting out of the house and into the fresh air will do you good. Also it would be nice for you to meet John."

Michael's words rushed through Lucifer's mind, returning to the time when he had spoken of saving John.

"Are you trying to tell me David that Mary and John live together?"

"Yes, Mary's caring for John."

A multitude of thoughts surged through Lucifer's head. He knew that by doing the Most High's bidding and saving John, he would have to come into contact with Mary again. But surely the reward of escape and freedom after saving him would outweigh the sickness he felt when he was around Mary.

"We won't be staying long, will we David?"

"No, not at all, you can even wait in the car if you want to."

"No, I think I would like to meet this John. It sounds like he has suffered quite a lot," Lucifer was trying to put on his best sympathetic voice.

"Okay," David sounded surprised, "I am sure he will be delighted to see you. I know Mary will be especially glad to see you again after last night."

"Erm, yes. Is she still angry with me?"

"I don't know. I guess we'll soon find out, won't we? Come on, let's go."

David stepped forward and switched off the television.

"Here, take my keys and go and wait in the car. I just have to get something from upstairs."

Waiting in the car Lucifer was thinking about the next day or so. He would use his powers to heal John, then when Michael and the Most High had rewarded him, he would take his angelic form and go and find General Silas to command him to start a nuclear war. He thought that if the Most High had forbade him to do any harm to humans, then a human substitute would make the perfect puppet to do his bidding.

"I am a genius," he started to laugh to himself.

"What are you laughing at?"

The driver's door had opened and David was getting in.

"Nothing much David, just drive me my good man. Take me to my destiny."

"Okay, are you all right?" David asked in a concerned tone as he looked at Lucifer.

"Yes, I am feeling great. And I will soon be on top of the world."

For the brotherhood, David thought, as he pulled out from his drive away, *For the brotherhood, I will prove myself and show myself worthy.*

"Are you okay Mary?" Ruth asked.

"I'm fine. I just have a strange feeling in my stomach, very similar to the one I had yesterday afternoon. It's a strange feeling, like excitement and fear mixed together."

"Perhaps you're just nervous about meeting Luther again?"

"Maybe, but I first had this feeling even before I met him."

"Do you feel it too, Mary?"

John had awoken and was looking at them both.

"I do John, but what is it?"

"I don't know, but when I have my dreams and I'm talking to God, I have the same feeling, but a lot more intense. It's like something is going to happen that you know is right, but it seems very wrong. I know it sounds strange, but that's the only way I can describe it."

"Well, how come I don't feel it?" Ruth asked, feeling a little left out.

"Maybe it's because you have been married to David for far too long," John said. Mary and John giggled.

"I'm sorry," John said, seeing the hurt in his sister's eyes.

"Yes, I'm sorry too," Mary took hold of her hand.

"They're here," John said as they heard the car pull up outside. He winked at Mary. "So I will finally meet the man for my sister."

"Stop it John," Mary said, gazing at the mirror, making sure her hair and make-up was in order.

"You look lovely Mary," Ruth said. "Now go and greet them at the door. I'll wait with John."

In the car David was again curiously looking at Lucifer,

"Are you sure you're okay Luther? You've been holding your stomach all the way here and the pain seems to have got worse."

"I'm fine!" snapped Lucifer, as he glared at David for his over concern "Let us get this over with."

"I can give Mary and John your apologies and tell them you wanted to stay in the car."

Lucifer glared another icy stare in his direction.

"Okay, let's go, they'll be waiting."

Mary was behind the closed front door with her hand on her stomach as the familiar feeling intensified. She heard their footsteps get closer and closer until they ceased and were followed by the sound of the doorbell. She counted ten seconds before answering the door. She didn't want to seem too keen, but she also didn't want them to wait too long in case Lucifer changed his mind.

As she opened the door, Lucifer thought his stomach

would explode as his eyes met Mary's and the feelings rushed back. He felt him feel awkward and not sure what to do.

"Hello Mary, how are you?" David reached forward and kissed her on the cheek.

"I'm fine, thank you David. Go through, Ruth and John are waiting."

"Thank you," he said and went inside.

"And how are you Luther?" Mary asked.

"I feel quite ill and sick in my stomach. I think it must still be the effect of the drink last night."

"Maybe, but me and John also don't feel too well. Perhaps there is some stomach bug going around."

"Maybe," he said and pushed past Mary without another word. Mary closed the door and thought to herself, *This is going to be a long afternoon.*

"Hello darling," Ruth stood up and embraced her husband.

"What was that for?" David said.

"Do you know how good it makes me feel when you tell me you love me?" Ruth said aloud, wanting everybody to hear.

"Well, I haven't said it for a long time and I really do appreciate everything you do for me."

She bent forward to whisper in his ear. "If you play your cards right, tonight I'll show you what I can really do for you."

"Ahem, are you going to introduce me to your friend David?" John discreetly interrupted their romantic moment.

"Sorry yes, excuse me John, this is Luther."

John tried to sit up and Mary rushed forward to assist him.

"Stop fussing woman. I can manage."

He held out his hand for Lucifer to shake. Lucifer looked at him and took hold of his hand. When their hands met, a strange energy resonated between their palms. To both of them, this energy felt like two magnets; one second they were repelling, the next they were attracting. Feeling uncomfortable at this sensation which challenged his own power, Lucifer broke the grip. John watched as Lucifer walked to the other side of the room and sat down.

"So Luther, I hear you made a bit of a name for yourself last night,"

Lucifer looked at John coldly.

"Do you like being ill, John?"

"Luther! That is not a very appropriate question," David had interrupted in John's defence.

"It's all right David. Why do you ask, Luther?"

"Well, if you had the choice, would you prefer to be ill or would you like to be healthy all your life?"

Lucifer was starting to enjoy himself now that the pain associated with Mary was dissipating, allowing him to play with John's mind.

"Well, if I was given a choice before birth, I would obviously choose to be healthy. But I don't think we are given a choice, we have to accept the life we are given by God."

"You see, now that is what I don't understand. God has given you this life and you accept it."

"With all my heart."

"Why? Tell me you hate the Most High for this affliction?"

"No, in fact I love God more. If I am meant to have this disease then I accept it. Maybe in another lifetime, I'll be healthy, which I will be grateful for. Can't you see that I am experiencing this disease and pain so that when I experience a healthy life I will appreciate it all the more?"

"But what if you could change your fate. Would you do it?"

"Of course. I think anybody would if they had the power, especially if it would stop the suffering and sorrow of my family and friends. Unfortunately, I don't have that luxury. Besides, I don't have to worry because God talks to me in my dreams and I have been told that

I will be saved and my suffering will soon be at an end."

"Can we please stop this talk?"

Mary walked over to John's bed to puff up his pillow. "You know it upsets me John, besides they are only dreams."

"They might be only dreams to you, Mary, but to me they are a sign, and if death is my salvation I gladly accept it. One way or another I will be free of this pain by the help of another."

"Another? What do you mean?" Lucifer asked, intrigued.

"I had a vision of a man standing over me. He had the darkest of a shadow surrounding him, so much so that I couldn't see him, but within this darkness was the most glorious of all lights. I couldn't see this light, only sense it was there."

Lucifer was listening intently. Michael had told him that he had to save this man, but who was John talking about? Was it him? It couldn't be, there was no light inside him, only darkness.

"What does this other person do?"

"He cures my pain. I don't know if he assists me to die or he actually saves me from dying. All I know is that my visions inform me that my pain and sickness have gone, but I don't know if that is through death or life."

Lucifer sat back in his chair and pondered. Michael had told him that the Most High wanted him to save John, so he already knew the answer to John's question.

"If you were to be saved and live, what would you do with your newfound lease of life?"

"I would rise up from the bed, dress myself and put on a very good pair of walking shoes because a new beginning and a long journey would be ahead of me. I would walk and walk and spread the word that God is good and God is great and is living in the hearts of men again. My new healthy body would be a testament of his love for mankind."

"What a wonderful dream, my dear."

Mary had interrupted as she thought the conversation was getting a bit heavy. "I am glad you have your dreams and hopes to comfort you in this painful time, but can we please now talk about something else?"

"Of course, Mary. So David, how is the brotherhood?"

"Come on Mary, if they're going to talk about the brotherhood, I'd rather be in the kitchen making tea," Mary took hold of Ruth's hand and they both left the room.

"It's going very well John, thank you for asking."

"That's great news David. Now Luther, what would you do if you were in my situation?"

David stood up.

"Okay, I can see when I'm not wanted. I guess I'll go and give the ladies a hand." His words fell on deaf ears. Lucifer and John were now locked together with their eyes staring, oblivious to what was going on around them.

"If I were in your situation John, and I had finally been saved, I would certainly not go around praising the Most High."

"Why would you not want to thank and praise the one who saved you?"

"Because that is hypocritical. Why would I thank someone for undoing what they had done to me in the first place? It would be like a child receiving a smack from a parent, then thanking that parent for taking the pain away. I would rather not have the smack in the first place."

"That's not the point. Surely it's what you learn from the experience. If you had been born blind and all your life you felt the pain of not being able to see this beautiful world, imagine how much more special it would be if you were given the power of sight and saw it for the very first time."

"You're missing my point. Can't you see that God is to blame for all the suffering in the world? Even Jesus, his only son, died on the cross from pain and suffering. For what? Now even today we have people killing in his name under the camouflage of religion. We have hunger, greed, rape and murder. I'm sure God and Jesus didn't save the world then and they never will."

"No, but they did free our minds and souls from sin, giving us free will to choose between good and evil. Unfortunately most of mankind has chosen the evil way, following the ways of Satan."

"Perhaps they want to believe in something other than a God who isn't evident in a sick world?"

"Don't you see Luther? That's why God gave us faith, because when we hold on to our beliefs and faith it reminds us and keeps us mindful of God and what love is."

"Love!" Lucifer snapped. "A word so overindulged. It serves nothing or nobody, it's like a sickness causing people more pain than any amount of evil in the world."

"Which one are you, Luther? Have you never been loved or did you lose a great love?"

Lucifer's anger and impatience started to grow as he found it hard to find an answer to John's awkward question.

"You're right. I don't know love, but that's only because I don't want to know it. If I had my way I would wipe its very name from the minds of man until it is never spoken about again."

"Luther, you were hurt weren't you? You must have been to hate love and God so much."

"I have never been hurt, it is my decision alone to be hateful and evil."

"What do you mean?"

"This!"

In one sudden movement Lucifer was on his feet with his hand around John's throat, throttling him. Looking down at John's frightened eyes, Lucifer started to smile.

"You see John, I choose to do evil. That is what I am. I am every man's darkest fear and I will see my will be done on earth."

"Please!" John managed to croak as he struggled against Lucifer's grip, pulling on his arm he lifted Lucifer's sleeve to reveal the angel tattoo. At once John's eyes were no longer frightened. Lucifer was confused when John gave up the fight and started to smile. He released his grip slightly and asked, "Why are you smiling?"

Coughing, John struggled to speak. "It's you! The one I've been waiting for." He took hold of Lucifer's hand. "Bless you. Please do what must be done. Into your hands I commit my soul."

This brief moment gave Lucifer time to reflect: if he saved this man John would tell people about the glory of God, which is something he did not want happening. The other choice was not to save him and suffer the consequence of staying a man. His made his choice without hesitation.

"I do this for me John, not for you and certainly not for God. I do it so that I can be released from my punishment."

"Whatever the reason, your choice will be the right one in God's eyes, thank you." He closed his eyes, "Let it begin."

Lucifer closed his eyes and concentrated on his power from within. "I call upon my power and the word from when time begun, assist me now."

The red glow started beating from his heart and made its way around his body until his hand, which was covering John's face, started glowing a bright red. The red mist made its way down his arm until it finally encapsulated both his and John's bodies. Time and eternity had now come together in Lucifer's mind and they were breathing the same rhythm of life. Lucifer breathed in; John breathed out. Now they were as one. In that moment, Lucifer's light entered John's heart, causing him to gasp in a mouthful of air. He opened his eyes and looked up at Lucifer and the light emanating from him.

"You are the one, thank God for his mercy –"

John suddenly groaned in pain. Lucifer broke from his concentration and looked down. John's whole body was now surrounded by a bright white light and his face was shining with a light that hurt Lucifer's eyes.

"Thank you," John said as Lucifer's eyes met his. John took hold of his hand and said, "You see I was right, God does care".

John's hand fell by his side as the white light left him, leaving only Lucifer's red aura alight in the room.

"What are you doing?"

Mary had rushed into the room on hearing John's cry, startling Lucifer who turned to see her rushing towards him. Mary's presence instigated a retreat of Lucifer's red glow and as his light was fading, Mary took hold of his arm.

"Get your hands off him."

Lucifer pulled his arm away from Mary's grip, but it was too late. Lucifer's receding power had pulled some of Mary's life force with it into his presence making him feel even sicker than he had before.

"John, John, wake up."

Mary was shaking John's shoulders as David and Ruth entered the room. Lucifer stepped slowly back from everybody and watched with terror as part of Mary's blue light aura forced its way into his body.

"Luther what were you doing? Why did he cry out?"

"We were just talking about his life when all of a sudden he cried out. That's when I got up to see if I could help him. Then you came rushing into the room." They all looked at one another to see who believed him, but concern for John took over.

"I'll call an ambulance," David was on his mobile phone, walking out of the room to get a better signal.

"Thank God, he's still breathing and he has a pulse, although it is a very weak one," Mary said.

Lucifer was now sitting back in the chair holding his arm and watching everything go on around him.

"The ambulance will be about ten minutes," David said, returning to the room. "How is he Mary?"

"Unconscious, but he is still alive."

"Are you all right, Luther?"

Ruth was looking at Lucifer who was still looking dazed and puzzled at what had just happened. Had he saved John or had his energy had the reverse effect and ultimately harmed him?

"Just a slight pain in my arm. John must have pulled it a bit too hard when he was having his attack."

"Don't worry about him!" Mary was angrily looking at him, "John is what matters to us, so get him the hell out of my sight."

David turned towards Ruth. "Darling, I'll take Luther home out of your way. Stay with Mary and go with her in the ambulance. I'll come and pick you up later when I hear from you."

"Okay I think that's a good idea. See you later, darling."

"Come on Luther, let's get you home. Things are a little sensitive here at the moment."

Still confused, Lucifer looked up at David who was beckoning him to go with him. Nodding, he stood from the chair and made his way to the hallway.

"See you later Luther," Ruth called out behind him. Lucifer didn't respond and Mary didn't even turn to see them leave.

"Are you sure you're okay, Luther?" David was holding the car door open to let Lucifer in.

"I am fine, just get me away from here!"

"Okay, I was just asking, there is no need to bite my head off."

"One day maybe I will," Lucifer said quietly under his breath.

"What was that?"

"Nothing, I was just thinking aloud about what had just happened."

"Yes I hope for Mary and Ruth's sake that this is the day when John will finally be at peace."

As they were driving home, an ambulance shot past them going in the other direction.

"That will be for John. I hope God will take care of him, as well as of Mary and Ruth."

"Don't hold your breath. God never keeps promises."

Mary and Ruth sat holding each other in the back of the ambulance as it headed towards the hospital with its blue lights flashing and siren sounding.

"Is he going to be okay?" Ruth asked the paramedic as he was wiring John up to a heart monitor.

"Well, he's unconscious but stable. The doctors at the hospital will be able to tell you more."

"It's going to be okay, Mary. Even if he does die, his pain will be no more and he will be free. If I'm totally honest, I hope he does quietly pass in his sleep."

Mary broke into a flood of tears. She realised that her sister was right and she thought that only God would know what was best for him now.

"Can I get you a drink of anything Luther?" They had both arrived back at David's house and were sitting in the lounge.

"Get me a whisky!"

"Are you sure? Don't you remember the effect whisky had on you last night?"

"I don't care. I want one and I want it now."

"Okay, would you like ice?"

"No, just a full glass of whisky."

"Tell me Luther, what really happened back at Mary's house? Why was Mary so angry with you?"

He handed Lucifer the glass of whisky.

"I guess she just panicked after hearing her brother cry out and seeing me next to him. It must have looked suspicious. But I was only seeing if I could help him."

Lucifer searched David's eyes for any signs of disbelief.

"Well thanks for trying to help. I'm sure when Mary's calmed down she'll appreciate what you did. I am just going upstairs for a quick wash and change. Will you be all right?" Lucifer looked at him with an air of contempt.

"I'll take that as a yes. Help yourself to whatever you like."

"Just leave the whisky bottle; that will be fine."

Lucifer watched and waited as David left the room and the sounds of his footsteps had drifted into the distance.

"Well Michael, I'm alone at last. Where's my reward?"

Nothing but silence.

"I know you're there Michael. Show your face, you're always there. I did what you and the Most High wanted, now where's my reward?"

Still nothing.

"What do you want from me? Do you want me to close my eyes, get on my knees and pray to the Most High? Where are you?"

His furious outbursts were met with nothing but silence. Then he remembered how he previously thought about saving John and then returning to angelic form and taking his revenge.

"Come on Michael. I didn't mean any of that. I was just playing with you. Now give me my reward."

Nothing.

"Hello Mary."

"Hello doctor, how is he?" John's specialist had walked into the waiting room after examining John.

"Please sit down." Mary gripped Ruth's hand tightly as the doctor started to talk, fearing the worst. "He's slipped into a coma. At the moment, he's on a life support machine. It seems like his whole body has just shut down for some reason. Did anything happen?"

"No, he just cried out then fell unconscious."

"Strange. Well, your brother is in very safe hands. My team are some of the world's best and will stop at nothing until we find an answer. I know it's hard, but try not to worry. We'll all be working on him round the clock. I must get back, but I'll let you know if there is any change in his condition."

"Thank you, Doctor."

Mary and Ruth watched the doctor disappear down the corridor. Mary turned to her sister.

"Why don't you call David and get him to come and pick you up? There's no point in both of us being here."

"Are you sure? I don't mind staying. David is big and ugly enough to look after himself."

"No, it's fine. Please go and call him. I'll come and get you if anything happens."

"Okay, I'll just go outside and call him. Get us a coffee from the vending machine. I won't be long."

The sound of the phone ringing in the corridor disturbed Lucifer. He listened to David as he answered it.

"Hello Ruth, how is he? Really, did they say what caused it? Okay, give me twenty minutes and I'll be there. Ruth before you go remember he's still alive and while he's still alive, there's always hope. Love you, goodbye."

The living room door opened and David entered. "That was Ruth. She says that John's in a coma. They don't know what caused it but at least he's still alive. I'm just going to pick her up. Do you want to come along for the ride?"

"No, I think I'll stay here with this whisky bottle."

"Okay, but promise you will be here when we get back. The brotherhood have charged me with looking after you. See you soon and don't go anywhere."

The front door slammed behind him.

"Do I have anywhere else to go?" Lucifer's shouted sarcastically as he left, a quiet voice above him started to speak,

"Do you have anywhere to go Lucifer?"

"Michael, how good of you to join me. I think you know the answer to that question. I don't."

Michael had now appeared in his full glory and was floating above.

"You are exactly where you are supposed to be for this

exact moment in time, so everything is going well and all according to God's plan."

"Yes, I know I am not in control. I've heard it all before. Now tell me what happened: did I save John or not? I was interrupted by that interfering Mary. I don't know if I completed my work or not."

"You did exactly what you were meant to do, no more, no less."

"Stop answering me in riddles, will he live or not?"

"He will live and the Most High is most pleased with your cooperation."

"I don't want to please the Most High. I certainly do not want his acceptance. Now Michael, down to business. When you're ready, I'll have my reward for saving John."

"My dear brother, did you not realise that you have already received it?"

"Is that some sort of joke? Because if it is, I'm not laughing."

"No Lucifer, I am not joking. You have already been rewarded for your work."

"So where are my wings and my freedom?"

"Nobody mentioned that your reward would be the same as before."

"I assumed it would be, because my ultimate desire is to be a fiery angel once again."

"I am sorry you thought that brother, but the Most High decided on a much more special reward, one that will enable you to rediscover yourself."

"Rediscover myself! What do you mean? I know who I am. Damn you and the Most High with your mind games. What is this reward that is so special?"

"Do you not feel it? Your reward is now running through your veins, slowly finding its way around your body until you finally accept it. Then and only then you will allow it to enter into your heart, look."

Lucifer looked down to where Michael was pointing. The arm Mary had grabbed was now glowing a bright blue which was pulsating all around his arm.

"What trickery is this? How can this be? What have you done to me?"

"It is a token of the Most High's love for you. It will remain there unseen until you decide to tap into your own energy. This is when it will reveal itself again. Lucifer, it is up to you whether you decide to accept this gift or not. Until then it remains a permanent reminder. Goodbye, my brother."

"Wait! A reminder of what?"

"In time you will know, in time."

"Come back, Michael, come back here and explain yourself!"

Michael had vanished and Lucifer was left in the room, surrounded by nothing but silence. He looked down at his arm. The blue light had vanished. What could have that meant? He decided to try and access his energy to see what would happen. Cautiously, he closed his eyes and began to slow his breathing. It was not long before he was at one with himself and his red aura was illuminating his whole torso. He sat in this quietness for a while before opening his eyes to look at his arm.

"Come on, Lucifer" he said to himself.

Opening his eyes, he looked down to his arm which was alive all in a perfect crimson red, and relief calmed his mind.

"You see Michael, my power is still strong enough to withstand anything the Most High imposes on me, look!"

He held his arm aloft to show it to the heavens in all its glory, then to his horror the blue glow started to appear much stronger than before, and this time it was interacting and intertwining with Lucifer's own red energy like smoke, slowly working its way up his arm.

"No! This can't be, I won't let it happen."

He tried to fight it, but the more he fought it the stronger it became. Lucifer switched off his own energy with an angry cry causing both colours to disappear. Feeling stunned and confused, he jumped to his feet and shouted at the heavens.

"I hate you, do you hear me? I hate you!"

His cry was so loud it startled some birds in the tree next door which took flight at hearing his screams.

Back at the hospital, David had arrived to pick up Ruth.

"Hello darling," Ruth had turned to see David walking up the hospital corridor towards her.

"How is he, Ruth?"

"He's still stable. They're carrying out blood tests and will be doing some scans later."

"How's Mary coping?"

They both looked through the glass window to where Mary was sitting next to John's bedside holding his hand.

"She's okay and she is very strong. I think she now accepts that John is finally going to die and there will be no more pain and suffering for him."

"Good," David said quietly. He tapped gently on the window to draw Mary's attention. Her electrifying blue eyes were magnified by the tears inside them. She raised her hand and waved to David and he responded with a gentle caring smile. "It's going to be okay," he said through the glass.

"I don't think she can hear you, David."

"Yes she can, look." Mary nodded and mouthed, "I know, thank you."

"Come on, let us get home. I'm tired and I told Mary that I will relieve her tomorrow morning. She's going to spend the night with him. You don't mind bringing me here before going to work?"

"Of course not."

Ruth tapped on the window to wave goodbye. Mary looked up and blew a kiss to them both then returned her attention to John, gently stroking his hand.

Lucifer awoke to the sound of the front door opening. He had felt drained and lethargic after his experience and had fallen asleep in David's favourite chair.

"Cup of tea anyone? I'm gasping." Ruth was putting her coat on the banister and calling to them both.

"I would love one thanks, dear. Do you want one Luther?"

"Yes, with lots of sugar."

"Two please, darling, and make Luther's very sweet. Is there any chance of having my chair back?" David's question was greeted with an icy stare. "Okay, I'll sit here."

He looked down to the whisky bottle and noticed it had hardly been touched. "Did you not fancy a drink then?"

"No, I have other things on my mind, things of great importance."

"Like what?"

"Things like how to get myself out of a situation I don't want to be in."

"What do you mean? You're not going to leave us are you? We need you here."

"We? What do you mean by 'we'?"

"Me and the brotherhood will assist you with anything, so it might benefit you to stick around."

"Oh yes, your benefit or mine?"

"Yours of course. Anyway, what situation do you need to get yourself out of?"

"It's beyond your comprehension, little man. Besides, it's something only I can do. Not something that you or your brotherhood can help me with. I'll skip the tea. I'm tired so I'll go and have a lie down. When I wake up I'll decide where I have to go and what must be done."

"Okay Luther."

Lucifer got up and headed upstairs. Moments later, Ruth walked into the room.

"Here's your tea. Oh, where's Luther gone?"

"He decided he was tired. He has the weight of the world on his shoulders. I only hope he decides to share that burden. Excuse me darling, I just have to make a quick phone call."

"To who?"

"Jeremiah, he'll know what to do."

"About what?"

"Keeping Luther here of course. What's with all the questions?"

"Nothing dear, I'll drink the tea on my own then, shall I?"

David had already left the room and made his way to the hall where he picked up the phone. "Hello Jeremiah, it's David. I thought I'd better phone you to let you know that Luther is thinking about moving on."

"What! That mustn't happen. It's imperative he stays with us no matter what."

"I know Jeremiah, but I can't physically lock him up in the house can I?"

"No, you can't. I think the best thing to do is when he wakes up, tell him the brotherhood has something to tell him about himself. If he wants to know the truth he has to stay with you until we can arrange a meeting, is that okay?"

"Yes Jeremiah, I only hope he listens."

"So do I. I'll pray he makes the right decision. Goodbye, David."

"Goodbye, Jeremiah. God bless."

David slowly and quietly put the phone receiver down and returned to the living room.

"Is my tea poured, Ruth?"

"Yes it is poured, your royal highness. Come and relax, you've been on your feet all day."

The hours had passed and Mary was still by John's bedside, stroking his hand and gazing at the monitors which were constantly bleeping. She looked at the clock, it was a little after nine. The hospital corridors were finally quiet from the feet and voices of busy doctors and nurses. She released John's hand to stand from her chair and stretch. Slowly, she walked towards the window where she rested her head on the glass and looked out towards the heavens. The stars were shining bright and the moon was resting in its black blanket of sky. Then she noticed one star shining in the east shining brighter than all the other stars. For some reason she was inspired to pray.

"I don't know if you are up there and listening God, but I ask you to please look after my brother in our time of need. I accept the outcome of your decision, but please make it the right one for John. If that means an end to his suffering by death so be it. I just ask that you look after him. Amen."

After she had spoken her prayer aloud, she returned to her brother's bedside and looking down lovingly at him.

"Good night brother, God and I love you and are with you no matter what. Rest now, be at peace."

She sat down again in her chair and rested her head on his bed, then sleepily she closed her eyes to the sound of the bleeps of the heart monitor and the ticking of the clock, which began to get fainter as Mary fell asleep in her own place of peace.

Chapter Fourteen

THE WARMTH OF THE morning sun caressed the back of Mary's head as it shone through the window. She started to stir from her slumber and raised her weary head for a full morning stretch. She felt for a moment like time had stood still. But panic quickly set in as she noticed John's bed was empty and he wasn't lying next to her.

"Oh my God, John where are you?"

"It's all right Mary, I'm fine. I'm over here."

She turned to where the voice was coming from. She shielded her eyes from the bright sunlight emanating from the window and engulfing the man standing in front of it.

"John, is that you?"

"Yes, it is me Mary, your brother John."

"My God," she screamed as she leapt off her chair and ran into his open arms. "But how can this be? Let me look at you."

She turned him away from the sunlight to get a better look at him. She couldn't believe what she was seeing. John's usual grey pallor had totally vanished; his eyes were shining like crystals and so full of life, looking like they did before he became ill.

"I can't believe it! How is this possible?" she asked as she hugged him tighter.

"I told you, Mary that God would take care of me.

It is a miracle, all those dreams and visions I had, they were all true, the ones you so easily dismissed."

"I just thought it might have been the medication you are on making you hallucinate. Besides it might not be a miracle, your cancer could have gone into remission."

"Forever the doubting Thomas, aren't you Mary? Don't you know God and I heard your prayer last night?"

Mary's face went pale. "What prayer?" she asked nervously. John then recited Mary's prayer word for word and even told her where she had been standing.

"I don't believe it," she stammered.

"My dear Mary, believe what you like but look at me, I am a walking miracle, alive and ready to spread the word of God."

"John, I must get a doctor to check you over. Please get back into bed. I'll be back shortly."

She waited until John had got himself comfortable back in his bed and then ran down the corridor to find a doctor.

After a long sleep, Lucifer sat on the end of his bed, staring at the picture of Jesus. He was trying to understand why someone would want to save somebody's life. He couldn't understand the concept of love and someone sacrificing their own life for the sake of others. *Well, you saved people because you wanted to, whereas I saved someone because I was forced to.* He rubbed his arm where the blue light had appeared. As he stood, he looked out of the window. The sun was shining bright and in the garden below, Ruth was sitting in a sun chair lying back absorbing the sun.

"Luther are you awake?" David's voice was accompanied by a knock on the door.

"Well if I wasn't, I am now with you hammering on the door. What do you want anyway?"

"Me and Ruth wanted to know if you would join us in the garden for breakfast before we go to the hospital to see John."

"I'll be down shortly."

"Okay, don't be long. I'll see you downstairs."

Lucifer listened as David's footsteps faded and took another look out the window. He watched David join Ruth and thought to himself, *It's time to make a big decision.*

To Mary, it seemed ages since the doctors had gone in to see John. Nurses were rushing in and out, carrying blood samples off to pathology for examination. Mary wanted to call David and Ruth but the battery on her mobile had died and she didn't have any change for a payphone. Her frantic thoughts were disturbed by the door of John's room opening. A group of three doctors left his room, the last one stopping to talk to her. He wore a puzzled look on his face.

"In all my years as a doctor, I have never witnessed what I have today."

"What do you mean? Is he all right?"

"Mary my dear, he's better than all right. He no longer has cancer. In fact there are no signs that he ever had it at all, apart from the weight loss, but when he puts on weight, I'm sure he'll have a body most men of his age would envy. I really don't understand it. Something like this defies all known laws of medical science."

"What? I don't understand." Mary was now questioning her own beliefs. *Could what John spoke about be true? Was she witnessing a modern day miracle?*

The doctor shrugged, then smiled.

"Can I go in and see him?"

"Yes of course you can. We will be keeping him in for a couple of days just to keep an eye on him."

"Thank you, doctor for everything you have done."

Mary watched as the doctor walked off down the corridor, still shaking his head in disbelief. When she walked in, she saw John sitting upright in his hospital bed, a smile across his face and a twinkle in his eye.

"You certainly know how to shock people don't you

John? That poor doctor, he looks as though he's whole belief in the medical system has just flown right out of the window."

"That's good," John replied.

"Is it, why?"

"Don't you understand, that is my purpose now, to get people believing in another faith besides science, and this is the reason why God sent someone to save me."

"Sorry John, you've lost me. What do you mean? I don't understand."

"Well, if I've shocked that doctor without as much as a word, and challenged his belief system, imagine what I can do if I start preaching to other people about the miracle that has happened to me? I want the world to know that God is good and God is great and merciful. I will tell them that I am that living proof."

"John, I understand that you're excited at what's happened to you, but don't you think you should slow down a little?

"I've spent the last two years in bed with that wretched illness slowing me down. It took my energy and it was destroying my body, Mary my love, but not any more. Soon I'll be out of here and then my pilgrimage can begin."

"Okay, let's just get you one hundred per cent fit again first."

Even though the doctor had told her that John was more than well, Mary couldn't help acting on the assumption she should be caring for and protecting him.

"Breakfast time for the miracle man." A nurse had entered the room with a breakfast tray.

"Miracle man," Mary said with an air of distaste and disapproval. The nurse turned to look at Mary.

"Yes, word spreads very quickly here on the ward and your brother has got everybody talking."

Mary looked at John, who clearly liked what he was hearing.

"You see Mary, it has begun. Already people are

talking about me, now they will listen to what I have to say, won't they nurse?"

The nurse smiled and laid his tray on the bedside table.

"Yes John, I'm sure we'll be hearing a lot more about you. Now is there anything else I can get for you?"

"Thank you, nurse. If you don't mind, my sister wishes to phone our sister Ruth. Unfortunately her mobile is dead and she doesn't have any money."

Mary gasped. "How did you know that?"

John gave a radiant smile. "God now talks to me when I'm awake, so I don't have to be dreaming to hear the voice of the Most High."

The nurse's smile grew bigger.

"I'll bring the ward phone to you as quickly as possible. Praise God for the miracle man."

Mary lifted her eyebrow as the nurse left the room in search of the phone.

"I wish she wouldn't call you that. It makes you sound like some sort of freak. Now tell me John, what's the hurry for me to have the phone?"

"Well, besides informing Ruth and David that I'm well, you have to speak to Luther. God has big plans for you two."

"Right," Mary said suspiciously, "what do you mean by that?"

"All God told me was that you should now speak to Luther on the phone and tell him it's not the right time for decision making It's imperative that Luther listens to you if he wants to gain his freedom. This can only be done after you two have met again."

"What! How can us meeting again gain his freedom?"

"Mary, I am not here to question the Most High. I am just telling you what was told to me. Will you do it? After everything that has been promised to me has come true, is it not evident that God loves me and knows what is right?"

"I guess so, I'm just finding it very hard to understand

why God would take such an interest in my personal life."

"Well my darling sister, there is only one way to find out isn't there?"

Lucifer had joined Ruth and David outside in the morning sun. Ruth was sitting sipping her orange juice and David was struggling with a very flaky croissant.

"So Luther," David said, "will you come with us to the hospital to see Mary and John?"

"I don't know. I have to make a decision of where to go from here. I feel I have to move on because there's nothing for me here now."

David nervously dropped his knife.

"Luther, please you can't go anywhere. You don't have a job and you don't have any money. Where would you go and what would you do?"

"I'm sure I'll find my own way. I always have and always depended on myself."

"Yes, but look where that got you. When I found you, you were waking up alone in a lion's cage." Lucifer looked at him with disapproval. "I'm sorry if I offended you Luther, but where are all your family and friends when you need them the most? From where I'm sitting, it looks like we are all you have right now. Tell him Ruth."

"I'm keeping out of it. I'm more concerned about my brother right now, more than anything in the world."

"What makes you think I need anyone David?" Lucifer retorted. "All my existence I have never needed anyone and I certainly don't now."

"Maybe that's your problem."

"What's that supposed to mean?"

"Tell me, have you ever asked yourself why you don't let people get close to you or why you don't have any friends around you?"

"I don't want people to get close to me. I want

everything and everybody near me destroyed. Nobody will ever get close to me. I would rather see them in hell first."

David's mobile phone started flashing on the breakfast table.

"Excuse me. Hello Mary. How's John?"

Lucifer watched as an astonished look grew on David's face.

"I don't believe it. Hold on, I'll put the phone on speaker so Ruth can hear you too." David pushed a button on his phone and laid it on the table.

"Ruth, are you there?" Mary's voice called out.

"Yes, what's wrong?"

"Nothing, on the contrary I have great news." Mary paused. "It's John, he's made a total recovery. There's no more cancer and the doctors reckon in a couple of weeks he will be fitter than ever."

"What! How can it be, did the doctors tell you why?"

"No, they don't know, they say it defies all medical history and knowledge."

"Hello sis, it's the miracle man."

Lucifer watched Ruth eyes swell with tears as she sat close to the phone.

"Is that really you John? Are you really well and cured?"

David had gone over to his wife and put his arm around her.

"Yep, it's me John, the miracle man."

"Stop it, John," Mary interrupted in a joking tone.

Lucifer took hold of his arm as his heart began to beat fast, sending the same familiar pain around his body while he watched the love and emotion on David's and Ruth's faces. Suddenly, both David and Ruth leapt to their feet and grabbed hold of Lucifer and held him in a warm embrace. The feeling he was experiencing intensified, so much so he could see the blue glow returning around his arm.

"Get off me! Leave me alone."

He pushed them off and watched as they danced around the garden, embracing one another.

"Go on Mary, it's time." They heard John's voice on the other end of the phone.

"I don't know if I should."

The embracing had stopped and now all of them were listening to Mary and John talking.

"Trust me Mary and trust the Most High. You know it is what God wants." Lucifer's full attention was concentrated on the phone. "Okay John, David is Luther there? I need to speak to him."

"Yes Mary, he's sitting here listening to everything."

"Can you give him the phone? I want to speak to him privately."

"Oh, okay." David replied with disappointment at not being allowed to listen. "Tell you what, me and Ruth will go and get ready indoors to come and see you while you talk to Luther. See you soon Mary and John, love you both."

Lucifer watched as Ruth and David ran indoors and closed the door behind them.

"Are they gone?" Mary asked quietly. Lucifer didn't answer, the pain from his heart was still troubling him and the blue aura around his arm was shining even more brightly.

"Try again Mary," John said. "I know he's listening."

"All right, be quiet John. Luther I know you're there. I have a message from John."

"No! Not from me, from God."

"Sorry, I have a message from God given to John. The message is that it is not the right time for a decision. If you truly want to gain the freedom you so desire, you have to meet up with me again. Only then will be the right time for the decision."

Lucifer waited and lowered his head for a while contemplating with suspicion at what Mary had said.

"And me meeting up with you again will grant me my freedom?"

"Yes, that's what God told John."

"Can you explain to me how someone like you could release me and give me my freedom?"

"I don't know! And what do you mean someone like me?"

" I just don't trust what God has to say. I'm very suspicious of why God the Most High would choose you to save me."

"I don't know either, but after seeing all the things that have happened to John, I can't ignore what God is telling him."

"Go on, and the rest," John was again forcing Mary to speak.

"All right I was just about to. Luther, I want to say sorry for being angry with you when you were trying to help John back at the house. Things have been crazy lately and I've been so emotional. Believe me, I don't know what's going on, but John assures me that everything will become clear when we meet."

"I'm sure it will, "Lucifer replied ironically, "Mary, if God's word is spoken to John, prove it. Tell me something I would only know."

"Now, now, Luther. You know you shouldn't test the Lord," said John. "God did tell me to remind you of your name which is being held in a safe place for you until you want and are ready to receive it again."

"My name? How intriguing that you and God think I don't know my own name?" Mary and John could tell Lucifer was mocking them.

"Okay, tell us your name then."

"Very well, it's Lu ... Damn, I can't tell you. God has forbidden me to speak it aloud."

"Luther, it's okay, we believe you and ..."

The lined bleeped as the phone was running out of money. "See you soon, the man with no name," John said with a chuckle.

"Stop it, John. See you soon, Luther."

The phone went dead leaving nothing but silence.

Even the birds in the trees had silenced their song. As he sat in this moment of quiet, Lucifer thought to himself, *How could Mary, a mortal, and the one who causes me so much pain whenever she is around, save me?* He concluded it was another one of God's deceptions to add to his suffering. He wondered if there was no end to the Almighty's wrath against him. David poked his head out of the door.

"All done, Luther?"

"Well, they're no longer on the phone if that's what you mean."

"Okay good," David said as he came outside and switched the phone off. "Are you all right? You look very pale. What did Mary want?"

"I'm fine, and stop fussing. If you ask me another question I swear I will..." He paused before adding, *Tear your heart out.*

"Well, I just have one other question, are you coming to hospital with us to pick Mary up?"

"No, I'll wait here. I have some more thinking to do."

Lucifer could tell what David was about to say. "Don't worry, I'll still be here when you get back. Just don't bring Mary round. I'm not ready for that yet."

"Whatever you say is fine with me. We'll go round to Mary's house and leave you to have some time alone."

"Are you two ready?" Ruth was calling from inside the house.

"Coming darling, see you later, Luther."

"Go! Before I rip your soul out," Lucifer growled.

David nervously laughed and ran into the house to his waiting wife.

"Come on David, I want to go and see my brother. Is Luther not coming?"

"No, I think he wants some time to sulk and be on his own."

"Oh well, let him be on his own. Anyway, did you find out what Mary wanted with him?"

"I don't know, he wouldn't say. But I think it must

have been something very important. He said he didn't want to see Mary right now."

"The sooner we get to see Mary and John, the sooner we can find out from Mary what she said. Now let's go and meet the miracle man."

They left and shut the door behind them.

On his own in the garden, Lucifer sat staring at the ground. He noticed a spider emerge from behind a brick and ran across the ground in front of him. Without thinking, Lucifer raised his size eleven shoe and bought it down on the defenceless spider. For a moment he paused and smiled while twisting his foot side to side to make sure the spider was dead. Lifting his foot, he bent down to look at what was left of the creature. It was a mass of blood amongst black bits of flesh.

"God didn't save you I see. You're just another very small victim of a godforsaken world."

Just as he finished speaking, a blue light surrounded the remains of the spider. Its legs started to move and its body parts started to join together again. Finally the blood rolled back into its body, bringing it back to life. Then it ran off across the garden like nothing had happened.

"Okay Michael, where are you?"

"Hello, Lucifer my brother, I'm afraid it's not Michael, but me Gabriel."

Lucifer looked up and saw Gabriel's angelic face shining above him.

"I thought you knew that God had forbidden you to harm any living thing while you were earthbound?"

"I just had an urge to vent my anger and show that I still have the power to kill. Anyway what are you doing here, where's Michael? Is he too high and mighty now to grant me an audience?"

"He is giving another important message to someone else, someone who is going to play a very important role in your salvation."

"Who?"

"That isn't for you to know right now. I have come to tell you that the message you just received from Mary and John was true. Eventually you will have to meet up with her and the inevitable will come to pass."

"Yes my brother, the inevitable will happen. And when it does I will be glad when you and Michael and his pathetic army will be begging for mercy with my sword at your throats."

"Peace be with you my brother. Before I go, I have to instil some discipline in you for attempting to kill the spider. I must remind you of pain."

He brought down his hand and with his finger he touched Lucifer's wound on the back of his head, immediately causing a vision to rush into Lucifer's mind. He saw himself alone in a desert. Above him was a blood red sky darkened by the shadows of vultures circling their food below; dead and rotting corpses were scattered all over the desert floor. As the vision intensified, the pain in Lucifer's head got worse and he could now see a wall of flames making its way across the dunes of the sand like a wave. As it got closer it got bigger and hotter until it finally engulfed him. In this horrific moment the sound of the fire's roar hurt his ears. The roar eventually turned into the screams of tortured souls causing him to fall to the ground on his knees, covering his ears with his hands. In this moment, he was trying his best to control what was happening to him but the screams just got louder. Then he looked at his hands and the flesh was melting off his bones from the heat of the fire. He cried out and fell to the floor then there was silence. The vision had ceased and there was no sign of Gabriel.

CHAPTER FIFTEEN

THE CLOCK PROVIDED the only sound resonating through the dark room where General Silas lay asleep. In his deep slumber, he wasn't aware of what was happening above his head.

"General, General," a gentle voice spoke from above, "Come on, wake up. It's time."

General Silas eventually opened his eyes to see Michael's face looking down on him.

"What!" he shrieked. "Who … who are you? Get away."

He sat bolt upright and shielded his face with his arms and hands.

"Don't be afraid. I am not here to harm you, do you not recognise me?"

Terrified, he turned to see the face again, peering through the darkness. His eyes widened as he recognised the face before him.

"I remember you, but how can this be? You're the reporter who asked me that question about doing God's work, aren't you? But where's your body? Are you a ghost? I must be going mad."

He shielded his eyes again.

"I will answer your questions, but first you have to look at me."

Shaking with fear, he lowered his arms and looked at the face glowing in the dark.

"Do not be afraid, I am the Archangel Michael. I came to you before in human form because I did not want to frighten you. Now I appear to you in my true form to give you a message from the Most High."

"I don't believe it. I must be dreaming, am I still asleep? Why would God want to give me a message?"

"You are not asleep and this is a very real. The time has come for you to answer your calling and do God's work and prove how much you love the Most High. Do you remember telling me at the news conference that you would do God's work even if it meant the death and destruction of you and your people?"

"Yes, I remember, but I thought I was talking to a reporter not a messenger from God."

"So you are telling me you did not mean it?"

"No ... no, on the contrary if this is real, I will certainly do God's work. It is just that I'm a little confused about what's going on. Why would God choose me?"

"God is very pleased with the devotions you have performed daily. Your prayers and actions have been observed from above. That is the reason why you have been chosen, because God sees what is in the hearts and minds of men, especially yours."

"If God knows what's in my heart and mind, then you must know what I already want."

"Yes, precisely. You see what you want, think and feel are all what God intended you to feel. This was done for you to be able to carry out the great work which is intended for you and mankind."

"Tell me what to do and I will do it without question."

"God is very displeased with the way men have been treating each other. Even though free will was issued to man, God did not expect man to become so full of hate and act in such an evil and violent manner. As men have been given free will, God cannot intervene personally, so it was decided that a mortal would do God's work on earth to act as an avatar of his wrath."

General Silas' body began tingling with excitement at the prospect of doing God's bidding.

"What do I have to do?" he asked eagerly.

"God wants you to instigate a war with the West and cause the inevitable; a nuclear war among nations."

"What! A nuclear war? Are you telling me God wants me to start Armageddon?"

"Exactly. God wants the message to be loud and clear, a message to remind men that the faith and the word of God have been ignored far too long."

"If God sees in my heart, then it is known that I am the right man for the job. I will accept God's mission and I feel very honoured to have been chosen. I myself have also seen what man is doing to man and nothing would satisfy me more than to destroy the disease of mankind in a glorious martyr's death. I will fulfil my destiny and finally sit in the Most High's presence and be rewarded for my work and obedience. Michael, when do I start?"

"Soon Silas. I will visit you on the eve of a great dawn when men will die and be reunited with their one and only true God. Speak of this to no one until I return. God bless you, Silas."

"No God bless you, Michael. And thank God for the great reliance that is placed in me. I will not let the Most High down."

"I know you won't, Silas."

In a flash Michael had disappeared and the General's room was filled with darkness once again. Only the sound of the ticking clock in the distance could be heard. Right, he thought, no time like the present. He got up out of bed and summoned his guard.

"Get me the Captain at once and tell him to meet me in my office immediately"

"Yes, General."

In an instant the guard was off to find and wake the Captain.

Back in London, Ruth and David had arrived at the hospital.

"I can't believe it. Let me look at you." Ruth had

tears in her eyes and was holding John at arm's length, looking him up and down to see his new rejuvenated state. "You look so well and you have that great smile back again."

"It's a miracle John. Welcome back." David held out his hand and firmly shook John's.

"Thanks David, I feel great. Have you heard my new name? I'm being hailed as miracle man."

"Yes, all the nurses were talking about you as we arrived. Quite a celebrity now, aren't we?"

"Great, the more people that know about God's power and love, the easier it makes my job to spread the word of God."

"I also have good news," Mary said, as she entered the room "I spoke to the doctors this morning and they said it's fine for John to return home today. Obviously he will have to come in for more tests, but in the meantime it's safe for him to go home."

"That is great news, Mary," Ruth said as she hugged her sister. "When shall we leave then?"

"There's no time like the present. I think I've got all of mine and John's things together. Let's get out of here."

"What's the hurry?" John interjected, turning to Ruth. "I think she's eager to see Luther."

"No John, I've just seen enough of hospitals to last me a lifetime. Besides you want to start your mission right?"

She pushed John to the door and the rest of them followed.

All four of them left the room and walked into the corridor. They couldn't believe their eyes as they saw that the corridors were lined with nurses, doctors and patients, all pointing at John and whispering to one another. Mary hung her head in embarrassment. David and Ruth just smiled nervously at the people as they walked past. John, however, was smiling and greeting everyone with his head held high.

"Nice to meet you. Yes, I am the miracle man and please don't forget to tell your friends about me."

"Stop it John," Mary was trying to pull John's hand away from greeting any more people.

"Mary, I'm afraid you are going to have to get used to all this attention because this is only the start of it. Just you wait and see."

"I'm sorry John, but I've never liked people staring at me."

"What? From where I'm standing, I'm the one getting all the attention and I'm loving it!" He started shaking more hands and even kissed a nurse as he walked by.

"I give up. Come on Ruth, let's get out of here quick. Maybe then we can get him home and our lives back to some form of normality."

"Okay Mary," Ruth said. "David, you run ahead and get the car started." David kissed her on the cheek and ran off ahead. "Mary, I agree with John, I don't think our lives are going to ever be the same again."

"Enjoy it, Mary. Soon the whole world will be seeing me and they will listen to what I have to tell them about God's work."

They opened the main door of the hospital entrance and were blinded by an array of flashing lights. David was still trying to fight his way through the throngs of media.

"Is it true you were cured of cancer in one day?" asked one reporter.

"Why do they call you the miracle man?" asked another.

"Is this a sign from God?"

The reporters were firing their questions at John who just smiling while holding his head high and bathing in his newfound fame.

"How could all of this have happened?" Mary shouted to her sister above the chaos and noise.

"Well I suppose one of the doctors or nurses must have contacted the press."

"Come on John, let's get out of here!"

Mary and Ruth wrapped their arms around him and started to pull him through the gathering. To their relief, the crowd started to separate as David sounded his car horn and drove towards them.

"Hurry up and get in."

David stopped the car and opened the doors. Mary scrambled across the back seat, Ruth got in the front and John reluctantly got in next to Mary on the back seat.

"Get out of the way!" David shouted to the reporters in front of the car whilst sounding his horn again.

"Wow, look at them all. God's word will be around the world sooner than I thought."

"At last." David was relieved to see an opening which allowed him to put his foot on the accelerator. John had turned to look out of the back window where he noticed a reporter writing something on his pad. He looked at John and smiled.

"Yes, I will be seeing you soon too my friend," John murmured.

"What was that John?" Mary asked puzzled.

"Nothing Mary, just thinking out loud." He rested his head on the car window and looked out to the sun, then took him a deep breath and smiled. "Wake me up please Mary when we get home." Then he gently closed his eyes.

General Silas' captain was making sure his uniform was correctly ironed, his buttons were shining and his beret was positioned correctly before knocking on the door. He was wondering what was so important for him to be summoned at such a late hour. Had he done something wrong? *Well there is only one way to find out,* he thought.

Feeling satisfied everything was in order, he nervously knocked on the huge door in front of him. There was a brief silence, then he heard the general call. "Enter." The captain opened the door to find the General pacing his chambers with a strange transported expression on his face.

"Come in Captain, thank you for coming so promptly. I have some important news. Would you like a drink? Please sit down."

"Thank you," the Captain took hold of the glass of whisky the General offered as he sat down.

"I have summoned you here to ask something of you, something which will test your character, obedience and fidelity to me and our beloved country."

"My General, you know that I am totally faithful and will do anything you ask of me."

"Good, that's what I thought. So I can take it that you're with me when I tell you that we are going to start a nuclear war."

The Captain stopped drinking his whisky and looked at the general who sat stony faced behind his desk.

"Excuse me General, did you say a nuclear war?"

"Yes I did, the war of all wars." The captain rested his glass on the General's desk and nervously prepared himself to ask his next question.

"Forgive my reasoning General, but why?"

The general gazed at his second in command, observing the puzzled look on his face.

"Before I will tell you why, I need to know that when the time comes you will push that button with me no matter what."

"General, you know I will. You are like a father to me and took me under your wing when my whole family were killed in that bomb blast. Can I ask you something, General? Would this mean my own death?"

"It might do, that I can't answer for sure. All I can say is that we have to play an important part in what God wants."

"What do you mean?"

"Do you believe in God? I mean do you really believe in God with all your heart and soul?"

"Well no not much since my whole family were wiped out, so if there is a God I don't see this God as a loving one."

"I understand you fully my friend but ask yourself this, what if everything happens for a reason? No matter how painful that reason might be at the time."

"I'm sorry General, but I'm not sure I follow."

"Well, let's take the example of your family. They were all killed and taken away from you. Why? I will tell you why this happened. So you could be here now with me and be my second-in-command, the only one I can trust to launch the missiles with me."

"But why would God be so sadistic? What reason would God have to ask you to wipe out the entire human race?"

"I will tell you something now and it is imperative you believe everything I say. I would hate you to think of me as a madman. Can I be assured you will not think that way of me?"

"Of course not, General."

"Today, you my friend, you can call me Silas not General, okay? Do you remember the other day when I was giving the news conference and you thought I was talking to myself?"

"Yes, I remember trying to prompt you and asked you if you were all right."

"That's it, well I was talking to someone. I don't know if it was a vision or if he was really there, but I was asked if I would do God's work even if it meant forsaking my own life."

"Who asked you Silas? Me and your bodyguards did not see anyone."

The General paused for a second while looking at the young man in front of him and wondered if he would accept what he was about to tell him.

"It was the Archangel Michael." Again he paused, but the Captain sat calmly and focused on his every word and his eyes widened as he listened to Silas' story. "Michael told me that God is very displeased with the human race, especially the way we are all killing, robbing, raping and destroying the very home that was made for us. God wants mankind to be taught a lesson and through me, a mortal with free will. God's lessons will be learnt as I reveal God's judgement on earth. God also instructed Michael to tell me that God sees what's in my heart and my actions have been observed from above. This is the reason why I have been chosen. Do you see now what I meant when I said about everything happening for a reason?"

The General stopped speaking as he noticed the Captain's eyes beginning to fill with tears. "What's the matter my friend?"

"It is just all these years I have hated God for what was done to me and my family, but if what you are saying is true, then I feel very humbled that I, along with you, have been chosen for such a task."

"Come here, my friend." The general removed himself from behind a desk and held his arms open. At once the Captain was on his feet and in his arms, sobbing. "That's it, let it out. Now you see why you should feel honoured that your family were sacrificed in order for you to be driven into my arms and be by my side at the end of time. Then if we die we will be remembered for eternity and reunited with our loved ones in Paradise."

"Forgive me Silas for my reaction, but I have built up so much hate and resentment in my heart all these years. I have forgotten to feel anything but somehow what you are saying feels right and makes perfect sense. It is true that I have missed my family so very much that I would do anything to be reunited with them."

"That's what I thought. Now dry your eyes soldier, have another glass of whisky and let us talk some more."

"Thank you," the Captain said and took hold of another glass of whisky from the general. "When do we begin?"

"That, I don't know. Michael told me that he would visit me again on the eve of a new dawn, so for now let us raise our glasses and drink a toast to God, sacrificed families, our friendship and, most important all, the destiny of mankind and our part in it."

Chapter Sixteen

Ruth and David had arrived back home after dropping off Mary and John at their house. David turned off the engine and put his head in his hands.

"What's the matter, darling?"

"I just have a headache. Mind you, it has been a crazy day."

"Yes, it has been unusual, but I'm happy John's physical health is better. However, I'm not sure about his mental health."

"What do you mean?"

"Well, all this talk about doing God's work and sounding like some kind of prophet. I could understand it when he was on all of his medication for the pain, but now without the drugs he is starting to sound more and more like a madman."

"I see what you mean." He rubbed his forehead again.

"Come on, let us get you inside. I think I have some painkillers in the kitchen cabinet."

"Yes, I want to see if Luther is still about. I must not let the brotherhood down."

Ruth raised her eyebrows at his constant worrying as they headed for the front door.

Lucifer heard the front door opening from where he was lying on the couch in the living room.

"Luther are you here?" David called out as he opened the living room door.

"Do you know you are worse than a wife? Always wanting to know where I am."

"I'm sorry, it's just that I promised –"

"Yes I know," Lucifer interrupted, "the brotherhood how could I forget?"

"Anyway, I forgot to tell you that I spoke with Jeremiah yesterday. After you had retired for bed, he told me that if you want to know the truth about yourself, you must meet up with him and three other important brothers. They have something to show you."

"What do they have to show me? What could be of such importance?" *What do these people think they know about me?*

"I'm sworn to secrecy, but you'll know when you see them and when they show you the very thing they possess, your eyes will be opened."

"I'm starting to get a little tired and angry at all of this nonsense. First of all I have to meet with Mary where I will allegedly rediscover my true name. Now I have to meet up with your irritating friends to find out who I am. Don't you think I know already?"

"Well okay, tell us your name and who you are." Ruth had walked into the room, Lucifer glared at her angrily. "Come on tell us, after all we know nothing about you."

"Stop it Ruth," David was getting a little concerned at Lucifer's growing anger.

"You see, he can't answer."

"Why you impertinent human, if I were my true self I would ..."

He stopped in mid-sentence as he saw the blue light energy around his arm.

"What is it Luther, what's the matter?"

"Can't you see the light around my arm? Here look."

He held out his arm to show them.

"There's nothing there," Ruth replied. "I'm going to

have a bath. I'll leave you and Luther to discuss his little drama."

"Ruth! I won't tell you again. Go and have your bath and get me some tablets and leave us alone."

"You don't have to be so rude David," she snapped angrily. "I'm not your servant. Just call me when things are back to normal."

She left the room and headed upstairs. With Ruth out of the room, Lucifer started to calm down and the blue light quickly faded.

"David, I must go to the zoo again. I want and need to see my friend, the lion. He is the only one who truly understands me."

"What! Why on earth would you want to do that?"

"I need to feel a connection again. If you want me to stay around to meet your brotherhood, I suggest you take me there straightaway."

"Okay, give me ten minutes. I just have to change my clothes and tell Ruth where we're going."

Lucifer watched as David left the room and rubbed his arm. He knew Ruth was right, because he couldn't speak his name out loud – God had made sure of that – but going to see the lion felt so right because the lion already knew his name.

Upstairs, David knocked on the bathroom door.

"Ruth my darling, can I come in?"

"Certainly dear, it's open."

A smile made its way across her face. Was he wanting some passion? She lifted the top half of her body out of the water to reveal her shining soapy breasts.

"Do we have any painkillers in this cabinet? My headache is getting worse and now Luther wants me to take him to the zoo."

"What! Whatever for?"

"Don't ask, he's very complicated." He bent down to the bathroom sink to drink some water from the tap and swallow his tablets. "Hopefully, we won't be long. I'm just going to get changed."

"You're sure there is nothing I can do to make you want to stay?" She ran her finger between her breasts in a seductive manner.

"I would love to stay, but ..."

"I know, the brotherhood. I tell you when Luther is out of our lives, you're going to make up for lost time, you understand?"

"I will my love, see you later, darling." He bent down and kissed her moist forehead as she slowly let her head go underwater.

Outside, John sat in the garden on an old wooden chair. His eyes were closed and his face was looking towards the sun. He was gently breathing in the warm air and relaxing in the heat.

"Can I get you anything?" Mary called from the open kitchen window as she stood washing the dishes.

"No thank you and please stop fussing. If I wanted something I'm now quite capable of getting it myself. So forget the dishes and join me outside, I have something to tell you."

"Okay, I'm coming."

John got out of his chair and pulled another out of the garden shed for his sister to sit on.

"What is it, John?"

"You know I've already told you about God talking to me when I was asleep? Well now God talks to me even when I am awake. On the way home from the hospital, God told me that I would soon be on television with an important message to tell the world."

"What's the message?"

"God would not tell me. All I was told was that when a man comes calling I should accept his offer and when the time is right, I will know what to say."

Their conversation was interrupted by the front door bell ringing.

"Who can that be?" Mary said. "If that's more photographers, I'll call the police and have them arrested."

She angrily walked back indoors and as she did a smile made its way across John's face. He knew who had come knocking on their door.

Back at David's house David was collecting his keys off the kitchen table

"Are you ready Luther?"

"Of course I am. You took your time, come on let's go. I have to get out of here."

"Okay, I've got my keys. Now do I need anything else?"

"No! You have everything," Lucifer had opened the front door and was pushing David outside.

"So how long are we going to stay at the zoo?"

"I just need you to show me the way, then I want to be on my own."

"But I told Jeremiah that I would keep an eye on you."

"David, I am going to the zoo and nowhere else. I am willing to meet up with Jeremiah and his three peers just to satisfy my natural curiosity, but for now I just want to be left alone."

"Okay it's only a twenty minute walk or I can drive you there in five minutes."

"Drive, the sooner the better."

"Okay come on, get in then." David opened the car door for Lucifer and ushered him in."

"You're lucky I know the manager of the zoo. He belongs to our fraternity and I'm sure he'll let you in for free, but you'll have to wait until the zoo closes in a couple of hours, then you can meet up with the lion."

"All right, but please tell me – when we get there, you will leave me alone, yes?"

"Yes Luther, if that's what you really want."

"Yes it is."

Mary angrily opened the door to tell any photographer where to go, instead she found a smartly dressed man with no camera. He was wearing a smart grey suit and shiny shoes. His clean shaven face gave way to a warm friendly smile lighting up his brown eyes.

"Hello, am I at the miracle man's residence?"

"I don't know what you're talking about. Now can you please go away, I'm busy." Mary tried to close the door.

"It will only take up ten minutes of your and your brother's time." He put his foot in a doorway.

"Excuse me, if you don't move your foot I'll be forced to call the police."

"It's okay Mary, let him in." She hadn't noticed John behind her.

Mary spun round to face her brother.

"Why? We don't even know this man or what he wants. I bet he's here to tell lies about you."

"This man is different, aren't you?" The reporter nodded even though he didn't know what John was talking about. "Please come in, it's all right Mary, let him in."

She stood aside at her brother's request, then closed the door behind them.

"How did you know how to find us?" Mary asked.

"I was at the hospital earlier when your brother was released. I took down the car registration number of the car you left in. It only took one quick phone call to a friend of mine in the police force to get the address. Unfortunately, it wasn't the right address, that belongs to your sister Ruth, I believe."

"How do you know my sister's name? You certainly know a lot about us."

"Well, when I knocked on the door there was no answer. That is when a neighbour came out of her house to ask me what I wanted. After explaining myself she informed me that the house belonged to David and Ruth, and I could find John and Mary living at this address."

"Friends in the police giving out personal information? I should report you and your friend to your superiors."

"Calm down Mary," John interrupted, and gently put his hand on Mary's shoulder to reassure her, "Don't you remember what I was just telling you in the garden?

When a man comes calling, we should meet with that man."

The reporter looked at John in a curious manner then looked at Mary to see if this was some kind of joke.

"Don't you look at me," Mary snapped. "I just wish you people would leave us alone."

She pushed past them both and stormed into the kitchen.

"She'll be okay. I'll get her to make us a cup of tea when she's calmed down. Now tell me what you must."

"I'm a news reporter for Global News. After another tipoff from a friend working in your hospital about the miracle man, I rushed to the hospital to find you. Unfortunately, more of the media had also heard about you and the miracle cure. I've contacted my boss and she's given me permission to grant you an exclusive interview to a global audience tomorrow night in a prime time slot. So my friend, how does that sound?"

John could hardly keep himself from jumping up and down with excitement, but struggled to regain his composure.

"What would the interview entail? What would I be asked and what am I allowed to talk about?"

"Easy tiger, one question at a time. Before that, you need to understand if you agree to do the interview you'll have to sign this document to say that you won't be interviewed by anyone else. You won't speak to anybody else regarding this matter until tomorrow night."

"Of course," John said, feeling himself tingling all over with excitement.

"Naturally there will be a large amount of money in it for you. My boss has agreed to pay you £250,000 for exclusivity."

"The money is immaterial to me, but I'll give it to my sister Mary."

"That's your choice, but can I safely say we have an agreement?"

"Yes my friend, I think we do."

John took the pen from the reporter's hand and neatly signed the contract on the table in front of him.

"Well, that's the formalities out of the way. Did I hear you mention tea earlier?"

"Oh yes of course, Mary!"

Mary reluctantly appeared in the doorway.

"Yes John, you called," she said sardonically while giving a sideward disapproving glance to the reporter.

"My dear sister, I was wondering if you could make me and my new friend here some tea please, then join us we have something to celebrate."

"Celebrate?"

She noticed the smug look on the reporter's face and was holding the newly signed agreement in front of him.

"What's that, John? What have you done?" Mary said, alarmed.

"I've been given the chance to put mine and God's message out to the whole world. This young men here works for Global News. They're setting up an interview with me which will be aired tomorrow night. What do you think of that then?"

Mary gave a look of horrified despair. "I don't think you should let our privacy, or what is left of it, disappear even further."

"Exactly! Don't you see that is what God and I want?"

"Precisely," the reporter started to speak, "John will not only become globally famous overnight, you will become considerably richer as well."

"Mary, they offered me £250,000 for exclusivity, but I said I would rather you had the money to make up for all those years you spent caring for me."

"John! I did it out of love, not money. All the money in the world couldn't pay me for the time I cared for you."

"But think what you could do with all that money," the reporter interrupted.

"And you can shut up," Mary angrily snapped.

"Mary! Don't speak to a guest in that manner. This is so unlike you," John turned to the reporter. "I'm sorry but would you mind waiting in the kitchen for five minutes to give us some time alone?"

"Not at all, just give me a shout when you've finished. I'll help myself to some biscuits."

They both watched him walk out the door and head for the kitchen.

"Argghh! That man. John, forgive me, it's just that I am so used to it being me and you alone in this house. I'm having a hard time in sharing you with other people, if not the whole world."

"I know it feels strange to you, but it does to me too. You know how much I love and respect you. I also respect your wishes. However, I am doing this interview tomorrow evening, no matter what anybody says. Take the money and give it to some charity if you wish, maybe cancer research. Don't you see that this man is giving me the opportunity to spread the word of God to a worldwide audience? It's imperative they hear God's message through me."

"I understand that John, it's just that everything is happening really quickly. I feel like my feet haven't touched the ground since yesterday."

"That's another reason why I have to do the interview tomorrow."

"What do you mean?"

"Well, like you just said, things are happening very quickly, not just with us but on a global scale. Politicians are making decisions with some urgency, almost as if they're in a panic. And people, including you, are always remarking about a year seeming like a day."

"Yes, I'm always complaining I don't have enough time."

"Exactly. There's a reason for this. Mankind's consciousness is being quickened to prepare them for what is to come, and when it does come it will alter the way mankind thinks forever."

Slightly fearful Mary asked, "What is coming, John?"

"I do not know yet. All I know is that it's coming very

soon: an event that is going to change mankind for ever. God has told me that I will know more tonight."

"Okay, I guess we'll know more in the morning. But if you don't mind, I'm going to have a shower. You can deal with our unwanted guest. I will see you in a little while, darling."

She bent forward, kissed her brother on the forehead and went upstairs.

John returned to the reporter in the kitchen.

"It's okay, my sister's gone upstairs. Now let's discuss the final details."

The reporter followed John back into the living room and sat down.

"Well, I'll be carrying out the interview with you myself. We'll give you structured questions that you will be asked about two hours before you go out live. This will give you time to prepare your answers. We expect you there about five o'clock, is that all right?"

"Yes, that's fine."

"Here's my card, you can get me on my mobile any time, even through the night if you have any questions."

"I do have one question now if you don't mind. After I've answered all your questions during the interview, will I get five minutes of my own to address the world about something?"

"What sort of something?" the reporter asked cautiously.

"I don't actually know yet. All I know is that I have a message from mankind that has to be heard."

"A message about what?"

"That also I don't know because God hasn't told me the whole story. I'll probably know more in the morning."

"God, you say?" the reporter asked, startled.

"Yes, how else do you think I was healed?"

"What a great angle. Not only were you cured by God, but God also talks to you. Of course you can have your five minutes, John. It would be good for you to put your side of the story forward, the public will love it."

John's face slightly sorrowed as he spoke gently and with regret. "I'm not so sure that the message will be something they will like."

"Great, this just gets better. Listen, I have to get back to headquarters to sort a few things out with my boss."

"Okay, thank you."

"No, not at all John, the pleasure has all been mine. Thanks again for agreeing to do the interview with us."

"It is what God wants and who am I to disagree with the power of the Most High?"

"I'll see you tomorrow night and remember, not a word to anyone. Especially any other reporters."

"I promise," John said and held out his hand for a firm handshake. "Goodbye. I am sorry, I don't know your name."

"It's Andrew."

"See you tomorrow then, Andrew."

John watched Andrew walked down the garden path before closing the door. Andrew seemed a genuine and sincere person to him. The perfect person in the perfect place to create a perfect situation tomorrow night.

Chapter Seventeen

Lucifer paced back and forth at the zoo's entrance as he watched David talking to his friend from the brotherhood. Security guards were ushering people out of the exit doors as the zoo closed. In the distance Lucifer could hear the roar of the lion, which made him even more impatient.

"Excuse me sir, if you don't mind we are closing." Lucifer turned to see one of the security guards directing him towards the exit gates, "Please, sir."

"It's okay Eric. He's with us." The zoo manager and David had joined them.

"Oh, okay sir. I think that's everybody. I'll make a final sweep of the grounds then I'll lock up."

"After you've done that," the zoo manager said, "bring the keys to me because I have to return later on."

"Isn't this a little unusual sir? We've never done this before. May I ask why?"

"You can, but I won't answer. It's a private matter between friends. I'll return the keys to you later on tonight so you can open up in the morning."

"Very good sir, as you wish. I'll see you later tonight."

"Goodbye Eric."

Lucifer was pleased to see the back of the interfering security guard. "I thought he'd never leave."

"Luther, it's a pleasure to see you again. I hope

you enjoyed the ceremony the other night, although the food wasn't up to much was it?"

Lucifer just looked at the zoo manager with contempt.

"Well, okay," the zoo manager continued awkwardly, "David tells me that you want to spend some time with Samson."

Lucifer gave David a puzzled look.

"That's the name of the lion whose cage you shared when I first saw you." David reminded Lucifer,

"Oh right, can we go now?"

Lucifer was looking over his shoulder towards the lion's cage.

"Robert has agreed to leave you here for as long as you wish. He will wait over there in his office. When you've finished, just knock on the door and he'll let you in. He'll then phone me so I know when to come and pick you up."

"Fine, fine. I just want to go to the lion now!"

"Come on Luther I'll take you to see Samson again ..."

Before he had chance to finish what he was saying, Lucifer was running towards the lions.

Lucifer could feel his heart beating faster as he got closer and closer to where the lion was resting. The anticipation of seeing the graceful beast again was almost too much for him to bear. It grew stronger as Samson let out a deep roar as he approached. It wasn't long before Lucifer had climbed the safety fence and was crouching down in front of the lion's cage, nose to nose with the noble beast. The lion was intently staring at him through the wide cage.

"Hello again."

Lucifer blew air into the lion's nostrils, and the lion breathed it in. He then let out an almighty roar that moved the hair on Lucifer's head and sent a shiver down his spine.

"Where is that damn zoo manager?"

He put his fingers in the cage to stroke the fur of the

beast. The lion looked over Lucifer's shoulder cautiously watching the zoo keeper approaching.

"At last, I thought you'd never get here."

Robert was very nervous at seeing Lucifer so close to the lion.

"David told me and the brotherhood about how he first saw you in this cage. I must say some of us doubted the validity of his story, but now seeing you with Samson, it utterly inspires me. He is usually very bad-tempered and aggressive. It makes a change to see him so calm."

Robert had spoken too soon, as at that moment Samson pinned his ears back and threw himself growling at the cage.

"I don't think he likes you," Lucifer said with a smile as Robert got closer.

"Are you sure you want to go in there?"

"Yes, I am sure and once I'm in there. I think it would be best if you left as soon as possible. Samson and I want privacy."

"Okay, follow me."

Samson was angrily watching Robert's every move. Clearly he did not appreciate Robert's intrusion and wanted him to leave immediately.

"Here we are."

They both stopped at a large green padlocked iron door.

"Before you go in Luther, I just want to tell you that I am honoured to be in your presence, whether or not you're the one the prophecy talks about."

Lucifer's heart was nearly beating out of his chest as he waited for Robert to unbolt the door and let him in – he didn't have time to listen to niceties. Robert unbolted the door and let Lucifer in, quickly closing the door behind him.

"Mary?"

"Yes John, my dear, I'm in the kitchen."

John opened the kitchen door to see his sister preparing some sandwiches. "I'm really looking forward to my television interview tomorrow night. This talk show is one of the world's most watched. Now God's message will soon be beaming into millions of households."

"Are you sure you know what you're doing?"

"Mary, do you still not believe in God's word?"

"You know I do. There has been so much evidence to renew my faith in God, but it's you I'm worrying about." Mary handed him a plate of assorted sandwiches.

"Why do you worry about me?"

"It just seems like you're being used and being told what to do rather than thinking for yourself. Imagine what would happen if tomorrow night you are asked to give some evidence of your special relationship with God and nothing happens. The whole world would think of you as a fraud – or worse a fool."

"I thought you said you had a renewed faith."

"I do, it's just that I am so used to seeing you so vulnerable. I accept I have to let go of that over caring side of me."

"Never! You must never lose that side of you. It's what makes you so special and why I love you so much. More importantly that side of you is the very thing that is going to help Luther."

"What do you mean John?"

John's face suddenly went blank and emotionless; his eyes were fixed on one spot and his pupils dilated.

"John!" Mary cried out while shaking him.

His head just rolled back and forth as she clumsily tried to find his pulse in his neck. To her surprise there was a perfect rhythmic beat and she could hear him breathing. It was like he was in a trance. She rushed into the corridor to phone for an ambulance, but as she was dialling the number John let out an enormous cry.

"Mary!"

Dropping the phone receiver she rushed back into the kitchen to find John slumped on the table. His head was buried in his arms and he was sobbing.

"John, I'm here. Are you all right?"

"I am, Mary."

He lifted his head to look at his sister. Mary took a step back on hearing a strange voice that was not John's. He now had a completely different face. His usual brown eyes had now turned blue and his facial skin was glowing with a golden aura lighting up like the sun. Terrified, Mary struggled to speak.

"It is all right Mary, don't be afraid," a deep resonating voice sounded from John's lips.

"Who, who are you? What have you done with John?"

"He is fine, his soul has been temporarily taken over by me."

"Taken over by who? What have you done with John?" Mary was now full of panic almost to the point of fainting.

"Mary!" The voice had now become authoritative. Mary looked deep into the blue eyes, and at once she began to feel serene and calm.

"Sit down Mary, I have something to tell you."

"Who are you?"

"I am a messenger from God, my name or identity is of little importance to you."

"Is this really happening?"

She turned her head side to side, looking at the strange face that had imposed itself on her brother. It was like she was in a hypnotic trance herself.

"Yes Mary, it is really happening. Your brother has a very important message for mankind which he will reveal tomorrow night, a message sanctioned from the Most High, this message when revealed to all mankind will tell of a great event that will change the way man thinks forever."

"Why are you telling me this?"

"Because you have a very important part to play in preparing the one for what is to come."

"The one, who is that?"

"Mary, do you still not know what I'm talking about? Have you not felt love for the first time in your life over the last couple of days?"

Mary looked down to the floor trying to hide her embarrassment, then she looked back up with her eyes wide. "Yes, I know, Luther."

"Yes, God has spoken to John before and told him to tell you that when you and Luther meet he might find love again."

"Yes I remember. But Luther is very arrogant and I thought I couldn't possibly help him. Who is Luther anyway, and why is he so important?"

"Only I and the Most High know Luther's true identity and hopefully soon he will too. Luther still has a great deal to learn. That is why God has sent me to instruct you what to do."

"Instruct me? I thought I just had to meet up with him and he would remember."

"It is not that simple. What is demanded of you takes great courage and faith, but remember this is bestowed upon you from the Most High with infinite love."

"What is demanded of me?"

"First let me explain, Luther is lost and has been for thousands of years. His anguish, hate and envy have kept him from remembering and feeling love again. He cannot discover this for himself. He needs to be shown an example of love in its purest form. That example is you."

"Me an example of love? I'm just a woman who hasn't known a man yet."

"Precisely, and that is what the Most High had planned for you. You needed to be untouched, pure and unsullied. Only then you could be a perfect example demonstrating that love for Luther."

"And just how am I supposed to demonstrate this love?" Mary's cheeks had now flushed a vibrant pink in anticipation of an answer.

"You must go now to meet Luther. You will find him at the zoo. There you will find the zoo manager in his office. He will let you in and tell you where Luther is."

"What if he doesn't let me in?"

"Trust me, he will."

"What do I do when I meet up with Luther?"

"That, my child is up to you. A choice has to be made and all I can tell you is that you must search your heart for courage and faith. Look for that truth which has been buried since time begun. Then and only then will you know what to do. If you fail, all mankind will fail. The Most High and angels will weep at the end of time and the end of the human race."

"If I fail? I don't understand."

"If your faith and courage fail you, we are all lost. Good luck, Mary. I am sure the trust the Most High has placed in you will not be unwarranted. Go and fulfil your destiny. We will pray for your life."

"My life? What do you mean? Where are you going?"

The light around John's face started to disappear; the blue colour was leaving his eyes returning them to their natural state.

"Wait!" Mary shouted but it was too late, the angel had disappeared. John began to cough as he regained his own consciousness.

"John are you all right?"

"I'm okay, can I have some water? My throat feels like sandpaper and my head is pounding."

"Of course, wait there while I get you some."

She went to the kitchen sink and poured John a glass of water then rejoined him at the table.

"What?"

Mary was staring at John's face intently.

"Do you not know or remember what happened to you a few minutes ago?"

"What are you talking about? The last thing I remember was that we were talking about you helping Luther, then my mouth and throat went dry. That's why I asked you for some water."

"You stopped talking to me ten minutes ago when you were taken over by an angel. The angel told me I had to go and meet with Luther now."

John's mouth fell open.

"Are you really telling me I was taken over by an angel?"

"Yes your eyes turned blue, you had a different voice and your face was shining like the sun."

"Wow, that's amazing. I feel so honoured to have been chosen and used in this way. Tell me, what did the angel say?"

"He told me that I should meet up with Luther now at the zoo and be an example of true love in its purest form. I have to find my faith and courage because the destiny of mankind shall be decided by my choice."

"Did the angel tell you his name? Did he tell you anything else?"

"Stop all the questions. He didn't tell me his name, but he did tell me that your message to mankind tomorrow night is of great significance."

Mary sat back as John leapt to his feet and started dancing around the kitchen like a child who had just received the best news ever. He leant forward and grabbed his sister by the hands and pulled her up to dance with him.

"John stop it, please. The angel said that he would pray for my life."

In an instant John stopped dancing around and looked deep into his sister's eyes.

"What! Are you telling me the angel said you were going to die?"

"No, but any fool can guess if someone tells you that they will pray for your life, it suggests there is a chance you could die."

"Mary, I more than anyone else, do not want that to happen. So if you decide not to go through with it, I understand"

"It's not as simple as that. If I don't go through with it, it won't just be me that fails. The entire human race will fail. Anyway, the angel might have been metaphorically speaking about the salvation of my soul and not the death of my physical body."

"That's the spirit Mary. That's what the world needs, more people with positive thinking. So what are you going to do?"

"Well I believe there's a man waiting for me to show myself in my purest form, no matter what the cost. Now where's my coat?"

Lucifer had sat face-to-face with the lion in the cage for ages. They were both intently looking at one another; the large golden eyes of the lion stared curiously at Lucifer. To Lucifer, it seemed as if the lion wanted him to talk about his problems and worries.

"I wish you could talk, Samson. Maybe you could tell me how to get out of this mess I have found myself in."

The lion lowered his head and rubbed it against Lucifer's head.

"My only desire is to return to angelic form and be myself again, Lucifer the Almighty." Lucifer was momentarily confused because here in the presence of the lion he was able to say his name again.

"It looks like you are the only one who is allowed to hear my true name."

The lion let out a little growl, acknowledging Lucifer's statement, then he laid his massive body down flat on the straw. Lucifer noticed he was using his old black coat as a pillow.

"I see you have kept it safe, my friend. I think I will rest here with you for a while."

He lay on his back and positioned his head on the stomach of the beast. He looked up at the darkening sky and shut his eyes.

Mary arrived at the entrance of the zoo to find everything locked up for the evening. Maybe she had arrived at the wrong time? Or worse still, she was not meant to be there at all. Her faith was slipping again. Just as she was about to turn away, a voice sounded from behind.

"Can I help you, miss?"

She turned back to see the zoo manager looking at her through the holes of the fence.

"Yes I hope so. This is going to seem a very unusual request, but first tell me is Luther here?"

The manager looked at her suspiciously.

"Who are you?"

"I'm Mary, David's sister-in-law. I was told that Luther would be here."

"Of course. I remember seeing your face briefly after the meeting the other evening. Please come in. What was your unusual request?"

"I have to meet up with Luther, wherever he is."

"That might be a little bit difficult at present."

"Why is that?"

"He is with Samson. Maybe you should wait with me until he is finished."

"Samson, who is Samson?"

"Only the fiercest and biggest lion we have here."

Mary's eyes widened with awe.

"And Luther is safe with him?"

"When I was walking away from them both, Luther had his arms around Samson in a warm embrace around his neck. I've never seen anything like it before."

"Do you think you could take me there? I would love to see such a sight."

"No I don't think –"

The manager stopped in mid-sentence; his arms dropped by his side and his eyes went blank staring at nothing.

"Are you all right?"

After a long silence, he spoke in a zombie-like voice.

"Here is the key to the lion's cage. I will wait for your return in my office."

Mary took the key from the manager. Shaking her head, she thought that after what had happened with her brother, anything was possible.

"You will find Samson's cage in the big cat area. Follow that path until you get to the feline enclosure, Samson's cage is the last one on the right." He turned and walked off to his office closing the door behind him.

The lights illuminating the path up as Mary began walking. It wasn't long before she had reached the signpost for the big cat area. She held the key tightly in her hand and nervously began walking to the right.

Back at the cage, Samson's head shot up, his eyes wide with alertness, as she approached. He sprang to his feet, sending Lucifer sprawling across the floor in front of him.

"What's the matter with you?" Luther asked, anxiously.

Samson was frantically placing the length of his cage and roaring, then all of a sudden Lucifer felt that all too familiar feeling coming from his heart. Someone was approaching and he knew who it was.

Mary's heart was also beating fast as she heard the roars getting louder and closer. She could now see the lion walking side to side in its cage, and as she got closer she could see a silhouette of a man in the cage watching her. The lion now looked aggressive. His ears were pinned back and he was watching her every move.

"What do you want?" Lucifer asked with contempt.

"I have –"

She stopped talking as the lion threw itself at the fence with an almighty roar. She thought she was going to faint. After a while she managed to compose herself and waited for the lion to become quiet.

"I have come to meet with you. Remember we spoke on the phone and I said that we have to meet again and then you will know love."

Samson roared again, foam was coming from his mouth and his claws revealed themselves as he swiped at the fence.

"Yes, and I distinctly remember asking, how could someone like you show me love?"

"I don't know, but I was just told by an angel speaking

through my brother John that I must come here and meet with you in a test of faith and courage. Then and only then would you understand."

"You say an angel? Did the angel tell you his name?"

"No, he said that was of little importance, but he did have the most beautiful blue eyes."

Lucifer groaned.

"Michael, still the puppet of the Most High. So Mary, what is this test of faith and courage you have to perform?"

When Samson had stopped roaring again, she looked into the lion's eyes who stared intently and aggressively back at her. She almost fainted again at the thought of what she was about to say and do.

"Well, I have been given a key to this lion's cage. I guess I have to join you in there." Samson seemed to give her a look of defiance, as if to say *Just you dare.*

"Are you crazy? He'd rip you to bits in seconds. Look at him. Only I am allowed the privilege of being here in his company. But if you're crazy enough to believe a deceitful Michael and his lies, be my guest. But I won't save you."

She could hear her heart pounding in her ears as her whole body shook with fear and as she struggled to speak, Samson let out another roar. For an instant she thought about running away as far as possible, then she remembered seeing Michael's eyes earlier.

"All I know is that God cured my brother from a dreadful illness and the evidence I have seen up to this point has renewed my faith and taught me everything is possible. Now I am willing to blow my world of doubt apart and see truth again."

Mary could see the metal door vibrating from the intensity of Samson's roars. She put the key in to its hole and closed her eyes. Then with a deep breath, she turned the key. Before pushing the gate open, she said a little prayer in her head: *God all that I am and all that I have ever been, make this known to me now, for now*

I surrender my beliefs in an act of faith. Let thy will be done, for me and the sake of mankind.

Then, still with her eyes closed, she pulled the handle and opened the door. Her body shook at the sound of the roar of the lion in front of her as she walked in. Just then she heard a voice in her head commanding her to open her eyes and see the truth for the first time in her life. Immediately she opened her eyes and saw the lion six foot in front of her. Lucifer was standing behind him, watching the scene being performed in front of him. The same voice sounded in her head, again instructing her with courage in her heart to walk the path of faith. She took one step forward and the lion roared even louder, standing his ground. And yet he didn't attack. Mary took another step. Tears ran from her eyes at the thought of being devoured. This could be the last moment of her being alive. Samson took a massive swipe at the floor in front of her, throwing up dust and straw. Lucifer began laughing as Samson edged even closer. He became quieter with anticipation as Mary took another step, then another and then Samson took another swipe with his large claw, tearing at her clothes with his claws

Impatiently he shouted, "What is the matter with you? Why don't you attack?" He could not contain himself any longer. "What are you waiting for? Kill her!"

On hearing this Mary looked at Lucifer, standing there with so much hate for her. She smiled and said in a whisper to Lucifer, "I love you."

She closed her eyes and said, "God, into your arms I commit my soul."

She then dropped to her knees in front of the lion. In despair Lucifer threw himself at the lion and pushed him. "God dammit, I order you to kill her!"

Samson leapt forward, mouth wide open and his claws ready to rip, but as Samson got closer to Mary her blue light started to emanate from within. The aura began to shine all around her body like a force field. The perfect blue sapphire colour reflected in Samson's eyes as he made contact. In a moment which seemed to last a lifetime, everything stood still. Samson was repelled off Mary in a shower of sparks of light and bounced off her to the edge of the cage.

"How can this be? Lucifer said as he looked at Mary who was now glowing the brightest possible blue. He then turned to see Samson sitting bolt upright calm as if he were a statue. Samson looked at Mary and bowed his head in submission. Lucifer couldn't believe his eyes when Samson started to glow a golden colour like the colour of the sun.

"What's going on?"

He shielded his eyes as both of their lights became even brighter, then the light started humming and resonating, vibrating in Lucifer's ears. Just when Lucifer thought he could stand it no longer, Mary's and Samson's lights shot into one another. They were joined together by a beam of light like a laser pulsating between them. They both opened their eyes and looked at Lucifer lovingly.

"What? What do you want from me? I can't give you what you want. In fact, I don't know what it is you want."

In his frustration Lucifer became angrier. His own red light started to shine from within until his whole body was surrounded in a ruby red glow.

"Why are you both looking at me that way? Please stop it, I'm in agony."

He fell to his knees in pain and rolled on the floor, screaming. On hearing Lucifer's cries for help, Mary and Samson looked at each other and nodded in mutual respect and agreement. Mary then opened her arms while Samson tilted his head and looked towards the heavens. He opened his mouth and let out an almighty, deafening roar. Lucifer watched with a mixture of awe and pain as the evening clouds above parted and a white beam of the purest light shot down into Samson's mouth. The light continued from Samson's mouth into Mary's left arm which was outstretched. It raced through her body and left via her right arm which was now pointing at Lucifer.

"No, no!" He screamed as the light entered him. It pulsated around him then continued out of his body, re-entering Samson's mouth. The three of them were now joined together in a perfect triangle of light originating from above. Mary's eyes were now totally blue, Samson's were flickering golden yellow and Lucifer's eyes were shining totally red. All three were in a silent trance. The more Lucifer tried to impose himself and his red light, the more the blue colour fought against him. It was like the beginning of time again, when the two atoms of matter and anti-matter fired against each other.

"No, get away!" Lucifer shouted in his mind as he concentrated and surged his red energy forward. *I am winning,* he thought when he saw Mary recoiling on the ground in pain.

Mary managed to focus, and in a last desperate act, she spoke to God in her mind. *Although I am feeling the pain, I still love Luther even to the point of my own death.* In an instant Mary was bolt upright on her knees again and energy flowed from her. Her blueness lit up the whole cage and the dark trees surrounding it. Lucifer felt his pain getting stronger and his power faltering as he struggled to control what was happening. The vibration of the light resonating around them got stronger and the noise hurt his ears. In one final attempt, Lucifer pushed his last bit of energy forward to Mary, then it all went black.

Lucifer started to dream about what had just happened. His mind went back to Mary as she first entered the cage. Why didn't Samson attack her? Was Samson afraid? No that could not be so, he could have killed her easily. But he seemed afraid. What was he afraid of? So many questions went through Lucifer's head. What did Mary have inside her and why would she put her own life in danger? The dream moved to the memory of Mary just before kneeling in front of Samson. He could see Mary moving her lips in slow motion and his heart became heavy when he read her lips saying, "I love you". Lucifer felt his soul begin to weep. *She did it for me, she was willing to sacrifice herself for me, but I have shown her nothing but contempt and hate. Why would she do that? I am not worthy of saving, you only have to see all the evil acts and deeds I have done in my existence.*

Visions of burning and mutilated bodies were played in his mind. The sad faces of those who had lost their loved ones through evil were crying in front of him. As these images faded, Lucifer saw the image of a grotesquely wicked angel. How could Mary love that? *If she could love me, then she must truly love everything, and her selfless love knows no bounds.*

As he was trying to register all this in his mind, his heart began to slow until it eventually ceased. For a moment he was reunited with that mysterious veil which the eye of human reason cannot penetrate. There was silence. Then out of the silence, Lucifer's heart began to beat again. This time it now started to beat a different beat, one that was not painful but joyful. The new feeling he was experiencing started to excite him. His mind was beginning to open and as it did the vision of himself dissipated in a flash of light. The memories of the mutilated and burnt bodies returned to his mind. *I am sorry, please forgive me. I still do not know why I did these things to you, but I am truly sorry about what I bestowed upon you. I hope in time, when I truly find out who I am, you will find it in your own hearts to forgive me.*

The visions began to fade. Lucifer's heart started to feel lighter, no longer heavy or burdened with a guilty conscience, freeing his mind for new visions to enter. He saw images of people in love and mothers lovingly looking at their children. Lucifer found these acts of love were giving him a different kind of power.

With the help of Mary and Samson's love, courage and strength now rushing through his veins, he could find himself again. He smiled as he said, "I love you too". The dreams started to fade and Lucifer began to regain consciousness.

The redness had started to fade as he opened his eyes to see Mary and Samson looking at him. The light from above had disappeared. Mary was still glowing a glorious blue, Samson was still an elegant statue surrounded by an aura of gold. Lucifer then looked down at his own body. Instead of glowing red, he was now shining a beautiful violet colour with a beautiful gold border of light emanating out of the edges of the purple. When he looked at his chest he could see his heart. It was shining with the same beautiful light that had previously descended from the sky above. The beauty of the light reflected on Lucifer's hands as he held them out in front of him. He looked back at Mary who was smiling at him. As a tear rolled down Lucifer's face, his own colour shone the brightest of all. The three of them sat for a while enjoying each other's energy, then there was nothing. All the lights had vanished and they were left in darkness surrounded by the noise of the animals at the zoo.

"I can't believe that just happened." Mary was the first to speak. "I feel I truly know myself for the first time in my life."

"Yes I feel the same, I feel like I have been reborn and yet this all seems so familiar to me."

"I know what you mean. It's like we have done this before and not just the once."

Samson walked up to Mary and nudged her with his muzzle in an apologetic gesture for his previous aggression.

"I understand, big fella," she said and threw her arms around him. After a while she turned to Lucifer, "Well, are you going to join us?" Awkwardly, he moved towards them.

"You have to be patient with me. I'm not used to this. I'm just starting to remember all those feelings I lost a long time ago. I have not felt like this for more than a millennia." He slowly moved towards them both and put his arms around them both. The three were as one again, at peace with each other and the world. They stayed embracing for a while, then Samson pulled away and walked to the end of the cage where he bent his head forward and took something up in his teeth and returned to them.

"What's that?" Mary asked.

"That is my coat given to me by a friend and now it is being returned to me by a true friend. Thank you."

He ruffled his hand through the lion's mane and took the black coat from his jaws.

"Well, I must say it could do with a clean," Mary said with a giggle.

"Yes," Lucifer answered after moving the coat away from his nose to avoid the unpleasant smell.

"I think it's time we headed back home. It's getting cold," Lucifer lifted the coat to put it around her cold shoulders.

"No it's okay, thank you," she laughed again, "but you can put your arm around me as you walk me home."

They both left the lion's cage and locked the door and they stopped at the fence where Samson was resting with his head turned to face them.

"I bid you farewell my friend and thank you for making me see the light."

Lucifer put his fingers through the cage and played with the beast's ear. Samson rubbed his head against Lucifer's finger in response.

"Goodbye Samson, love to you my friend," Mary blew Samson a kiss.

Samson let out a deep breath of warm air, looked up at the moon in the night sky blinked and started to close his eyes for a good night's sleep.

"Come on Luther, let's get home. We need to speak

to John about what has just happened and what to do next."

"Okay, I'm coming. I'm just wondering if I will ever see Samson again."

"I think you most probably will."

"Yes, you're right, let's go."

He climbed the safety fence and helped Mary over it and started walking.

"Well?" Mary said. Lucifer looked at her puzzled.

She was standing with her hand on her hip and her elbow sticking out.

"Oh yes," he awkwardly put his arm around Mary's shoulder and placed the coat in his other hand. They both headed home.

Chapter Eighteen

THE HANDS ON THE CLOCK seemed to be going around very slowly as John nervously waited for his sister's return. He was drumming his fingers on the kitchen table not knowing what to do with himself. He was just about to walk to the phone when he heard the key turning in the front door.

"Mary is that you?"

"Yes John, I'm back."

He rushed into the hallway to see his sister smiling the biggest smile he had ever seen. Then as she stepped forward, Lucifer entered the doorway. John stepped back with his mouth wide open; he couldn't believe what he was seeing. Lucifer's face was almost glowing and his eyes were now a darker brown with a hint of gold just like a tiger's eye.

"You have found your way, haven't you? John asked excitedly.

"Yes, John. I have your sister and an old friend to thank for that. I can't believe how good I feel. Feelings long forgotten have resurfaced and I no longer feel like I want to kill and destroy everything. My evil side has definitely subsided and given way to my true nature."

"Come here," John grabbed Lucifer in a warm embrace. Lucifer awkwardly stood with his arms down by his side as John held him tightly.

"Okay you two, it's time to talk about our next move," Mary spoke quietly.

John broke off the embrace and held Lucifer at arm's length.

"Come on, let's retire into the lounge where we can talk."

John watched as Lucifer led the way and Mary took hold of his arm, then looked skywards.

"God, you are wonderful," he said quietly under his breath.

The three of them sat talking for hours about the events of the evening. John's eyes widened with awe at what he was hearing.

"So my little sister, how do you feel?"

"Fine but I'm still a little confused as to what I'm supposed to have done."

"Well after restoring your own faith and courage, you then found it in your heart to help Luther find his again. Don't you see, Mary? You only had to be your true self for this transition to happen."

Lucifer interrupted them with an intense look in his eyes.

"The most profound thing for me was that Mary proclaimed her love for me. That I couldn't understand. If she'd known half of the things I've done during my existence, she would most probably turn away in disgust."

"Perhaps I already know unconsciously. I have always said since I met you, I felt I had known you, even connected by something, maybe it was love."

"Yes, I think it most probably was," John answered, "and maybe the Most High intended this to happen."

The phone began to ring. John got out of his chair to answer the call. Mary could feel Lucifer's eyes upon her while John was in the corridor.

"Why are you looking at me like that?"

"I am just looking at somebody that has been untouched by man and the influence of evil. Somebody who has remained in innocence. It is as though I was seeing something I have lost, something that feels so familiar."

"Luther, I see in you a beautiful light that has faded for some reason, but I do feel that this light will shine bright again once you find what you are looking for."

John entered the room again.

"That was David worrying about you Luther and where you were. He was panicking because he thought you'd run off. He'll be round shortly to pick you up."

"I suppose it would be good to get my head down. I'm exhausted."

"Yes, you'll need some sleep Luther, because what you discover tomorrow will take even more strength and fortitude than today."

"What do you mean John?" Mary asked.

"Well Luther has his meeting with the brotherhood. What they are going to tell and show him will require an inner strength of the highest level."

"I am intrigued," Lucifer answered with apprehension, "how can they tell and show me what I already know?"

"Tomorrow morning, I guess you will finally know."

"Yes, I suppose I will."

"Anyone for tea while we wait for David?"

Mary had risen to her feet.

"Yes please Mary and lots of –"

"Yes I know Luther, lots of sugar," Mary headed to the kitchen and closed the door.

John turned to Lucifer.

"So Luther, how does it feel to be this new you?"

"It is a paradox. I feel strange and yet normal, the only way I can explain it is that I feel as if I have been living with a hood over my head in complete darkness, so much so that my mind, eyes and heart accepted that darkness as normal. However, now that darkness has been lifted I am seeing the world in a different light. Although it still does feel there is a piece of me that is missing. I can't quite put my finger on it. Hopefully tomorrow I will get my answer."

"For your sake Luther, I hope you do."

It wasn't long before Mary returned with the tea and the three of them started chatting. Time flew by and David was soon knocking on the door.

"Well Luther, it looks like your ride is here."

"Yes, thank you for the tea and conversation."

He bent down to pick up his coat.

"Please leave it here Luther, I'll wash it and return it to you tomorrow."

"Thank you," he handed her the coat, "Mary I want to say –"

Mary put her hand to Lucifer's mouth.

"Please you don't have to say anything. What I experienced tonight told me everything I need to know, but I will have another hug before you go."

She threw her arms around Lucifer and squeezed him tight. This time he responded and squeezed her back.

David was impatiently knocking on the door again.

"I think we'd better let David in before he knocks down our door," John said. He went to the door, and David stormed into the house to find Lucifer.

"Thank God..." David stopped in mid-sentence as he observed Mary and Lucifer in a warm embrace. "What's going on?" David asked John.

"It's a long story. I am sure Luther will tell you on the way home."

"Are you ready, Luther?"

Lucifer turned back to Mary. "Will I see you tomorrow?"

Mary smiled. "Nothing will stop that from happening. Now go and get a good night's sleep and when tomorrow comes you will finally find out who you truly are."

He walked to the doorway and took hold of John's hand with a firm handshake. "Please take care of her, John."

"I will and I'm sure we will both see you tomorrow."

"Goodbye," he said and stepped outside, then stopped and turned to see Mary smiling at him. She whispered, "I love you". A tingling went down his spine and then he turned and headed down the path to the car.

"Wait Luther, wait for me." David was eagerly following closely behind him. "You have to tell me what happened today."

"This happened today."

He turned around, took hold of David and lifted him off the ground in a warm embrace. David didn't quite know what to do as he struggled with his feet dangling off the ground.

"You see David, I am a new man and I feel good for the first time in my life."

"I'm feeling that. I see you like me now, it's a start."

Lucifer laughed and let go of him.

"Now David, please take me to your brotherhood. I feel I am ready for them now."

Chapter Nineteen

THE FOLLOWING MORNING, Jeremiah, Daniel and the three other brothers, Timothy, Mark and Peter, were gathered at Daniel's house, sitting quietly talking. Jeremiah had a look of anticipation on his face as he looked at the other brothers.

"Well gentlemen, I do believe it is time that I made the most important phone call of my life."

The four other men looked at Jeremiah as he rose from his chair. Daniel assisted the ageing man to his feet.

"Thank you Daniel and thank you for agreeing to have the meeting at your house."

"Jeremiah, the pleasure is all mine. I still can't believe that I could be potentially witnessing the change of mankind starting in my own house."

"Yes Daniel," Peter said, "we all have been vigorously studying the scrolls and the signs are all there. I feel this is going to be a very special day for mankind."

The other two men nodded in agreement.

"I am all right from here, Daniel." Daniel let go of Jeremiah's arm and sat back down. "I'll only be a few moments on the phone. Please excuse me and talk amongst yourselves."

They watched him walk off into the corridor, closing the door behind him

"Will I be allowed to be present when the scrolls are presented to Luther?" Daniel asked Mark nervously.

"We've spoken about this and we are all in agreement that you and David will be present. You must be present to secretly record what takes place and David will be entitled to be here because of his patience and fortitude. That's what led him to Luther in the first place."

"I am so excited." Tears of joy and anticipation ran down Daniel's eyes again.

"You won't have to wait much longer now, my friend."

Back at David's house, Lucifer was still lying in bed after a restful night's sleep. His eyes flashed open just before the phone began to ring downstairs. It was as though he had somehow expected the phone to ring. He heard the sound of David's voice.

"Hello Jeremiah," David said, then paused. "Yes, he is still with us. Okay we'll be there in about an hour." There was another brief silence. "Thank you so much, I'm honoured. I also have some great news about Luther and what happened yesterday. We'll tell you when we see you. Goodbye."

Lucifer heard the phone receiver click down.

"I'll be down shortly." Lucifer anticipated David calling up to him and shouted downstairs before he had the chance.

"Okay, I'm in the kitchen with Ruth. Do you want anything?"

"Just some tea and toast, thanks."

David walked into the kitchen where Ruth was sitting at the kitchen table.

"Is there any more tea in the pot, my love?"

"Yes sure darling, does his majesty want anything else?" Ruth jokingly asked.

"Ruth stop it. If you hadn't gone to bed early, you'd have seen him last night. It's like looking at a different person. He even gave me a hug, can you believe it?"

"This I have to see," Ruth said.

"And yes, his majesty would like some toast. That was Jeremiah on the phone. The brothers have gathered and we should leave in about half an hour. I'm so nervous."

"Why?"

She turned to her husband as she put Lucifer's bread in the toaster.

"Because today we really find out if he is the one. From what he told me about what happened last night, he surely has to be."

"What happened last night? Oh apart from the hug, of course."

He lifted his eyebrows at her.

"I can't tell you. Luther was very secretive, but he did say he would tell us today at the meeting."

"You boys and your secrets. I expect I'll find out from Mary or John anyway. So what's so important about today?"

"Again I can't tell you too much, partly because of my vows of secrecy and partly because I don't know myself. All I can tell you is that what Luther sees and learns today will make a difference to mankind."

"What difference would that be?"

Lucifer had opened the kitchen door and stood looking at them both quietly talking in the corner. Lucifer smiled as he saw Ruth's eyes widen on seeing him in a new light.

"Good, you're down," David said. "We were just talking about the meeting. Are you nervous or excited?"

"Very good," Lucifer retorted, "answering my question with a question. Now tell me what difference were you talking about?"

"I don't know. All I know is that when you have had the meeting you will know."

"Riddles and half-truths. I suppose I'm intrigued. Good morning Ruth, you're looking fine this morning."

Lucifer smiled again when Ruth's mouth dropped open in astonishment at his compliment. "Thank you." She glanced at David with a look that made him feel as if he wasn't complimenting her enough.

Lucifer sat down and poured himself a cup of tea and spooned in his usual six teaspoons of sugar. He could feel Ruth's eyes on him as he sipped his tea.

"Is that my toast burning?" Lucifer asked as he looked over her shoulder to see smoke rising from the toaster.

"Oh, I'm sorry." She quickly pushed the eject button and two pieces of black toast shot into the air.

"Don't worry Ruth. I don't feel that hungry any more."

"Are you sure? I can make some more."

She was opening the window to let the smoke out.

"No honestly, it's fine. This tea will keep me going."

"Why don't you feel hungry any more Luther?" David asked with a concerned look on his face.

"I don't know, I just feel strange. Like my fate and destiny is about to be revealed to me."

"Like what?" Ruth had joined both of them at the table.

"I just feel that the news I receive today is not going to be all good."

"Really, who for?"

"I think it could be most probably me."

"Don't be silly," David scoffed, "the brotherhood would never let anything happen to you, especially if you are the one scripture talks about."

"What scripture?" Ruth asked with interest.

"Oh nothing. I've said too much already. Come on Luther, it is time for you to finally meet your destiny."

The two of them got to their feet. David kissed Ruth on her cheek before she could enquire any more about the scriptures.

"Goodbye then," she shouted as they closed the door behind them.

Jeremiah had rejoined the four other men in Daniel's lounge, who were all waiting patiently.

"Are you okay, Jeremiah?" Peter had noticed that Jeremiah was looking slightly pale. "Yesterday and today, I've noticed you're not your usual self."

"I'm fine, Peter. Thank you for asking. However, I do feel my existence in this mortal frame will soon come to an end."

"Never!" Daniel replied. "I think you will outlast all of us. The Most High has still got great work for you to perform."

"That is very kind of you Daniel, but I feel my work is nearly complete. I have lived a full life and remain true to our order. I am glad to be participating in this occasion."

"We are honoured you are still with us Jeremiah." Mark was at the window watching for David's car. "You are very fondly thought of in the order."

Jeremiah began to blush at all the compliments.

"Thank you all for your kind words. I am very proud to be a member of the brotherhood with so many good friends."

"So how will we present the scroll to Luther?" Mark asked.

"When he arrives we will introduce ourselves informally, then we will introduce ourselves ritually. After this we will hand him the scroll and tell him the secrets. Hopefully after that he will know his true name. The most important thing we must achieve today is to get Luther to discover his true name and for him to translate what is written at the bottom of the scroll. If he's the one, he will certainly know what it says."

Mark turned to the window at the sound of a motor outside. "They're here." Mark released the net curtain of the window and sat back down.

"Okay, remember," Jeremiah lowered his head to speak to them discreetly. "If he isn't the one, we will have lost nothing. The scroll will mean nothing to him and afterwards we can go our separate ways. Are we all in agreement?"

"All hail," the four of them said aloud.

Outside, David had pulled up opposite Daniel's house.

"Are you sure you are all right Luther? You look pale and you were very quiet on the way over here."

"I am a little nervous of what I'm about to discover."

"Well my friend, there's only one way to find out. Look, there's Daniel at the door. Ready?"

Lucifer looked at David.

"Yes, let's go and find out the truth. If Mary can face a ferocious lion, I'm sure I can be strong enough to face my truth."

"That's the spirit. Come on then."

They both left the car and joined Daniel at his front door.

"Hello, Brother David."

"Hello Daniel." They greeted each other with a welcoming handshake.

"And how is Luther?"

"I'm okay, thank you." He took hold of Daniel's hand and shook it firmly.

"Come in, we have three very excited people inside, desperately wanting to meet you."

They walked past Daniel who closed the door behind them and then all three walked into the lounge.

"Hello again Luther," Jeremiah said. "I hope you don't mind if I don't get up."

"No, not at all, please stay seated."

This time Lucifer held out his hand to the frail old man.

"Hello, I'm Peter." They exchanged handshakes as did Timothy and Mark after introducing themselves.

"Please sit down," Daniel gestured to David and Lucifer.

"David told me on the phone there something special happened last night. Would you find it in your heart to relate the story to us?"

Lucifer nodded, then began to relate an account of the previous night at the zoo. The brothers sat wide-eyed as they listened intently to his story. Daniel recorded it in the usual big black book. David in particular couldn't believe what he was hearing. After he had finished, there was a brief silence which was eventually broken by Jeremiah.

"Well gentlemen, after hearing that do we still doubt that this could be our man?"

They looked at each other and shook their heads.

"Luther what happened to you yesterday was remarkable. I feel confident that now we can impart our intelligence to you, but first we have to introduce ourselves by the names which we and our fathers and mothers have had since time began. Afterwards we will present you with the scroll and the writings that have governed our faith since the beginning of time. Daniel, would you mind closing the curtains? We need the room in total darkness. David, take these two candles. Light one at the table and give one to Daniel so he can see what he's writing."

Before long, they were all sitting in a blacked-out room in which the only movement was their shadows flickering and dancing on the walls.

"Gentlemen, shall we begin?"

"All hail."

Timothy stood up, took hold of Lucifer's hand and led him to the centre of the room where the candle was resting on a table.

"Just stand there," he whispered to Lucifer, then went back to join Mark and Peter who were all standing in a row. Peter held Jeremiah's hand to support him as he stood unsteadily on his feet.

Daniel was in the corner busily writing in his book and David was sitting wide-eyed at the ritual being acted out in front of him. The four men standing all looked at each other then bowed their heads in Lucifer's direction. Mark was the first to break the line. He stepped forward and shook Lucifer's hand.

"I greet you well Master of Masters, I am Fly-Isis-Fly the guardian and ruler from the West. I am of the air we breathe and the four cardinal winds, especially that which blows from the West."

He bowed and returned to the line and Timothy stepped forward.

"I also greet you well Master of Masters, I am A-Mia-Hey the guardian and ruler of the North. I govern the rain and the water that falls from the northern skies to the ground giving birth to Mother Earth's oceans."

After bowing and returning to the line, he took Jeremiah's hand so Peter could step forward.

"I for the third time greet you, Master of Masters, I am Set-Death the guardian and ruler of the East in the absence of the One. I govern the Earth on which we all stand and that which supports us in life and consumes us in death, when we give up our flesh deeply buried in its bosom."

"Thank you Peter, I can manage."

Jeremiah steadied himself then joined Lucifer in the centre of the room, then with a tear in his eye he spoke.

"I for the final time greet you well Master of Masters, I am Our-Ra-Knew, the guardian and ruler of the South. I govern the fire which is but a spark of that which comes from the sun. It gives us warmth to our mortal bodies and spirit and fuels the passion in our hearts."

He bowed then stood for a while looking into Lucifer's eyes. He returned to the line where they all bowed for the last time then sat down.

"Please sit at the table, Daniel would you mind,"

"Of course not." He stood up and took a wooden chair for Lucifer.

"Now Luther, do you remember when we first met and I examined that wound on your head?"

"Yes, I remember."

"I wasn't only looking for a physical wound. I was looking for a specific kind of wound."

"I did wonder at the time. I remember you looking at it and dropping your stick on the floor in shock."

"I had very good reason to react the way I did, but first tell us who you really are and how you really got that mark on your head."

"I feel that I can tell you as much as I can and as much as the Most High will allow. I am Luc..." Still, he was not permitted to speak out his name, but he continued. "I was and had been a rebel angel, the head of an angelic order committed to the overthrow of the Most High. I and my army of angels committed many atrocities against mankind and made them do evil things to one another. I even committed the ultimate sin of killing my angelic brethren in pursuit of establishing my own will on earth. I succeeded, at least I thought I had succeeded, when I conquered man and the Archangel Michael and his army of angels. That is when the Most High struck. In my moment of triumph, God deceived me and took all that away from me. For me it was irony, the great deceiver had been deceived. Before I knew what was happening, I was taken up in God's presence where I was told that I only existed because man had created me in their minds. God had decided that my image in man's mind was getting too powerful, so to readdress this I was to return to Earth in mortal form and help save lives of men who I hated so much."

"May I speak, Jeremiah?" David nervously asked.

"Of course, David."

"So, Luther, you were the one who cured John of his cancer."

"Yes, now you can see what my predicament was. I was the one doing the healing and yet God is getting credit for it. I had to keep doing this and save myself, only then could I return to my angelic state of being. As for the mark on my head, I have no clue where that comes from."

"Well that I can now explain to you," Jeremiah said, "but first we have to present you with the scroll that has been in our possession since the beginning of mankind. Here, written in the words, you will at last discover your true name."

Jeremiah lifted a briefcase from beneath his chair and clicked it open. He put on his protective white gloves, opened it and removed the four separate pieces of scroll.

"David, put on these gloves."

David looked at Jeremiah and realised Jeremiah wanted him to handle the pieces.

"Oh no, I couldn't, it's such a precious thing. Surely someone else should have the honour of that?"

"Ritually, it should be my honour, but I feel that it's right for you to present it to Luther as you were the first person to discover him."

David looked at the other brothers who were all smiling in agreement, then like an excited boy he stood up and put on the gloves. The excitement didn't last long when his nerves took over at the realisation of what he was handling. Tentatively, he took hold of the four pieces of carefully sealed scriptures and carried them gently to where Lucifer was sitting. He laid them on the table in front of him and returned to his seat.

Lucifer sat in his chair for a while looking at the men in front of him. He was deliberately stalling the inevitable, it was as though, paradoxically, he didn't want to know the truth, and yet he desired it so much. The eyes of the men in front of him were watching his every move.

Finally Lucifer took in a deep breath, exhaled and turned to the table. As Lucifer was slowly reading the ancient parchment in front of him, the other men in the room sat forward in their chairs in anticipation of Lucifer's response.

"I am sorry, these mean nothing to me," Lucifer finally spoke, "it's in a strange language I can't read or understand."

Some of the men sat back in disappointment, but Jeremiah and David still sat forward.

"Perhaps you need some more time, Luther," David stated.

"Yes, keep looking Luther, it will come to you. While you're looking, I'll tell you about the mark on your head."

"I'm listening," Lucifer replied while he continued looking at the ancient scroll.

"Well cast your mind back to the meeting you attended the other night when you heard the story of which our ritual was based."

"Go on," Lucifer turned his attention to Jeremiah.

"I can now inform you that it isn't a story but the truth, a truth about a special man from the East that God loved so much. Luther, that man was you."

Jeremiah again paused to see Lucifer's reaction in the candlelight. Lucifer didn't say a word, but his face started to show signs of intrigue and worry.

"Remember, the ritual tells us how this incredible man was slain by the hand of the Master of the West by a fatal wound on the head."

"Yes I remember. He and his two companions were all murdered."

"That's it. Well the mark on your head has been carried with you throughout your entire existence. You now carry it with you today in your human form. Would you like to see it?" Lucifer nodded. "Daniel, if you don't mind."

Daniel stepped forward and showed him some writing in his book.

"When I examined your head when we first met, I saw this word."

He pointed to a word in the book. "It was written in the centre of your wound."

"Sorry again it means nothing to me."

"I know, but look it is exactly the same as the third set of writing and symbols on the scroll."

Lucifer took the book from Daniel and matched the writings together.

"How can this be? I want to make sure myself. Do you have a mirror?"

"I thought you might ask that," Daniel smiled and removed his hand from behind his back and handed Lucifer a mirror. The both of them held the mirror at the correct angle to read what was written on the back of his head. As he moved his fingers through his hair, the candlelight revealed the word written there.

Lucifer's eyes widened.

"Thank you," he said and handed back the mirror to Daniel who returned to his seat. "What do these words and symbols mean?"

"That we don't know because it is written in a language we don't understand. We were hoping you might be able to enlighten us."

"Jeremiah may I be so bold to speak?"

"By all means, David go ahead."

"Maybe Luther is not looking at them properly."

"What do you mean?"

"Perhaps he can't understand them because he's in a human body."

"Of course David, you might be right."

"Luther, remember you said last night about the magical things that had happened at the zoo. You said this was only possible with assistance from the light above. Maybe, it is time to try to contact that light again."

"I can try," he said and spent several minutes looking upwards but nothing happened. Everybody could tell that Lucifer was getting frustrated.

"Come on, show yourself!" he shouted.

Still nothing. Then Lucifer started to get angry, allowing his old nature to reappear.

"Show me!" he shouted again.

In an instant, his eyes flashed red and his body began to radiate a red light all around the room. The other men in the room sat spellbound in the red glow while Lucifer sat staring at them. He removed his attention from the men and turned his head to look at the scrolls.

"The letters have moved. I can see them differently, but I can't still understand what they say."

Lucifer was squinting his eyes.

"You must be able to understand them, try harder," Jeremiah was now getting frustrated and impatient. "Can't you see them through your red eyes? Surely God gave you those eyes for a reason."

"I'm trying my best!" Lucifer angrily snapped at

Jeremiah, causing him to sit back in his chair. "Something is missing. What am I not seeing or understanding?"

Lucifer concentrated harder.

"Wait!" David said. "Luther, in your experience with Mary and Samson, didn't you say that Mary had a blue light around her and some of that blue entered you?"

"Yes, I remember allowing the heavenly colour to enter my aura."

"What happened after that?"

"My angelic light turned purple, surrounded by the white light from above."

"My God. David, you're right," Jeremiah patted David on the back, "Lucifer, you have to concentrate your energies and bring back that purple essence. Then maybe you will understand the writings fully."

"Okay, I'll try."

He closed his red eyes and sat for a while in silence, pleading with the Most High. It wasn't long before Mary's face appeared in his mind. The image of her loving eyes started to make his colour vibrate more as she whispered that she loved him. The energy around him now started to rotate like a whirlwind. All of a sudden Lucifer's head shot back and he let out a deep roar. Sparks started flying off him and shot around the room and everyone in the room sat back in amazement. The whole room was shook on its very foundations. The chairs started vibrating to the energy that was flying around the room, Lucifer's red glow now gave way to a beautiful purple light surrounded by a white light which hurt everybody's eyes. The vibrations in the room ceased as Lucifer lowered his head. His eyes were now open, a perfect purple in colour.

"This is amazing, what a beautiful sight." Jeremiah said, weeping at what he was seeing in front of him. "Luther, now in this state, please look at the scroll."

Lucifer nodded and looked at the scroll. As he read, his aura started shining even brightly as the words and symbols all changed again. This time they glowed in the light of his aura and he now could fully understand them.

"Daniel, get ready to record what is about to be said," Jeremiah instructed Daniel.

"I'm ready," Daniel sat with pen poised ready as Lucifer began to read.

"I am Joshua and this is a true account of what has come to pass. It was given to me when the light passed over me. I am writing the word of God so that when the One reveals himself, he will understand what is written and will know his true names. These names will be revealed when all the signs are in place and the time is at hand when God's will has to be established on Earth again. To the one who is reading this, remember your name well, as it comes with love from that light which is from above.

Your first name given to you from the Most High is Altithronus, meaning 'one enthroned on high, seated in heaven'. God gave you this name because you were loved the most of all the angels. God saw in you the love and light in your heart which shone the brightest. The Most High and his angels were discussing creating another form of life and, after long deliberation and discussion, God decided to create a life form which would be called man. It was decided that when mankind was created, people would need guidance and a leader to watch over them. When the Most High asked his angels for a volunteer to be this leader of man, they all refused to take such a transformation except one. Most thought it was dirty and unclean to give up their angelic status and become flesh. The one who accepted was you, Altithronus. You loved God so much you would even sacrifice being an angel to please the Most High and remain in favour. So God decided to give you another name by which you would be known by when you went down to Earth. You were to be called Agonotheta Luminar 'champion of light'.

You were then sent into the universe where you

became atoms of anti-matter. Here you clashed together with atoms of matter. For light years you had battled, trying to impose your will against matter. Finally anti-matter and matter accepted one another and the Most High's plan had started. It was the beginning of the creation of life. It was there on Earth, when joined by other men and women who had also left their atomic form, people came to know your name. You were loved by your people as much as you loved God."

Lucifer paused in his reading, staring into space.

"What is it ...?" Jeremiah asked. "Goodness, I don't even know what to call you now."

"I don't know," he replied. They could see tears in his eyes as he spoke. "I'm just starting to remember it all. My people who I loved so much, I can hear their screams in my head." He wiped away a purple tear and continued reading.

"Your people grew in numbers and it wasn't long before some of them travelled. In doing so, they moved away from the light that was bestowed upon you every day. Then in the west, a man proclaimed himself leader of people who had settled there. Year by year, he grew more and more jealous of your people's love for you. That is when it was decided he would kill you and claim your name and power. But the Most High's love for you would not let you die. After forty days and nights of contemplation in Earth's cold bosom, the Most High brought you and your two faithful companions back to life. This is when you chose your third name and your previous two were to be forgotten, hidden away from you and the eyes of mortal men. You chose the name Ulcisor Mano, 'to take revenge on men'. You had now given up your mortal body and returned to an angelic state. The Most High sorrowfully gave you the courage and ferocity of the lion and the blood of your people ran through your veins and lit up your eyes. You then decided to wreak your revenge on mankind for what they had done to you and your people. The Most High allowed you your freedom to punish them for their wickedness. However in your rage you forgot where you had come from.

The Most High wept as the darkness in your heart grew, fuelled by a lust for death and revenge. So much so that you started to hate and deny God, the one you had loved so much before. It was not long before other angels who were attracted to this new darkness joined your cause. They left their heavenly bodies and joined you on Earth to rid the world of dirty flesh and soon all of mankind was feeling the full strength of your wrath. It was here when you were given your new name. In the confusion of you losing your old names, man decided to call you Lucifer or Satan, that great darkness and evil which all men were to fear and hate even though it was mankind's fear and hate that created you. On hearing yourself being called this, you adopted this name and started to believe that this was your true identity. So you decided that your angelic brethren and any man that would follow you would call you this as a lasting reminder of man's evil in their mind. I, Joshua, have now stated what has gone before. Now I will tell you what is to come. The one reading this must know that his power will not last. You will win a great battle and briefly be a king and ruler on earth."

Lucifer stopped reading the text and looked at the men in the room.

"So now you know my name and who I am. I am Lucifer." He could not believe that he was actually speaking his name aloud. "Yes, I am Lucifer."

"Technically, that is not true, is it? If you think about the other names you've had," Jeremiah boldly replied.

"But if I'm not Lucifer, then what am I to be called?"

Daniel sat forward. "Perhaps the time will come when you will get a new name?"

Lucifer was surprised at their reaction, he was telling them that he was lord of all darkness and yet they remained in his power helping him. His memory went back to the orphanage when Angela had recognised him and spoke his name. She was not afraid. Did she know the real him?

"Can't you see? Lucifer was the name given to you by man. It is an illusion. You are real and the name is only an illusion."

Jeremiah's kind words gave Lucifer heart.

"If you don't mind, we shall call you that until you get your new name." Lucifer nodded and then returned to reading the scrolls.

"After this brief rule on earth, you will be taken into God's presence. You will be told about your former existence, but still you will remain in your arrogance and think God is lying to you. After much discussion and deliberation, the Most High will bestow a punishment on you where you will be ordered to return to flesh, the thing you have come to hate so much. On Earth, you will have to carry out God's work in order to return to your true self and more importantly readdress the balance of good on earth. This will get men believing in God again. If the right person is reading this, then the brotherhood I started have done their job well, and I would like to thank them for guarding and preserving the sacred writings. I, Joshua, would love to thank all of the brethren from the North, East, South and West for their hard work and dedication and fidelity to the cause. "

"Jeremiah, imagine, your oldest known ancestors are talking now with us and thanking us?" Daniel was speaking like an excited boy.

"I know Daniel, it's quite remarkable. Sorry Lucifer, please continue."

"Now my friend, you will now be reading this in troubled times for man. A conflict will be growing which is going to change the very way man lives. Man will now have to prepare for their final fall. A man will rise in the east and will come to represent God's wrath on Earth. It is up to you."

At last Lucifer stopped his reading, and they all noticed his colour purple fading.

"What is it, Lucifer?"

"I just can't read the final piece of writing at the bottom. The words and symbols are too distorted."

"Please try and focus again," Jeremiah had now stood and was willing Lucifer to understand it.

"I can't, I really can't."

The purple had now given way to his own red which in turn was now also fading, until there was nothing but darkness again, save the candlelight flickering in the darkness of the room.

"Are you all right Lucifer?"

David stepped forward as Lucifer slumped forward onto the table in front of him.

"I am fine, just a little exhausted. That took a lot out of me."

"I am sorry I pushed you Lucifer." Jeremiah had sat back down. "I just wanted to know the whole prophecy. Are you sure –"

Jeremiah's question was silenced by Daniel placing his hand on the old man's shoulder.

"I think Lucifer needs to rest now, my old friend."

"Yes, you're right, forgive an old fool."

"Not at all, I also wanted to know the whole story, but maybe God didn't want us to know everything right now. What do you think Lucifer?"

"I think you could be right Daniel. If God had wanted us to know, I would have been able to read it."

Lucifer noticed Jeremiah looking at him strangely. He knew that not for one moment did Jeremiah believe that he was telling the truth, a truth which for now Lucifer would keep to himself.

CHAPTER TWENTY

WHILST LUCIFER AND THE BROTHERHOOD were contemplating what had just happened, thousands of miles away in the East, General Silas and his captain were talking about their own momentous events. They were sitting on the General's balcony watching people walk by below them. On either side of the General and the Captain stood two bodyguards.

"Well my friend, the time is close," the General said. "I have called you here because I have just had another visit from the Archangel Michael. So now I can tell you God's plan, which is to bring as much destruction on the Western world as possible."

The Captain sat forward eagerly.

"At twelve noon tomorrow we will strike. All of Europe will be obliterated. They will feel God's wrath burning down on them from heaven. We will meet at eight in the morning and will be driven to the Defence Ministry. At midday, we will launch the missiles."

"Can you be sure they will strike back at us?"

"As soon as their rulers are aware of the impending strike, they will retaliate and launch their own in defence. Why do you ask?"

"I am eager to die and see my family again. I miss them so much."

"I admire your bravery and your fidelity to God, especially your faith in the afterlife. I'm sure they are just as keen to see you. As for myself, I'm not concerned about seeing any of my family. I just want to sit at the right hand of God. I feel privileged and honoured that the Most High would bestow this on me."

"Yes General, and I feel honoured that you find the confidence in me to be at your side when the end comes."

"Here take this and keep it on you, keep it safe until tomorrow afternoon."

The General bent down under the table and pulled out a black briefcase and entered the digital combination. It clicked open and inside the captain could see two keys, one red and one blue. They were both attached to a chain and next to these keys was a black envelope.

"This key," he handed him the blue one, "and envelope are yours. Inside the envelope is one half of the death code serial number. My envelope contains the other half. You must not open it until tomorrow just before we launch, is that clear?"

"Yes, General."

The Captain took the key, then wrapped the chain around his neck. He took the envelope very carefully and placed it in his shirt pocket. "I will put the envelope in my personal safe when I return to my quarters."

"Very good. As an extra precaution, I will be stationing two guards outside your room along with one bodyguard in your room for the entire evening. I will have the same, just in case anybody hears of our intentions."

He looked at the two guards standing behind him and leant forward to whisper to the Captain.

"I think I can trust them. Anyway they have full knowledge that they will lose their heads if they ever repeat what is said in privacy."

"I think all your men are loyal to you, even to death. We are all sickened by the corrupt ways of Westerners and would all love to see them wiped off the face of the earth."

They both sat back and reclined in their chairs, watching the sun gently go down behind the horizon.

The warm evening breeze flowed in from the desert and caressed their faces as they sat back looking at the sun.

"It's a strange feeling, knowing you are going to die tomorrow. It gives you some perspective on life."

"What do you mean, Captain?"

"The sun rises every day and we take for granted that it will rise again tomorrow. It is only tonight that as I'm watching it go down for the last time, I am realising what a beautiful sight of nature it is. Such a beautiful creation from God given to us. I will certainly miss it."

"Yes, it is beautiful. But my dear friend, tomorrow when your spirit enters paradise you'll see a light brighter than any sun known to man. Now have a drink with me as we watch the sun hide its beautiful light for the last time. "

"Thank you, I will have just one. I want a clear head tomorrow. I don't want to make any mistakes."

"Me too, my friend, me too."

As the sun was going down in the eastern sky, it was still shining through the bedroom curtains of Mary and John's house.

"Mary, have you seen my red tie? The one with the gold stripes," John called into the kitchen to his sister.

"I think you left it on top of the sofa next to the television, that's where I saw it last."

"I've tried there already. Oh, why do things go missing when you need them the most?"

"You men are all the same. You always expect things to leap out in front of you. Have you checked behind the sofa? It might have fallen behind."

"No I haven't. Could you look please? I'm having trouble with these cufflinks. Damn, I hope we won't be late for this interview. The car will be here in half an hour to pick us up."

"Stop worrying, here it is," Mary said.

John turned from looking in the mirror to see his favourite tie dangling from her finger.

"Thank you Mary. I still don't know what I would do without you."

"What do you mean? I think we will be together until one of us dies or if the world should ever come to an end."

"Maybe you're a prophet too, Mary. You might be closer to the truth than you realise," John murmured to himself.

John had turned to face the mirror to put on his tie.

"What was that?" Mary asked.

"Nothing, I was just talking to my favourite tie and saying how much I had missed wearing it because of my illness."

"I must say, it certainly does look good on you."

Mary was looking over his shoulder at their reflection in a mirror. She pulled his collar down to cover the tie at the back.

"Are you really sure you want to do this interview John?" John looked at his sister in the reflection.

"If you ask me that one more time, I will put you over my knee," he said and quickly turned and started tickling his sister.

"Stop it John, you know I find it hard to breathe when you're tickling me."

"Are you going to ask me again?" He continued tickling her.

"No, I promise, John please! I can't breathe."

"Okay, now go and get my suit jacket."

"Sorry John, can you? I have to change into my dress."

"Anyone would think that you were the one having the interview. Hurry up!"

He shouted to her as she ran upstairs. He walked into the corridor and saw his jacket all neatly pressed hanging on the banister. Next to it was Lucifer's coat all clean and neatly pressed.

"Mary, whose coat is this?"

"It's Luther's. I thought it needed a good clean. Beautiful, isn't it?"

"Yes very nice," he said gently stroking his hand

across it. His thoughts were disturbed by the telephone ringing next to him on the hallway table.

"Hello David, how did the meeting go?"

There was a long pause while David explained as much as he could about the secret and what had gone on.

"Really! So now he finally knows his name? And what did the scriptures say? You can't tell me. Okay, I understand, but you say he could not read the final part? Maybe he will, sooner than we think. I'm sorry David, but Mary and I are getting ready for my interview. Will you, Ruth and Luther meet us later at the studio? Okay, see you later then."

He replaced the receiver and put on his suit jacket as Mary came down the stairs.

"Wow, look at you," he said. She was wearing a beautiful sky blue dress.

"Who was that on the phone?"

"It was David, they'd just finished the meeting."

"How did it go? Did David and the brotherhood get what they wanted?"

"David was very cautious not to tell me too much about what had gone on, but he did tell me that Luther had rediscovered his name."

"Really, what is it?"

"I don't know. David would not tell me that either. He did say though that he, Ruth and Luther would meet us at the television studios later tonight. Come on, here put this on."

He held out Mary's coat for her to slip her arms through.

"Thank you, always a gentleman aren't you?"

"Yes of course. Oh, my God. That's the car."

He glanced out of the hallway window to see a black limousine. The chauffeur was standing by the door patiently waiting for them.

"Do I look all right, is my tie straight?"

"Yes stop worrying, now come on John, or should I say, miracle man, the world awaits."

In Daniel's front room, Lucifer had now recovered his strength and was talking to Jeremiah and the other brethren. David had returned from the hall, having made his phone call.

"It's all coming back to me," Lucifer said. "Everything from being in the presence of the Most High where I was loved so much to loving my people in the east. I also remember the treachery which followed at the hands of the Master from the West which caused my evil transformation. I distinctly remember the battle I thought I'd won, then being told by the Most High that this wasn't true."

"So it is all true what the scriptures say?" Peter had stepped forward to pose his question.

"Yes, God told me only a half-truth. I was told that I left heaven because I was jealous of the Most High's light and I didn't understand why men could not receive this light. But I wasn't cast out of heaven, I chose to leave for the benefit of mankind and because I love the Most High so much. And now it would seem I have to face what awaits me. "

"'What awaits you Lucifer? Is it all right to call you that now?"

"Yes you can call me Lucifer. Only the Most High knows what awaits me now, but I'm sure we will know soon."

"Yes Lucifer, I am sure the Most High does know. Now I think all of us here present are unanimous in believing that you are the one that our ritual and scriptures talk about," Jeremiah looked around the room as they all nodded in agreement. "It just puzzles me that, you being the one, why were you unable to read the final part of the prophecy? Why would Joshua write an incomplete prophecy and why does it not mention what awaits you?"

Lucifer again felt Jeremiah's eyes suspiciously looking at him.

"Jeremiah, can I have a few moments alone with you please?"

"Certainly Lucifer, please gentlemen, if you don't mind." He motioned with his hand for them to leave. All of them stood and retired to the kitchen. When the door was shut, Lucifer turned to Jeremiah.

"I have noticed your suspicious looks and they are well-founded. I feel that I am able to tell you now what I read in the final part of the scroll."

"Are you sure? If the scroll tells you that you cannot divulge ..."

"It's okay, thank you for your concern. But you remember where I left off from the reading?"

"Yes, you started to say it is up to you."

"That's right, it went on to say it is up to me if I want to tell anyone about my death, which is dated tomorrow."

"What, no!" Jeremiah was shaking his head in disbelief, he trembled as he spoke. "That can't happen, I won't let it happen. The scriptures have no mention of this. They only talk about the One returning. You can't arrive and then die so quickly."

"Jeremiah, you know I can read the scriptures; I've proved that. But it does regrettably say at the bottom on the fourth part of the scroll that the prophecy will only be fulfilled after my death tomorrow."

"I still don't understand why God would allow this to happen."

"Jeremiah, were you not the one who was telling me that the Most High knows everything? God's word must not be questioned. I should know, as this is something I have been doing nearly all my existence."

"Yes, I understand. Perhaps you will give us our final answer on life before you die. How you are going to die?"

"That is not written there. All it says is that I will die tomorrow and only then will man know God again and the prophecy will be fulfilled."

"Then Lucifer, I will pray for you in your time of need. I thank you for sharing this confidence with me."

"It feels right that I should be telling you, as you are Joshua's only surviving relative. I hope you won't tell anyone of my fate. I feel it is not the right time to divulge it to anyone else. I don't want anyone trying to stop me or try to persuade otherwise."

"It goes without saying Lucifer," Jeremiah replied and began to weep.

"Why do you weep?"

"All my life I have waited for the prophecy to come true and to meet you. Now it has, only to be taken away so quickly. It seems such a travesty, but the Most High is all-seeing and all-knowing. We have to let God's word come true."

"Who knows, we may even see each other again in another existence. After all, I have lived three times before haven't I? Shall we call the others back in?"

Lucifer stood up and walked over to the kitchen door. Jeremiah watched him, as it began to sink in that Lucifer would be only alive for one more day.

"It is okay you can come back in now," Lucifer told the others, "all that has to be said has been said and will stay between me and Jeremiah."

Without hesitation they all agreed that the communication between Lucifer and Jeremiah would stay a secret between them and even Daniel put his book to one side.

"So Jeremiah, where do we go from here?" Peter asked.

"Lucifer, you will remain with David, it only seems right. The rest of us will remain here with Daniel until after tomorrow's events. Daniel, do you mind if we will stay here this evening? The brotherhood is going to need each other more than ever."

"Of course you can Jeremiah, you can have my bedroom. Peter and Timothy can share the spare bedroom and Mark can have the other. I'll sleep on the sofa; I often rest on it in the afternoons, it's better for my back."

"Okay, that's settled then."

"Sorry Lucifer we have to go," David turned to Lucifer. "John and Mary are expecting us later on, but first we have to go and eat. Ruth is preparing a great dinner for us, then we will leave for the television studio and watch John address the whole world."

"Okay gentlemen, it's been a pleasure meeting you all." Lucifer stood up and shook all their hands. "I would also like to thank you for your fidelity to the cause and the sacrifices you have made to bring the scroll to my attention. I hope I will be able to fulfil your expectations."

David turned to Timothy, Peter and Mark. "It has been an honour to meet you, men of such a stature. As a young brother, I could have only dreamt of meeting the likes of you."

"Not at all," Peter replied, "if it hadn't been for you and your perseverance, your faith would not have led you to discover Lucifer. Take care, and David, look after him."

"Goodbye Jeremiah," David looked back at Jeremiah who had sat on a chair in the corner of the room with a sad and pensive look on his face. "Jeremiah," David called again.

"Oh yes, sorry David, take care and see you soon."

"Come on, I'll open a door for you." Daniel was on his feet and walking into the corridor.

"Thank you, Daniel." David was the first to step out the door. Lucifer stopped to shake Daniel's hand.

"Please tell them all in their how much they all mean to me. If it hadn't been for them I wouldn't have remembered who I was. Tell them I will miss you all very much, but we will see each other again."

He walked out the door but before closing it he turned to Daniel,

"Daniel, don't forget to have your book and pen ready tomorrow to record that is what is to come."

"Thank you Lucifer. God be with you the Master who was lost but is now found."

In the car Lucifer could tell David was aching to ask him about what Jeremiah and he had spoken about in private.

"David my friend, do not worry about what Jeremiah and I spoke about. I just told him about a great thing that is going to happen tomorrow, a special event which you will see yourself tomorrow."

"Okay, thank you, it was just that Jeremiah looked so sad as we left."

"It must be the fact that he was tired more than he admitted. It's been a very exhausting afternoon for all of us and I'm starving. Did you mention that Ruth is doing us dinner?"

"Yes, it should be about ready by now. I'm famished also, though I am very excited about seeing John on television this evening. I don't know if I will be able to eat."

The other brethren watched from Daniel's living room window as David drove off.

"Jeremiah," Mark said, "is it just me or do we all feel that the whole prophecy has not been told or fulfilled?"

"You're right, Mark," they all turned to Jeremiah as he spoke. "What I and Lucifer spoke about in private will remain in private, but what I can tell you is that after tomorrow we will know the prophecy in its entirety. That is why I wanted you all here together tonight and tomorrow, for when the time comes we have to unite and be strong and send our thoughts out to Lucifer in his time of need."

"But –" Timothy put his hand on Peter's shoulder to stop him asking his question.

"I think we all should get some rest now don't you think?" said Timothy.

"What a splendid idea. I'll make some tea and afterwards I'll prepare dinner for us," Daniel said making his way to the kitchen.

Chapter Twenty-One

THE TELEVISION STUDIO was like a maze as John and Mary made their way with the security guard who was escorting them to Andrews' office. The lights above slightly blinded them as they weaved their way through one corridor after another. Cameras were standing lifeless on either side like big black beasts asleep. It wasn't long before they were approaching a glass paned office where they could see Andrew sitting at a desk reading some papers.

"Great to see you again John," Andrew held out his hand as John and Mary walked into his small office. "Hello again Mary. I trust your drive here was comfortable."

John held out a chair for his sister to sit on. "Please sit down, can I get you anything?"

"I would love a cup of coffee," Mary replied.

"John, anything for you?"

"No I am fine, thank you."

"Okay the coffee will be along shortly. I'll just go and get my boss Rebecca, then we can discuss the final points about tonight's interview. You know the general do's and don'ts, I'm sure. I won't be long."

Andrew left and shut the door behind him.

"Well, this is cosy," John said, leaning back in his chair.

The office had glass windows on all four sides,

and Andrew's desk was covered with papers scattered everywhere.

"Look, Mary," Mary turned to see where John was pointing.

People had gathered by the windows looking in on them.

"Stop encouraging them John. Doesn't it make you feel weird, those people staring at you like that?"

"No, not at all. Hello, how are you?"

He waved his hand at one of the ladies, who in return waved back at him, then all of a sudden the crowd gathering outside parted.

"Where are they all going?" Mary asked, confused, then they saw Andrew and a lady heading their way.

"Now that is a woman who demands a lot of respect from her workers. I wonder where she keeps her whips."

"Stop it, John," Mary giggled as the door swung open and Andrew gestured his hand for Rebecca to enter first.

"Rebecca this is –"

"Let me guess Andrew, is it John? The one you have been going on about the last twenty-four hours?"

"Yes," he sheepishly answered.

"Shall we begin?"

She sat down at Andrew's desk. John studied her face as she sat in front of them. She was about forty and had long black hair which was tied back in a ponytail. Her brown eyes were behind thick black-rimmed glasses, her nose was pointed and her lips were covered in a thick red mass of colour.

"I gather from what Andrew told me that you are aware of some of the procedures regarding this interview tonight."

"Yes, he told me briefly about some of the structure and what's expected of me."

"Um, no doubt he has left some of the important detail out, knowing him."

Mary looked at Andrew who stood awkwardly in the corner of his own office like a boy waiting to be scolded.

"I am sure my brother and I are fully aware of what is expected of us, Andrew did his best to relate to us what was necessary."

Andrew looked at Mary and managed to smile.

"Really! Well done, Andrew," Rebecca sarcastically remarked, wiping the smile from Andrew's face.

"So you are aware and happy with the amount of money we are paying you?"

"Yes, but me and Mary have decided to give the money to cancer research. We would be grateful if you could make the cheque payable to a local hospice."

"Okay if that is what you really want."

"Yes it is," Mary replied abruptly.

"Take this then Andrew and make sure it is written out to the appropriate people, but only after the interview is complete and I'm happy it has gone well."

"Sure, Rebecca. Right away."

"Now I've been watching the news very carefully. I'm curious to know more about you, miracle man, and how you were miraculously cured of your cancer in one evening?"

"God always told me in my dreams that I would be cured of my illness and I always saw this happening, but I never saw the face of the person curing me."

"What do you mean?"

"When I had my dreams I was only allowed to see the hands on me doing the healing, I never saw who this person was."

"Well now you are healed and this miraculous thing has happened to you, do you now know whose hands they were?"

"Yes."

There was a long pause.

"Well?" Rebecca broke the silence.

"You'll have to wait for the interview, then I might tell you that."

"Well I really would like to know now and I usually get what I want." Her words were met with silence. "Okay, fine, if you insist. I just wanted you to get a feel for what the interview will be like, that's why I asked you those questions. Here are the structured questions you'll be asked." She handed him an envelope. "I compiled them myself and I think you'll find they'll enable you to put your story out there in the public eye. I want the world to know your story John: how you felt before, during and after your illness."

"I don't know if Andrew mentioned to you that tonight is not only going to be about me and what has happened to my cancer."

"No, Andrew didn't mention anything."

She gave a stern look in Andrew's direction making him feel even more uncomfortable.

"So what did he forget to tell me?"

"I have a very important message for mankind."

Mary looked at Rebecca's face to see if there were any signs that she thought John was a complete madman, Rebecca was looking anxiously at Andrew with her arms folded in an angry stance.

"Go on."

"I don't know what this message is. All I know is that when I am having this interview, God will tell me what is to come."

"Intriguing, are you telling me you will be prophesying on television about the fate of humanity?"

"Yes I am."

There was a brief uncomfortable silence broken only by a glance at one another.

"I'm not entirely sure about this, but we'll go with it and mark my words, I'll be closely watching, ready to cut anything inappropriate and make sure you answer those questions first. Heaven knows it took me ages to compile them. You have two hours to think of some answers. It's nice to meet you. Andrew and word in my office now please."

She stood and waited at the door for Andrew to open it for her.

"See you in a bit," Andrew whispered to them and quickly followed Rebecca to her office.

"That was certainly different. I think the word witch comes to mind."

"Mary, how could you say such a thing? More like a dragon."

They both giggled, then watched as some of the other workers outside started to gather by the window again.

"Don't look now Mary, my freaky friends are back."

"Ignore them, come on let's look at the questions."

In the office down the corridor, Rebecca was sitting at her desk and Andrew was standing awkwardly in front of her.

"Believe me Andrew, I'm not too happy about you doing this interview. I feel I could make a better impression. However as you managed to get the scoop and with the pressure from my bosses, I had to agree to you doing it."

Andrew knew that although Rebecca was very good at her job behind the scenes, her bosses knew that she wasn't a people person and they wouldn't allow her in front of the cameras.

"You will stick to the structure and not deviate from it, is that clear?"

"Very clear, boss."

"And if our prophet wants to do his piece towards the end, allow him. The public will decide if he's a man of God or a total madman. You'd better go and keep them company and get them to sign some forms. I'll go and do a studio check."

Andrew went back to his own office to rejoin Mary and John.

Back at David's house, they were finishing their meal.

"Ruth my love, that was a meal fit for a king."

David was sitting back in his dining-room chair, Ruth was drinking the wine and Lucifer was finishing the last scraps of food of his plate.

"So," Ruth asked, "you two aren't going to tell me what happened this afternoon?"

"Sorry gorgeous, let's just say it was very revealing, not only to our brotherhood, but more importantly to Luther here."

"Ruth." Lucifer turned in Ruth's direction,

"Yes Luther."

"I promised everything will be revealed tomorrow, that is the only thing I can assure you of."

"I'll leave you boys and your secrets. I'm going to get ready. David you can wash up and I'll see you in a while."

"I suppose I'd better do as the boss says. Have you finished Lucifer?"

"Yes, thank you," he handed David his empty plate.

"You are coming with us tonight, aren't you?"

"Yes, I'd like that. It'll take my mind off about tomorrow."

"Yes, ever since we got in the car, you've had a concerned look on your face. I know you've told me as much as you can, but if there is anything I can do, just let me know?"

"Thank you, but I'll also go and get ready and leave you to your womanly chores."

David laughed. "Very funny, I'll see you in a while."

David left the kitchen with the plates piled up in his hands. Lucifer started to slowly walk up the stairs, still contemplating the forthcoming events. He knew that he was going to die tomorrow, but how and why were the two questions burning in the back of his mind. In the bedroom, he sat on the bed and put his head in his hands. For the first time since being cast into human form, he didn't want to leave it. Lifting his head, he noticed once again the picture of Jesus. This time he didn't feel hate and contempt at the face looking at him, but instead he felt empathy for the suffering that Jesus had endured while being nailed on the cross.

"Well brother, it looks like I'm about to meet my fate tomorrow. Then maybe we'll see each other again and you'll find it in your heart to forgive me."

His thoughts were disturbed by a knock on his door.

"Bathroom is free."

Ruth had finished having a shower and was heading back to her bedroom. David was still downstairs washing up; Lucifer could hear the plates knocking together in the kitchen sink. He told himself to pull himself together, grabbed a towel and headed for the bathroom.

Back at the television studio, Andrew had returned to Mary and John and was discussing the upcoming interview.

"Andrew, you have a real charming boss there, don't you?"

"She's okay really. She might seem a bit harsh on the outside, but inwardly I think she cares too much. If it wasn't for her, this studio wouldn't run at all."

"Still, I think she still could be a bit more polite."

"I agree," John joined in the conversation. "Anyway, let's forget about Rebecca and concentrate on tonight's interview."

"Yes, we'll be on air in about two hours. After we've finished up here, I'll show you where the green room is. That's where you'll be before you're called in front of the cameras."

"Wow, this is really exciting. I can't believe this is actually happening."

John was again acting like an excitable schoolboy, Mary thought.

"First, you have to sign some forms. One is to say you agree to the amount of money, the other is a form telling you of your and our rights. Basically, what goes out on air is agreed by both parties. I know it's live television, but if anything embarrassing happens we have the right to stop transmission. Is that clear?"

"Yes, give me the forms. I'll sign them straight away."

"Don't you want to read them first?" Mary had a concerned look on her face.

"No, I am where I am because God wanted me to be. I have every faith in what's going to happen tonight."

"Okay, if you're sure."

She nervously watched as John put pen to paper and scribbled his name in the appropriate place.

"Good, now that's done, I'll take you around and show you the studio so you can familiarise yourself with it. Studios can seem quite daunting, but some people feel right at home in the surroundings. Are you ready?"

"Ready, as I'll ever be."

John was at the door opening it before the other two had chance to get to their feet. Outside the office was a long corridor with desks on either side, some workers had their heads and faces stuck against a computer screen while others watched John the miracle man walk by.

"He's really excited about tonight, isn't he?" Mary looked up to Andrew's remark as they both watched John ahead of them introducing himself to whoever took an interest.

"Yes I think tonight is the most important night of his life."

"Mary, did God really cure him?"

"That I don't know. All I know is that I prayed on the night of him being admitted into hospital and in the morning he was completely cured. It was certainly some kind of miracle, whether God was involved or not, who knows?"

"Yes, he was!" John shouted down the corridor to them.

"How did he hear that?" Andrew marvelled. "He was too far to hear what we were saying."

"Yes, it is a little unnerving. He seems to know what people are thinking. He told me that God tells him what people are thinking and talking about."

"Interesting and slightly uncomfortable. I don't want him knowing my innermost thoughts, though I must say I am really looking forward to doing the interview myself, it's my biggest story so far."

"And it will be the biggest one you will ever do," John called down the corridor again. Andrew lifted his eyebrows and Mary laughed.

"John, turn left, there. That's the make-up department. This will be our first port of call, then I'll show you the studio and introduce you to some of the ground crew and the camera operators."

"I must say," Mary confessed to Andrew, "as it's getting closer I'm getting a little excited myself. Even though I won't be in front of the cameras, just being there for my brother is a very proud moment for me."

"Come on sis, take a seat."

John was already in a big black leather seat and one of the make-up artists was putting a towel around his neck.

"You know that Luther will be here soon. Imagine what he would think seeing you all dolled up?"

"Who's Luther?" Andrew asked.

"Oh, just a close friend I've recently met."

"More than just a friend Mary. I've seen the way you to look at each other," Mary could see John's smiling face reflecting in the mirror.

"That is mine and Luther's business.

"Of course it is. I just have to go and check on something. I'll be back in about half an hour."

"Thank you Andrew, see you soon."

"Luther will be here soon and you have to look your best for him," said John.

"I know, I can't wait to see him again."

She held out her hand to her brother and they held hands with their heads back, enjoying the moment.

Back at the house, Lucifer was ready to leave.

"David, have you changed yet?" Ruth called.

Lucifer and Ruth were downstairs waiting for David who was upstairs putting the finishing touches to his look.

"He is worse than a woman when choosing what clothes to wear, especially when we're going somewhere important. David!" she shouted again

"I'm coming, I'm coming."

David almost ran down the stairs, while moving the top part of his tie side to side to make sure it felt comfortable. "Come on you, Mr Beautiful," Ruth had grabbed him by his arm and was pulling him away from the mirror.

"Yes come on David, Mr Handsome," Lucifer joined in the fun and ruffled David's hair with his hand.

"That is not funny." David pulled his head away from Lucifer's intruding hand. Lucifer laughed, but he felt more serious when thoughts of tomorrow raced back into his mind.

"Ruth have you got the car keys? I left them on the kitchen table."

"Here they are." David looked to see Ruth dangling them between her finger and thumb.

"Thank you," he said and grabbed them from her as he rushed past. "You two coming?" he called out halfway down the path.

"After you," Ruth gestured to Lucifer.

"No please," Lucifer returned the gesture and let the Ruth leave the house first.

At the studio, Andrew had returned to see how the make-up session was going.

"How are you two getting on?"

"Fine I think," John said, eyes shut as the make-up artist was applying the last of the foundation.

Mary couldn't speak; she was having the last of the red lipstick painted on her lips.

"Next, I'll show you the studio where all the action happens."

"There you go, all done. You can open your eyes now," the make-up artist said, pulling off the white cloth and spinning John around in his chair.

"How do I look?"

"Still the same old John, but now you have a very feminine glow about you," Mary joked as she got up from her chair.

"Wow look at you. Do you realise how gorgeous you are Mary?"

"No I'm not, it's only the make-up."

"Actually, you're pretty without the make-up," Andrew said before rushing off ahead to save himself embarrassment. Mary and John followed him arm in arm, giggling.

"Okay, this is Studio Two." Mary and John looked around in the very darkened room. The black walls all around them were imposing as their eyes adjusted. "You can see from the red light above the door that they're recording, so we can't enter. Along down here on the right is Studio One where you'll be. Come on, I'll introduce you to a few people. Over there's Mike, he's the lead cameraman. Mike! Have you got a minute?"

A scruffy man wearing jeans and a black t-shirt walked up to them.

"Mike, this is John, who's being interviewed tonight."

"It is a pleasure to meet you. My aunt works near the hospital. She's told me everything about you, the miracle man. I was supposed to be on holiday this week but when I heard you were coming here for an interview, I cancelled it so I could hear what you have to say."

"I'm honoured you would give up your holiday for me, thank you."

"Not at all and who is this beautiful flower you've brought along? Please tell me it isn't your wife."

"It's my sister Mary and she's not interested."

"Really?"

He ran his hands through his long black greasy hair to try and make himself more presentable.

"Anyway," Andrew continued, "so that's my cameraman. Moving swiftly on, over there is Janet the floor manager." She had her head down looking at some papers and had a headset on which she was talking into.

She briefly paused to acknowledge and wave at them and then carried on talking into the headset. Walking away from Mike, Mary started to feel a bit easier. "Janet makes sure everything runs smoothly on the ground here and if you look up there ..." they both looked up to where Andrew was pointing to, above them was an office with a massive glass window, "... that's where Rebecca will be barking out orders to us all through our earpieces."

"Not everyone," Janet said. "I assume you must be John."

"Yes, I'm John. This is my sister, Mary."

"Nice to meet you. Yes, Rebecca might bark her orders, but I just switch my earpiece off. I've been here ten years longer than her and I certainly could run that office a damn sight better than she does."

"I'm honoured Janet to be in your presence and in such capable hands," John said with a smile.

"I'll see you in a while. I just have to prepare a sound check. Andrew, why don't you let him sit in the chair so we can do a camera angle and sound check at the same time?"

"Great idea, thank you Janet. Come on, it's just around the corner."

The three of them slowly walked around a black wall until they saw a platform with two black leather chairs facing each other. As they were walking towards the chairs, the studio lights started flashing on above them.

"Are you all right?" Mary could feel John's arm getting tighter around her arm as they approached.

"Yes, I'm just getting a little nervous. It all seems so real and that chair is where I will be sitting in one hour's time with millions listening to my every word."

"Don't worry, you have your questions already. If we don't deviate from them and choose some good answers, there'll be no problem."

"Yes, I know, but is it still okay for me to have my speech at the end of the interview?"

"Yes, that's fine, here take a seat, this one will be your one and I will be sat here," said Andrew.

John slowly sat in the chair and its cushioned surface gave way to his weight.

"How does it feel?"

"Very comfortable, although it's a bit hot under those lights."

"Yes unfortunately they are very strong, but we need it for the correct lighting levels."

"Excuse me gorgeous," Mary turned around to see Mike moving a camera into position. It glided towards her like a silent robot and rested facing towards where John was sitting.

"Hurry up Jack," Mike said and looked behind him, calling to his assistant who brought another camera towards them.

"Andrew, can you sit down for a moment? So Jack and I can get the focus and angles right. Mary, you can come and stand next to me if you want."

Mary raised her eyebrow as Mike winked at her.

"I'm okay Mike, thank you. Perhaps it would be better if I went and stood on the other side."

"Please yourself," he said and put on his headphones and instructed Jack to do the same.

"So John, have you any more thoughts about what you'll say at the end of the interview?"

"No I have no idea. God will tell me in due time."

"But what happens if nothing comes to you?"

"I doubt that'll happen, but if it does I think we should work out some sort of signal that I can give you to tell you the interview is over."

"Okay great idea, so after all the questions have been asked and you realise there's nothing more to say, straighten your tie then I'll know that I should wrap things up."

"John, can you move your chair slightly to the left please?" Mike looked through his camera lens and adjusted the focus.

"Here comes Fiona, she's our sound checker."

"Hello there, may I?"

She bent down in front of John and attached a microphone to his tie.

"Okay your turn now, Andrew."

Andrew lifted his chin so Fiona could get a better view. "John, you know you're the talk of the studio." Fiona said. "Me and my mum are fascinated by your story. God must really love you."

"I think God loves everyone Fiona. I'm just fortunate to be the one chosen to relate God's message to the world."

"Still you are a very special person; you must be to have been chosen. Okay, that's you two sorted." She stood back and looked at both of them to make sure the microphones didn't show too much. "Could you just say a few sentences for me so we can get the audio input and output set?"

Mary watched her brother as he and Andrew talked into their microphones. She saw that John certainly looked special sitting there. In her heart she now felt that John was doing the right thing and that he was the right person in the right place doing the right thing. John noticed Mary looking at him and smiled, reassuring her he understood. She smiled back and her heart started to feel a all-too-familiar sensation: it began racing at a great speed. Luther, she thought, must be close.

Outside in the car, David wound his window down to speak to the security guard and show him his driving licence. In the back, Lucifer's heart beat the same rhythm as Mary's. Its strong beat helped to calm him and his worries about tomorrow.

"You say you've come as guests of Andrew Clayton?" the security guard said, looking at all three of them through David's open window.

"Yes, this is Ruth my wife and John's sister, the man who's being interviewed this evening."

"John?" The security guard had a puzzled look on his face.

"You know, the miracle man?" Lucifer sat forward, joining in with the conversation.

"Oh right, yes of course. Wait here a moment, I'll phone reception just to check if you are expected."

He handed back David's driving licence and walked to his phone inside his wooden hut.

"Why do you have a big smile on your face? David looked at Lucifer in his rear-view mirror.

"I'm just excited to be here and I can feel Mary close by."

Ruth just lifted her eyebrows and looked out of her window unamused.

"What's the matter dear?"

"Nothing. I'm just impatient. Where is that man?"

"Here he comes now."

David watched as the security guard returned.

"Okay, so that's fine. Andrew has confirmed that you're expected. Can you just write down your car number plate here for me please?" The security guard handed David a clipboard through his window and David scribbled his name down and handed it back. "The studio you want is down their second on the left, there's plenty of parking. Just follow the signs for reception. They'll issue you with a visitor's pass which you should keep on you at all times. One last thing, enjoy your visit."

Smiling, he pulled his head from the window and signalled to his colleague to lift the wooden barrier in front of David's car.

"Thank you." David closed his window and drove through the gate and headed for the car park.

John rejoined his sister after all the checks had been carried out.

"You're looking a bit flushed there Mary. Your cheeks are so red."

"I'm fine, it must be the heat from those lights. It's so hot in here."

"Or is it the fact that Luther is close by? Come on Mary, you know I can read minds."

"This Luther must mean a lot to you."

Andrew had now joined them.

"Yes you can say that we're close and we have a connection, but can we please change the subject onto something other than me and Luther?"

Mary could see the look of disappointment on Andrew's face.

"At least he'll be able to protect you from our resident Romeo, Mike. I'll show you to the green room where you can help yourself to some drinks. Please stay there until you're called. I suggest you use your time to go through the questions."

"Thank you Andrew, where are you going?" Mary looked back as Andrew left them at the green room door.

"I'm just going to meet your guests. I won't be long."

They both watched as he rushed off down the corridor.

"Do I look okay John?"

"Mary, you look a picture of beauty and grace. You're blessed with a beauty not of this world."

"Now I know you're exaggerating. A simple yes would have sufficed."

"Okay, yes, yes, yes. You are very beautiful. Anyway enough about you, how about me? Do I look respectable enough to be God's messenger in front of those cameras?"

"Yes, very respectable. When I was watching you earlier talking with Andrew, I felt for the first time that you were completely doing the right thing. It's as though your destiny will be fulfilled tonight."

"It certainly will," Ruth said. They hadn't noticed the door behind them open.

"Ruth, come here," John held out his arms for a loving embrace.

Next through the door stepped David who walked over and gave Mary a hug. As she was held tight, she looked over his shoulder to see Lucifer slowly walking in. She felt her heart would burst as he looked at her with a smile. She stood back from David so Lucifer could see how she looked after her makeover, then she was in his arms holding him tightly.

"It's good to see you again. You look amazing and beautiful," he whispered in her ear.

"It's good to see you too. I've missed you."

"Right," Andrew said as he returned. "We will be on air in about twenty minutes. John I will come and get you in fifteen. Don't forget to straighten that tie, if needed."

"What did he mean by that?" Ruth asked as he left the room.

"Nothing, he just wants me to look my best for the camera. Mary, is any chance of me greeting Luther now?"

"Sorry yes," she stood back as John took hold of Lucifer's hand.

"It's good to see you again, are you still happy with your new name?"

"Yes, thank you,"

"What new name?" Mary asked.

"I am sure Luther will tell you in his own time. Now tell me why do I feel a sense of apprehension about you? After all, I'm the one doing the interview."

"It's nothing," Lucifer said. "I just have something to do tomorrow, something which is playing on my mind."

"God hasn't told me what that is, so I expect we'll find out when we need to. Please everyone, sit down and try and help me forget my nerves."

Andrew was getting his final orders from Rebecca as he sat in the make-up room.

"So we're quite clear," she said, "that once all the relevant questions have been asked and answered, we will not under any circumstances prolong the interview for John to do his speech."

"Yes we've decided that if he finds that he has nothing to say, he will signal me by straightening his tie."

"All right, that's decided. Even though you should

have discussed that arrangement with me first." The make-up artist pulled a face behind her back which Andrew caught sight of in the mirror. "Are we nearly done here? Time is getting close."

"He will be done in about five minutes Rebecca. I will have him looking like a prince."

She winked at Andrew from behind him in the mirror.

"Just get it done and make him look more presentable. I'm on my way upstairs for some final checks." She put her head phones on and spoke into the microphone. "Janet, Janet where are you? Dammit, I swear she switches that thing off whenever I want to speak to her. Janet!"

They both laughed as she walked off, calling her floor manager's name.

In the green room, the minutes were ticking by and John heard more voices outside as the studio filled up with the production crew.

"I am so proud of you, John." Ruth took hold of John's hand and squeezed it tightly.

"Thank you Ruth, and thank you all for you all your support. I must say I'm really nervous but also excited at the same time."

"Have you got your answers ready in your mind?"

Mary had noticed that John had laid the envelope on the floor.

"Vaguely, I think. I hate structured questions because they don't allow you freedom of free thought and inspired talk. I'm not going to bother with the structured questions, I'll just go with the flow."

"Is that wise?" Ruth had a concerned look on her face.

"Very wise, Ruth. I am sure God will make sure everything goes right tonight."

They all stopped talking as the door behind them opened.

"Are you ready, John?" Janet said. "Your audience awaits. Andrew is already miked up and waiting for the cameras to roll."

"Yes, I'm ready Janet, lead the way. I have a message the whole world needs to hear."

Before leaving the room, he looked back at Lucifer who was looking down at the ground morosely.

"Hey Luther, everything will be okay. God did not save me just so I could live. There was a reason and you are part of that reason. Don't lose faith in the Most High. I'm sure you'll make the right choice."

"Please can we go John? We're cutting it very fine," Janet interrupted.

"Sorry Janet, see you all later."

Lucifer looked at John and whispered, "Thank you".

"Luther, will you join me here?" Mary patted the chair next to her with her hand.

"Of course," he stood up and joined her on the sofa.

Ruth pushed her husband from his chair.

"Come on David, turn the television on. We want to see our brother in action."

David flicked the switch on. As the picture cleared, they saw the final part of the news being read out.

"How much longer to go?" Mary asked and David looked at his watch.

"About three minutes and then the news will end and John will be on live."

All four of them sat in front of the television nervously watching the time tick by.

On the studio floor, Fiona made sure that John's microphone was correctly fitted. The whole studio had now fallen into complete silence. In the office, Rebecca flicked the switch and turned on the red light to indicate they were going on air, and then she counted down.

"On my mark, 10, 9, 8, 7, 6, 5, 4, 3, 2 and cue Andrew, you are on."

"Good evening and welcome to Inspired TV with me, Andrew Clayton. On tonight's show, we have the extraordinary story of a man who claims to have been miraculously cured of cancer by the hand of God.

No doubt you have read about it in the papers. He's being hailed as the miracle man. Tonight we get an in-depth exclusive story of this so-called miracle man and the events leading to his miraculous recovery."

"Good evening, John."

"Good evening, Andrew."

"First of all I would like to say how happy I am that you have beaten a dreadful illness. Please could you tell me and the people at home how long you had been suffering."

"I was diagnosed about three years ago. The doctors told me that it was terminal and I would only have about five years to live."

"So obviously you were suffering for a while. I'm sure some of the audience who are watching at home in similar circumstances can sympathise with the pain you endured."

"Yes I suffered tremendously. It was a very painful illness, although not all the time. It was a bit like a rollercoaster ride. One minute I felt I was going to die, the next I felt like I could live another year."

"It must have been difficult, how did you cope?"

"With lots of painkillers and the healing hands of my lovely sister Mary."

In the green room, they all looked at Mary. Ruth rubbed her sister's back in appreciation.

"Tell us a bit about your feelings aduring your illness."

"Like I said it was a bit like our rollercoaster ride, but it seemed when I was at my lowest ebb God would talk to me in my dreams."

"What did God talk about?"

"Are you seeing this?"

One of the producers sitting next to Rebecca in the office pointed to a computerised number on the panel in front of them.

"What?" she snapped.

"Our viewing figures. The highest it has ever been and people in other countries are now switching on to us."

"That's impossible. How come people in other countries got to know about this interview so quickly?"

"I don't care as long as these numbers keep rising, the bosses will be very happy."

"He's certainly living up to his name, the miracle man," Rebecca replied as they gazed down to John and Andrew in the studio below them who were still in deep discussion.

"God told me in my dreams that everything would be all right and I had a recurring dream."

"What was that dream about?"

"In the dream, I was first told that it would soon be all over and I would be free. At first I thought that this meant my death, but then I dreamt of a man standing in the shadows. I couldn't see his face because he was only a silhouette. But when he was standing in the darkness, a beautiful light still shone through. At first he would just stay in the darkness, then finally he emerged from the darkness and put his hands on me. The final thing I would see before the dream ended was a tattooed arm adorned with an angel, then I would wake up."

"So are you telling me and all the people at home God saved you via a dream?"

"No, those dreams prove to be just a premonition of what was to come."

"Are you saying this actually happened?"

"The evening before I was admitted into hospital, my other sister Ruth and her husband came around and brought along a friend."

"Who was his friend?"

"It was a stranger David had met. David is Ruth's husband and a very charitable man, and so being of this nature he took the stranger in, fed and clothed him."

"What happened next?"

"Me and Luther, sorry that's the stranger's name, were left in a room alone. We were having a philosophical debate about life, you know things like good and evil, then the next thing I remember is that I am choking and feeling like I was about to die. Then all of a sudden Luther was standing above me trying to help me. I took hold of his arm pulling on his sleeve and noticed a tattoo of an angel."

Lucifer watched intently as John carried on his narrative. He knew full well that it was his initial intention to kill John for his insolence, but he inadvertently ended up saving him.

"The next thing I remember was waking up in hospital with Mary by my side. I then found out that I had been completely cured of cancer."

"So there were no visions of God curing you when you were unconscious or anything like that?"

"No, although since waking up from my comatose state, I can now hear God when I'm awake. I also can feel and sense what is in the minds and hearts of men and women. I also have the ability to tell mankind of future events."

"Really?" Andrew continued, his voice filled with a sense of excitable intrigue, "Is there anything you can tell us and all the viewing people at home what the future holds for us?"

Making the link, Andrew wondered if John would give him the signal whether he should terminate the interview or not. John sat and waited for a while to see if he was going to get any information from the Most High. Just as his faith was fading and his hand was moving to his tie, his head flew backwards so he was looking up to the ceiling.

"John, are you all right?" Andrew said, scared that his interviewee was having a fit.

"John!" Mary screamed in the green room. She rushed to the door, but as she was about to open it, an invisible force threw her back into her chair. She tried to get up again, but all of them including Lucifer were held firm in their chairs by an unseen force.

Andrew and the rest of the staff in the studio were also frozen on the spot unable to move. In the office, Rebecca and the producers were all sitting motionless, only their breathing and eye movement allowed by the unseen power.

John started to breathe heavily as his head slowly came forward. His eyes had now turned a sapphire blue. He turned to the camera and blue light reflected out from his eyes like a lightning bolt and fired all around the studio. The light hit the cameras, causing them to spark and malfunction. Televisions worldwide were forcibly turned over to another channel. In dozens of countries, people got out of their chairs at home to try and switch over but to no avail. It was as though time had stood still.

In his office in the East, General Silas was watching. He lit a cigar and stared at John intently.

"To the people of the world I now speak to you in a universal language. It is the language which all men hear, the one that was born in their breast since time began. I am a messenger from God."

General Silas sat forward in disbelief and turned his television up on hearing these words.

"For a long time now, God has been watching man and his actions. He is very displeased with your evil deeds and the sins you have engaged in. It will no longer be tolerated and the Most High is saddened by your contempt for one another. Your actions unfortunately come with a price, that is why God's judgment is coming to the world tomorrow. A judgment that will see the end of man and their hateful ways. Not only will evil man and women be destroyed, but the blood of innocents will be spilled and sustained. Mankind, weep for yourself as your life on Earth is coming to an end."

General Silas fell to his knees on the floor in front of the television, as the world was told of the destruction he would be bringing tomorrow. He put his face against the television screen and spoke urgently to God.

"My God on high, you address the world and speak of my actions, how honoured and humbled I am by your very word."

He threw himself to the floor and started praying.

Back in London, the strange voice coming from John continued.

"I ask you people of Earth to repent and your souls might be saved in heaven. Repent not and suffer a fate worse than death."

The camera zoomed in automatically by some unseen force on John's face, and the blue eyes shone even brighter as he spoke into the camera. "Brother, join me here now."

Lucifer found that the invisible force holding him dissipated. He stood up and tried to release the rest of them in the room, but it proved fruitless. He again turned and looked at the television in front of him. He knew that John's eyes were staring at him in particular.

"Come brother, come hither, I have a whisper only fit for worthy ears."

He left the green room and slowly walked to where John and Andrew were sitting. As he got closer his own red energy started to glow. Mary, Ruth and the rest of the world watched as Lucifer walked in front of the camera. The camera followed his steps as he walked up to John.

"Bend to me brother, hear my words, for I must tell you something and the world can witness that I, as a messenger from God, have done my work."

Lucifer bent forward and put his ear to John's mouth. The camera zoomed in on John's mouth moving and Lucifer nodding in acknowledgment of what had been said to him. Lucifer's red glow began to get stronger as he pulled away from John.

"Now brother you have heard my word, remember it well, now go and retreat and contemplate your fate for the time is nearly at hand."

The camera stayed fixed on John as Lucifer left him and returned to the green room.

"Mankind you have witnessed the passing of the word from God. It now lies with my faithful brother. This is done at the end of time and I tell you to look to the east for God's wrath is coming. It will be swift and decisive, no man, woman, child or beast will survive that which comes from the east."

John's head shot back again. The lights on the ceiling started flashing off and on and the blue light from John started shooting around the room again. It blasted through the camera, smashing the glass lenses. The window of the office came crashing down on the floor scattering pieces of glass everywhere. Everybody in the studio still could not move and yet they were not being harmed in any way by the chaos going on around them. As smoke started to billow around the studio like a ghost, Mary, David and Ruth became free of their invisible prisons.

"Come on, let's get John." Lucifer led the way through all the chaos towards John who was slumped forward in his chair.

"David, take Ruth and Mary to the car. I'll get John."

He bent forward and put John over his shoulder and followed David. Before leaving, Lucifer turned back to Andrew and shouted, "Thank you, you have served God well and it will not be forgotten on judgment day." These words fell unheard because Andrew was slumped in his chair after fainting.

Lucifer then turned and kicked the exit doors open which led into the car park. David had started the car and was waiting for him to appear.

"Come on, get in." Mary opened the back door. Lucifer bent forward and gently laid John on the rear seat with his head resting on Mary's lap.

Lucifer jumped in and closed the door.

"Are we all in?" David asked.

"Yes David, just drive," Ruth snapped, panicking at

the chaos happening all around them and the studio burning into flames lighting up the dark evening sky. David put his foot on the accelerator and without stopping he smashed through the wooden barrier where the security guards were still unable to move. Ruth screamed as some of the window screen cracked and pieces of wood went flying either side of the car.

"Oh great," David said, looking in the rear view mirror.

"What is the matter David?" Mary asked.

"I think the police are after us."

Lucifer and Mary looked out the back window, and saw blue and red lights lighting up the night sky.

"It is okay, they're stopping at the studio entrance," Mary said.

As they got further away, fire engines and ambulances shot past them heading in the opposite direction to join the police. Soon the flashing lights had given way to the dark blanket of a night sky as they made their way home.

"Where am I? Ouch, my head," John said, regaining consciousness and slowly sitting up.

"On our way home. Do you not remember anything?" Ruth turned around in the front seat to speak to her brother.

"Now the last thing I remember was that I was reaching for my tie to give the signal. Why what has happened?"

John listened intently, his eyes wide open as each member of the car gave a short account of what had happened.

"So what was whispered in your ear, Luther?"

"That I can't tell you, it will be known when it has to be known and not before."

"Is it good news though? I noticed your energy came to life when John whispered in your ear," Mary smiled.

"I think it's not good news for the world after hearing John's prophecy," David remarked. "What are we going to do?"

"I don't understand it, why would God save me only so I would die the next day?"

"Let's just get home so we can think it through. If the end of the world doesn't come tomorrow, we'll have the police to deal with, not to mention scientists and clergymen all wanting answers about what has just happened. On the other hand, if death and destruction does come tomorrow, the police and other people will be the last of our worries. We will have our souls to worry about."

They weren't driving long before they could see the lights of their home town lighting up the sky in an orange glow.

"Do you believe this is last night alive on Earth?" Mary asked.

"I don't know Mary." John answered. "What do you think, Luther?"

Mary turned to look at him, David was watching him in the rear-view mirror and Ruth was facing him.

"Let us just say that man will face their fate tomorrow whatever that fate might be."

"Is there nothing we can do?" John sat up again.

"No, man's destiny is now in God's hands. The best thing you can all do now is pray."

"So if we are going to be spending our last night on Earth, we should at least spend it together. Let's all go back to Mary and John's house and wait and pray."

The car fell silent as David sped off to Mary's house.

Back at the studio, crew members were moving about again. No one was harmed, only shaken up about what had just happened. A policeman was interviewing Andrew.

"So you were the interviewer and you're telling me you can't remember the name of the person you were interviewing?"

"All I know that is his name was John and he called himself the miracle man. We do have his paperwork in my office, I can get that for if you like."

"That would be very helpful. The sooner we find out where this person lives the better. We will make some enquiries, hopefully we can get answers to this mess before MI5 get involved and start walking all around our crime scene, and this bloody awful mess, what the hell happened here anyway, can someone tell me? Before you go, just answer me one question: is this John we watched on television a true prophet of God?"

"I have no idea, but tomorrow I guess we'll all find out." Andrew shouted as he ran down the corridor to get John's paperwork from his office.

CHAPTER TWENTY-TWO

AS THE NIGHT DRAGGED on in the west, the sun began to rise in the east, dispelling the darkness of the previous evening. In his room, General Silas was nearly naked on the mystic symbol painted on the bare wooden floor. A lit candle was positioned on top of a drawing of the sun in the east and a candle in the west stood on the face of a moon. The general knelt in silence as he watched the sun getting higher and brighter. Its reflection made the shadows in his room seem like dark figures crawling up the walls.

"My God, I have heard you call for war. I am honoured that you should choose me to be your hand on Earth that smites its inhabitants. Lord, I know I will not fail when the time is right. Let your will guide my heart and give me the courage to execute my mission."

He held up a red metal key, the one he would be using to launch the nuclear missiles.

"With this key, I will unleash your wrath on Earth and no man or woman will be able to escape our work."

He moved the key slowly to his lips and kissed it. He then placed it around his neck and then leant forward to kiss the floor where the candle was alight in the east.

In a room not too far away, the Captain was alone, watching the sun rise. He sat on his chair on a balcony. He had told his bodyguard to wait outside so he could have a moment alone.

A tear rolled down his cheek as he ran his finger across a photograph he was holding, a picture of his family taken when he was a child. He was in the centre and his mother was behind him with her hands on his shoulders. His father had his arm lovingly around his mother and both his brothers were either side, one of them pulling a face.

"My family, how I've missed you. I'm so very honoured that I have been given the opportunity to be with you again soon in paradise. I hope you've been watching over me and are proud of what I've achieved."

He wiped the tears from his eyes and took hold of the blue key in front of him.

"You my friend are the key to my eternal life of happiness and a reunion with my family. I am not going to let you out of my sight."

He looked at his watch: it was approaching seven thirty. Another half-hour until he would leave to meet his destiny. He put the photo in his pocket and hung the key around his neck again. He reclined in his chair and enjoyed breathing in the morning air for the very last time.

Back down the corridor the general was still kneeling.

"Michael, messenger of the Most High, I am in this sacred symbol invoking your assistance. Come to me."

He repeated this several times but nothing happened. It was only when he was going to blow out his candle that the yellow flame turned blue and in the centre of this blue flame Michael's face appeared.

"Michael, I humble myself before you."

Silas bent forward without looking up.

"Why have you summoned me Silas?"

"Forgive me Michael, even though my faith is strong

and true, I was just wondering if it was still my charge to carry out what has to come."

"Yes Silas the Most High is pleased with your fidelity and still holds you in favour. Continue as instructed and you will receive your reward in heaven. Everything is going to plan and the prophecy will be fulfilled as God ordained it when time began. Fear not, be strong and do what must be done."

The blue light began to fade, returning to its yellow form. For a while Silas remained in a posture of submission then he slowly lifted his head. He stretched and breathed in the power he was feeling. Soon, he thought, I will literally be God on Earth and no one will be able to stop me. He bent forward and blew the candle out and replaced the rug over the floor, then turned to his uniform that was lying neatly ironed on his bed.

"Soon I will be wearing my sacrificial robes. You are the last thing I will wear at the end of time."

He picked up his boots to see if they were perfectly polished, then kneeled to replace them at the foot of his bed.

"Now for my final shower. I must clean my skin in preparation for meeting the Most High."

Taking one more look at his uniform, he smiled then walked off to the shower.

Back at Mary's house, they sat up talking and watching television into the early hours of Sunday morning. The news showed frequent reports on John's interview. Reporters questioned whether the whole event had been staged. Most of the public officials interviewed on television reassured the public that it had been a hoax and the end of the world was not coming.

"If only the world knew," John said disappointed. "If I was supposed to give God's message, why is it not being heard or believed?"

"Hold on a minute, John," David raised his hand to silence John as a reporter spoke on the television.

"We tried to speak to the television studio that arranged this interview about the events of the evening, but they have declined to answer any of our questions. They did state that their studios had been vandalised and police are following up enquiries. But all of us have one question left unanswered: was it an elaborate hoax or do we only have hours left to live? I think the most reasonable and stable-minded of us will think that God has no plan to wipe us off the face of the earth. This is Peter Jones, Global News."

Lucifer sat in a corner of the room not saying a word. He had been silent since arriving back at Mary's house. He smiled occasionally when Mary turned to him to see if he was still in the room.

"David, please switch the television off. I've heard enough of this nonsense." John asked David as he waved at the television,

David leant forward and switched off the television.

"Luther, can you tell us why the people watching this evening have not believed me? They heard the angel speaking through me and yet people still don't believe. They would rather live in ignorance in spite of all the evidence shown to them."

Lucifer sat for a while and pondered John's question, then he began to speak.

"John, we all know what happened tonight was genuine. The people at the television studios also knew this and yet the world has not heard your warning."

"Yes, we know that already," Ruth rudely interrupted.

"What I am trying to say is that mankind only believe what they want to believe. For instance, if John went around telling people that he was a man of God, those people would ask him to prove it. If eventually he did prove it, those people would be fearful and they would say it was a case of schizophrenia or John was crazy. They would rather deny the existence of God than having something strange happened in their lives.

Man has become so full of self-importance to worry about affairs of other people let alone the whole world. They have satisfied themselves with their possessions, so much so that the search for truth is no longer a priority. However, there are a few who are searching for truth and if they seem to be getting too close to the truth, scientists and governments, backed up by the police, step in to squash this newfound truth out of fear of losing control."

"But how do you account for people's belief in me as the miracle man?"

"That's different. Something happened that people didn't see. Admittedly, you were cured of cancer, but they didn't see how you were cured of cancer. So they put this down to their faith in an all-healing god. It's ironic that people would rather believe something they don't see rather than what they saw on television this evening. It's as if the human race after thousands and thousands of years is still not ready for the truth."

"Yes but..." John began.

Lucifer lifted his hand to avoid another question. "I'm very tired and if you don't mind, I'd like to spend my last hours alive on my own in contemplation."

"Are you telling us that John's prophecy is true? That the end is coming?" Mary asked Lucifer.

"Yes, I'm afraid the prophecy is true and what was whispered in my ear earlier this evening were my instructions."

"What instructions? Are you the one who is going to cause this mass extermination?" Ruth asked.

"Please. I just want to be alone. I suggest you find some time for yourselves to pray and ask for God's forgiveness."

"Luther!" Mary pleaded.

"Let him go Mary," John held back his sister as Lucifer left the room and went upstairs to be alone.

"Is he the one who is going to annihilate us?" Ruth looked around at John, Mary and David.

"Shut up Ruth," Mary said, "of course not, can you not see how sad he looks? I think he's just as scared as us."

"Please don't argue. We only have a short time left. Let's draw together and become closer in our time of need," John pleaded with Ruth and Mary.

Mary could see her sister had fearful tears in her eyes. "You're right John. Sorry for snapping at you Ruth. Come and sit here with me."

"I'm just going to phone Jeremiah." David got up out from his chair and headed for the phone.

"John, God speaks to you, have you heard any more since getting home?" Ruth wiped the tears from her eyes as she spoke.

"Now God has fallen silent," John said. "It's like the calm before the storm. Whatever is coming will be big."

In the hallway, David dialled Jeremiah's number.

"Hello Jeremiah, I hope I didn't wake you, phoning you so late,"

"No, it's okay."

"Did you see John being interviewed?"

"Yes we did. All of us sat and watched it and now we're waiting for the inevitable."

"Yes we are too. Lucifer has gone upstairs to be on his own. Jeremiah, maybe I shouldn't ask you this, but when you spoke to Lucifer this evening in private, did he tell you that he would be the cause of all our deaths?"

"No! He will be just like the rest of us at the end of time. He'll be suffering."

"So what was the point of the Scriptures? Why did Lucifer have to incarnate in human form? What have we learnt from all this mess?"

"I do not know, my dear boy. But all I can say is that maybe we are being shown our way back to God again on the eve of destruction."

"Yes I suppose faith is being called into question and I suppose Lucifer is the one who has to question his the most."

"David, I believe you're right. I will now return to my

brethren so we can pray. God be with you David and your family."

"And you, Jeremiah. When the time comes I will see you again in Paradise."

"Yes, goodbye, David. Good luck."

General Silas had just finished adjusting his black beret in front of the mirror when there was a knock on his door.

"Enter!" The door opened and in walked the Captain.

"Are you ready my General? The jeep is waiting downstairs."

"Yes Captain, do you have everything?"

The Captain lifted the black electronically-locked briefcase which was handcuffed to his wrist.

"And you have your key?"

The Captain smiled at the General and pressed his hand on his chest to show that the key was safely fastened around his neck.

"Okay Captain, it is time. Let's go and make history and meet our destiny."

Driving along in the jeep, the Captain looked along the streets. Beggars held out their hands in a desperate attempt for a donation. People with diseases were aligned all along the pathways watching them as they drove past.

"It's a shame, is it not Captain?" the General said. "And yet they will not be suffering for much longer. All their pain and suffering will soon be at an end because of our work and what we are about to do."

The Captain turned to look back at the people. Admittedly, these people were suffering, but what about the people who were not? The people who were happy with their lives, did they not deserve a chance? For the first time, his resolve wavered but he reassured himself that the General was right and the divine command he had been given was true. After all who was he to question the word of God?

An hour later, they arrived at the nuclear defence facility. Guards saluted them as they drove past. The sandy road sloped down into a tunnel. As they entered the tunnel, the roar of the engine bounced off the walls surrounding them. Their driver switched on their headlights and carried on into the darkness.

"Are you excited or afraid my friend?" the General asked his companion.

"A mixture of both. I am excited about seeing my family again, but afraid of the pain I will feel when my flesh is being burnt off my body while I'm alive."

"I am also afraid of that, but I do believe that the reward will outweigh any pain we receive before death."

The General tapped the driver on the shoulder to signal him to stop at the next turning. The jeep pulled up alongside an illuminated glass building. The Captain left the vehicle and held the door open for the General as he stepped out. The two guards saluted the General and Captain as they entered, then they made their way to a main office where the door was securely fastened. Either side of the door were two keyholes, one in blue and one in red. The General took his red key and signalled the Captain to use his blue one. They both turned at the same time and the door slid open. Inside the room were lots of computers with arrays of colours flashing. On the walls were maps of the Western world and in front of them was a massive window to another room where scientists were busily working and constantly watching a massive radar screen.

The General walked forward to the glass panel and switched on a microphone in front of him.

"Dr Amir, would you come to the red room at once?"

One of the scientists looked up at the glass window to see the General and Captain looking down at him. He waved and gave his clipboard to another one of the scientists and left the room.

"Please sit down Captain," the General told his second-in-command, "I just have to clarify a few things with Amir."

As the Captain sat down he could see on the computer panel in front of him the key holes to launch the missiles. They were securely locked by a metal frame. There was a knock on the door.

"Come in."

Dr Amir walked in and shook the General's hand and then stepped forward to shake the Captain's.

"It is good to see you both again, especially on a glorious day like today."

"Yes Doctor, it's good to see you too. Now tell me, are we ready to go and are all the coordinates set?"

"Yes, look," he said and pointed to a massive computerised map of the world, "as you can see we have highlighted certain points of the countries in the West in red. This is where the missiles will strike causing optimum destruction. Soon there will not be much left of the West as we know it."

"Excellent, so if everything is set we able to proceed on schedule. I would like to launch at twelve precisely when the sun is at its most high."

"Everything will be ready by then. I just have to finalise some systematic operations then we'll be ready."

"Thank you, Doctor, for all you have done and God be with you. I will address everybody at eleven o'clock."

"We all will be waiting. God be with you General Silas and you Captain," he said and turned and left the room.

"What time is it now Captain?"

"Ten, sir."

"Good, would you like a drink?"

"Yes, I would like one very much, my mouth is a little dry."

"Mine too," he laughed. "Mine too."

Lucifer lay on his bed looking up at the ceiling. He had slowed his breathing down until he was in an almost meditative state. The darkness of the room surrounded him as he lay there contemplating his existence. He thought it was ironic that he should be lying here on this bed in human form, waiting for the end of the world, where before he had been lying on the rock in the desert in angelic form. It was as though his existence had now come full circle. This time however it was different. Before, he was the one bringing destruction to man, now it was God's turn. God would be the one to bring destruction to him and mankind. His thoughts were disturbed by a gentle knock on the door.

"I thought I said I wanted to be alone."

"It's only me," Mary popped her head inside the door. "Can I come in? I've brought you a cup of tea with lots of sugar."

"Thank you, please come in."

She walked in and closed the door behind her and sat at the foot of Lucifer's bed.

"Here you go," she handed him the tea while looking at him intently.

"What?"

"Tell me what's bothering you? I know it's not just that we will all be soon blown to pieces. There's something else, I can feel it."

"I'd rather not talk about it."

"Why not think of it as your confession while you still have a chance."

"Very well, if you put it like that. Though you might not like what you are about to hear."

"We won't know that until you tell me, will we?"

"Earlier on today at the meeting with the brotherhood, I discovered some truths about myself, truths I had hidden away and forgotten."

"What truths?"

"My name is not really Luther."

"I know, you were going to find your true name, did you?"

"Yes, well one of them anyway," a confused look appeared on Mary's face, "I suppose the name you might commonly know me as is ..."

He paused looking at Marys' fragile face wondering whether she could handle what he was about to say.

"Well?"

"It is Lucifer or Satan, take your pick"

Mary sat back, confused and afraid. Lucifer sighed.

"You see, that is the reaction I was hoping to avoid. So what do you think of the monstrosity in front of you now?"

"I am a little stunned, especially now I have been told that I'm in presence of the devil."

"Are you not afraid?"

"No not at all, I'm just confused."

"Why?"

"If you are Lucifer, then how can I explain what I feel for you?"

"I expect I am the darkness and you are the light. They do say opposites attract."

"Hold on, let us rewind a bit. Did you not say this was one of your names?"

"Yes I am also known by others. I was told that I got the name Lucifer from man because they needed to give a name to all the evil that exists in the world."

"So what are these other names you have?"

"My first name was Altithronus, that is what the scripture helped me to remember."

"One seated in heaven on a throne, so now I should not be afraid but be honoured to be in your presence," Mary said. Lucifer looked at Mary, surprised. "Oh, I studied Latin and philosophy at university."

"Now it is me who should feel honoured to be in your innocence and presence. You are such a beautiful work of God, untouched by the evils of man."

"Please I deserve no praise. I have just followed my heart all my life and remained true to myself no matter what."

"I am so happy you had the privilege of knowing yourself. It seems my whole existence as all been about getting to know myself again."

Mary calmly sat and listened to Lucifer while he told her his whole story, about his confusion and feeling he had been betrayed only to discover that had not been the case, and the more he explained the more she felt for him,. She felt his pain when he told her about his people in the east being massacred and having to be buried for forty days.

"It must have been awful to have been a man so full of love only to lose it, a love hidden away inside you away from yourself and the world because of your revenge, hate and contempt of mankind. It must be even worse now."

"What do you mean?"

"Well you have only just discovered your true identity. Now in a matter of hours we are all going to be wiped of the face of the earth. Are you not angry?"

"Yes I am angry, but in turn I'm happy that I did get to know myself before the end. That's what is making my decision so hard."

"What decision?"

"That I can't tell you, but when it's all over, you'll know if I made the right one. But what I can tell you is that I have been given a new name. It was whispered in my ear just after receiving my instructions from the angel that possessed John tonight."

"Really! What is it?"

"It is –"

Lucifer suddenly screamed in pain.

"Luther, what's wrong?"

"The sun is beginning to rise. Where's my coat? I need it and I need to get outside. Quick Mary, get my coat."

Lucifer groaned again. Mary bolted out the door and descended the staircase two steps at the time. As she reached the bottom she noticed a red glow shining from the black coat hanging on the bottom of the staircase. It was lighting up the whole hallway with its red light.

"Mary!" Lucifer shouted. The others ran into the hallway panicking to see what all the noise was about.

"Mary," David called to her as she went to grab the coat. "What are you doing, it could be dangerous, don't touch it."

A lion-like roar came from upstairs, startling everybody.

"Lucifer needs it," she shouted.

Without a second thought she took it in her hands, and held it close to her chest as she rushed upstairs. As she reached the top, her whole body lit up with a beautiful sapphire blue. The rest of them followed her upstairs to Lucifer's room. The roars and cries were getting louder as they approached. Mary pushed the door open and saw Lucifer rolling side to side on his bed, his eyes shining like rubies in the dark.

"My coat do you have it?" he managed to ask between cries.

"My love, here it is."

"I need to put it on, can you help me?"

"David, will you and John help me please?"

Ruth stood watching, astonished, as her husband and brother helped Mary. David and John took hold of an arm each and pulled Lucifer to his feet. Behind Lucifer, Mary struggled to put the coat over his arms. Eventually the coat was fully on and Lucifer pulled the red glowing collar around his neck.

"Thank you, I must go outside now and witness sunrise for the final time."

Slowly David and John helped Lucifer down the stairs, Mary followed behind issuing orders to both men to be careful. Lucifer cried out again.

"Hurry, I must be outside."

They made their way through the corridor into the kitchen where Mary opened the kitchen door to let them outside. The sun was just breaking over the horizon as they got into the garden. Lucifer lifted his head to look at its golden glow. The heat started to warm his forehead as he breathed in the early morning scent.

"Please leave me now, I have to be alone, leave me on the grass over there."

"No! I won't leave you, you need my help and you are in pain," Mary cried.

"Go! Do as I say, I will call you if I need you, but now please just leave me. This will be my one and only holy moment."

"I understand. Come on Mary." John gently took her arm

John and David led Mary back into the house. Mary glanced back at Lucifer. He was looking at her with his red eyes shining. As they held their look Mary noticed a red tear roll from his eye down his cheek and onto the ground below.

"Can we not help him?" Mary said, still trying to persuade her brother to let her go.

"Now Mary, you heard him, he wants to be alone."

They all watched him from the kitchen window. One moment he was rolling on the floor the next he was kneeling praying to the sun as it made its way into the morning sky.

"What is that?" Ruth cried out.

They all looked to where she pointed. There was something moving underneath Lucifer's coat at the back. Lying on his stomach, the coat at the back was getting bigger. Then all of a sudden Lucifer let out a mighty roar as two wings pierced through his flesh and tore their way through the coat, all the time growing in size. Before their very eyes, the wings grew bigger and started to glow a golden yellow, reflecting in the morning sun as they gently moved side to side.

"It may be the end of the world soon, but I can safely say I'm going to die a happy man after seeing such a beautiful sight," John said, his eyes wide at the view before him.

Now on his feet, Lucifer's cries and roars ceased. He stood in a humble state of reverence, head bowed to greet the morning sun. His red glow was shining brighter than ever. He turned to face the people watching him. All of them, except Mary, did not know where to look. Humility made them feel unworthy of such a sight.

"Mary, what are you doing?" David nervously asked her as she went to open the kitchen door.

"It's all right, look."

Lucifer was beckoning them to come outside. Cautiously, they followed Mary outside to where Lucifer was standing.

"Behold you now, see me as Lucifer as I stand before you. I stand as a witness at the end of time. Today man's eyes will truly be open to how great God is. I want to thank you all for your assistance, especially you Mary, for without your love I would not have found myself again. Can I have a moment with Mary alone please?"

"Of course, come on David and Ruth. Let's give them a moment."

After they had all gone inside, Lucifer looked at Mary, his eyes now ablaze with fire.

"Mary, I soon have to depart from here to face my fate as do you and the rest of the world. But before I go I want to give you something."

He took hold of Mary and bent forward to her face. She closed her eyes and waited for a kiss. Instead he went to her ear and whispered, "I want you to know my new name."

"What's Luther doing?" Ruth called out to David and John as she watched from the kitchen window.

"Ruth, we were supposed to be giving them privacy," David said as they joined her in the kitchen.

As they looked out of the window, Mary's body became a beautiful purple colour, lighting up the kitchen where they were all standing.

"So Mary, you now know my new name. Guard it well for it may be called upon again." He kissed her on her cheek. "Sorry Mary, I now really have to be on my way. The time is very close. I will call you again when it is time for me to say goodbye."

He let go of her arms and she retreated sobbing uncontrollably back to the house.

"What did he say to you?" Ruth asked her sister.

"He told me a secret, a secret that has to be kept safe until it is time for man to hear it."

Chapter Twenty-Three

"IT'S TIME FOR MY SPEECH," the General pulled out a piece of paper from his pocket and switched on the microphone.

"My beloved friends and fellow countrymen, I stand before you today not only as a leader of a great country, but as a man destined to be at the right hand of God. We have all seen the suffering of man, we have all seen the evil of man, we have all seen men rape and steal nature's beautiful gift to us, mother Earth. So much so that Mother Earth has been brought to her knees.

My friends, let me tell you that this has not gone unnoticed. God has witnessed such scenes and is not pleased. You might ask yourself how I know this, so I will tell you. God has seen fit to send me an angel, an angel of great splendour and beauty. This messenger told me that God will no longer tolerate such actions in the beloved home made for us. I was then told that it is my duty to unleash a holy fire on Earth to once and for all cleanse and eradicate the evil of man. My actions will clean the Earth of all the hate and contempt installed in the men in the West.

Unfortunately, these actions will come at a price, the price which I hope your fidelity will keep steadfast at our last and finest hour. No doubt the West will retaliate, causing the death of us and our loved ones, but let me assure you that there is no better honour to receive than that of dying while doing God's work. Believe me my countrymen, today we will be sitting in Paradise, a Paradise where we will join past loved ones who have gone before. We will take our loved ones with us today and we will sit in the love and comfort of the Most High. So now it is time, I give you leave if you wish to go and be with your families. You have my love and respect and go with your heads held high. I will see you soon. Those who wish to remain here by my side please do and we will ascend on high together. God be with you all."

He switched off the microphone in the office above where the scientists had been working and watched through the glass window as some of the men left through the exit doors while others knelt on the floor to start to pray.

"So my Captain the time has come, are you ready to be reunited with your family once more?"

"Yes General, my very soul aches for it. I have for so long wanted to see their faces once more and be held once again in my mother's arms. So how do you feel knowing you are going to be seated at the right hand of God?"

"Strange, and yet I think I have always known that something as special as this would happen to me and be my destiny."

"What will you say to God?"

"That I don't know. I expect I'll thank God for allowing me the opportunity to do a great work on Earth. Sometimes my friend," he put his hands on the captain's shoulders, "words are not enough. Being in the same presence and power of God would be my reward. To share that knowledge of God is all I need to know. What time is it?"

"It is five minutes to midday."

"Then let us begin."

The Captain lifted the black briefcase attached to

his wrist onto the table in front of him. He turned a combination lock and clicked the case open. Inside was a metal cylinder tube with a keyhole at each end. The General removed the tube and placed it on the table. He took the red key from around his neck and instructed the captain to do the same. They both entered their keys to their respective holes and turned them. The lid on the metal cylinder sprung open to reveal a piece of paper neatly rolled like a scroll lying at the bottom. The general removed it.

"Here my friend is a six digit launch code. I can't tell you how long I had been waiting for this moment."

The general unrolled a scroll to reveal the number 798666 written in red ink. They both turned to see the clock: it was now three minutes to twelve. They stepped forward to the computer panel and the hidden red button.

"Remember we put the keys in and turn together to the left. The computer will then ask for the launch code. After keying in the numbers, we turn the keys to the right and that will then release the button. Is that clear?"

"Yes General, very clear."

The general could see his Captain's hands were shaking.

"God is with you my friend," he said and put his hand on the Captain's to reassure him.

"Thank you, General."

"Ready?"

"I am ready."

They both entered the keys and turned them to the left. The computer screen flashed in front of them prompting them to enter the six figure launch code. General Silas carefully typed in the number. More writing appeared on the screen asking them if they were sure they wanted to launch. If the answer was yes, they had to retype the six numbers and confirm the launch code. The General did as instructed and the launch code was initiated.

They both then turned their keys to the right and the metal casing imprisoning the button glided down into the computer panel and the red button slowly emerged from its hiding place.

"General, it has been an honour and a pleasure to be here with you today."

"You too, my friend."

They both once again turned to the clock. The second hand was approaching twenty seconds to midday.

"God be with you captain, I will see you again in Paradise."

"God be with you too, General."

The tiny hand on the clock made its way to noon and in the General slowly counted down: "8, 7, 6, 5, 4, 3, 2, 1.

Then with the click of the hour hand the General slammed his hand down on the button. The computer screen flashed up in red: "Missiles launched."

The roar from the rocket engines firing up made the building they were standing in shake on its foundations. The two soldiers watched, as missile after missile launched into the blue sky towards the heavens. The Captain took hold of his family photo and held it against his chest and whispered, "Soon my family, very soon."

Back at the house, Lucifer stood calling for Mary in the back garden.

"Mary, come quick, it's time for me to go."

Mary rushed out the kitchen door, the clock on the wall was showing a little after 8am.

"What is it?"

"I needed to say goodbye again."

"Where do you have to go and what do you have to do?"

"I have to go make my peace with God and then finally I can go home."

"Will death be painful? Will we see each other again?"

"So many questions. All I can tell you is that it won't be painful because you, John, David and Ruth will remain together no matter what."

Lucifer looked at all of them watching from inside. He lifted his hand for them to join him outside, one by one they came outside to where they were standing.

"It is time for me to go, my friends. I want to thank you again for what you have done..."

As Lucifer spoke, a scream came from next door. Then more and more screams started sounding outside in the streets.

"What is all the noise about?" Ruth ran back indoors and ran down the corridor to open the front door to see what was going on.

"It's coming," Lucifer said ominously, "it is time for you to prepare yourselves. Now I must fly."

Ruth ran back into the garden to join them just before Lucifer took flight.

"It's true, the end is coming, General Silas has launched his nuclear missiles and they are heading this way. Our government has retaliated and launched their missiles. Grace from next door said that the reporter on the television has told everybody to prepare for the worst. David hold me."

Ruth threw herself at David wrapping her arms around him.

"I must fly now and go make my peace. God be with you."

"Oh Lucifer," Mary took hold of him and put her head on his fiery chest, "I will pray for you and you will be the last person I speak about in my prayers."

"Mary, you will be the last picture in my mind as I meet my fate."

"Come on Mary." John gently pulled her away from Lucifer into his arms. "Goodbye Luther, I think we will all sit out here together to see last moments alive in the radiance of the sun."

Lucifer let out an almighty roar and, as he channelled his energy, the red colour around him started to pulsate quicker and brighter.

"Do not forget, take my love," Mary put her hand on his chest causing a blue colour to enter him, soon spreading until he was shining a beautiful purple. He bowed his head, spread his wings, took one last look at them then took flight, almost knocking over his friends with a blast of air.

As he flew higher and higher, his body began to grow. His wings expanded behind him. Soon Mary and her family were just like small dots as Lucifer's flight gained momentum. With a cold morning air whistling in his ears, he was thinking about what the end of the scripture had told him. It had instructed him to fly to the exact centre between heaven and earth and the exact centre between east and west. It went on to say that is where he would meet his death. He looked down at his body. Covered in the black coat, the purple still radiated all around him. Soon, he thought, there would be nothing of this left. The very body that had initially imprisoned him would soon be ashes.

"Lucifer."

Lucifer looked up to where the voice sounded.

"I call upon you to make your choice. Fly here now and consider your decision."

Lucifer immediately recognised the voice of the Most High. On approaching the point within the centre, he started to see something shine down from above and as he got closer he recognised what he was seeing. From a break in the clouds, his sword started to descend. It shone in all its glory, the red rubies in the handle were electrifying and the metallic surface radiated from the light of the sun.

"Animositas! Come to me, I have missed you," Lucifer shouted.

He held out his hand and flew even faster to be reunited with his trusty blade. Closer and closer he flew until the coming together of hand and sword sent a white flashing light into the heavens, opening the clouds above him. Then there was a silence. Hovering in the morning sky, Lucifer held his sword close to his chest until the silence was broken by a movement in the clouds above. He watched as the angels led by Michael descended from the parting in the sky. One by one, they surrounded him on either side.

"Hello Lucifer, welcome back. It's good to see you in your new light."

"Thank you Michael. It's good to see you again and it's even better to see you without having the wish to destroy you."

Once all the angels had descended, they all hovered in position with their heads bowed, then there was a silence that covered the sky.

"Lucifer, I, the Most High," the silence was broken by the voice of God, "and the brethren here have come to witness the end of time. We have come here to see my will on Earth be done. It is time to make your choice, Lucifer. In your hand you have the sword which is claimed to be alive. I now give you back your power and free will to do as you wish. You can use the sword to wipe out all man on earth or you can choose to save them. Whatever your choice you will lose the body you possess and return to our heavenly home."

On hearing the words of the Most High, Lucifer pulled the sword closer to his chest and closed his eyes and began to contemplate. He had now been granted his wish to return to his angelic status. He also now had the power to choose man's fate. Whatever he decided he would still be returning home. Would it be better to return home as the new Lucifer with a clear conscience or as the old Lucifer covered in blood of man? As he was thinking, he started to hear a strange noise. It started off like a high-pitched scream then the sound became recognisable: it was the sound of Angela's voice, the girl he had saved at the orphanage.

"Lucifer if you can hear me. Once before you made your choice and chose to save me, do you remember the feeling you felt? It was not a feeling of pain but a feeling of love, I know that you now know what love is and I know now you will make the right choice."

Then another voice began.

"Lucifer, if you can hear me, it is me Mary. I am praying for you. I hold your new name in my heart and my mind, I hope we will see each other again my love."

"Lucifer," the Most High's voice sounded aloud, "you have to decide."

"Why must it be me? I am not questioning your decision Most High, but I just don't understand."

"All will be explained after you have made your choice."

Lucifer looked around at all the other angels who are now holding each other's hands in a circle with Lucifer in the centre.

"Lucifer, see what approaches."

Lucifer turned to the east and then to the west. On both horizons he could see the metallic surface of the nuclear warheads getting closer. The roar of their fire deafened his ears as they got closer and closer.

In one final thought, he remembered the people in the east who he had originally loved so much. So long now he had sought revenge for them, but was this what they wanted? He had been their leader who had loved and respected them. Did they want to see him turn into something so horrible? The answer came to him within an instant. He realised he was not fighting to avenge them. He was fighting the weakness in himself for letting this happen to his people. His eyes flashed open.

"My choice is made."

He held out his sword and started to fly to the exact centre between heaven and earth and between east and west. On approaching the centre his speed gathered momentum. In the blur of his speed, he saw all the faces of his tribe from the east; they were all smiling at him and sending him so much love. This love made his flight get even faster, closer and closer he approached that perfect point. From his chest, a beautiful white light started to radiate. It was the light he had received from the Most High when he and Mary were in the lion's cage. This light grew brighter and brighter and as it did, it reflected on the missiles causing them to change direction and head straight towards him.

The other angels watched with a mixture of sadness and joy as the inevitable was soon to come to pass. The light from above grew brighter, then with one final flap of his wings he held out his sword in front of him and closed his eyes.

"In the name of God," he screamed, "I was Lucifer now I am no more. In time people will come to know my true name."

There was a brief silence which seemed to last for a lifetime then an almighty explosion erupted. The fire in the light from the explosion ripped through the sky and headed towards the Earth. The inhabitants of the Earth cried out in fear as the approaching fireball got closer and closer, Jeremiah and the other brothers were watching from Daniel's house, Mary, David, John and Ruth held each other tight. General Silas and the captain were watching from the launch area. The General held out his chest to bravely accept his fate and the Captain held his photo against his heart. The flames engulfed the entire planet, but instead of the flames killing people, they danced around them like a warm blanket in a loving glow. The sound of a roaring fire sounded in their ears but the flames comforted them rather than hurting them.

In one moment, the fire entered the hearts of man, making everyone fall to their knees. Every evil thought the men had conceived was abolished from their minds and memory. Every evil man and woman now had no perception of evil any more. All the hurt, both physical and emotional, that had been exercised on man by man was now healed. The darkness in man's mind was now being eradicated to give way to a new light and a new love. As this light and love grew in man's mind and hearts, the angels above began to weep. Their tears fell to the earth like raindrops extinguishing the fire all around the world. The light from the explosion faded and out of its centre fell a black figure. The wings were not moving and the body fell next to his sword downwards to earth. Faster and faster it fell, falling lifeless until it and the sword hit the Earth, sending an enormous boom around the world, like the Earth's new heartbeat.

"It is done," Jeremiah said and took hold of his chest. He closed his eyes and breathed his last breath. Angela was crying as she looked out of her window holding her doll. Mary, John, David and Ruth looked towards the heavens. All of them now could see a new light in the sky shining down upon them. From a hole in the ground in the desert, Michael appeared with Lucifer lying lifeless in his arms. As he ascended towards the light above, Lucifer's body began to burn away into ashes. Michael lovingly looked down as Lucifer's face began to fade and floated away into the wind.

"You did well, my brother," said the voice of the Most High.

The light behind Michael faded as the opening in the clouds closed as he entered heaven. The people of the world now began to weep as they fell to the ground on their knees praising and thanking God for their lives and salvation, for the start of another day and the new dawn of man.

Chapter Twenty-Four

"Welcome home Altithronus. It has been a long time, but I am glad you have found your way home."

Lucifer opened his eyes to see he was once again sitting in his heavenly place, but this time he was not being held down with chains. He was sitting on a glorious golden throne.

"Is that my name again?" Lucifer said to the Most High who presence was hidden behind a white light.

"Yes Altithronus, I could not tell you before because it was up to you to rediscover your old name."

"But what about the people of Earth, what has befallen them?"

"Look," God said and parted the clouds beneath their feet. "You see, men are alive and well thanks to you. They are once again living in perfect harmony now the balance has been restored. I am very pleased that people believe in me again. Your actions have invoked a new belief in me and I am alive again in their minds."

"How did that happen? I only saved them from a physical death."

"Is that what you really think? You did more than that. In your selfless act of sacrifice, you were willing to destroy your own evil. This showed them that the evil inside themselves was no longer needed. You helped them to face up to their own dark side and spiritually gave them the strength to destroy that within them. It was my intention to let you feel unloved during your existence in order so that when you found that love again you would appreciate it much more. This was done so that at the time of your death that feeling would resonate in the hearts and minds of man. For so long man has felt abandoned and unloved by me, they had turned to evil or worshipping false idols in pursuit of happiness.

Altithronus, you were my firstborn when you decided to be incarnated in matter and eventually into human form. We have travelled a long journey together but now we have come full circle and now man is born again."

"Yes, but I do have one question for you. How come I know of good and evil, but can still be in your presence?"

"The reason you can be here in my presence, higher than all the other angels, is because at the beginning, you were the only one who had enough faith in my love for you to sacrifice your angel status. You knew that you would move far away from me, but deep down you knew your love for me would bring you home. Michael and the other angels only know good. They had not been down to earth and seen the evil of man. I am not saying I think any less of Michael and the other angels, I love their fidelity and their love for me, but you decided to share your knowledge and my love for man by your own sacrifice."

Altithronus began to weep.

"Why do you weep?"

"I am just glad to be home. I have travelled a long journey and my heart is humbled in your power, my God. But before I take my leave answer me this, will man now finally be at peace?"

"That even I am not sure of, because of their free will, but I am sure one day you might have to answer another call."

"Until then I will meditate and remember the only one person on Earth who knows my new name. I hope she will pass it on from generation to generation, so it will be kept safe until we meet again and man is in need of it and the world will finally know the truth."

Back down on Earth, the shimmering heat danced on the sand like a mirage of water as a convoy of jeeps and lorries grew nearer. The sand was thrown up behind them as they were being driven at great speeds. It was not long before they came to a halt in the middle of the desert.

"The sword must be here somewhere," A man in uniform and wearing glasses was studying a map and talking to the general next to him.

"Are you sure?"

"Yes, according to the readings and the alignment of the stars, this is where the impact took place here within a mile radius."

"Okay men dismount and set up camp, we start digging in the morning." The General barked his order.

"General Silas, do you think we will find the sword we are looking for?"

"I am sure and I will not let my friend's suicide be in vain."

General Silas pulled out the Captain's family photo which he had taken off his friend's dead body after he had shot himself in the head when realising that the end was not coming.

"Believe me, when we find it, I will use its power and I can assure you that I will not be fighting on God's side. I will raise an army on Earth, a terrifying army that will make God quake in the heavens, then I will take my revenge into heaven and bring God and the angels to their knees. Then, and only then, will I hold that sword and take my revenge on a deceitful God."